The Road to Lavender

Recipient of the **2020
Southwest Book Design
Production Award** from the
New Mexico Book Association

and

third place winner in the **2019
Rocky Mountain Fiction Writers'**
Colorado Gold Writing Contest

Praise for *The Road to Lavender*

The
Road to
Lavender

The Road to Lavender

Book One
in *The Four Corners Mystery Series*

D.P. Benjamin

ELEVATION PRESS
OF COLORADO

The Road to Lavender
By D.P. Benjamin

Ordering information: Quantity sales. Special discounts are available on quantity purchases by book clubs, corporations, associations, and others. For details, contact the publisher at the address above.

ISBN 978-0-932624-02-4

1. Main category— [Mystery-Cozy] 2. Other categories— [Colorado]—[Female Detective]

ELEVATION PRESS
OF COLORADO
Cedaredge, Colorado
www.elevation-press-books.com

For information on services offered by Elevation Press, please see the final page of this book.

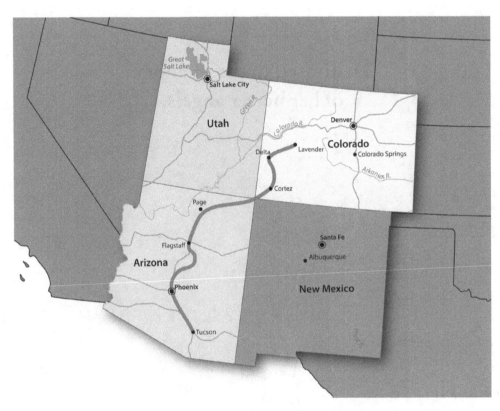

The road to Lavender, Colorado from Tucson, Arizona, July 2018

Dedicated to the memory
of her better angels.

Prologue

Midnight, July 14, 2018
Tucson, Arizona

Clark hadn't killed a man since the war and never at close range. His sedentary lifestyle had made him soft. The big Russian would be armed. Clark's attack would have to be swift and sure. Taking a deep breath, he wished he had a drink but couldn't risk it. In a matter of moments, his four decades of unstinting service as a renowned and respected university professor would be reduced to ashes. His concessions had sealed his fate and tonight, with a final irredeemable act, he'd cement his legacy as traitor to his profession. But he'd made too many compromises and it was much too late to turn back now.

He'd have to kill the Russian. It was his only option.

Hiding in the unlit interior of his Tucson ranch house, Clark rolled his shoulders and tried to relax as he sought to reduce the tension of waiting for his victim to arrive. Standing erect in the dark recesses of his walk-in closet, he took a deep breath and indulged in a self-congratulatory smile. He'd been cavalier but also clever. It hadn't been easy but, just when the future looked darkest, he'd invented a plan to extract himself from what had become a wildly complicated situation.

So far, so good, he told himself. *Just pop my unsuspecting visitor and I'll be home free.*

It was his fault of course—his blunder. He and he alone had transformed his Russian customers from mere annoyances into a lethal threat. But that was what it was and soon he'd settle things. He tightened his grip on the croquet mallet in his right hand. Just one clean swing was all he needed.

As seconds ticked away, the professor considered the unlikely journey which began with a remarkable twist of fate and ended with his scheme to profit from his unexpected stroke of luck. Finding the thing and arranging to sell it should have solved all his problems. Before fortune smiled on him, legions of creditors had been nipping at his heels and his professional life was in tatters. Then, literally overnight, his extraordinary discovery changed all that. With his treasure in hand, Clark spent months online, trolling the dark web as he sought to market his prize. Shunning legitimate connections, he worked in secret because no reputable dealer would have agreed to participate in his sacrilege. Anyone with an ounce of scruples would have turned him down and also turned him in. He'd had enough of the establishment with its rules and ethics. He needed cash, so he turned to the underworld, seeking the highest bidder.

Eventually his efforts attracted the attention of the Scarlet Brotherhood—a shadowy Russian cartel. The Brotherhood had contacted him with a multi-million dollar offer and within days they'd sent their man Fyodor to examine the treasure. One look had convinced the big Russian that the professor's merchandise was genuine. So, the deal was well on its way to a swift conclusion until Clark got greedy and threw a wrench into the transaction.

Thinking back, he could see that he'd been reckless. What had seemed like a good idea at the time he now recognized as a tactical error. It had been a mistake to aggravate the dangerous mobsters by demanding a down payment. Asking for two million dollars upfront had been a foolhardy thing to do, but a growing flock of creditors and their carnivorous lawyers were circling the professor's feeble bank account like an ever-descending spiral of vultures. After years of abuse, his wastrel lifestyle was rapidly coming home to roost and Clark desperately needed cash. So, he'd insisted on half down, as if he were haggling over the price of a carpet in a foreign bazaar. Half down, he'd demanded, with the balance due when he delivered the treasure.

Astonished by Clark's demand, the Brotherhood had hesitated and that, the professor recalled, was when things got complicated. Fearing the cartel was losing interest and pressed by his mounting debts, Clark had taken the perilous step of opening negotiations with another buyer. And he'd just concluded a new arrangement to sell to a renegade Saudi prince when the irritated Russians reconsidered his demand. To Clark's utter surprise, the cartel grudgingly forked over the down payment, but their compliance came with a price as they attached an unwelcome condition. The Russians were adamant that the professor let them examine the merchandise a second time. The Brotherhood had grown anxious—so anxious that they were sending someone tonight to take another look at the treasure. But Clark was convinced that the impending visit would be more than a simple buyer's inspection. He was certain it would be a deadly confrontation because he'd pushed the treacherous cartel too far and now, they were pushing back.

He'd received the bad news a few days ago. The niggling scoundrels had awakened him with a late-night phone call on his seldom-used landline.

"Your decision?" the impatient Russian had demanded after delivering the Brotherhood's ultimatum.

"I'll take the meeting," Clark had said, his voice thick with resignation.

What choice did he have? The cartel had him over a barrel. He'd have to deal with the Russians and the Saudis, a dilemma which saddled him with two dangerous buyers and only one treasure to sell. Disheartened and apprehensive, Clark had been about to end the call when he had a sudden inspiration.

"Yes, I agree to another inspection," Clark told the caller, "but I need an additional day to make arrangements and you must send someone I know and trust. You must send Fyodor," he insisted.

His Russian contact had grudgingly accepted Clark's conditions and the professor had taken advantage of the delay to organize his escape.

The additional day had flown by and his hand-picked examiner was coming tonight. Allegedly, Fyodor was coming to scrutinize and photograph the artifact, but the professor was certain the Brotherhood had no wish to continue the transaction. Despite their supposed friendship, he was convinced that the big Russian was coming tonight to terminate the deal. In moments, the loyal mobster would be crossing Clark's threshold with unambiguous orders to seize the treasure and kill the troublesome seller. As the troublesome seller in question, Clark wished Fyodor luck since he had no intention of surrendering either the treasure or his life. Already he'd acted to smuggle the desired object out of town. By now, it would be far away and, once the professor settled with his midnight visitor, he'd be off like a shot to retrieve it.

For a moment, waiting there in the darkness, Clark wondered what his fanatical customers would do when they realized that their precious treasure and their impetuous seller had both disappeared. But almost immediately he ceased wondering. It didn't matter how they reacted because, from now on, the professor would be calling the shots. Hastily improvising, he'd devised a plan to keep the Russian down payment and string the cartel along. Then, in short order, he'd jilt the Brotherhood and sell to the Saudis for a handsome profit. Already his plan was in motion and he'd pulled it off by doing something which—to the casual observer—would appear completely normal.

Remembering the beauty of his plan, Clark sighed with satisfaction.

For a decade he'd been challenging his advanced classes in field archaeology to master a geocaching exercise. Preparation for the exercise called for a mature student to transport a dozen nondescript toolboxes from Arizona to Colorado and stash them at predetermined coordinates. This summer, he'd selected Anne Scriptor, his trusted graduate assistant, to fulfill that role. In a typical term, once the boxes were hidden, other students would be dispatched with instructions to locate the caches using orienteering techniques. But this term would be anything but typical. This time he'd not be sending a gaggle of undergraduates to traipse through the Colorado wilderness. This time there would be no student searchers at all. Only their professor, Clark himself, would be taking the field, and his attention would be exclusively focused on one special cache.

Box number one, he thought. *I trust that you have placed it well, Miss Scriptor—placed it good and well and within easy walking distance of these chubby legs of mine.*

To safeguard the treasure, Clark had used toolbox number one to conceal it, then placed the gray metal box with the other caches. Unaware that her cargo included a priceless treasure, the dutiful young woman had shown up bright and early that very morning, loaded the toolboxes into her little plaything of a Volkswagen, and driven out of Tucson at precisely 6 a.m. With no idea that she was being used to smuggle Clark's clandestine treasure out of Arizona, the innocent young woman had driven northward. Her goal was to reach Colorado, then spend the long July day hiking through mountain wilderness to place each cache—including the treasure box—in remote locations known only to the two of them.

Once Anne had hidden the first six caches, she was to telephone her professor and report her progress. Having done this, she would spend the night in Delta City, Colorado, then arise the next morning and drive on to continue stashing the rest. Anyone following her would be drawn north and thus further away from the toolbox containing the treasure. He'd trusted Anne to do her part, even going so far as to give her his personal smartphone number.

In the end she came through, although it had been a near thing. It was a long drive from Tucson to Colorado, but even so, Clark had expected Anne to report in much earlier. This first day's caching should have been completed before sundown and yet, despite Clark's expectations, Anne had taken much longer. As a result, it had been uncomfortably late when she finally called to say that she'd reached the half-way point of her assignment.

Anne's tardiness had been vexing and nearly unforgivable since her belated call had come well after eleven. It was a delay which nearly scuttled Clark's plan. He'd promised to give the Russians a second look at the treasure no later than midnight. There was no telling what the unpredictable Brotherhood might have done if they hadn't heard from the professor before the appointed deadline. Waiting for Anne's call, Clark had chilling thoughts as he pictured a murderous missile-bearing drone hovering ominously in the Arizona sky while it zeroed in on his isolated ranch house.

When Anne's call came at last, the exasperated professor had been tempted to pick up his smartphone and soundly reprimand his student for her delay. But he let the call go to voicemail and, hearing Anne's contrite tone on the speaker, he merely listened while she apologized. When her message ended, Clark had grumbled to himself that she'd cut things pretty-darn close. Then he'd used a burner phone to call the Russians and confirm that he was ready to receive their representative.

"It's nearly much too late and your call is not coming from a recognized number," the man who answered had protested in his thick accent. Clark imagined him glaring at the clock in whatever time zone he occupied. It was an unfamiliar voice—one which Clark hadn't encountered before.

Crap, he'd thought, *how I hate dealing with this endless parade of Russian underlings—and always a different person!*

"Well, pal," he'd said aloud, striving to communicate his sarcasm, "I'm obviously calling now, using whatever phone I please, so deal with it."

There was silence on the other end and Clark had grinned as he suspected the man was fuming.

"Hello," Clark said.

"Yes, Dr. Clark," the man answered, his voice dripping with disdain.

"So, comrade, tell me that you're sending Fyodor, right?" Clark reminded the operative. "And listen carefully—when he's nearby I want him to text to this number. Got that? Don't have him use my smartphone, understand? I need to recharge my personal phone, so be absolutely sure to have him use this line—you can see the new number, right?"

"We are aware of your requests," the man assured him. His tone was icy.

"Just do it, comrade," said Clark. He ended the call before another righteous Russian could chastise him for calling from an unfamiliar number or object to his language. Apparently, the mobsters hated being called 'comrade' which is precisely why Clark enjoyed using the term.

He saw the Scarlet Brotherhood as a bloodthirsty Russian gang and yet surprisingly priggish. Based on his assessment of their moralistic overtones, Clark envisioned his prudish buyers to be a collection of lapsed-saints— a schizophrenic group, willing to kill at the drop of a hat, but somehow unwilling to utter profanity and detesting the label 'comrade.' He suspected there might be a point when the Brotherhood would tire of his taunting. He was fully aware that his salty and politically incorrect language offended them, but he couldn't resist.

The sanctimonious gangsters are already annoyed enough to kill me, he thought, *so why should one more insult make any difference? What are they going to do? Kill me twice?*

Clark's musing ceased as his burner vibrated with a text message announcing that his visitor was fifteen minutes away. Clark didn't recognize the sending number, but the overly cautious Russians were constantly changing phones on their end and the exotic area code was correct. It had to be Fyodor, so he dictated and sent a return text.

"Park behind the shed, old friend. Walk up the driveway. Front door is open. Room on right."

Those instructions would compel Fyodor to conceal his vehicle, then channel the unsuspecting man straight into Clark's ambush. His secluded ranch house was a rambling structure with few exterior windows and shadowy interior hallways. Soon the big Russian would open the front door and cross the entryway. After his target took a dozen steps down the hall and turned right, he'd be inside the darkened study and Clark would spring from his hiding place to knock the startled man senseless.

Earlier, when contemplating his murderous plan, Clark had momentarily felt a twinge of guilt at the need to sacrifice Fyodor. The big Russian had been his one and only face-to-face contact with the Brotherhood. It was Fyodor who'd been sent to conduct the first examination of the merchandise—an inspection which took all of three minutes. Then the two of them had spent a comfortable afternoon poolside at the Biltmore Resort in Phoenix, drinking margaritas and swapping jokes. But this passing notion of regret had dissipated quickly. Clark was a man in a deep hole and there was no climbing out. All he could do was keep digging and hope that he would eventually reach the safety of China—or Saudi Arabia in his case—because he had every intention of double-crossing the Russians.

Clark glanced at the luminous dial of his watch—any minute now. Waiting there in the dark closet, he adjusted his grip on the croquet mallet. He had a pistol, but he'd use the mallet to avoid the risk of anyone hearing a gunshot. His ranch house was secluded, but not, he knew, unobserved. Balancing the wooden weapon in his right hand, he reached forward in the darkness, carefully placing his left hand on the closet doorknob, and tensed his muscles, preparing to fling the door open.

Then he had a thought.

Why keep the door closed?

He quickly turned the knob, pushed the door open, and left it ajar. The house was deadly quiet and there was no need to alert Fyodor with the sound of unlatching. The study was dark, and it was darker still in this corner. So long as Clark kept quiet, he would be completely hidden until it was time to sprint from the shadows and wallop his visitor. Waiting there, the minutes seemed to pass slowly, and Clark grew uncertain, so he took one last precaution to increase his odds of success. To make sure he was adequately armed, he reached back into the closet and pulled a second mallet from the croquet set.

Fill both hands with weapons. Keep the door ajar. Fyodor is a big guy. No sense taking chances.

Once Fyodor was down—ideally dead or at least unconscious—Clark planned to don the Russian's suit and hat, take the man's car keys, and slip out of the ranch house. He'd specifically requested that the Brotherhood send Fyodor because he and the big man were nearly the same build which made the portly Russian an ideal body double. To the watchers it would look like Fyodor had come and gone, leaving Clark alone in the house, exactly where they expected him to be.

And they would be watching—of that Clark was certain.

When Clark was clear, he'd use his smartphone to activate a fuse, igniting the ranch house along with the ambushed Russian. Thinking of his newly enhanced pyrotechnic skills, Clark grinned. His military training had already provided him with a nodding acquaintance with explosives and it was simply amazing what a person could learn by surfing the world-wide web.

With the house and his double in flames, it would take considerable time to extinguish the blaze and even more time for anyone—cops or the Brotherhood or whomever—to notice the switch. By then Clark would be far away and he would have escaped right under the noses of the men assigned to watch him. The watchers would be out there tonight, just as they had been for more than a year. The cautious professor had noticed them from the beginning, even though he'd yet to discover who coordinated the surveillance. It could be the Russians, or it might be the Saudis, or the cops, or what's-his-name—the man the Saudis feared. Whoever the spies were, he knew one thing for certain. Starting tonight he was taking steps to evade them.

It was for the benefit of his mysterious watchers that Clark had, for weeks on end, been maintaining the appearance of a predictable work schedule and a dull home life. Forced to keep tabs on his regimented and redundant life, he was certain the watchers would soon tire of his exasperating consistency. He counted on them growing so accustomed to his repetitive routine that they would begin to see what they expected to see and miss what was really happening. Early this morning, for example, as Clark sent Anne Scriptor on her way, the watchers would have believed they were witnessing the start of one of his routine geocaching assignments—a repetition of something he did every term. But Anne's cargo was not routine and tonight, in a matter of seconds, everyone, including the unlucky Fyodor, was in for a surprise.

"Tick-tock," Clark whispered to himself.

He heard the front door open. Then came footsteps followed by the telltale creak of vintage floorboards in the entry hall and the study door was opening and a voice sounded in the darkness.

"Dr. Clark?"

And instantly C. Arnold Clark, PhD, past curator of the Paleo-Indian exhibition, past director of the Cactus Canyon Ruins project, and full professor of The University of Arizona's division of archaeology, brandished his weapons and sprang from his hiding place.

Part I: Anne's Story

Chapter 1

July 15, Morning
Western Colorado

The little Volkswagen Bug lurched sideways as Anne Scriptor tried to remember whether she was supposed to steer into a skid or in the opposite direction. Whatever she did—and she had no idea what it was—she survived the sharp corner and was still on the muddy road when the next curve loomed before her.

Rain fell in sheets, drenching the windshield, blotting out the July sun, and muting the morning light. The wipers worked frantically, but the tiny blades made little headway. Anne could barely see the road ahead and she was beginning to wonder if she was on a road at all, because the car's lack of traction suggested she might have inadvertently plunged into a river. The rain had been hammering down for an hour and Anne should have remained on the pavement or at least pulled over to wait out the storm. Instead she'd impetuously turned left and driven straight into the clutches of a steeply descending and thoroughly muddy roadway.

"Here we go again," she sighed as another curve seemed to emerge from the gloom surrounding her.

Early this morning, before the mud, before the rain, and before this accursed road, everything had been proceeding like clockwork. Anxious to begin the second half of her caching assignment, she'd awakened before dawn and gone for an invigorating run. Feeling energized, she'd showered, checked out of her Delta City motel, and discovered a cozy restaurant where she shared a table with locals. During breakfast, the conversation had been dominated by complaints about the persistent drought which was strangling Western Colorado ranches and farms. Nobody could remember such a dry spell. Everybody was praying for rain—in fact they literally joined hands and prayed for it—right there at the breakfast table. Now, within an hour of that invocation, Anne had managed to drive smack-dab into a punishing rainstorm and onto a seemingly endless hill of liquid earth. Faith could move mountains it seemed, or possibly turn one into mud.

Drought? she asked herself as she leaned forward to study the gloomy sky.

An hour earlier, the summer sun had been beaming—a bright new penny in an otherwise clear and impossibly blue sky. Then abruptly the wind rose, dark clouds materialized, and thunder growled. In moments, her idyllic mountain morning was battered by an ominous downpour and, in the chaos of the storm, she'd become disoriented and turned onto this primitive dirt road where the mud was slick and deep.

What was she thinking? Why had she left the pavement? Her little car was no match for this narrow dirt road. It was precipitous and winding—a primitive rollercoaster minus the luxury of guiding tracks and guard rails—a down-bound slip-and-slide with a rain-soaked hill on one side and a sheer drop on the other. As the Bug relentlessly descended, the dissolving roadway took control of her steering wheel. It was all she could do to hang on each time the car slipped to the edge of the road, then toward the hillside, and back again. One minute she was teetering on the outer rim of the road, only a few feet from falling into the ravine below. Seconds later she was sliding the other way, her front tire boring into the hillside and spewing a plume of mud up and over the hapless car.

Surviving yet another sweeping curve, she reached a drop in a road and saw nothing ahead but sky as, caught in the grip of gravity, the car plunged over. She clutched the steering wheel, downshifted, and fought to stay on the road. There was no other choice. There was only one way out of her dilemma and that way was down. No chance of stopping. Any hesitation would mire her in mud, and it might be days before someone showed up on this remote roadway to pull her out. So, she kept the Volkswagen headed downhill, feeling the tires slip, and trying not to think what would happen if she lost control and plummeted over the edge.

"Should'a stayed on the pavement," Anne told herself. "Should'a kept an eye on the weather. Should'a, could'a, would'a."

The rain showed no sign of stopping and, as the downpour thundered on the vintage Volkswagen's rounded roof, she reached yet another sharp corner. As she careened around, the car teetered sideways causing the bobble-head wildcat figurine on her dashboard to sway like a storm-tossed ship. The grinning plastic souvenir of her undergraduate days seemed to shake its head and she guessed at its meaning.

"I suppose," she complained, "you're going to say, 'Well, Miss Anne with an 'e' and Scriptor with an 'o,' here's another fine mess you've gotten us into.'"

With sweaty palms, Anne gripped the vibrating steering wheel and sighed. It was hot inside the Volkswagen with the windows rolled up and no AC and...

"Again?" she asked aloud as another corner waited ahead. "Does this blessed road ever end?"

She wanted this trip to go well. She wanted to please the prominent man who had entrusted her with the responsibility of driving hundreds of miles from Arizona to Colorado to hide his semester caches. C. Arnold Clark, PhD was more than her mentor. He was a campus legend, a tenured professor with impeccable credentials as a field archaeologist, not to mention an internationally renowned author and lecturer. Anne herself was a departmental nobody and just beginning her advanced academic career, a fledgling graduate student with a shiny new B.S. degree.

"B.S. is right," she said aloud. "And we all know what that stands for. And M.S. is more of the same and if I ever achieve it..." She managed to wink at the wildcat figurine, "PhD stands for piled higher and deeper."

She was, by all accounts, the youngest student Dr. Clark had ever trusted to drive to Colorado and hike through the rugged wilderness to place his caches. She'd felt unbelievably fortunate to be chosen from a host of applicants who'd been clamoring for the chance to assist the celebrated professor with his famous term project. She knew that success on this field assignment would earn her a prestigious University of Arizona fellowship—which would mean a tuition waiver and a generous stipend, plus a coveted accolade for her resume. She desperately needed the financial benefits as well as the honors. With luck, all those precious rewards would be hers. If she didn't screw it up.

"Ah hell," Anne shouted as she fought her way around the next tight curve.

The deluge continued and two more merciless corners lay ahead, so Anne held her breath and struggled with the steering wheel while the Bug wobbled toward the next hairpin turn. The VW slithered, regained the roadway, then swerved like a pig on ice as she survived another curve and aimed for the final corner. At last she reached the bottom of the winding roadway where the car bounced over a bump and landed on solid pavement. Gaining traction, the VW surged forward, and Anne had to jam on the brakes to discourage the seemingly enthusiastic vehicle.

"Nice landing, pal," she said as she turned off the ignition. Then, despite the still pouring rain, she wriggled into her coat, put on her cap, and got out to survey the damages. "Shoot," she exclaimed as she walked rapidly around the car, struggling to keep her footing on the rain-soaked asphalt.

The lower half of her vintage 1968 sky-blue Volkswagen Bug was covered with a thick layer of clinging mud. Squatting awkwardly in the pouring rain, she could see that the car's undercarriage was so thoroughly encrusted that the tires were within inches of being glued in place. She examined all four wheels and was just lifting the rear hatch to check the engine for damage when the rain abruptly ceased. Instantly the overhanging clouds dissolved, the sun reappeared, and the wet pavement began to steam.

The engine seemed okay, so Anne closed the hatch and stood for a moment beneath the brightening sky considering her alternatives. Clearly, she had little choice. The pavement was steaming and the mud beginning to congeal. To keep driving, she'd have to get dirty. The July heat was rapidly reasserting itself, so she stripped off her jacket and cap. She'd keep those items clean at least. She glanced at her blouse, durable jeans, and running shoes. The top was a favorite, but rather than dig through her luggage, she decided her present outfit could fend for itself.

Should she move the car?

Anne looked around. She seemed to have landed in the middle of nowhere. She hadn't encountered any traffic on the way down and she doubted any would appear on this lonely road. Deciding that the unpaved shoulder was as muddy as the hill, she left the car in the middle of the asphalt and set to work. Donning a pair of cloth gloves, she knelt next to the rear tire, scrunched up her face, and reached tentatively up into the wheel well. The mud was dense there, like a slab of raw clay on a pottery wheel.

Another fine mess, she thought.

With effort she broke a clump free. Pulling it apart, she discovered a jumbled mixture of clinging mud and sizable pebbles. No telling what kind of damage such debris would do to her Bug. The mud would have to come off and that would take more than bare hands. Standing up, Anne tossed the mud aside and opened the front bonnet.

Chapter 2

Diak Hodell was in position.

Parked on a side road, his camouflaged Toyota 4Runner was well obscured in a thicket of oak brush. He rolled the window down and poked his head out to study the cloudless morning sky. Since dawn, Diak had been reviewing his map and waiting for the girl to appear.

The girl, he thought.

His macho German heritage left little room for gender equality and he grinned to himself thinking that the modern and liberated young woman whom he'd come so far to locate would undoubtedly bridle at being called a *mere girl.* But he'd seen her photograph and read her dossier and, given the difference in their ages, he was content to consider her a girl, no matter her objections. In all likelihood, the German would never have occasion to discuss with her the political correctness of his opinion. If things went well this morning, he would allow her to continue and the two would never meet.

Was she overdue?

He glanced at his watch. Then he folded his map, returned it to its case, and fastened the snaps. Allowing his hand to linger on the dusky timberland leather, he observed that his skin and the case's outer surface were the same tawny shade.

"Zigeuner," he mumbled to himself. "The dark skin, the dark eye, the untouchable gypsy. Untouchable," he repeated as he ran his fingers over the smooth leather before moving the case aside.

He was growing mildly impatient as he drummed one hand on the steering wheel while absently fingering the hilt of his Damascus knife with the other. He unsnapped the keeper on his belt scabbard, pulled the blade free, and held it up in the morning light. Twisting his wrist, he examined first the spine, then the razor-sharp edge. Looking closer, he was pleased to see that the blade was flawless—a thing of perfection in marked contrast to his reflected face with its disfiguring scar. Taking care to avoid dwelling on his reflection, he returned the blade to its scabbard and snapped the keeper in place to immobilize the weapon once again. Then he instantly drew it forth again and just as quickly replaced it.

If needed, he could smoothly unsnap the keeper and pull the blade with one hand. It was a maneuver he'd practiced so often that he could draw the knife without looking and wield the weapon before an adversary could blink. In an instant, the blade would appear in his right hand as he drew it back, poised to kill with the swift thrust of a single forward jab. With the blade at the ready, he would circle his victim, crouching slightly, assuming a taut Marine Corps stance, keeping the opponent at a slight angle, ready to step forward and back again in tandem with the movements of his blade. His muscular body would become a lethal spring, tightly coiled, and perfectly positioned to defend or attack.

The Damascus blade was his riding weapon, purposely truncated to allow him to wear the knife while seated and, when standing, to obscure the blade and scabbard under the hem of a jacket. It was a stubby blade but serrated and deadly. At present, he had no need for the knife because he was convinced the girl would be no trouble. The map too could remain in its case because he was certain she would take this county road. It was the route routinely used by the university—not the shortest and certainly not the most efficient—but rather the most traditional. Knowing the university and its dependable students, he had every expectation that the girl would adhere to tradition.

Earlier that morning, before first light, he'd driven through the vacant streets of Delta City and spotted her blue Volkswagen. It was an old Bug, from the late 1960's he guessed. The small vintage auto had been sitting beneath a light pole in the cramped parking lot of the Starlite Budget Motel.

Sandwiched between two semi-trailer trucks, the diminutive vehicle looked fragile and a bit forlorn. Seeing it there had briefly reminded him of his unhappy days in Berlin.

"Think on something else," he'd told himself.

He'd passed close enough this morning to confirm the girl's Arizona license plate. Then he'd driven further through the slumbering city and crossed the Gunnison River. Driving over the highway bridge, he could see the full moon reflected in the dark current and, poking his head out the Toyota's open window, he glanced up to see the object itself riding high in the midnight sky. Beyond the bridge, he checked into the luxurious Pine Lodge, ate the complimentary pillow mints, and lay down on the king-sized bed. An hour's sleep was all he could risk, so that would have to do. He didn't bother to undress. He set his cell phone alarm and closed his eyes.

Awake at 5 a.m. he'd found no restaurants open, so he put on a ball cap, donned dark glasses, turned up his coat collar, and purchased a make-shift breakfast at a 24-hour convenience store. The clerk hadn't looked up when he rang the German's purchases and the surveillance video would be inconclusive. Leaving Delta City, Diak had avoided the four-lane highway and taken the narrower county pavement instead. Heading north, he located an elevated spot where he could monitor traffic traveling in both directions. He'd wait for the girl to pass then follow her. There was a chance she knew nothing about the treasure, a chance that the conniving professor was keeping her in the dark. Was she aware of Clark's scheme and did she know the jaded man was on the run?

Time would tell.

The German's thinking called for the girl to pass by this morning and keep going. That would mean she was adhering to her route and such obedience would convince the German that she'd already played her part and played it innocently. If she behaved, he'd let her go and turn his attention to Clark. Her actions in the next hour would guide him and, if all went well, he'd let her live.

In the meantime, he would wait.

His position was ideal. Well-hidden and far above the pavement, he could watch for the girl and watch also for Russians. The Scarlet Brotherhood could be on the prowl and they might appear from either direction, driving their prominent Bentley automobiles, traveling in the conspicuous style that was so typical of them. It was probably too soon for the Brotherhood to be in Colorado but, just in case, he'd watch for the Russians too. After all, this was a treasure hunt and the field might become crowded. Thanks to Clark's unexpected behavior, the Russians would be scrambling. Even the German—once so certain of his ground—had been forced to improvise. Like his Russian competitors, Diak had been surprised by Clark's disappearance. As a result, he'd missed the opportunity to intercept the wayward professor. With the professor gone, the German had persuaded himself that locating the girl was essential, even though she herself was of no importance. She was merely a pawn, a marker, a means of confirming that he understood her route and had correctly guessed the timetable she was following. So long as the girl kept to her schedule, he'd have no need to contact, let alone harm her.

If she kept moving as expected, the German could forget about her. But, if the girl deviated from her route or bolted or came between him and the treasure, the German would not hesitate to do what was necessary. She would not be the first woman he'd killed, and she would undoubtedly not be the last. It might not come to that, but, if the girl misbehaved, he would act accordingly.

The morning sun was bright. Diak stretched and yawned. He needed sleep, but he must remain alert. The day was warming. He rolled down his window and reached for his water. Unscrewing the cap, he raised the canteen in a mock toast.

"Here's to the elusive Dr. Clark," he smiled. "You may be cunning, but you are no match for me. You may be an intriguer, but you are also greedy, and that fault has made you careless."

For all the professor's planning and scheming, for all the effort the man had expended in smuggling the treasure out of Tucson and then eluding those set to watch him, it seemed apparent that the careless man had yet to realize the German had inserted himself into the hunt. It had been almost too easy to monitor Clark's personal smartphone. In Diak's estimation, the professor was apparently too cheap or too naïve—possibly both—to purchase, use, and discard an array of so-called 'burner' phones. Instead, the foolish man doggedly persisted in using one and only one smartphone.

The German had only to utilize a basic surveillance app to detect and monitor communication traffic in and out of Clark's smartphone. The application was so efficient that Diak had no need to access the target device. All that was required was to discover the professor's password and, for that information, Diak was indebted to one of his Arizona contractors. Acting under the German's strict instructions, his Tucson operative had shadowed Clark and watched over his shoulder with telescopic enhancement while the unsuspecting professor sat at his desk with his back to an un-curtained window, and went through his morning routine of activating his smartphone to retrieve messages. And, just like that, the German had been connected. Now, whenever Clark made a call, the German would be listening. If needed, Diak could even reroute a given call, answer pretending to be the recipient, and extract intelligence from the transaction.

The German smiled as he capped his canteen and considered the foibles of human nature. Dr. C. Arnold Clark had once been an incorruptible darling of the archaeological world until his own government betrayed him. It was a shock which drove the disillusioned professor to drink and financial ruin. Fearing bad publicity, The University of Arizona had forced Clark to take a sabbatical. It was a banishment from which most assumed the pathetic man would never return. Shunned by his campus, abandoned by fair-weather friends and a fickle young lover, deeply in debt and desperate for cash, the faded professor was on the ropes until he somehow experienced a reversal of fortune.

Virtually overnight, Clark had been able to rekindle his existence, regain a measure of self-respect, and resume his duties at The University of Arizona and all because he'd managed to stumble upon a priceless artifact. Buoyed by his discovery—which he intentionally kept a secret—the professor had managed to make a comeback while also leading a double life. By day Clark had been playing the role of a gracefully aging professor, content to teach a graduate class and seminar while mentoring younger faculty and advising students. Meanwhile, off campus and after work hours, he'd been pursuing a clandestine calling as a dealer in black-market artifacts. In particular, he was hawking one singular piece. Clark implied that it was a rare Clovis projectile point. To Diak, the uproar over what, to his thinking, amounted to an ordinary arrowhead was a bit puzzling. But, if others considered it valuable, who was he to question the notion?

Since his triumphant return to campus, the moonlighting professor had been attempting to sell the Clovis to the highest bidder. It was a scheme which obliged Clark to explore the dark web which, in turn, attracted the German's attention. Soon Diak was closely scrutinizing Clark's every online move as the greedy professor trolled the dark underbelly of the internet for customers. When the professor's proposal had seemed to go unnoticed, Diak decided to intervene. To test the waters, he'd placed a bid. His offer was well under the asking price, but this was an auction after all, and someone had to prime the process. If Clark was having trouble attracting customers, perhaps Diak could strike a bargain. At the very least, he expected to initiate a conversation and open negotiations. Dangling the professor on a string would help the German keep tabs on the venture, allowing him to take advantage should the opportunity arise. Having submitted his bid, the German had expected a measured and civil response, but Clark's answer was immediate and patently flippant.

"LOL," was the extent of the jaded professor's dismissive reply. If Diak had at first been mildly interested in the venture, Clark's frivolous message cemented the German's determination.

"Sehr erfreut," Diak had emailed in his written response. "Very pleased," he wrote, although he was, in truth, far from happy with the impertinent man. Desiring no further correspondence, the German instantly cut off communication by closing the bogus email account he'd concocted strictly for the purpose of prodding the professor. Returning to his clandestine surveillance, Diak continued to secretly monitor Clark's unfolding scheme, biding his time, looking for an opening to shoehorn himself into the process.

The Scarlet Brotherhood had responded next. The Russians were Diak's old nemesis, a gang which had plucked him off the mean streets of East

Germany. To the German's surprise, the otherwise cautious and typically frugal Russians had offered millions to secure the Clovis. By some stroke of fortune, Clark had turned up a buyer and a more dangerous customer could not be imagined. The Scarlet Brotherhood was a treacherous mob with a dodgy reputation. The extraordinary risk of dealing with the cartel provided the German with a telling measure of the depth of Dr. Clark's desperate desire for cash.

Whatever the professor was thinking, Diak was content to let the opening stanzas of the hazardous transaction run its course. He would let the Brotherhood take the monetary risks, let them verify the authenticity of the artifact, and propose the details of the handoff. Then, when the deal went down, the German would swoop in and seize the treasure. Once in possession of the Clovis, Diak would re-peddle the artifact—sell it to the Russians if they were willing to meet his inflated price. If the Brotherhood balked, he would be more than happy to market it elsewhere.

That had been the German's original plan: to monitor Clark, interrupt the transaction by cutting the Russians out, and steal the Clovis. A few hours ago, relying on experience, he'd been certain how the Russians would behave, and he'd been equally certain that he understood the professor's plans. But, in the wee hours of this morning, all that certainty had evaporated.

It had vanished the moment Clark disappeared.

The professor's unexpected disappearance had forced the German to leave his headquarters in Northern Arizona and drive pell-mell through the night in the vain hope of intercepting the fleeing Clark. But he'd been too late to catch the professor. Now his only option was to find the girl and he was certain he'd find her soon enough. If she behaved as expected, that would confirm that she'd already stashed the treasure and was continuing north to create a diversion. After verifying his assumptions, Diak would let her go and turn back to take up residence in Delta City. In an hour or two, he'd be back in the city and ideally positioned to steal the smuggled treasure the moment Clark contacted the Russians.

Dr. Clark's phone call was the key.

Soon the professor would use his smartphone to call his Russian buyers and disclose the location of the Clovis. The girl had stashed it somewhere, probably unaware that she was doing so. Rather than waste time searching, Diak would wait for and intercept instructions. One phone call and the professor would inadvertently surrender his treasure. One phone call and Diak would be in the driver's seat and Clark would be on the outside looking in. For a moment, the German wondered if he'd once again been guilty of mixing his metaphors. To take his mind off his grammatical lapses, he glanced at his watch.

Seconds later, a breeze began to stir as clouds roiled overhead. Instantly, thunder grumbled, and it began to rain hard. Diak hurriedly rolled up the Toyota's window as the storm settled in. The rain drummed down and another hour passed before the German spotted the Volkswagen. He waited until the compact blue vehicle rounded a sweeping curve, then he drove down from his hiding place and fell in behind. He tailed the girl for five miles through the pouring rain and was about to cut her loose when he saw the VW turn sharply left. He slowed as he approached the spot and could see the crest of a dirt road leading precipitously downhill. What was she playing at? Why leave the pavement in this storm? Why deviate from her route to take such an unlikely road? Had she spotted him? Though the muddy road looked unappealing, he'd been on the point of rushing after her when he noticed a Bentley approaching from behind.

Assuming he was being pursued, the German increased his speed and watched as the reflection of the conspicuous black automobile diminished in his rear-view mirror. He was still watching when the Bentley abruptly veered off the pavement and skidded to a stop at the crest of the hill down which the girl had disappeared. The Bentley showed no signs of moving, nevertheless the German pulled his hat down, slumped in his seat, and drove on. Glancing back a third time, and just barely able to discern the outline of the Bentley, he realized that he needn't have taken such pains to obscure his identity because the attention of the black car's single occupant was totally focused on the side road.

So, the Russians are here, he thought. *So, let them follow the girl. She is expendable and I have no desire to get between them.*

"Better they are finding her than me," he said aloud as he drove on.

In twenty minutes, if the Bentley did not reappear and he was certain the Russians were pursuing the girl, he would make a U-turn and return to Delta City. In the meantime, he was content to put as much distance as possible between himself and the dangerous Brotherhood.

Chapter 3

The downpour continued as the German drove further north. He endured the storm for another six miles until the rain suddenly diminished. Taking the change in the weather as a sign, he was about to turn back when he came upon a roadblock and a detour sign directing traffic to exit to the left. Like the girl leaving the pavement, this roadblock struck him as an unexpected development. He parked his 4Runner, turned off his wipers, and killed the engine. Looking through the windshield, past puddles of standing rainwater and beyond the glistening pavement, he saw that a portion of the highway was blocked by piles of sand and gravel, three piles on this side of the barricade, four more on the far side.

As the sun reappeared, he got out his map and walked forward for a closer look. Examining the piles and the barricade, the German frowned. If road repairs were in progress, where were the machines? Where were the workers? Where were the damages to be repaired? He decided there were no damages and therefore no construction. Someone had tried to make the scene appear legitimate, but there could be only one purpose for this roadblock.

It was intended to divert traffic to the west, but why?

He scratched his head, consulted his map, and the map made it perfectly clear. Both this detour and the unexpected turn the girl had taken led to the same place. If she'd continued driving this direction instead of making her sudden turn, she would still have been diverted to the little village of Lavender. Clearly, someone wanted her to go there.

The Russians perhaps? The German folded his map. Then he walked to the far side of the road, cautiously approached the sheer drop, and looked over the precipice.

"Ha," he whispered.

Far below on a parallel stretch of pavement sat the little blue Volkswagen. The girl had stopped at the base of a road which zig-zagged down the side of a steep dirt hill. He could see her down there, walking around her vehicle, in an agitated attitude which, even at a distance, communicated her distress.

"Was ist das?" he asked himself aloud. What was he seeing? Seeking context, he looked beyond the girl for a moment and studied the dirt road down which she must have come. How did she manage to drive through all that mud? And where was the Bentley that he presumed was pursuing her?

"No doubt afraid to get his wonderful machine dirty," Diak guessed aloud at an explanation of the Russian's absence. That would be so typical of the star-struck Russians who coddled their shiny Western vehicles with a passion approaching worship. "This unwholesome love of material things," he decided, "is what happens when peasants are given a taste of decadent luxuries."

He watched for a moment more as the girl opened the VW's front bonnet, to gather tools to fix a flat perhaps. *If she delays much longer,* he predicted, *the Brotherhood will surely overtake her.* If the Russian thug caught her alone on the isolated roadway, he could imagine the girl's fate. *That,* he decided, *would be a tragedy and a waste of good flesh.* The aftereffects of his accident had long ago cured him of sexual stirrings, but he was not immune to the girl's visible charms. Her flattering photographs, and even this long-distance view of her backside as she leaned over the bonnet, showed a lovely young woman in her prime.

"Think on something else," he said aloud.

Abandoning the girl to her fate, he turned from the precipice and walked back to consider the barricade. For a moment he toyed with the idea of pushing the wooden obstacle aside to signal to the unknown plotters that their ruse had been detected. But he decided it would be better instead to leave the false barricade undisturbed and take the Lavender detour. Something told him the little village was important and he was determined to discover why. Pocketing his map, he was about to return to his vehicle when a second Bentley appeared.

Bentley number two was traveling south as it worked its way toward him from beyond the barricade. It came fast, moving erratically while the driver sought to avoid the far piles by swerving off the asphalt, onto the roadway's narrow shoulder, and back again. There was no chance the occupants wouldn't see him standing there in the middle of the pavement and even less chance they would fail to recognize him. Regardless of his reluctance to interact with the Russians, the bastards seemed to be forcing his hand. Now they were not only behind him but in front as well. He had only a moment to think before the Bentley reached him, but it was time enough.

"Good day, my friends," he shouted as he waved enthusiastically and quickly buttoned his jacket to obscure his scabbard and blade. The Bentley turned sharply and skidded to a stop next to the barricade, and so near that the driver's window was mere inches away. The vehicle idled ominously as the German leaned casually forward and counted four men in the car—too many to risk a fight—so he maintained a cheerful air as he addressed the driver through the open window. "This is a happy accident! I was just now on my way to find you. Wait a moment while I get your prize."

He saw confusion on the man's face, which is exactly what he hoped for. Without waiting for a reply, the German turned away and strode confidently to his Toyota. With the Russians watching, he opened the rear hatch and removed a small toolbox from its protective packaging. As he held the box, a single drop of rain, the last remnant of the fading storm, fell from the sky and splashed onto the metal lid.

"Aus dem Regen und unter dem Auslauf," he whispered to himself. "Out of the rain and under the spout."

The unpredictable Russians were clearly in the neighborhood, but why now and why in such force? As he walked slowly back toward the waiting Bentley, he had a moment to consider the box he carried. He'd padlocked it to make it resemble a university cache, but he'd also rigged it to explode upon opening. He'd intended it as a devious surprise for anyone who showed up to claim Dr. Clark's hidden treasure. The German took a deep breath realizing that he'd have to alter that aspect of his plan. But the Russians left him no choice, so he carried the deadly box back to the Bentley and addressed the same man again.

"Here it is," he said as he handed the toolbox through the open window. "You will find the key taped to the bottom. Enjoy your prize." The German started to leave and then he turned back, got eye contact with the Russian, and added, "But, whatever you do, be absolutely certain you do not open this box until you have delivered it to your superiors."

Trusting his caution would go unheeded, the German turned away and headed toward his Toyota. As he walked unhurriedly, he counted silently to himself. When he reached fifteen seconds, he was convinced the Russians weren't going to shoot him in the back. When he reached thirty seconds, he was certain someone was about to open the bomb, so he picked up his pace and leaped behind the nearest sand pile.

Chapter 4

With a heavy sigh, Anne rummaged through the VW's trunk, moving her professor's precious toolboxes aside as she searched for the metal rod that served as the handle for her scissors jack. Finding it wedged beneath the spare tire, she fished the handle out and tucked it under one arm. Then she put everything back in place and was about to close the bonnet when she paused to address the toolboxes.

"Proud of yourselves?" she asked the row of metal boxes with their dull gray finishes and matching padlocks. The boxes appeared identical. Only a painted number on each lid distinguished one from another. There had been a dozen boxes to start with. Now she was down to six. Six more of Dr. Clark's boxes to cache in the wilderness, six more trails to hike to fulfill her professor's assignment. Anne's adventure on the muddy hill had put her off track and behind schedule and those problems were her own fault. It was pointless to blame someone else, let alone the inanimate objects she'd been assigned to cache, but she did it anyway.

"This is entirely your fault, you know," she chastised the innocent toolboxes giving the nearest one a disgruntled tap with the jack handle. It was a half-hearted blow, but strong enough to cause its padlock to swing from side to side. "All in the name of science," she frowned as she closed the bonnet.

Before she drove a foot further, she'd remove as much of the disagreeable mud as possible. Then she'd travel on and find a carwash to finish the job. She knelt on the damp pavement, pried with the handle, and wrestled with the intractable muck. A sticky clump seemed to yield so she laid the handle aside, reached up under the car with both hands, and strained to dislodge it. The clump came free just as a resounding boom pierced the mountain air, causing Anne to sprawl face first onto the asphalt.

The blast had been near enough to shake the pavement and rattle the Bug's windows. Its echo reverberated, then gradually faded. In the silence that followed, Anne remained motionless, lying on the sodden pavement, and getting thoroughly soaked, until she began to shiver.

"Here's another fine mess," she said, picturing a vintage comedic film in which a rotund Oliver Hardy in coveralls chastised his diminutive partner Stan Laurel for getting the two of them into yet another jam. She loved that cinematic pair and she loved old movies in general, but she was beginning to regret her role in today's unwelcome script.

Struggling to her feet, she looked back toward the hill and its sodden road but saw only mud and sky. She cocked her head and heard only mountain wind. A moment ago, birds had been chirping in the roadside foliage. Now the silence was complete. Something had exploded—something big but thankfully not too close. Curious but determined to return to her task, she shrugged and was about to continue freeing her VW from its mud cocoon when she spotted smoke on the far horizon. Leaning in that direction, she listened more closely and seemed to hear the faint sound of heavy machinery.

"Hard rock miners," she said to herself as the explosion, the smoke, and finally the imagined sound of clanking machinery conspired to evoke unhappy memories of her childhood.

Years ago, sitting in the family's dilapidated truck, she'd experienced similar sensations as she waited for her father to finish work. In those days, her father and an army of fellow miners labored long hours to extract copper ore from a sprawling open pit mine in southern Arizona. Her father and the others were long gone now, but she was certain that the trench was still there, a mile-deep scar in the high desert just north of the Mexican border.

Every evening when Anne was a girl, families arrived in secondhand trucks and automobiles, parking on the upper tier of the pit while the miners below changed shifts. In the gathering dusk, the rumble of distant explosions and the clatter of working machinery reached those who waited high above on the dusty rim of the ever-expanding mine. As a child, Anne had sat alongside her mother in the family's old Ford pickup. Waiting there on the rim of the Bisbee mine, she'd listened to the distant sounds of igniting dynamite, the rumble of dump trucks and rock crushers, the grating of blast-hole drills, and the relentless pawing of steam-shovels. Caught in a cycle of never-ending work, men and machines labored around the clock, rapaciously assaulting the earth far below, and accompanied all the while by an unholy and unceasing racket. On those long-ago evenings she'd closed her eyes and imagined the unseen mechanisms to be huge prehistoric monsters trapped in the enormous pit, lamenting their fate, and bellowing in agony.

Despite her efforts to stifle them, memories of those long-ago evenings came surging back. She remembered waiting above the pit and, though she tried to suppress her thoughts, she also recalled the rest. She remembered the moist package in her lap—a folded towel filled with ice cubes and wrapped around two unopened bottles. Young Anne was in charge of the cold beers which her father would be expecting at the end of his shift and she shuddered at the memory of that icy towel balanced between her legs.

She remembered her father cursing as he yanked on the truck door then slammed it shut. Once inside, the exhausted man—his overalls stinking of sweat, his face a mask of dirt—pushed against his timid daughter. Angrily grasping both beers in one thick hand, he used his pocketknife to uncap them. No one spoke. Her mother started the pickup. As they left the dust and noise of the mine behind and turned onto a gravel road, her father would tip his hardhat back, guzzle both beers, belch raucously, and toss the empties into the darkness.

For twenty miles the family rode in silence, her mother driving, her father snoring. When at last they arrived at the cabin, there was inevitably a third beer and then more. Everything came flooding back and Anne remembered the nights she'd trembled beneath her blanket with her bedroom door locked while the cabin filled with the echoes of her hard-drinking father devolving from a gloomy giant into a volatile, unpredictable monster.

"Think about something else," she instructed herself. This was the mantra she repeated whenever her mind strayed into unwanted memories.

That mantra, and her religious routine of daily running, these were the things that centered her, the things that calmed her and guided her to suppress the past and concentrate on the present. Today's explosion stirred old memories. Under other circumstances, she would have preferred to leave the car behind and, pursued by the past, run as far away and as fast as she could. But running was not an option at the moment. She needed to refocus on the task at hand. There were no more explosions and the roadside birds piped up again. After hesitating a moment longer, Anne resumed her work until she was satisfied that she'd done what she could to free the Bug from its mantle of clinging mud. Then she rinsed the jack handle in a nearby puddle and wiped it clean.

"I like a man which looks after they tools," her unschooled father used to say.

She soaked her gloves too, wrung them out, and put them and the handle into the trunk. Then she frowned at the mud on her jeans and shoes.

"At least I didn't sit in the crap," she decided, although she reached around and felt her backside just to make sure.

Anne climbed into the Bug and took a moment to get her bearings. According to her map, the next village was Lavender—a tiny place and not on her itinerary but closer than any other option. With a final look back toward the treacherous road she'd survived, she elected to go forward. Under no circumstances would she chance the muddy hill again. Somehow, she'd get back on track. Except for her muddy detour, she'd been adhering faithfully to her schedule. It was true that, since leaving Tucson yesterday morning, she'd dawdled a bit, but she made up the time and managed, by late last night, to reach the midway point of her assignment. Checking into her motel, she'd nervously telephoned her professor to report her progress.

"It's Anne, Dr. Clark," she'd said when her call to the professor's smartphone rolled over to voicemail. "It's a bit late—sorry—but I'm spending the night in Delta City. I've got caches one through six all in place. No problems.

Good weather. Halfway done. Not real good cell service here so I'm using the motel phone and I'm really sorry for calling you so late, but everything's all right here. Well, okay then. So—once again sorry and have a good night." She hung up and glanced at the clock. It was well past eleven—she'd just managed to get her call in before midnight.

Dr. Clark hadn't called back, but that was to be expected. He was a busy man, so it was up to her to keep him informed. No need for him to call her.

Studying the map as she sat in the VW, listening to the music of the roadside birds, Anne prayed the place ahead would have a carwash and a restaurant. Then she started the Bug and pulled away, leaving a jumble of discarded mud behind. As she drove further, a handful of gunk dislodged from someplace she hadn't been able to reach, but she kept going. No way was she going to pull over. Once she had her mind set on something, there was no stopping and no turning back. She rolled the window down and let the warmth of the summer day wash over her. Drinking lustily from her water bottle, she belched audibly, and began to sing aloud a song from her undergraduate days.

"By the light, of the Tri-Delta moon..."

As she shifted through the gears, the VW's earnest engine hummed industriously and pushed steadily from behind, seeming to guide her onward. She put her shoulders back and pressed on the accelerator as a final glob of mud and pebbles spurted from beneath the Bug and collided noisily with the passing pavement. Then she heard only the rhythm of the engine and the rush of the wind. Eager to be on the move, she felt determined to complete her task and a little feisty. The story of her journey through Colorado was about to open a new chapter. She was ready to go to Lavender and for Lavender's sake she sincerely hoped that the people there were ready for her.

Chapter 5

When the echoes of the explosion had dissipated and the Bentley and its occupants were reduced to smoldering wreckage, the German started his 4Runner and abandoned the mangled vehicle and its murdered passengers. With renewed purpose and no hint of remorse, he obeyed the detour sign, steered left, and drove downhill. With four Russians eliminated from the equation, he would see for himself why someone was so anxious to have traffic go in this direction. As needed, he'd confront the girl and deal with the Russian who followed her.

"Zwei Fliegen mit einer Klappe," he said aloud. Two birds, one stone.

His pistol in its holster lay on the passenger seat. He moved the weapon closer and glanced over his shoulder at the arsenal in his back seat. His shotgun and rifle were still in their cases. Additional explosives were secured in banded crates. His knife, of course, was where it always was, in the scabbard on his hip. He was ready for Lavender and he wondered if they were ready for him.

Chapter 6

The mid-morning sun was shining brightly, and the temperature was pushing eighty when Anne reached Lavender. The village was situated in a broad valley surrounded by low hills on three sides with the slopes of the towering Grand Mesa dominating the northern edge. She crossed over a bridge spanning a small stream and turned toward a cluster of buildings. Lavender was small and yet it had both a carwash and a restaurant. In fact, the two conveniences were on the same property. She slowed down for a moment and then, even though she was starving, decided to wash the car before the remaining mud dried in place.

To reach the wash bay, she was obliged to drive through the restaurant parking lot. She could see that the vintage establishment—an old pancake house—had a bank of large windows with stools at a long counter and several booths facing her way. The lot was full, and Anne was certain the diners inside were watching the passing spectacle of her Bug with its mud cocoon. They'd be laughing at her expense and winking at one another in the knowing way locals do when they can clearly see that an uninformed tourist has taken the wrong road. Anne crouched down as low as possible and continued toward the carwash. She was anxious to finish her chore, but her plans were derailed when she arrived at the wash bay. The Jiffy-Spiffy Carwash required quarters and there was no change machine.

"Figures," she said aloud.

She'd have to swallow her pride, return to the restaurant, and ask for change. Resigning herself to the necessity of walking back, she was just beginning to dig through her purse to gather some folding money when someone tapped on her window. Without thinking, she rolled it down.

"Looks to be a five-dollar job, I reckon." She detected an accent—a foreign influence mitigated by a smattering of western slang—that was interesting. The man was tall. He'd leaned over to tap on the Bug's window but had immediately straightened up again. Anne could hear his voice but couldn't see his face or his shoulders for that matter. She sat stock still for a moment before she realized she was staring directly at his crotch. "Ma'am?" he asked.

"Yes, sorry." Anne opened the door, clutching her shoulder bag in one hand and a fistful of dollar bills in the other. Feeling flustered, she climbed awkwardly out of the Bug, stepped into a graveled puddle, and immediately lost her footing. A strong arm steadied her. She looked up and wanted to say thank you, but instead she remained silent and stared.

Despite his unfamiliar accent, the man might have stepped out of central casting for a vintage American cowboy movie. He wore tight jeans and sturdy boots along with an authentic western shirt—everything needed to complete the part except a Stetson and a horse. His complexion was dark, and his hair was graying ever so slightly at the temples. And his eye was blue. She could only see one. Where the other should have been, a weathered scar angled across his otherwise handsome face.

"Sorry to come up on you so sudden-like," he said. Then he smiled. It was a warm smile and her thoughts of the scar vanished. "I am Diak—Diak Hodell." He offered his hand and she shook it and introduced herself. His fingers were thick and warm and rough. She held his hand a little too long. The accent—was it German?

"I am going to need that back," he said and smiled again.

"Of course," she blushed and let go of his hand.

"I saw you come across the pancake lot and I wonder might you be in need of these?" He held out a roll of quarters. "I ask Madge to give me some from her cash register and I wonder if you might need a handful."

"How much can you spare?" Anne asked.

"How much ones you got?" he responded.

After making change, the stranger realigned the wash bay's adjustable ramps to accommodate the Bug's narrow wheelbase.

"We do not have many of these baby cars here," he explained.

He used hand signals to guide Anne as she steered slowly up onto the ramp until her car was safely in place with its nose in the air. When she'd set the emergency brake, he helped her out of the Bug and down off the ramp. Then he fed the timer and motioned for her to stand back while he wrangled the high-powered nozzle and began to blast mud from the Bug's wheel wells and undercarriage.

It was a nasty and noisy job, but he aimed the water skillfully and he moved gracefully—like a dancer she thought. As he worked around the car, he managed to remain dry by deftly dodging ribbons of ricocheting water and sprigs of diluted mud. He was doing a splendid job and he looked good doing it. Still, she was surprised by how quickly she'd accepted the stranger's help. She liked to think of herself as a liberated and independent woman and, under normal circumstances, she'd have resisted an ordinary male's wrong-headed attempt to rescue a damsel in distress. And yet, since the rainstorm, her circumstances had been anything but normal and something told her that this particular male was anything but ordinary. But it wasn't in her nature to stand idly by and she couldn't resist making a comment.

"Pardon," he said. Anne had said something which he didn't hear so he released the nozzle trigger and interrupted the noisy spray.

"I said, it looks like you've done this before," she shouted.

"Yes. If anybody here—including and especially myself—claims they have never been caught in the rain on Old Goat Trail, they would be lying," he yelled back as he resumed his task.

"Old Goat Trail," she shouted. "Is that what it's called?"

"Yes, ma'am!" he said and grinned.

My gosh, Anne thought, *I wonder how long this guy needs to know me before he stops calling me ma'am.* Then she frowned. The ma'am business was probably her own fault. Moments ago, when she introduced herself to this handsome stranger, she'd blurted out her standard "Anne with an 'e,' Scriptor with an 'o'" spiel. She'd picked up that annoying habit as a college freshman during sorority rush. She figured everyone she met would be judging her and she wanted to make certain that, if she was going to be rejected, at least her detractors would remember to spell her name right. Anne thought about her college days as she watched the dexterous cowboy hose down the Bug.

Five years ago, she'd been a younger-than-average and extremely pessimistic freshman when she threw caution to the wind and dived into the tumultuous activity of visiting prospective sorority houses. She'd entered the so-called 'rush' activity with low expectations. She was expecting to be dismissed by all those rich, trust-fund girls from genteel homes. She was just a skinny kid from a mining camp with a drunkard father and a docile dropout mother, both dirt poor and both dead. Intelligent but shy and never a scholar, she'd applied to The University of Arizona with average grades and lackluster test scores and been admitted entirely on the strength of her heartfelt essay which contained as many misspellings as articulate ideas. In short, she was convinced that she didn't belong on campus and absolutely certain that no sorority would want her.

But she was pretty and personable and pleasantly surprised when all five houses she rushed invited her to pledge. Looking back, choosing the Tri-Deltas turned out to be one of her better decisions. She'd grown up longing for a sister—and suddenly she had fifty. She was reminiscing about her sorority days and humming, 'By the light, of the Tri-Delta moon,' when she realized that the stranger had finished.

"I know that tune," he said as he opened the Bug's door, released the emergency brake, and stepped clear, allowing the little car to roll gently down the ramps.

"It's a college song," Anne said. "Our sorority changed the lyrics a little, but the tune is the same. Thank you so much for your help and—and—oh, please excuse me because I just remembered I have to make a call."

The stranger put a few more coins in the timer and proceeded to dilute the piles of dislodged mud, explaining that he didn't want to leave debris clogging the wash-bay drain.

Watching him as she dialed her professor's number, she thought, *'I like a man which looks after they tools.' That saying again, will it ever leave me? Probably not since it's the only remotely fond memory I have of my father.*

"Think about something else," she sighed.

Chapter 7

Through his spotting scope, the German watched Anne drive to the carwash. He was about to abandon his cover and move closer when he saw a tall figure walking toward her and instantly recognized the scarred face.

So that's how it is, he thought. *Well, she has chosen the wrong bed-fellow and this interloper who masquerades as me will bear watching. There is only one Diak Hodell.* He frowned. *And I assure you, he is not amused. It seems that I must linger for a time in this backward village. This man could interfere with my plans, as might the girl, and meantime, there is no sign of the Russian who was following her. Many things are converging here, and something is amiss, and I had best discover what.*

With such thoughts in mind, the German decided to stay put. Instead of returning to Delta City, he'd remain hidden and continue to observe the girl and the imposter. After a few minutes, if they behaved normally, he'd break off his surveillance and explore the little village, cautiously searching for a suitable place to conceal himself and his vehicle. For the time being, he was content to remain in Lavender, the better to keep an eye upon the girl, the cowboy, and—as needed—the Russian, wherever that dullard might be.

Chapter 8

It was almost ten and Anne had nearly forgotten her plan to telephone Dr. Clark. She'd last reported her progress around midnight and it was time to update her professor. She dialed his smartphone number again and again she got his recording. She waited for the beep, then left a message saying she was taking a short break in a place called Lavender.

"Don't worry," she said. "I know—I know it's July 15 already but, like I reported last night, I'm already halfway finished, and I'll be back on schedule in no time..."

She paused, unable to think what to say next. Dr. Clark had been her mentor for years and she admired and respected him, but they hadn't grown close. That was probably her fault since she tended to keep older men at arm's length and Lord knows she had her reasons.

Think about something else, she thought and aloud she said, "So anyway I hope your summer is going well."

Ending the call, Anne returned to the wash bay and sensed that the helpful stranger was about to leave. She wracked her brain for an excuse to prolong their acquaintance, but "I'm starving" was all she could think to say.

"Me also," he said.

As they left the carwash, the sound of the harmonica surprised her. The stranger must have had the portable instrument in his pocket because he suddenly produced it as he walked alongside the Bug. And, while she slowly drove toward the pancake house, he played a familiar tune.

By the light, she thought to herself, *of the Tri-Delta moon.*

As she drove, Anne imagined herself as a starry-eyed coed again, joining with her sisters to serenade a gaggle of horny fraternity boys. When she sang long ago in the university quad as part of a sparkly and doe-eyed sorority chorus, she'd scanned their male audience hoping to see a kind face, a face of someone who wouldn't hurt her.

Think about something else.

Returning to the reality of Lavender, she offered the cowboy a ride, but he insisted on walking.

"I do not think I can fold up that way, ma'am," he said as he stopped playing but continued walking and leaned over to examine the Bug's cramped interior.

I've had bigger than you in here, she thought to herself, and then her face reddened at the memory of her college days and the fevered night she'd made-out in the Bug with Clarence, the six-foot-eleven second-string center of the Arizona Wildcat basketball team. Not only was the heavy petting unsatisfying but, looking back, it had been nearly anatomically impossible.

When they reached the parking lot, she stopped, and the stranger opened her car door and called her ma'am again. Anne grabbed her shoulder bag and followed him to the restaurant door, which he opened for her.

A gentleman, she thought.

Once inside, he excused himself to wash up and she watched him amble down a narrow hallway toward the restroom. As he walked away, she couldn't help noticing his broad shoulders, solid back, tight buns, and sturdy legs.

And he would be how old? She found herself speculating.

Anne was so intent on watching her new companion traverse the hallway that she failed to notice everyone else in the restaurant was staring at her. Only when she turned toward the main dining area did she realize the extent of their attention and utter a little yelp of surprise. Obviously, she must look terrible. In rapid succession, she covered her mouth, turned away, and rushed briskly down the same hallway. Ducking into the ladies' room, she bolted the door with trembling hands and switched on the lights.

"Oh, my god," she said aloud as she beheld her image in the murky mirror. The rain and wind had done their worst and her hair had been whipped into chaos. It was such a mess that even the most charitable observer would have the impression that her ordinarily well-kept pixie cut had been processed in a blender and then struck by lightning.

One side of her head looked like a matted helmet and the other resembled a frazzled rat's nest. She wasn't vain about her appearance, but why in the world hadn't she thought to check herself in the VW's mirror? What was she thinking? Thanks to the gloves, her hands were clean but her poor face! Her flawless complexion was marred by an unflattering patina of mud which blemished her cheeks, nose, and forehead. Her ivory top was splotched, the unsightly mud trailing across the front of her blouse and up both arms to the elbows. Her jeans and shoes were soiled too. She could live with that and she could manage somehow to rearrange her hair but, short of dining in her bra, there was nothing Anne could do with her filthy blouse. She was about to dash back into the hallway in search of a rear exit when she heard a familiar tap on the bathroom door.

"Ma'am?"

Anne opened the door a crack.

"This was washed only this morning."

The stranger was offering her his shirt.

"What will you...?"

"Oh, I have eaten here in my undershirt before now. I will go and get the coffee up."

His shirt was huge. The ample garment hung far down until it brushed her knees. Her own shirt was damp. His felt comfortably dry and it had a pleasant aroma that she couldn't place. She took off her blouse and hurriedly washed her face. Inhaling the aroma of his shirt, she buttoned it up, then tucked it in, stuffing it down past her butt. Then she reached in front and pushed the fabric across her stomach and further down until she felt a warm tingle.

Easy, girl, she told herself.

Anne rolled up the cozy garment's ample sleeves then took time to comb and brush her hair until it looked more presentable. She rinsed her grimy blouse in the sink, used paper towels to press and blot it, and finally folded the distressed garment as neatly as she could into her shoulder bag. At last, after one final look in the mirror, she emerged into the hallway wearing the cowboy's shirt and as much of a casual smile as she could manage.

Her benefactor was waiting in a booth which, she noticed, was set apart from other diners. She imagined this was his idea, a gentlemanly gesture to save her further embarrassment. Nevertheless, the restaurant fell silent the moment she entered the dining area and she was certain everyone was once again watching her. This impression was confirmed the moment she slid into the booth opposite him because, as soon as she disappeared from view, the restaurant again sprang alive with chatter.

"Well," she said, "here I am."

"And my shirt, it never looked so good," he said.

"Well, thanks," she said as she reached for a menu. She should have acknowledged his obvious compliment with more enthusiasm. She should also have taken time to admire his muscular physique, which his sleeveless undershirt made all too apparent, but suddenly she was absolutely famished.

"Chicken fried steak is good, unless you do not eat the animals. And the pancakes are very good also." he suggested.

"Well, it's pancakes for me," Anne decided. "No contest."

"Pancakes please," he told the waitress. Then he and Anne shared a smile and he added, "Well now, I think I should say to you: welcome to Lavender."

Chapter 9

As they waited for their meal, Anne's mind was racing. Time was passing and her schedule was blown. If she'd been thinking more clearly, she'd have brought her map along in order to ask her dining companion—who was obviously a local—for advice on how to resume her route back to the main highway.

She was anxious to resume her route—wasn't she?

Plus, other questions were crowding her thoughts. How could she discover this attractive man's age without asking directly? And why was that so important? She couldn't say why, but it was, so she kept talking and smiling while her mind tried to parse it out. Given his hair and complexion and solid build (no middle-aged belly she noticed), her best guess was thirty. That would make him eight years her senior and that was doable. But why did it need to be doable? Then again, maybe he was thirty-five. That would be pushing it, but his body was...

"Thirty-one," he said.

"Excuse me?"

"I see it in your eyes," he said. "You are wondering two things: which county road to take out of town and how old am I. The answer to both is thirty-one."

"How...?"

Their order arrived and—faced with a generous stack of golden-brown pancakes—Anne's appetite temporarily overruled her curiosity. They dined without conversation, the two strangers exchanging an occasional glance as Anne ate with abandon. Like a starving child, she savaged her pancakes, chewing heartily and making 'yummy' sounds, until at last she pushed her plate away.

"I can't eat another bite, or I'll burst," she said. "Now, tell me how on earth you guessed what I was thinking."

"I saw the map in your little car," he said as if that settled the matter.

"That might explain your advice about the road, but how did you guess the other—that I was curious about your age?"

"It is a natural question."

"It is?"

"Yes. And, to your next most natural question, I will answer, riding a bull."

"How you lost your eye do you mean?"

"Yes."

"Details?"

"The bull won."

Anne hesitated for a moment and then burst out laughing. He followed suit and the two were still chuckling when the waitress returned.

"Dessert, you two?" she asked.

"With pancakes?" asked Anne.

The waitress raised an eyebrow.

"We will take two slices of your fine apple pie," he said.

"Uh-huh," said the waitress with a doubtful tone and the obviously irritated woman walked away.

"So where are you from?" asked Anne, carelessly slipping into singles' bar banter before she could stop herself. It was an awkward moment and the two shared another laugh.

"The same question for you," he said. "But let me guess—you have Arizona license plates I notice—so my guess is Tucson."

"How...?"

"Your wildcat bobble-head and university parking sticker."

"Ah, so you're a detective?" she speculated.

"Yes."

"A thirty-one-year-old, one-eyed, detective."

"That sums me up, yes, ma'am."

"And what will it take for you to call me Anne?"

"You could pay for my pie," he suggested and there was that smile again.

"Deal," she said.

Chapter 10

The day wore on and pancake house customers came and went until the place was practically empty. Anne and her new companion remained in their booth, sated with pancakes and pie, fortified with coffee, and chatting like old friends. She was instantly drawn to the handsome stranger whose charm and wit kept her centered in the present. Not once, as they talked and laughed together, was she tempted to admonish herself to think about something else. Not once was she tempted to dwell on the past. She was living in the moment in Lavender and he too was present, and it felt like home.

Just when Anne was beginning to wonder where all this was leading, the stranger's attention was drawn to the restaurant window as a black Bentley turned off the pavement and rolled through the parking lot. Anne turned to follow his gaze and saw that the lower part of the Bentley, like her Bug, sported a skirt of tawny mud.

"Old Goat Trail?" she asked.

"Seems like."

"Lost?" she speculated.

He didn't answer. Instead he turned from the window and looked past Anne, avoiding her gaze, and with an expression that seemed to cloud his features. She sensed something new in his demeanor, something dark—not exactly sinister—more like determination. Anne tried to follow his gaze, but suddenly he was on his feet.

"Excuse me," he said.

She turned to watch over her shoulder as he started down the hallway in the direction of the restrooms. *Too much coffee,* she imagined. She looked back toward the window and was reaching for her cup when she heard a rasping sound and turned again. She was just in time to catch a glint of sunlight before the exit door at the far end of the hallway slammed shut with a resounding bang.

"You want your check?" The waitress' voice startled Anne.

"Uh..."

"Never mind. I'll put it on Halloween's tab—as usual," the waitress said as she turned away.

"Halloween? But I...wait."

The woman seemed not to hear, so Anne grabbed her shoulder bag, jumped to her feet, and pursued her.

"Miss?" Anne called out.

The waitress stopped, turned around, and crossed her arms as Anne approached. "It's Ms. if you don't mind."

"Sorry."

"Can I help you?" the waitress asked. She was a stout woman who towered over Anne. Her tone sounded impatient.

"You said 'Halloween.'"

"What of it?"

"That man I was sitting with—you called him Halloween."

"Well, ain't he in that get-up?"

"I..."

"Oh, I see. You ain't in on it, I guess. Well, come closer." The waitress looked right and left as she motioned for Anne to sit down at the counter. Then the woman leaned toward her and continued in a conspiratorial whisper. "You want some advice, dearie? Forget the check. You just get that perky little butt of yours back into that teeny-weeny car and blow town right now. And don't be talkin' to any strangers on the way out."

Chapter 11

The cowboy didn't return, and the Bentley too had disappeared. It was mid-afternoon when Anne arrived at a crossroads where she stopped the VW and studied her map. Confused, but determined to resume her route, Anne had found County Road 31 easily enough and the map showed that this two-lane pavement made a perfect diagonal cross-country to link up with the highway. No mud. No problem. So why was she sitting at the intersection, blocking the road, with the Bug's motor running? A horn honked behind her and a farm truck wheeled around. Through her open window, she caught a profanity as the driver sped on.

"Dumb bitch," she repeated the insult. "That's me all right."

Anne had taken Madge's advice. What was Madge's problem anyway? At least she thought the waitress' name was Madge. Her name tag said so, but Anne was beginning to doubt that the residents of Lavender were entirely truthful. Anyway, she hadn't taken the woman's advice precisely. Instead of immediately getting her butt into the Bug and blowing town, Anne had taken time to get her suitcase and change clothes in the ladies' room before she left. Then she'd driven twelve miles until she came to the county road where she hit the brakes and sat there wondering two things:

What the heck just happened back there?

And why the heck am I keeping it?

After posing the second question to herself, she glanced at the passenger seat. Diak—or Halloween depending on who you believed—would probably be missing his shirt about now and wondering where she was. *Where,* he might be asking himself, *is the ma'am who ate pancakes and pie and, despite her promise, didn't pay for either?*

For a moment she considered calling Dr. Clark to let him know she was decidedly off-schedule, but she couldn't bring herself to report her dereliction of duty. Maybe there would still be time to resume her route. She wanted to resume it didn't she? She shook her head and tried to dislodge the nonsense that was rattling around in there.

It didn't work.

Anne waited a second more. Then she made a U-turn and headed back to Lavender. Retracing her route, she was only mildly surprised to see her mysterious one-eyed companion sitting on the front steps of the pancake house in his jeans and undershirt. She pulled to a stop as the stranger stood up and, with some effort, got into the Bug.

"Where to?" she asked.

"Turn right for now."

She obeyed. "Where are we going, may I ask?"

"You may. Turn left here."

"So, you won't tell me where we're going. What shall I call you at least?" she asked.

"What shall you—oh—I reckon you've been talking to Madge."

"Yes, indeed I have," she said and, despite feeling piqued, she smiled.

"If you're smiling, does that mean you ain't mad?" he asked.

"I'm not smiling and I ain't not mad and I'm stopping this car until you answer one question!" She slammed on the brakes and the Bug skidded to an abrupt halt.

"Ask away."

Anne took a deep breath, then blurted out, "Am I crazy? Or are *you* crazy? Or is Madge crazy?"

"Well, technically that's three questions and the answers are, in the order asked, no and maybe and probably," he said.

"Hmm. I thought knowing the answers would help, but it doesn't seem to," Anne said as she put the car in gear and continued on. "And is it my imagination, or has your English improved?"

"Turn here. Under the archway."

As they passed underneath, Anne tried to read the metal sign, but all she could discern was *Lavender H—something*.

"Your place?" she asked.

"Looks like."

Leaving the archway behind, Anne drove uphill. Nearing the top, she was conscious of a pleasant sensation. "Tell me," she inquired, "what's that delicious aroma?"

"That, my girl, is lavender," he grinned.

Anne guided the Bug up a steadily rising and bone-dry gravel road. Apparently, this morning's storm had not reached this far. When the road crested, she was delighted to see a vast field of lavender plants surrounding her. Bright rows of bluish-purple flowers stretched out on both sides of the roadway, creating a striking contrast to the subdued pallor of nearby hills. She slowed the Volkswagen to gaze at thousands of tightly knit shrubs which graced the ground like an immense plush carpet, forming a luxurious oasis in an otherwise featureless desert.

"They're beautiful," she gushed.

"Eyes on the road please."

"I suppose there's a castle at the other end," she speculated.

"Just a small one," he said, his words strangely muted.

Hearing his muffled voice, Anne turned to look at her passenger and discovered that he'd retrieved his shirt from the seat and had it draped over his head, like a cold sufferer breathing in vapors. He seemed to be struggling with the garment, unable to pull it on, and literally wiping his face with it. She stopped the car.

"Can I help you?" she asked.

"No thanks," he replied. "There—that's better." He poked his head out, turned to face Anne, and caught her as she fainted.

Chapter 12

Anne was lying on a sofa, propped up by pillows. She wasn't sure how much time had passed, but one thing was certain—she was holding an ice pack to her forehead.

"That dang gear shift knob," she said aloud. "Now I know what too-tall Clarence was complaining about."

"Who's this Clarence?" asked her host, who arrived with a tray full of tea and biscuits. He placed the tray on a low table alongside the sofa, poured two cups, and handed one to his visitor.

"Never mind Clarence," she retorted, placing the ice pack aside and accepting the proffered cup with a frown. "Who's Halloween? And who's Diak Hodell?"

"Touché," he said. "You vant I should go get him?" He scrunched up his left eye.

"You can drop the phony accent," she said. "And I think I liked you better with one eye. However, this tea is delicious."

"Lavender, my girl."

"You're kidding," she said.

"Not at the moment."

"Tea from lavender?" she asked.

"Part of the harvest of Lavender Hill Farm, my humble piece of heaven and our little village's namesake: fields of delicious tea, healing tinctures, natural remedies, skin care lotion, potpourri, and essential oils—a beautiful plant with many virtues," he assured her.

"Ah—virtues—such as truth-telling—now there's a fine old-fashioned virtue," she chided.

"So, it's the truth you want? Where to begin?"

Anne stared at him, set her tea cup down, folded her hands together, and expounded: "'Begin at the beginning' the King said gravely, 'and go on till you come to the end: then stop.' Oh, my god," she realized. "I'm quoting from Alice in Wonderland. What's next I wonder? A rabbit with a watch-chain? Invisible grinning cats? Caterpillars and talking playing cards?"

"You should hear yourself."

"Oh, no you don't—I'm not the one who's maybe crazy," she said.

"So, I understand that you insist on an explanation."

"I insist," she said, and she felt her face flush as her feelings vacillated between confusion and anger.

"So, I…" he began, but she interrupted.

"I'll tell you what," she demanded, "let's start with your real name."

"You're not buying Diak, I take it."

"Not at any price," she said.

"Would you believe Trinidad—Trinidad Sands?"

"Maybe—we'll see—it's not a bad name, but I'll let you know after I hear the rest."

He began again, but again she interrupted.

"And, furthermore, I insist on a *logical* explanation," she said and crossed her arms to emphasize her determination. Despite occupying a threadbare couch in a sparsely furnished living room which literally screamed bachelor-pad, she refused to be cowed by this mysterious stranger and was resolute in her attempt to make sense of a confusing situation.

Who is this man? What's with his former disguise? Why does he intrigue me so? And what am I doing here, sitting in a stranger's parlor, when I should be on my way?

"Hmm. A logical explanation?" her host continued. "Now that's going to be a bit difficult. I'll tell you what, to assist logic, I'll need your map and, luckily, I have it here. Excuse me." He carefully pulled her map from beneath the serving tray.

"You were using my map—my map—for a tablecloth?" she protested.

"Only temporarily, I was studying it in the kitchen and wanted to bring it along, but my hands were full. So—may I?"

Curious but also perturbed, Anne nodded her ascent. He moved the tea tray aside, opened the map, and spread it out on the coffee table. She sat up and frowned.

"Well," she said, "now what?"

"I can see that you have clearly marked your route," he observed.

"Yes." She sounded impatient.

"And this route was recommended to you by..." he prompted.

"Dr. C. Arnold Clark," she said.

"Who is..." he prompted again.

"My graduate advisor," she answered.

"And a professor of..."

"Archaeology at The University of Arizona," she answered with a raised eyebrow, suggesting she was on her guard.

"And what, pray tell, is your assignment?" he asked.

"My assign...oh..." Anne hesitated.

"Precisely."

"But my assignment is so...so..."

"Innocent?"

"Yes—I was going to say ordinary—but it's innocent as well," she declared.

"Would it surprise you to know you're being followed?" he asked.

"Followed? What..." she began.

"Yes, followed. And would it surprise you to know that four of the men pursuing you were killed this morning?"

"Killed? But I..."

"Killed in an explosion?" he added.

"That sound—it wasn't miners?" she asked.

"Miners?" Trinidad asked as he took a seat beside her. "Whatever gave you that idea?"

Chapter 13

Anne seemed lost in thought, so Trinidad gave her a moment before he continued. In the hallway, a relentless grandfather clock was striking four.

"You're not going to faint again, are you?" he asked.

"No," Anne declared, still uncertain why she'd swooned in the first place. Was it the shock of seeing the sudden transformation of her enigmatic one-eyed cowboy? *Can't be that,* she thought, *must be the altitude.*

"Hello," he said to the attractive young woman who sat on his couch but seemed to be somewhere else.

"Sorry," she said. "Have you said something true? Did I miss it?"

For an instant their eyes met, and they might have sat there transfixed for some time, but the sound of Trinidad's hallway clock broke the spell.

"Four-fifteen already," he noted.

"I should get going," she decided.

"Listen," he said, "I'll tell you what. You insist on the truth, so I'll make a list of truths if you like."

"I like," said Anne, as she regarded the handsome cowboy and tried to suppress a smile.

"Very well," he took out a pocket notebook and a stubby pencil and made an elaborate show of compiling a written list. "First truth: I am a detective."

She raised an eyebrow.

"No really, I am—a real honest to goodness detective. Second truth: I am thirty-one years of age and, I know from reading my reports, that you yourself have just turned twenty-two—much too young for me, so put that idea out of your pretty head at once."

"Reports? What reports?" she asked aloud, but to herself she thought, *what idea and does he think I'm pretty?*

"Don't interrupt please. Now, where was I? Oh yes, here's the third truth: I was once thrown while riding a bull."

"Shooting the bull don't you mean?" she said, then screwed her face into a disapproving scowl.

"A clever interruption—I commend you—but an interruption, nevertheless. And such a face! May I please continue?"

"If you must," she allowed, but she didn't alter her expression.

"Such a face," he repeated, as he paused to count on his fingers. "So, as for a fourth truth—hmm—I forget...but I'm positive I've told you at least four truths," he claimed.

"And maybe one big whopping lie—is your name really Trinidad? Or is that just one more gigantic falsehood?" she asked.

"Oh, it's Trinidad all right. I'm named for a town in southern Colorado, once a famous crossroads in the Old West. Well, they tell me I was born there. So naturally the name stuck. Trinidad has a nice ring to it don't you think?"

"Well—I think someone is ringing the bell alright, but there's nobody home," she scoffed. "So why the fake name and why appear to me in disguise in the first place?"

"You mean the eye scar prosthesis? Oh, that wasn't for you, dear girl. It was intended to fool our friend in the Bentley. Of course, I wasn't expecting either of you to come from that direction, through the mud I mean. You and the Bentley were meant to encounter the highway roadblock that the Feds had so lavishly prepared and which they are even now disassembling and..."

He paused and found Anne staring at him.

"I have no idea what you're talking about," she said.

"Sorry, you wouldn't know about the roadblock, would you? The Feds thought up that idea to force you down here but, anyway, I'm getting ahead of my story. Now think back," he said. "Your map clearly suggests that you were instructed to travel on paved highways—correct?"

She started to answer, but he continued speaking.

"If you'd followed your map, you'd have encountered the roadblock which would have brought you here to Lavender, but on the pavement and from the opposite direction, of course. If you had adhered to your assigned route, you'd have come into town from the direction we were expecting and with the Bentley behind you and without either of you traipsing through that mud. But you fooled us and if Madge hadn't seen you and alerted me—well, anyway she did..."

"Madge? Do you mean to say...?"

"But—come to think of it—it's actually better that you didn't continue on the highway. If you'd gone that way, you would have arrived at the barricade where this morning's explosion occurred—now that's interesting. That explosion was unanticipated. Our mission is to stifle the opposition, of course, but not by blowing the buggers sky high. And you..."

He paused and considered Anne.

"What about me?" she asked.

"Well, to put it mildly, you're full of surprises and, of course, I have to wonder if you took the Old Goat Trail turnoff because you suspected something might happen—but never mind—we'll sort that out later. In any event, of course, what happened at the roadblock was a clumsy attack."

"Not only clumsy but also pretty darn loud as I recall," she said.

"Loud for you maybe," he clarified.

"Maybe not loud enough to be heard here in Lavender," she admitted, "but the blast was just over the hill from me and—say, what exactly are you accusing me of—and why do you keep saying 'of course' and who got blown up and are you disappointed it wasn't me and who is this 'we' you keep talking about?"

Trinidad ignored her torrent of questions. "So, where were we? Oh yes, instead of following your map—as instructed—you took what you're asking us to believe was an unrehearsed shortcut. But look here..."

He moved the map aside, took three cubes from the sugar bowl, and placed them on the coffee table an equal distance apart. When the cubes were in place, he pointed to the center one.

"This is you," he said and then he put his finger on the cube beside it. "Now we have Bentley Number One traveling south and full of bad guys, rushing to intercept you." He slid the cube a few inches. "But they come to the detour—a diversion staged by us—whereupon, instead of taking the turn to come here, as we expected everyone would do, these fellows try to drive around and for their trouble they get blown to smithereens. But that makes no sense because..."

"Now look, I..." she interjected, but Trinidad held a finger aloft.

"A moment if you please. I'm just beginning to ponder the logic of this for the first time. Who blew up the Bentley and was the ambush intended for the Russians or for you? Well, never mind, we, that is, I'll leave that for the others to sort out. Luckily—and certainly it was luck that it was them instead of you—and..."

Trinidad seemed to lose his train of thought but only for a moment. Then, before Anne could get a word in edgewise, he continued. "And, if it had been just you at the roadblock, then maybe there wouldn't have been an explosion at all and probably you would have taken the detour as we intended. No reason not to. The Bentley tried to drive around and, instead of coming here as we intended, they were determined to press forward, which must be what got them killed."

"Now see here..." she began.

"Ah, but we're forgetting Bentley number Two." Trinidad moved the remaining sugar cube toward the middle one. "This Bentley is tailing you northward and sees you turn unexpectedly onto Old Goat Trail. The plan was obviously for the Bentleys to close in from both directions and catch you in the middle. But suddenly you do the unexpected. You leave the pavement and it's still raining hard up there and, instead of following you down that muddy hillside, Bentley Two hesitates at the top. Your turn is surprising. The road is virtually impassable. Your pursuer is driving a company car and not sure he wants to get it dirty, so he stops at the top of the hill to call for instructions. Yes, that would explain his delay in arriving here—explain what kept him—and that would also explain how you managed to make it here safely, thank goodness."

"Thanks, I think, but I..."

Trinidad abandoned the sugar cubes, stood up, and began pacing as he warmed to his recitation. He was obviously, and literally, thinking on his feet.

"Now Bentley Number Two calls for instructions, but the boss is out, see? So, he leaves a message and sits and waits. After several minutes, nearly an hour maybe, the boss calls back. The boss is furious. The boss chews out the underling and tells him he absolutely better get after you. It's stopped raining by then, but Old Goat Trail is still a mess and Bentley Two is under orders, so he dives in, slips and slides his way to the bottom, picks up your trail, and hurries into town."

"And we saw him come by, headed for the carwash?" Anne suggested.

"Nope, I figure he spotted your Volkswagen right away in the pancake lot. Probably he was planning to circle around back, wait there out of sight to pick up the chase again, or maybe do worse, until I persuaded him otherwise." Trinidad stopped pacing and rubbed his knuckles.

"Persuaded him how? Never mind, I don't think I want to know. And who's following me and why? And how do you know all this?" She abruptly lost patience and was on her feet, confronting him, both fists in the air, and apparently looking for something or someone to punch.

"Take it easy!" he said, raising both hands in self-defense. "Look—you've got questions and I've got answers, but to hear them you'd better sit back down."

"I am not sitting down!" she declared.

"Okay, sister, but don't say I didn't warn you."

Chapter 14

Trinidad side-stepped Anne's aggression and left her fuming in the middle of the room while he pushed two easy chairs together and took a seat. Though she was reluctant, Anne sighed and sat too, facing him, their knees almost touching.

"Comfy?" he asked and flashed that smile of his.

She blushed and thought, *my God, I can't be falling for this guy. Pay attention!*

"As for why you're being followed, your assignment is the key," he began.

His smile, she thought, *I could absolutely get lost in that smile and his eyes—they are so gosh darn blue.* For an instant the room was silent until she said, "I'm sorry—what?"

"Your assignment—your assignment—try to focus on what I'm saying here. Clark sent you on your way with a map and padlocked toolboxes numbered one through twelve and with explicit instructions to place each one at a specific set of coordinates, correct?"

How does he know about the toolboxes and how does he know they're padlocked, she wondered? *Did he snoop while I was out of it?*

"Is all that correct?" he asked again.

"Yes," she answered and dismissed romantic notions as her temper began to rise. "And he's *Doctor* Clark if you don't mind. And I'm guessing you already know this, but what I'm doing—my assignment—is called geocaching. I'm setting up the caches as an exercise for a student fieldtrip scheduled for later this summer. It's a standard navigation drill."

Trinidad raised an eyebrow.

"Well, isn't it?" she asked.

"You tell me," he responded. "How would you describe the process?"

Detective at work, she thought, *guiding me to tell my story, probing for facts he probably knows already, exploring to see if I'm involved in something—but what?*

"Don't overthink it," he coached. "Talk to me like I'm an undergraduate without a clue."

"Okay, if it's important," she said.

"It is," he assured her.

"Okay then." She took a deep breath. "I'm positive you already know that geocaching is essentially a high-tech game of hide-and-seek. I use the GPS— the Global Positioning System—to hide—that is cache—something at a particular set of coordinates. I put each toolbox at an intersection of latitude and longitude. And then other students seek the boxes out, except they must use orienteering skills. Using a GPS device to locate the caches would be cheating—they must use a map and compass and protractor."

"So, what do you hide?"

"The cached box itself is usually a compact container—in this case a small toolbox. It typically holds a logbook and a pencil so that the person doing the concealing and the finder can communicate with one another."

"Go on," Trinidad prompted. "Is there always a logbook inside?"

"Not always, the university's cached containers are sometimes filled with trinkets that hiders and seekers trade. For example, I find a cache that contains a toy car and I take the car and leave a bit of costume jewelry in its place. Like a human pack-rat."

"That explains the caching," said Trinidad, "but how about the 'geo' part?"

"What you're calling 'the geo part' of geocaching is a nod to the practice of hiding the caches cleverly in a variety of landscapes. And often in remote locations requiring not only orienteering skill but also physical stamina to hike fair distances to locate them. Plus, in about twenty years of activity, the practice has become so widespread that geocaches can be pursued at diverse geographic locations all around the globe."

"Pursued by treasure hunters," Trinidad suggested.

"Not really. The purpose of the activity is to accurately hide and efficiently locate the cached container. The objects hidden and found have no real value and..." Engrossed in her description, Anne had picked up the sugar bowl and was using it as a prop, focusing on it, imagining it to be a geocache. She broke off her narrative when she sensed that Trinidad was staring at her. She put the bowl aside and looked up.

"What?"

"Do you know what's in your toolboxes?"

"They're locked."

"Aren't you curious?"

"Yes, of course I am," she seemed irritated by the question. "Naturally I hefted each one when Dr. Clark and I loaded them up in Tucson. And I shook each one again when I hid it—like you'd shake a wrapped Christmas present. But I heard no telltale noises, and nothing moved, so I naturally assumed from the weight that they contained exactly what I'd expect."

"Like trinkets or logbooks?" he asked.

"Yes, a trinket or a logbook, and probably taped in place which would explain why I didn't hear anything loose or rattling around."

"Hmm. Are the caches usually locked?"

"Not usually, although—now that I think about it—it was odd."

"Odd how?"

"I asked Dr. Clark about the locks and he said something odd."

Trinidad waited while Anne collected her thoughts.

"He said, 'Not to worry, I have the key.' 'I have the key,' he said. As if he—and not the fieldtrip students—would be the one opening the boxes."

"So, he wasn't planning to go along on the recovery fieldtrip?" Trinidad asked.

"No—that is, I guess I don't really know—he never went in the past. That's a job for grad assistants."

"Like yourself."

"Yes," she said.

"Did he say anything else?"

"Only to remind me that he, as usual, was thinking outside the box," she recalled.

"Hmm. Does that mean anything to you?" Trinidad asked.

"It's something he says all the time. It's a reminder to his students to think creatively."

"Were you and Clark close?" he asked. "Was he..."

"Well—*Doctor* Clark is my advisor so yes, I guess I know him pretty well and we get along and I respect his work. He's my mentor and I like him well enough. We're colleagues. You might even say we're friends. Now what's all this about?"

"Anne," he reached out and touched her hand. "Anne," he continued, "I have..."

"Wait—wait—you asked, 'were we close.' You said—oh, no—no—no!" She pulled away from him and put her hand to her mouth as she stood hurriedly. Taking an awkward step, she bumped the table and sent the sugar bowl clattering to the hardwood floor.

Trinidad was on his feet too and moving toward her, but she held out a hand to fend him off.

"No, no, no! Stop! Stay right where you are! Just—just stay back. Oh, my God—he can't be—I—I—need some air!" She turned then and fled out the front door and across the lawn until she encountered a wall where she stopped and leaned against the stones.

Trinidad followed slowly and stood a distance away. She didn't look up but kept her forehead pressed to the wall as she stared at the grass at her feet.

"I don't understand. I don't understand any of this. I-don't-under-stand. I-don't-under-stand." She was punctuating each syllable by striking her open palms against the immovable wall, as if the stones themselves were blocking her path to comprehension.

Fearing she would injure herself, Trinidad strode toward her, stood behind the trembling woman, and held her shoulders. She dropped her arms, then turned around, buried her face in his chest, and said in a very small voice.

"I don't understand."

Trinidad held Anne close and she felt a tingling sensation as he gently kissed the top of her head. Bewildered and feeling faint, she looked up to meet his eyes. She would never clearly recall what happened next. It might have been an accident, an inadvertent intersection of two faces as she looked up in confusion and he leaned down out of concern. Whatever happened, she seemed to levitate skyward to meet his lips.

Chapter 15

Once again Trinidad must have carried her inside. Anne had no memory of passing over the lawn, let alone climbing the stairs to reach this second-story room. She seemed to have lost track of time. She could hear the hall clock striking the quarter hour. She looked at her watch, struggling to comprehend that it was after six o'clock and unable to account for the missing hours. She was lying beneath a single sheet. There was no blanket. A fan whirled in the ceiling above her. It was hot in the room. A vague memory—something about her professor—seemed to float just beyond her recollection. She seemed to have dreamed that Dr. Clark was gone—and if gone, where did he go? *Surely not...surely not...*

Unwilling to consider the possibility, she shook her head and tried to think about something else. Which caused her to remember Trinidad's kiss. Which caused her to sigh. She lay still for a moment, watching the ceiling fan as it rotated above her. Then she peeked beneath the sheet to take inventory, feeling a bit disappointed to find she was more-or-less still fully clothed. She was wearing everything except shoes. Her blouse and bra were intact, as were her jeans, panties, and socks. She moved the sheet aside, swung her feet out, and sat on the edge of the bed.

Her dash across the lawn had ended at the wall. The sprint had been a short one and, depending on how long she'd slept just now, it might be more than twelve hours since she'd taken a proper run. She doubted if she'd get a chance anytime soon. So much for her normal exercise routine. So much for anything approaching normal. For one thing, she'd lost consciousness twice—once in her VW when she saw Trinidad's suddenly wholesome face pop out of his shirt—and now again at the wall. This business of fainting was entirely new to her. She was fit and lean. She was no shrinking violet.

Got to be the altitude, she told herself.

A day ago, she'd driven a marathon of 700 miles from the low Arizona desert to the high mountains of Colorado, plus she'd traveled several more miles on foot to set out her caches. To reach most of the cache sites, she'd walked three or four miles one-way and sprinted back the same distance. She was used to vigorous exercise, but not at five-times the altitude. Dr. Clark had warned her to take it easy in Colorado, but she hadn't listened. She'd pushed herself and—since yesterday's running had produced no ill effects—she figured the altitude thing must be a myth. Last night she'd slept like a baby, arisen at dawn, gone for a vigorous run, showered, and had breakfast—following her desert routine to the minute. Then she'd endured the stress of surviving Old Goat Trail and...

Maybe that's what triggered my fainting spells, she realized. *Maybe my body was still adjusting and the drama on that muddy hill set something off. Whatever it was, I'm okay now—I think.*

Just to be sure, she took several deep breaths. Then she slid onto the floor and assumed a lotus position. She inhaled expansively, then breathed out, forcing her lungs to empty. She decided to do a lion pose. Sitting up straight, she let her palms rest against her knees. She splayed her fingers to emulate claws. She inhaled deeply through her nose while simultaneously opening her eyes and mouth widely. Then she exhaled slowly through her mouth, stretching her tongue down toward her chin, forming a 'ha' sound, and feeling the expelled breath glide over the back of her throat.

She did three repetitions before changing her leg position—crossing the left ankle over the right—and repeating the exercise. Then she closed her eyes and remained in lotus on the floor, controlling her breathing. Feeling relaxed, she sought her bearings. If Dr. Clark was dead, she'd need an explanation and she wondered if it would do any good to ask Trinidad. What would he tell her? Could she believe anything he said? The house seemed deadly quiet until she listened further and detected rhythmic thumping—fingers on a keyboard—someone typing—someone typing rapidly—someone who knew how.

She could see one of her shoes under the bed, but she left it there and went downstairs in her stocking feet. Reaching the main floor, she followed the typing sounds to a small room, apparently a home office. Anne stood in the doorway until Trinidad looked up.

"Good afternoon," she said. "Is it still afternoon?"

Trinidad looked down at his laptop, applied a few more keystrokes, and then closed it. "Sleep well?" he asked.

"Yes. Did you give me something?"

"Lavender tea."

"Naturally," she said as she crossed the room and moved behind him to place her hands on his shoulders, partly to see if he would appreciate her touch, but also hoping to get a glimpse of what he was working on. The laptop remained closed, but she could see a Colorado map tucked beneath it—a brand new map, still wrapped in a plastic sleeve. "All roads lead to Lavender, yes? Are you working on my case?"

"Your case?"

"The case of the mystery caches, not to mention the fate of my professor," she said as her voice faltered.

"Just catching up on some paperwork," he said flatly. His tone was business-like. He seemed unsympathetic and she felt a tinge of disappointment.

"Hmm," Anne said. Convinced that her indifferent host was being uncooperative, she decided to try another tact. *Time to play the romance card,* she thought as she began to playfully caress Trinidad's shoulders.

"Look, maybe we should just..." he began, but she interrupted.

"Tell you what," she said. "Since you refuse to enlighten me about the caches or Dr. Clark, I've got another mystery for you."

"Which is?"

"Who kissed who?" she asked.

"Is that even proper English?"

"Depends—was it a proper kiss?"

"Seemed like a good idea at the time," he said.

"Hmm. Older man takes advantage of confused and grief-stricken maiden —how would that look in the headlines?"

"What headlines? And who's this maiden you're going on about?"

"A maid of twenty-two," she said as she continued to massage his shoulders, "lured to a Cyclops' castle and plied with lavender extract."

"Are you drunk?" he asked.

"Possibly."

"Unlikely, unless you brought in your own liquor," he said.

"A dry castle?" she asked. "Is that by choice or by design?"

"What's the difference?"

"A teetotaler spurns liquor by choice and a recovering alcoholic by design—which sometimes works and sometimes doesn't," she said as an image of her drunken father appeared unbidden in her thoughts.

Trinidad didn't say which he was. Instead he closed his eyes and rolled his shoulders. "You have magic fingers. Are you flirting with me?"

"That's the wrong question," she smiled. "You should ask if I'm acting by choice or by design."

"Well—which?" he asked.

"By design of course," she grinned. "My design is to ply you with caresses until you tell me honestly what you're working on so feverishly down here while I'm lying alone upstairs in your bedroom, sans shoes but otherwise untouched, unsullied, and unblemished."

"That must have been some kiss you experienced," he laughed.

"That must have been some tea you poured down my throat."

"Such a lovely throat," he said.

Now who's flirting, she thought?

"You were upset," he continued. "I offered you tea."

"And put me to bed?" she asked.

"Let's say I helped a little."

"So now what?" Anne asked and she was genuinely perplexed.

"So now we wait," he said and, when he stood up, she was pleased to see that he too was in his stocking feet.

"So, we just wait here?" she asked. "Just wait here standing around in our stockings. And we're waiting for what exactly?"

"For another shoe to drop," he said.

Chapter 16

After supper, Anne was pouting in the upstairs bedroom. There was no other word for it. Having prepared a meal for them, Trinidad had said goodnight as she climbed the stairs and he showed no inclination to follow. He apparently intended to return to his work and then sleep down there. They had shared a quiet supper, he'd played a mellow tune on his harmonica, and now her handsome host was ignoring her. He was being a perfect gentleman and that was driving her crazy. Besides, as if Trinidad's lack of attention wasn't aggravating enough, she was troubled for another and vastly more important reason. She was profoundly disappointed with herself for being at first shocked by the news of Dr. Clark's death and then lapsing into what she could only condemn as callous indifference.

She'd been so busy trying to get her bearings and flirting with Trinidad, that she'd acquiesced to her host's reluctance to discuss the demise of her mentor and hadn't asked a single pertinent question about the subject. She'd expressed no curiosity about the fate of the learned man and trusted colleague who'd helped her through her undergraduate days, and had, in some ways, been like a father to her. She hadn't wept, nor could she honestly recall the last time she cried. Over the years, she'd tempered her emotions by shedding crocodile tears while engaging in conscious ploys designed to bolster her various masquerades. Now, when she really needed to cry—ought to cry—she found herself unable to weep for Dr. Clark. Was it her ambivalence about her own father's death that muted her response?

Think about something else, she reminded herself.

After supper, she'd been napping when she needed to exercise. Her recurring exhaustion might be a symptom of the altitude, but whatever was bothering her, she'd been uncharacteristically tired and unable to keep her eyes open. She wasn't sure how long she'd slept, but she felt listless and unfocused. After putting on one running shoe, she couldn't locate the other one and couldn't be bothered to search for it. So, she remained on the bed, in violation of all decorum, with one shoe off and one shoe on, feeling weary and sorry for herself.

Anne tried to comprehend that her professor was dead, but the possibility seemed so unlikely, so remote. She'd last seen Dr. Clark only yesterday when she set out from Tucson and headed north. What could have happened since?

Before coming upstairs, she'd paused to retrieve her things from the living room. Reaching into her shoulder bag, she took out her map, unfolded it, spread it out across the rumbled bed, and retraced her route.

Yesterday morning, the marathon drive from Tucson had initially taken her along remote stretches of Arizona's Interstate 10, until she reached Phoenix where she caught northbound I-17 and battled waves of urban traffic. Recalling the trauma of Phoenix congestion, she traced the multi-lane highway with her finger. She'd hated the tangle of vehicles and the heat and the concrete and was glad to leave the sprawling metropolis behind. Next, she'd traveled further north through the less populated Verde Valley and climbed steadily higher in elevation toward the mountain city of Flagstaff, Arizona.

Arriving at noon, she'd bypassed Flagstaff and eaten lunch at a Navajo taco stand north of town, then set out on Highway 89 toward the Reservation. After dodging sheep on a narrow two-lane road, she'd turned east, and gassed up in Navajo Land at Kayenta. Emerging from the station restroom, she encountered a large yellow dog lying next to the VW, trying to beat the July heat by taking advantage of the small patch of shade spawned by the tiny car. Taking pity on the friendly stray, she filled a paper bowl with water and then went back inside to buy the animal a sandwich.

"You'll make a friend for life," the clerk said when she guessed what Anne was up to.

"You never know," Anne said.

Traveling on, she played tourist, briefly visiting the Four Corners Monument, then crossed the border into Colorado. Eventually, she reached U.S. 491 and headed for Cortez. Just south of the mid-sized town, she'd left her first cache at latitude 37.331922 North, longitude 108.845197 West. She walked to the spot within sight of a county road and placed toolbox number one under a pile of dry leaves in a grove of cottonwoods next to McElmo Creek. Then she sat beside the muddy stream and double-checked her coordinates. It was curious that Dr. Clark wanted this particular cache so close to the road, especially since he'd instructed her to place the other toolboxes at least two miles from civilization.

"Guess he knows what he's doing," she said aloud, giving a well-deserved benefit of the doubt to her famous mentor.

The McElmo Creek cache was not much of a challenge. It had only required a quarter-mile round trip, walking there carrying toolbox number one and then running back. It was a walking-running pattern which she'd repeat for the rest of the day and one which, on the longer caches, would test her endurance.

In Cortez, she'd bought two burritos, which she left wrapped in tinfoil to eat later for supper. Then she'd treated herself to an ice cream sundae, caught Colorado 145, and headed north to the tiny settlement of Dolores where she stopped for gas. Driving still further north, she passed through the even smaller burg of Rico. Traveling higher, she reached Lizard Head Pass, where she hiked four miles through a broad beaver meadow to reach the base of the stark rock formation which gave the pass its name. Arriving at the lofty location, she'd been caught in a brief flourish of fickle Colorado weather. It rained hard and the mountain wind howled as she placed cache number two in a rocky crevice. Propelled by the storm, she ran four miles back to the trailhead only to top a final rise and see the VW basking in the warm July sun.

"Don't care for the Colorado weather?" she'd laughed as she stripped off her soaked top and donned a dry sweatshirt. "Just wait five minutes."

Following 145 as it veered west through an oddly placed roundabout, she'd skirted past the resort town of Telluride. Traveling on, she parked the

Volkswagen and secreted her third cache beneath a latticework of dead-fall logs along the icy San Miguel River, three miles downstream from the hamlet of Sawpit. She ran back along the river, hopped gracefully across midstream rocks, and drove on. Turning north onto Colorado 62, she steered her VW through the scenic vistas of the San Juan Mountains until she reached Last Dollar Road.

The dirt road led her to a spot far from the pavement where she parked and hiked four miles to stash her fourth cache at coordinates 38.091166 North, 107.906186 West. The distant Last Dollar site turned out to be a luxurious alpine meadow and, pausing there immersed in mountain beauty, Anne decided to take a break. Clad in her sweatshirt, shorts, and running shoes, she knelt on a hillside of wildflowers.

"It's okay," she whispered as she avoided the fragile plants, choosing instead to stretch out onto a patch of fallow ground. It was tempting to lounge on a floral mattress but leaving an impression in the natural garden would be trespassing, so she resisted. While harmless bumblebees flitted about, filling her ears with their diligent buzzing, she measured her breathing and closed her eyes. The sun warmed her face as she inhaled the pungent wild aroma of alpine lupine, paintbrush, and fireweed. Absorbed in nature, she dozed for over an hour before she awakened and ran back as the July sun was beginning to set.

"Gotta love these long summer days," she'd said aloud, but she knew she was falling behind schedule, so she quickened her pace. Reaching the Bug at a dead run, she hopped inside and made a U-turn.

Though she'd tried to hurry, it was nearly dark when she reached Ridgway and ate her cold supper in the town park. Then, continuing north on U.S. 550, she used a flashlight to place another toolbox, rushing back and forth to reach a spot three miles east of a game crossing structure. It was past ten o'clock when she reached Montrose where she switched to Highway 50. Traveling further north, she used the flashlight again to leave another cache several miles west of Olathe in an area of rolling dirt hills the locals called 'the 'dobies.'

That made six.

When at last she arrived at her motel after 11 p.m., she'd checked in and called Dr. Clark's smartphone to leave a message saying she'd reached Delta City. The Colorado portion of her trip had been a marathon journey through matchless mountain beauty, and she'd yielded to that beauty with an unscheduled nap. She should have reached her halfway point much earlier and shouldn't have been forced to place her last two caches in the dark. Nevertheless, she'd made it and reported in without mentioning that she'd dawdled along the way.

She'd stayed overnight in Delta City and this morning she'd been heading along a county road toward Grand Junction and Interstate 70 to begin the second half of her caching activity. She'd been making good time when it had started to rain, which caused her to take a side road, which took her down Old Goat Trail in the mud, which led her to Lavender, which brought her to Trinidad's bed.

Well, to his bedroom anyway.

A polite knock interrupted her inventory. "Come in," she said as she hid the map under her pillow. What did it matter if she was looking at her own map? Why was she keeping secrets? Why was he?

"I have a file for you to look over," said Trinidad. "If you're up to it." He seemed apologetic.

"Sure," she said, "I'll have a look. Maybe it will help with whatever it is you think you're doing." She tried not to sound sarcastic, but her tone betrayed her.

"Sorry I can't tell you much just now," he said. "It's complicated."

"Hmm," she sighed and held out her hand. "Give me the dang folder."

Trinidad handed it over, but didn't release his grip until he added, "If you're ready."

"I am," she assured him as she took it. Then, while Trinidad turned to go, she opened the folder but instantly called him back. "What am I looking at?" she asked. "Who is this supposed to be?"

Trinidad returned to the bed and looked over her shoulder. "What do you mean?"

"This man in these pictures here," she sounded exasperated.

"I don't understand," he said.

"I mean, who is this and this and this supposed to be?" She pulled three images from the folder and tossed them on the bedspread. The images laid there, one yellowed photograph and two pencil drawings, sprinkled across the blanket like discarded wedges of thinly sliced cheese.

"Aren't these pictures of Dr. Clark? Isn't this your professor?"

"What in the world are you talking about?" she exclaimed. "I've never seen this man before in my life!"

Anne claimed not to recognize the images and Trinidad seemed incredulous. "Look again. Are you certain?"

"What do you mean am I certain? Is this some kind of test?" asked Anne and she sounded equally perplexed.

"You're telling me that this man is not your Dr. Clark." He studied the images and looked just as intently at Anne.

"I don't know who this skinny runt is," she avowed, "but he ain't my Dr. Clark. Who does your research anyway? Didn't they tell you my Dr. Clark is chubby and six feet tall with white hair and a flowing beard? My Dr. Clark looks like Santa Claus. This guy looks like one of the elves, and not in a good way."

"Then who's the corpse we found in Dr. Clark's ranch house with the professor's wallet in his pocket?"

"Beats me. Like I said, I've never seen this guy before."

"I—I've got to make a phone call," stammered Trinidad as he gathered up the images, grabbed the file folder, and rushed from the room.

"I guess so," Anne called after him. "Amateur hour," she mumbled to herself. She heard Trinidad downstairs on his cell phone. She couldn't catch the words, but her host's distressed tone was pretty clear. There had been a major screw-up. Two screw-ups, if you counted yesterday's explosion.

Anne got to her feet, closed the bedroom door, and locked it. Then she drew the drapes and sat in the dark. Sitting there alone, she meant to stay awake and vigilant, but instead she fell asleep and endured a troubled dream as her mind turned to those nights long ago when she'd been compelled to put a locked door between herself and a man.

Chapter 17

When Anne awoke, she moved the drapes aside and peeked out the window. The sun was approaching the horizon. It was growing late, and things were getting weird. And—despite the momentary flights of romantic fancy that followed in the wake of Trinidad's impromptu kiss—she didn't relish the idea of spending the night at his isolated farm. With no clear idea of what she was doing but feeling suddenly unsafe, she left the window and knelt beside the bed. This time she put on both shoes. Then she grabbed her shoulder bag, intent on sneaking quickly but quietly downstairs and out to the Volkswagen. She'd start the Bug and drive fast to put as much distance as possible between her and Trinidad and Lavender.

Anne felt confused, but two things were certain—she was through listening to Trinidad's incomplete explanations and she was through hiding caches. She needed answers and she'd start with someone she trusted—and that would be Dr. Clark whom she was convinced must still be very much alive. So, she was determined to return to Tucson. She would carry the remaining boxes back south and, on her way, she'd pick up the caches she'd already stashed and... Anne stopped.

Making plans to escape, she'd been tip-toeing downstairs and was nearing the front door when she saw them. The remaining toolboxes were there in a row, all six of them, lined up along the baseboard. On the floor beside the caches—next to Dr. Clark's property which had been entrusted to her—she saw a pair of bolt cutters. And next to the bolt cutters, lay a pile of fractured padlocks.

She stood in the hallway for a moment before looking quickly over her shoulder. She could hear Trinidad typing in his office and she could see that his door was closed. She knelt and carefully lifted the lid of the nearest toolbox.

Empty.

No need to check the others. Clearly, while she'd been asleep upstairs, Trinidad had somehow opened the VW's bonnet, stolen the boxes, and broken into them—opened them without her permission and removed the contents. If Anne needed conclusive proof the man was not to be trusted, the debris in the foyer settled it. Without another thought, she sprang to her feet and rushed out the front door. A volatile combination of anger and fear gripped her as she ran across the porch, down the steps, and into the driveway with the VW key in her hand. Yet another man had violated her trust. Yet another man had betrayed her. Would she ever...?

Think about something else.

The driver's side window was down, and she tossed her shoulder bag inside. Then she hurriedly pulled the door open, jumped in, and eased the latch shut to avoid the noise. The Bug was pointed down the sloping driveway, so she released the emergency brake, engaged the clutch, and coasted for several yards before she started the engine. As she pulled away, she glanced once in the rear-view mirror, but there was no sign of pursuit. Gunning the engine, she reached the base of the steep road which connected the main house to the field above and started up. She had only to top the hill and pass through the lavender field to escape. And she would have made it too if someone hadn't been blocking the way.

Chapter 18

A black Bentley sat there, an immovable mass straddling the narrow roadway, an ominous obstacle and solid as a boulder. Anne skidded to a halt, causing the Bug to teeter on the crest of the hill as she tried to throw it into reverse. But the little car lurched, and the engine died as two men exited the Bentley and started her way. Sensing danger, she turned the key again, but the engine merely sputtered, leaving her feeling helpless as she watched them come. They were thick broad-shouldered men, one tall and portly and one short. Both were dressed identically in black suits and throwback twentieth century fedoras. They walked briskly toward her and neither man said a word.

Hoods from central casting, her mind told her.

They came rapidly forward and split up, the larger man walking straight toward the Bug and the short one angling to her left, until he stopped next to the driver's side window. The large man pressed both hands on the Bug's front bonnet and leaned forward, glowering menacingly through the windshield at Anne. Staring straight ahead, transfixed, she failed to anticipate the movements of the short man who reached into her open window and deftly snatched the key from the ignition. Sporting a mocking grin, he seemed to taunt her by dangling his purloined prize tantalizingly near but, when she irritably raised her hand to snatch it back, the impudent man pulled the key away and tossed it to his companion, who opened the bonnet.

Anne gasped as she suddenly realized what they were after.

"Shite," the large man exclaimed.

"A problem?" asked the other.

What accents? she wondered.

"Bring the girl!" the large man shouted.

As the short man leaned forward, she caught a whiff of hydrochloric acid. It was an odor she'd encountered often enough in her university science labs, where undergraduates habitually overused and frequently spilled the cloying chemical. Despite her tenuous situation, she wondered whether it was probable that the little guy who'd so expertly stolen her ignition key could also be a clumsy chemist. But her fleeting thought was interrupted.

"Step out, miss," the short man ordered.

Anne inhaled sharply and was on the verge of protesting when she saw the pistol bulging in his shoulder holster.

"Out now," the midget ordered.

Anne had only seconds to think, but it was time enough. The bonnet was up. The large man was still fuming out front. She could hear him pawing through the empty trunk. She couldn't see him, and he couldn't see her. The pip-squeak had ordered her out, but she had no intention of getting out. She'd take her chances right now.

She smiled, shrugged her shoulders, and rested her hand on the door handle. *Time to be ornery,* she thought. Suddenly shoving the door open, she knocked the short man off his feet. Yanking the door closed again, she jammed in the clutch and rocked in her seat, urging the little Volkswagen to roll back. Instantly, the Bug—which had remained teetering all this time—gave way to gravity and started to roll backwards down the steep hill.

"Halt!" The short man bellowed as he tried to regain his feet, but the Bug—propelled backward by the weight of its rear engine—gathered momentum. A pistol fired and she heard the slug hit the upturned bonnet which remained open and erect like an improvised battle shield.

One of the men shouted, "No noise!"

As the Bug rolled rapidly away, the pair gave chase. Halfway down, the car hit a bump and the bonnet flopped closed and Anne could see that the men were gaining ground. She kept the clutch in and steered backwards as best she could. Hoping the Bug would stay on course, she ducked down, fearing another shot. Then she heard someone cry out and looked up to see the large man stumble and fall heavily onto the graveled road.

"Sensible shoes, my foreign friends." She offered this advice aloud knowing that neither man could hear, let alone appreciate, her sarcasm.

Leaving his companion behind, the short man ran on, breathing raggedly but making progress. She was nearing the bottom of the hill where he nearly overtook her before he too went down. And—the oddest thing—as the Bug continued to roll downhill, she noticed that neither man rose to resume the pursuit. In fact, both men remained absolutely still, lying sprawled on the road precisely where they had fallen. It was only when Anne reached the bottom of the hill and had time to ponder this turn of events that she noticed a figure walking toward her.

It was Trinidad. He had discovered her, and he was cradling a rifle.

Chapter 19

Anne remained in the stranded Bug as the descending sun highlighted the scene with a patina of golden light. She reached for her shoulder bag and clutched it protectively to her breast. It would make a poor shield, but she wanted something between herself and this unpredictable man and his weapon. When Trinidad arrived, she avoided his gaze and looked instead at his rifle, then up the hill in the direction of the fallen men.

"Are those two dead?" she asked, trying without success to moderate the anxiety in her voice.

"Theoretically they're okay—although they'll have one peach of a headache," said Trinidad, "when they wake up, that is." He got her attention and pointed to his vest and the cluster of feathered syringes hanging there.

"Tranquilizer darts?" she asked. She'd seen the projectiles used on deer when she took courses in her zoology minor.

"Yup," he confirmed.

"I suppose you're proud of yourself. Although I must say, you took your time putting that second desperado down," she critiqued.

"This is an air rifle, so you need to pump it in between shots," he grinned. "But I had a plan. I got the big guy first and saved the midget for last. Figured his legs were shorter. He was a gamer though. As it was, I managed to get off two clean shots and plinked them both in the shoulder. Usually you want to aim for the butt, but these fellows didn't seem the type to turn around and run backwards. Still, given the range, I made two pretty fine shots, if I do say so myself."

"I don't suppose you could suppress your ego for ten seconds and put that thing away?"

"It's not loaded I assure you," he said.

"Guns make me nervous," she said.

"Okay," he complied as he walked toward the VW's nose.

She momentarily lost sight of Trinidad as he opened the bonnet, so she leaned out of the window and asked, "How did you...were you following me?"

"I'm afraid I was," he said as he placed his air rifle and dart vest inside. He closed the bonnet and made certain it was latched. Then, just as the big foreigner had done, Trinidad stared at her through the windshield.

Anne felt a sudden chill as she reached for the ignition key, only to remember that it was still in the bonnet. She tried to maintain her composure and look calmly through the windshield while Trinidad stared back and continued speaking.

"Funny thing about these vintage Bugs," he said. "They make a pretty distinctive sound starting up. So, I heard you go and, given the hill I knew you had to climb, I figured I could cut across country and stop you."

"Stop me? You don't mean? You wouldn't have..."

"Used a dart on you? Not sure," he admitted. "I just grabbed the first non-lethal thing that came to hand and started running."

"I suppose I should be grateful that you didn't have a bazooka handy," she scowled. "Or bolt cutters."

"Hmm," he said. "As for the bolt cutters, I can explain that. And as for the bazooka—that would've been much too noisy."

"Funny," she observed, "that's exactly what the bad guys said. The question is: are those two the bad guys?"

"Bad as they come."

"So, theoretically, I suppose that makes you one of the good guys," she said.

"Theoretically," he agreed. "But will it lessen your good opinion of me to learn that I'm being paid to look after you?"

"That depends," Anne said. "How much and by whom?"

"Secret," was his cryptic reply.

"For how long?" she asked.

"Until it's over. Until you're safe."

"Somehow I don't find those answers reassuring."

"Well, the sheriff will be here soon," he said. "I texted him as I was leaving the house. You can ask him for a reference if it'll make you feel any better."

"Don't you think the law will be a bit curious about the mysterious Bentley parked in your precious lavender field and those two comatose gorillas lying in the road?"

"I doubt it," said Trinidad as he pulled the ignition key from the bonnet lock and held it up. "This is yours I presume." He walked to the passenger door, climbed in, and handed the key to Anne. "I doubt if Jack—my friend the sheriff—will care much. Especially since he already has a Bentley in his impound yard and one gorilla in his lock-up."

"So that would be the muddy Bentley from yesterday and our Old Goat Trail gorilla I presume?"

"The very same."

"Don't tell me how you managed to corral that joker," she said. "I don't want to know."

"It was quite simple really. I sauntered out the back door and tapped on his window. He didn't recognize me when I asked for a match and, while he was looking at my fake scar, I cold-cocked him."

"Hmm. And why in the world, I wonder, would you think that one of our bad guys might be able to recognize you?" she asked.

"Slip of the tongue," Trinidad added. "I meant to say he didn't recognize me as a threat."

"I see. Tell me, did you take classes in lying or does it just come naturally?" she asked.

Trinidad didn't answer. Instead he stared at the frightened young woman sitting next to him, avoiding eye contact, and clutching her shoulder bag to her breast as if her life depended on it. "You able to drive like that?" he asked.

"Fine," Anne growled as she pitched the bag into the backseat and started the Bug. "*Now* she starts?" she complained. Turning the car around, she hesitated and nodded in the direction of the prostrate men. "How about our sleeping friends?"

"No worries. They'll be out for hours," he said.

"Hmm—I'm beginning to envy them already," she said. "Beginning to wish I was sedated too."

She gunned the engine and they traveled in silence for a time.

"Angry?" he asked as they neared the farmhouse.

"Seething," she answered. "So, don't speak to me again unless it's to tell me why you felt compelled to take bolt cutters to things entrusted to me. And don't utter another syllable unless it's to confess what you did with the contents."

"I'll answer the last part first," he said as they came to a stop. "As for those particular boxes—the cargo you've been assigned to systematically cache across untold miles of Colorado territory. Allow me to report that, when I opened your precious boxes, I found all six to be absolutely, totally, completely, and also utterly empty."

Chapter 20

From his hiding place, supine in the lavender field, Diak had been watching the drama unfold.

Earlier that day, after dispatching a carload of Russians at the roadblock, Diak had driven to Lavender in time to see the Volkswagen arrive. He'd watched the girl interact with the shameless impersonator and instantly adopted an abiding interest in her, her presumptuous companion, and Lavender. When the couple moved toward the restaurant, he'd discontinued his surveillance for a time in order to search for an ideal spot to take up residence in the little village. His plan was to establish a hideout, then return to keep an eye on the girl and confront the pretender, plus, somewhere, there was at least one nosy Russian to contend with.

Searching through the village, Diak drove to the outskirts where he'd spotted an abandoned house. Situated on the edge of town, the tiny dwelling sat at the rear of a narrow lot—a ramshackle place squatting between two towering grain elevators which screened it from view. It was far enough from the main street to avoid prying eyes and its back windows offered a view of the road in and out of town. He'd unloaded his gear and had just been walking back, being careful to avoid being seen, intending to keep an eye on the restaurant, when he saw the girl leaving town. Chasing after her would have required him to sprint back to his hideout. Instead, he seemed rooted to the ground as he stood in the shadows and watched the VW roll out of Lavender.

Deciding to let the girl go, he'd walked for another block without spotting either the imposter or the Russian. The summer sun was hot, and his head was beginning to swim as he turned into a shady alley and leaned against a crumbling brick wall. Diak's long day was devolving into a confusing swirl. On the go since midnight, the German was starting to lose focus. Having invested years in delegating the mundane task of surveillance to hired contractors, he soon discovered that his field tactics were rusty. Lacking the patience to conduct even a cursory stake-out, he abandoned downtown Lavender, walked back to the isolated house, and placed his bedroll on the dusty floor. Feeling exhausted, he closed his eyes, half expecting that the professor's call would wake him. But there'd been no call and his nap, however necessary, had been excessive.

Finding he'd slept the afternoon away, he arose in a disoriented state and stumbled out back to a tangle of bushes. As he relieved himself, he resisted the temptation to look down at his damaged loins. He'd grown accustomed to the odd sensation of not being able to feel his bladder at work. Zipping his fly home, he'd spotted two Russians cruising into town in their Bentley, a big man and a small one, looking sinister and obscenely out of place. Remaining hidden, Diak watched them drive past and sighed. Here was yet another pair of Russians who'd require his attention. Suddenly the Brotherhood was crowding into Lavender and they needed watching. Grabbing his daypack, he jumped into his 4Runner and gave chase.

Discreetly tailing the Bentley, he'd watched it turn under a broad archway marking the entrance to Lavender Hill Farm. He passed the entrance and continued downhill to park behind a thicket of willows. Setting off cross country, he wore sunglasses and carried his daypack and single lens spotting scope. He left his guns behind. If anyone asked, he was scouting for pheasant hunting sites.

He'd climbed a steep hill then walked upright through a thick stand of July corn until he reached a broad lavender field. Crouching down, he entered a furrow which ran between rows of the thick, knee-high plants. The heat of the day was beginning to moderate and the vibrant purplish flowers swayed languidly in a gentle summer breeze. He could appreciate the sight. But, unfortunately, he could also smell the blossoms, and, in the quantity of this vast field, he found the aroma cloying. He much preferred the earthy smell of the furrow, which his dependable nose told him was lined with granules of natural limestone. Crawling along the furrow, his senses nearly overwhelmed by the lavender, his thoughts turned inward.

Years ago, as a young detective of counter espionage, he'd been immersed in the Scarlet Brotherhood and had paid a steep price for his involvement with the unpredictable gang. The so-called accident which disfigured his face and robbed him of one eye had required surgery to restore his damaged cheek. After the operation, although it was small consolation, he discovered that his sense of smell was greatly enhanced.

"You've lost half your sight, comrade," the Russian surgeon had told him, "but you'll find that your other senses will compensate for this injury. And, if I do say so myself," he bragged, "I've worked a miracle here."

"Thank you," was all Diak had managed to say through his mask of bandages. In truth, he'd caught a glimpse of the doctor's handiwork in the sordid clinic's fly-specked mirror and was shocked by the image of his damaged face. "Thank you," he'd croaked, while longing to retrieve his trousers, unsheathe his serrated Damascus knife, and slip the blade between the ribs of the pompous surgeon. *Worked a miracle?* Diak thought. *That was some miracle, Herr Doctor. Just you try looking at this face in the mirror every morning.*

Shaking off thoughts of the past, the German returned his attention to the lavender field. Well-concealed by the thick plants, he removed his sunglasses and put the scope to his good eye. Propped up on his elbows and looking across the field he could see the Bentley clearly. The bulk of the jet-black luxury automobile contrasted sharply with the airy fields of luminous purple surrounding it. The Bentley sat near the crest of a steep hill, in the center of a narrow gravel road which bisected the field. The two men inside seemed to be waiting for something.

Diak's gaze followed the road as it continued downhill to a farm where he saw a two-story house, a sizable garage, a small barn, a few scattered out-buildings, a stone wall, and a corral. There were no animals. There seemed to be only one road in and out, so whoever was down there was trapped.

Then he spotted the blue Volkswagen. The little car was parked close to a house of the same color, making it nearly invisible from this high angle. It could be a coincidence. This might be another Volkswagen entirely, because Diak believed that the girl had left Lavender. Hadn't he watched her go? Hadn't he decided then and there to let her go? And yet the Russians had dispatched one of their pervasive Bentleys to this isolated spot. So, the chances were good that the Volkswagen below was the same one he'd followed to Lavender, only to watch it depart the village. Obviously, while he slept, the girl had returned.

Lying in the lavender field as he sought to organize his thoughts, Diak glanced at his watch. Then he pulled out his cell phone to make certain its ringer tone was set to vibrate. Dr. Clark's call might come at any moment. This out-of-the-way settlement was not Delta City, but it was as good a place as any to wait to eavesdrop on the illusive professor's call. Re-pocketing his phone, Diak had to admit that—where Clark was concerned—he'd miscal-culated. He hadn't expected the professor to disappear, hadn't expected him to run. But he was rapidly improvising and certain that, wherever Clark was, the missing man would soon be telephoning his Russian customers, and the German would be listening.

Meanwhile, here was the little Volkswagen again. Somehow the girl was back. Diak reprimanded himself. He was growing careless and that would never do. Letting the girl go and indulging in a nap, such oversights tended to accumulate and amalgamate into failure. Frowning as he lay in the lavender field, he scanned the house and farmyard, chastising himself for his negli-gence and looking for signs of occupation.

Scriptor, he thought.

Yes, that was the troublesome girl's surname. He'd remember her Chris-tian name in a moment. For the time being, he was more interested in the Russians and what they were doing, so he abandoned his surveillance of the farmhouse and returned his gaze to the Bentley. As a result, he was scoping the lavender field and the black automobile when he heard the distinctive sound of the Volkswagen engine revving to life. Swinging his scope back toward the farm, he saw the blue car in motion and heading for the hill. Soon it was trailing a cloud of dust as it labored up the incline. He could see that the girl—or some girl anyway—was driving. When she reached the top, she would be in for a surprise and, with his weapons far away in his Toyota, there was nothing he could do to help her.

Not that he was inclined to help. Whatever role the girl was playing in this treasure hunt, she was beginning to get on his nerves, so it would be better to let the Russians deal with her and save him the trouble. After they accomplished their ambush, he would deal with them. Thinking these thoughts as he watched the little VW chugging up the hill, he slipped his daypack off, unzipped it, and examined the contents. He had his knife, of course, and inside the pack was his portable detonator, a generous length of blasting cord, and a brick of C-4 plastic explosive.

Just the typical arsenal of your average pheasant hunter, he smiled.

He'd assembled these items earlier with the intention of booby-trapping the entrance and cellar of his Lavender hideout. When the Russians appeared, he'd instinctively grabbed his pack and pursued the Bentley.

Remaining concealed in the lavender, he watched the VW climb and waited for the girl to top the hill and meet her fate. Suddenly, he saw a figure emerge from the farmhouse. The man was running full speed, not directly toward the blue car but rather along the far side of the hill and parallel to the road. He was fit, this man, because his strong strides were rapidly closing the distance.

"This one understands his spatial geometry and can calculate an intersection angle. Also, he runs to the rescue swiftly—like an ardent lover," he whispered aloud as though he were narrating a film. "Liebe eilt die Uhr—love hurries the clock—but who knows if he comes in time?"

The man ran well and the girl ascending the hill was also rumored to be a sprinter, but soon the two of them would discover there was nowhere left to run. Returning his gaze to the crest of the hill, he could see that the VW had reached the top where it immediately came to a stop. The Russians were out of their Bentley and advancing toward her. And now they were searching the little blue car. And now...

"Was ist los?" he slipped into German as he wondered aloud what was happening.

With its front bonnet still open, the little blue car was suddenly rolling backwards and gathering speed as the men followed in pursuit. Diak looked up from the spotting scope in order to take in the panorama of the rapidly unfolding scene.

"But where is the lover? Where is the hero?" Diak continued to whisper his narration. "Ah! One Russian is down and now the other is in the dust. And now the Volkswagen comes to rest at the base of the hill and—ah—here is the hero at last!" Diak put the spotting scope to his good eye and stared for several moments before he added, "And behold the hero is armed!"

Over the years the German had studied and fired thousands of weapons and his expert eye quickly discerned that the man below carried an air rifle especially designed to deliver tranquilizer darts.

"Ach," he chided. "This will never do. You do not sedate the enemy. No, once they are down, they must stay down."

After delivering this critique, he waited until he was certain the little blue car and its two occupants had returned to the farmhouse below. Then he shouldered his pack and made his way through the lavender, moving rapidly toward the fallen men and the Bentley.

Chapter 21

As Diak hurried through the dwindling light to deal with the fallen Russians, Anne and Trinidad stood together in the front hallway of his farmhouse. Their arms were folded. They were staring at the empty boxes.

"How is this possible?" she asked.

"Search me," Trinidad said. "Does your professor ever send them out empty?"

"No, I told you, never," she insisted. "A geocaching exercise is like a big scavenger hunt. It's a put-and-take experience. You take something out, you put something in—the more ingenious the better. You keep track of your exchanges and everyone gathers afterwards to drink beer and display their finds. It's unbelievable that I've been hauling empty boxes around."

"Well, they are definitely empty," Trinidad observed.

"No wonder I didn't hear anything. You're absolutely sure there was nothing inside? No trinkets? No logbooks?"

"Nothing. Zip. Nada. Zilch," he said.

"Boxes completely empty. Dr. Clark missing. People dead on my route. Three thugs in jail—or one in the slammer anyway and two sleeping on the hillside—what does all this add up to?"

"A second-rate mystery novel?" he ventured.

"If only—but doesn't a mystery require a crime?" she asked.

"Well, we've got murder and a missing person. That's a start," he said.

"Murder," she remembered. "Yesterday's explosion...and I almost forgot about the elf in Dr. Clark's house."

"Yes—well, the medical examiner said the Tucson fatality was a heart attack. But the cops are treating the incident as a suspicious death."

"Because..." she prompted.

"Because of the look on the elf's face," he said.

"I don't follow."

"Oh, he died of a heart attack all right, but you should have seen that face. It was so distorted that we had to use an old passport photo and a pair of police artist's sketches for his file."

"The pictures I saw yesterday," she ventured.

"Yeah," Trinidad admitted. "I—uh—well—anyway from the look on the elf's face it's clear that his heart failed, but it didn't crash on its own. Something stopped his heart—something that scared him to death."

A sudden peal of nearby thunder shook the hallway and made Anne jump. So unexpected was the sound that, when the echo died away, she found herself clinging to Trinidad.

"Sorry," she said as she released him.

"No problem," he said. "That was unexpected."

"So, you didn't do that on purpose, for dramatic effect?" she asked. "Quite a trick. You say, 'scared to death'—and then—boom?"

"I confess," he said, "I control the weather. Watch this..." He grinned and struck a pose, gesturing toward the unseen sky.

"Nothing," she said. "Just as I suspected you're a..."

Another boom sounded, vibrating the front windows, sending hallway knickknacks clattering to the floor, and setting the pendulum of the grandfather clock swinging violently like a palm tree caught in the grip of a hurricane.

"Holy cats!" Trinidad shouted. "Get down!"

Chapter 22

After the echoes of the explosion died away, Trinidad and Anne remained hunkered down in the hallway until they heard sirens. Even then, Trinidad counseled caution until he confirmed by return text that the sheriff and other first responders were on the scene. When the two of them emerged from the farmhouse, they stood for a moment and looked in the direction of the lavender field. Along the top of the road, just visible in the gathering dusk, they could see a thick skein of black smoke billowing across the dim horizon.

"Almost dark," Trinidad said. "I think we'd better walk up this time. Hold on a minute." He went back inside and returned with a rifle—a real one this time—and a sizable flashlight. "Just in case," he said and, seeing her alarm, he added, "Sorry. Would you rather wait here?"

"Not on your life, buster," she said. "Just stay in front of me where I can keep an eye on you."

"You can't think I'd shoot you in the back," he protested.

"Stranger things have happened," she answered. "I don't trust guns. When I was a kid my father used me like a bird dog—out in front, beating the bushes to flush the pheasants—you think I'm joking? I don't like being out front. I've got shotgun pellet scars on my shoulders and scalp to prove it. You go on ahead. I'll be fine back here out of range."

"Suit yourself but keep up."

"Think about something else," she said under her breath.

"Pardon?"

"Nothing," she said. "Let's go."

It was a long slog up the hill. They heard more sirens arriving, followed by the unintelligible squawks and static of emergency radio chatter. As they climbed, they passed the spot where they had last seen the two Russians lying on the roadway.

"Where...?" she asked, but Trinidad kept walking and did not answer.

It grew steadily darker and the presence of emergency vehicles became more apparent. Up ahead, a multi-colored glare dominated the horizon like a weird pulsating sunset. With each step, the gathering gloom appeared to amplify the caustic sounds of radio chatter. As they neared the top, Trinidad seemed to come to a decision.

"I think I'd better go up alone," he said.

"Why?" she asked.

"I didn't tell you everything the sheriff texted me," he admitted.

"So, it's business as usual." She frowned. "What don't I know this time?"

"Those explosions destroyed the Bentley," he said, "along with the two men who accosted you."

Anne was unperturbed. "I've seen a dead body before," she said.

"There's dead and there's incinerated," he said. "I think you should skip this one."

"Look, I'll come as far as the top of the hill," she insisted. "Then I'll stop there, like you say. But I won't stay down here in the dark."

"Okay," he said. "That'll work. And, as for the dark, take this." He handed her the flashlight.

When they reached the top, she was surprised to see that the crime scene was far away from the crest of the hill where she'd encountered the Bentley. Obviously, the men whom Trinidad had supposedly put to sleep had regained consciousness and moved the car further down the road. *Either that or...*her thoughts were interrupted.

"Find a place to sit and shine the flashlight my way now and then so I know you're okay," he said.

"Yes, sir," she said, and he walked on.

Chapter 23

As he stood at the edge of the crime scene, Trinidad kept glancing over his shoulder, staring into the darkness in the direction of the flashlight beam that occasionally flickered in the distance.

"Tell me again how much this girl knows," said Jack as he puffed on a cigarette. Sheriff Jack Treadway's uniform was rumpled, and he sounded tired. Both men watched the coroner's crew as they pulled body parts from the still-smoldering wreckage of what had once been a luxury automobile. Trinidad counted two dozen first responders in all, including a tow truck driver who stood by, even though there was little left to tow away.

Too many ears for this conversation, Trinidad thought. Then, unaccountably, he found himself seeking to deflect the sheriff's attention from Anne as he asked aloud, "What do you guess happened here?"

"I can tell you this much, there were two victims. Russians—just like at the roadblock," said Jack. "What's left of a driver's license on the tall one says his name was Fyodor. No second name—just Fyodor. And we got nothin' on the short guy."

"Tall and short," Trinidad repeated.

"Hard to know which was which now," said the medical examiner as he joined them at the barricade. "Anybody got a smoke? Jack?"

The sheriff handed over a pack and a lighter.

"These pesky Russian bozos are dropping like flies," the examiner said a little too loudly, his words waffling as he lit a cigarette. "Already six stiffs and counting. First the dang roadblock goes south and now this here blow-up at Lavender Hill. Where in tarnation is all this headed?" he asked.

"World War III," laughed one of the paramedics as she drew within earshot of the conversation.

"Nobody asked you, Miss Jackass," growled the examiner. Then he added a defiant whisper, "Little jerk—after my job, probably."

"Let's get out of this darn cross traffic," said Jack. "Follow me." They left the examiner and the rest of the responder crowd behind as the sheriff directed Trinidad to a pop-up canopy. Jack shooed the occupants away. "Everybody out! I said out!" He reached up to pull the flap down and, when Trinidad didn't immediately follow, the sheriff added impatiently. "Get in here, now!"

The detective took one last look over his shoulder, pinpointing the position of the flashlight, knowing he wouldn't be able to keep an eye on it for a while. Then he followed Jack inside.

"Now," the sheriff asked again, "how much does she know?"

"She's convinced that her assignment is exactly what her professor told her it was: setting out caches for a university fieldtrip."

"Hmm. *She's* convinced—the question is: are *you* convinced?"

"No reason to doubt her," Trinidad said.

"The light's kind'a bad in here," said Jack. "I can't quite read you. Are you sayin' that with a wink?"

"I'm saying it straight," Trinidad insisted. "I'm saying I believe her."

"Hmm. A pretty young thing, so Madge tells me."

"To Madge, any woman under sixty-five is a pretty young thing. And, by the way, when your deputy was impersonating her waitress and I was busy dealing with our friend in the muddy Bentley, our intrepid Madge nearly blew everything by suggesting our young miss leave town."

"Madge has a crush on you, of course. Don't all the ladies, includin' this girl?"

"Trust me, I know what I'm doing," said Trinidad.

"Well, okay. It's your funeral, Slick. What do you need from us?"

"We can forget about the boxes I opened. And I also searched the Volkswagen from top to bottom, so whatever the professor's hiding, it has to be in the first six caches. I'll get the coordinates tonight. She trusts me and I'll get the numbers from her and text them to you. Then it'll be up to you to collect the missing boxes. And remember somebody out there is handy with explosives. So, watch your step while I keep the woman safe."

"Crazy people runnin' around our neighborhood with explosives," said Jack. "And my team's gonna deal with these pyrotechnic nut-jobs while you handle the girl. So, maybe we'll have the easy part."

"Could be," Trinidad said, unable to suppress a smile.

"You can grin all you want, Slick, but I think you're being led down the garden path."

"I doubt it," said Trinidad. "I know for sure that every last one of the boxes she had with her was empty. And sending out empty caches is something Anne insists is a total change in Clark's usual routine."

"So, it's Anne now, is it?" asked Jack and it was the sheriff's turn to grin.

The two talked for another fifteen minutes, then Jack looked at his watch and they parted company. Trinidad remained under the canopy, wrestling with his conscience—wondering if he had done the right thing to withhold information from the sheriff. If Jack knew half of what the detective had discovered about Miss Anne Scriptor, the young woman would probably be in custody right now. There was a coffee urn on a nearby camp table. Trinidad poured himself a cup, found a chair, sat down, and raised his cup in a mock toast.

"Here's to Anne with an 'e,' Scriptor with an 'o,' whoever the hell she is."

Earlier that day he'd been putting the finishing touches on Anne's dossier when the woman herself had padded into his home office in her stocking feet. He'd hurriedly typed 'Anne McDougal' as the file name and quickly saved the document. Moving swiftly, he just had time to close his laptop before the impetuous young woman had crossed behind him and put her hands on his shoulders. Under ordinary circumstances, he'd have responded warmly to her touch and been thinking of ways to encourage her advances while plotting a few moves of his own. As it was, he'd suppressed his desires, deciding it was much too soon to get involved with a—what was she—a client, a suspect, or something else? Whoever she was, she wasn't Anne Scriptor.

A computer search for "Scriptor" had led him to the McDougal reference. The first internet document he'd uncovered was a 2009 clipping from the *Bisbee Observer*. The Arizona newspaper ran a three-column story about a spectacular fire, a two-alarm blaze which blackened several acres, destroyed a family home, and killed one Hendrix McDougal, a hard-rock miner. Almost as an afterthought, the article mentioned that the dead man's teenage daughter was missing, reported a rumor that the mysterious girl had changed her last name to Scriptor, but offered no description of her whereabouts.

Digging further, Trinidad found that, a month earlier, the newspaper had published a 100-word item on the suicide of Anne's mother—an unhappy woman who had driven herself over the edge of an open-pit mine. The *Observer* closed its succinct report by noting that the woman's death marked the tenth suicide that year among miners and their spouses "so far." As near as the detective could determine, Anne had kept her first name out of sympathy for her mother. But after her father died, the orphaned teen apparently couldn't wait to change her surname.

Scanning online archives, Trinidad did a keyword search on both last names but got no further hits. Then he did a thorough visual search of virtual copies of the weekly newspaper and confirmed what he suspected. It was not so much what he found but what was missing. There was no further speculation about the fate of young Anne and no mention whatsoever of a search having been launched to locate the missing girl.

It was as if she'd fallen off the face of the earth.

Alone under the canopy, he finished his coffee, tossed the empty cup, and absently retrieved his harmonica from his shirt pocket. Playing it sometimes helped him think. He held it to his lips, then immediately dropped the idea as too macabre for the current circumstances.

"Whistling in the graveyard," Trinidad told himself as he buttoned the harmonica back into his pocket, picked up his rifle, and ducked out from beneath the canvas. Leaving the crime scene behind, the detective walked toward the distant flashlight which remained steadily shining as he grew nearer. A little too steadily—so he slung his rifle across his shoulder and broke into a trot. He found the flashlight propped on a pyramid of rocks with its beam pointing toward the crime scene. He picked up the light and swung it into the darkness.

"Anne!" he called. "Anne! Anne!" But she was gone.

Chapter 24

Anne hadn't intended to run. She'd intended to do as she was told. To sit in the dark and wriggle the flashlight like a good girl. She'd intended to do as she was told; to go out in front of the men, the drunken men, and flush the pheasants.

She'd implored herself to think about something else. But it didn't work.

As she waited at the top of the hill, she'd grown tired at first. Then she grew cold, then she became uneasy. Trinidad hadn't said how long she'd have to wait there. It could be all night—hours alone in the dark with her increasingly troubled thoughts. It was a bleak prospect. She wasn't afraid of the dark. It wasn't that. She feared the memories that were crowding in on her. Memories that always seemed to return to her after sunset, after the lights in her girlhood cabin were extinguished, after the drinking.

Sitting there in the dark, Anne was a girl again and alone in the family cabin while her mother was miles away tending to a sick neighbor. She was twelve and old enough to drive—although not legally. With her mother away, it fell to her to operate the old family truck, to drive her father to work and pick him up when his shift ended at the mine. At first, she'd dreaded the prospect of spending time alone with her father, but, to her surprise, days passed, and her old man stopped drinking. He even shaved and bathed more regularly, and he praised Anne's middling cooking and complimented her on her appearance.

She should have seen it coming. Why did she not see it coming?

Think about something else, she begged herself, but she knew that her mind would betray her there in the dark and keep returning to play the thing over and over again in her head. She had to subdue her thoughts. She had to run.

She flicked the light one last time and then she quickly gathered stones until she'd constructed a cairn. It was too dark to make a proper one, one with archaeological significance, but she reminded herself that she wasn't building a landmark or a grave marker or even an end-of-journey pile. All she needed was a pedestal sturdy enough to hold a flashlight. Once she had the flashlight in place, she rapidly descended the hill, stumbling twice in the dark as she rushed back to the farmhouse. Hurrying inside, she gathered up the empty toolboxes, leaving the ruined padlocks where they lay. The boxes may be empty, but they were still her responsibility and she'd take them back before Trinidad or anyone else could defile them further.

She didn't know for certain what she was feeling as she extracted Trinidad's air rifle and vest from the Bug's front trunk. Tossing the odious weapons aside, she packed in the toolboxes. Was she frightened or angry, or both? Whatever it was, she felt used and trapped and then suddenly she stopped what she was doing.

What was she thinking?

There was no way she'd be able to escape Lavender Hill Farm by driving the VW up through that crime scene mess. They'd stop her up there, confiscate her vehicle, and take the boxes. Maybe they'd arrest her. She'd have to leave the Bug behind and abandon the boxes unless...

Something seemed to snap in her as a combination of anxiety and resolve took hold. Closing the bonnet, she opened the VW's passenger door, reached into the glovebox, and took out her own flashlight. She snapped it on. The batteries were weak, but it would have to do. She dug a change of clothes out of her suitcase and grabbed her packs. Anne's hands were shaking as she donned her jacket and cap, then emptied the contents of her shoulder bag into her daypack. She unzipped her fanny pack and checked to make sure her

GPS navigator was inside. She strapped the fanny pack on and put a water bottle in each of the side holsters. Wriggling into her daypack, she hurried inside the farmhouse and rushed to the fireplace where earlier she'd spotted a box of extra-long matches.

She took them all.

She went back outside and removed the Bug's gas cap. Then she took off her scarf and stuffed it into the open neck of the filler tube. She'd seen this done in a movie and was hoping she remembered it correctly. It was just as well that she brought the entire box because it took several timid tries and several wasted matches before she got the tail of the scarf blazing. Then she grabbed her flashlight and ran, not wanting to see the Bug go up.

Earlier that day, from the upstairs bedroom window, she'd seen a pathway leading away from the farm. It started behind the house and led through old corral pens, then along a ditch bank. She had no idea where it went or how far. She couldn't see the end of it. All she knew was it led in the opposite direction of the hill, away from the lavender fields, and away from Trinidad—a man surrounded by death—a man she'd decided she could no longer trust. She'd trusted her father—too many times and long ago. She'd trusted Professor Clark—see how well that worked out. She was through trusting men. It was time for her to be on her own. As she ran, she heard a muffled roar behind her and then an explosion—bigger than she expected—but she didn't look back. The boxes were gone. Her beloved VW was gone. But she'd get money and somehow, she'd buy another car. Then she'd retrace her steps, retrieve yesterday's hidden caches, return them to Tucson, and undo whatever it was she'd done before anyone else got hurt.

Chapter 25

The moment the blue Volkswagen returned to the farmhouse and the occupants went inside, the German had rushed through the lavender field and set to work. The daylight was fading and there was much to do.

After placing the two sedated Russians inside their Bentley, he divided his brick of C-4 into two portions. He packed the smaller slice into a crevice beneath the gas tank, purposely positioning the plastic explosive to create a maximum upward spray of shrapnel. The remaining C-4 he molded into a gap between the engine and the front axle. Then he wired a standard impulse detonator into the smaller charge and inserted a delayed ignition pencil fuse into the larger one.

Diak's idea was a simple one. He would puncture the Bentley's gas tank by using his plunger to directly ignite the small charge. Moments later, in order to take full advantage of the leaking fuel, a delayed fuse would ignite the larger charge. The first explosion would be focused and subdued, but the second would be an enormous blast which would obliterate the Russians and send the Bentley skyward.

To begin, he set the delayed fuse and left it working toward ignition as he quickly moved back into the lavender field. Playing out his detonator cord, he hurriedly attached his plunger and ignited the first charge. Exploding with a low rumble, like distant thunder, it instantly spawned an odor of leaking gasoline, saturating the pristine summer breeze, and permeating the alert nostrils of the crouching German. The next explosion would be huge and, knowing the bigger blast would attract attention, Diak retrieved his cord, grabbed his pack and plunger, and moved further into the lavender. Then he waited for the delayed fuse to do its work. Lying still, he consulted his watch and counted to himself, *thirteen-twelve-eleven-ten-nine-eight-seven-six-five-four-three-two...*

As the second charge split the air with a thunderous roar, Diak kept his head down and covered his ears. He didn't look to see the car fly up, nor did he look to see where it landed. He had too much respect for the arbitrary flight of shrapnel, and his ears and nose told him all he needed to know. He didn't really care what happened to the Bentley or the car's hapless occupants. He was more curious to see what response his explosions would bring, and so he remained hidden and waited. Within twenty minutes, emergency vehicles began arriving until Lavender Hill was saturated with activity. The German watched from a distance as emergency vehicles filled the narrow roadway and the margins of the cultivated field. He wasn't worried about being detected. Even if he hadn't carefully limited his movements to the furrows and the edges of the road, the wholesale incursion of so many tires and boots onto the scene would obliterate any trace of his presence.

Clearly, he'd poked a bee's nest, but the swarm of people and machines that infested the scene was surely more than the incident warranted. After all, his explosions had only destroyed a single automobile and terminated a pair of Russians. Only two victims had been annihilated, not exactly mass murder, so there must be another reason for this feverish reaction. Of course, the German had to admit that things were adding up. Earlier in the day, and not so very far away, he'd killed twice as many, which added to six in all. That rising statistic might account for tonight's crowd, but Diak guessed there was another reason.

He might have underestimated the importance of the girl.

Although new to the area, this seemingly inconsequential female had quickly attracted a host of protectors. She was beautiful, of course, and that might account for some of the attention. She'd acquired one champion in particular—the man who appeared to reside at Lavender Hill Farm, the runner and tranquilizing marksman, the car cleaner and masquerader, the presumptuous jackal whose attempt at impersonation so annoyed the German.

Unaware that Anne waited in the dark, wriggling her flashlight, while Trinidad conferred with the sheriff, Diak lingered briefly in the lavender field before crawling away. When he could safely stand erect, he paused and looked back. Darkness had fallen and the far horizon was aglow with flashing lights. He watched the show for a moment more. Then he shouldered his pack and slipped back through the corn toward his hidden vehicle. Reaching the Toyota, he stowed his gear and decided to return to town by another way. Unwilling to have his vehicle spotted so near the crime scene, he left his headlamps off and steered an alternative route by the light of the moon, driving cautiously through a bewildering tangle of back roads. When at last he reached Lavender, Diak was exceedingly tired and hungry, but he bypassed the pancake house, knowing he couldn't risk dining in such a public place.

Tonight's meal, he thought, *will be a Spartan affair of apples and cheese, chips and salami, and warm beer.*

Avoiding the main street, he parked behind his isolated hideout in a tangle of tumbleweeds and entered through the back door. It was darker inside the tiny house than out. His remote hiding place had an active electrical hookup, but there were few lights and no appliances. A single bulb hung from the kitchen ceiling and there was another primitive fixture in the basement, but he kept the upstairs dark. Probably the dilapidated structure was on someone's list to tear down but, if Lavender's empty streets and boarded-up storefronts were any gauge of the village's marginal condition, his little house would have to wait in line to be demolished.

The German sat on an unsteady wooden chair, the sole piece of furniture in the place, and ate his modest supper. Then he stretched out on his bedroll and reached into his pack. He extracted an amber-tinted pill bottle and rattled it next to his ear. Still plenty left. The back-alley dealer had called the drug 'Jackpot,' one of the many street names for a prescription pain medication which was exponentially more powerful than morphine. It was a drug no sensible person would take in quantity unless his face was on fire. Diak had begun using the drug to control his facial pain, but he quickly began misusing the medication and grew increasingly dependent on the pills. Over time, his addiction became less about banishing pain and more about experiencing a fleeting feeling of euphoria. Lately, even that sensation had begun to fade. Now he took the pills for one reason only.

He took them in order to sleep.

This night was typical. He'd been fatigued in the wake of his early morning rush to Colorado and his busy day at the roadblock, but his afternoon nap had failed to refresh him. Then he'd hurried to the lavender field and back again and, even though his exhausting day was ending, he couldn't find sleep. He lay awake in the empty house, which was deadly quiet, except for the whine of a single stalking mosquito. It was tempting to take a handful of pills and wash them down with tepid beer. He'd done it before. Would he be foolish enough to repeat that abuse again?

Not this night, he decided.

Steeling his resolve, he put the pills aside and pulled his bedroll closer to the wall. Using his bunched-up jacket as a pillow, he created a make-shift headrest. Then he grabbed two six-packs, sat with his back against the wall, and opened the first bottle. Tonight, he'd induce sleep the old-fashioned way, by getting irredeemably drunk on cheap beer. Tomorrow he'd wake up early, return to the lavender farm, and settle scores with the occupants. By then the law enforcement crowd would be gone, leaving him free to deal with the girl whose persistence was beginning to annoy him, and also free to eliminate the hero who had mocked him by attempting to steal his identity. With luck, he might be able to dispatch the troublesome couple before it was time to intercept the professor's phone call.

By the tenth beer Diak was, as they say, feeling no pain. He shoved his bedroll away from the wall and stretched out full length on the filthy floor. Cradled in the embrace of an alcohol-induced stupor, he was just nodding off when he imagined he heard the percussive thud of a distant explosion.

"Cannot be my work this time," the weary German muttered as he surrendered to sleep.

Chapter 26

In the wake of her exploding VW, Anne's flight from Lavender Hill Farm led her through Trinidad's unused corrals to an irrigation ditch. Scrambling down the bank, she followed the dry bed southward. The sky was clear, the full moon riding high, and she found she could use the flashlight sparingly.

When she reached a sluice gate barring her way, she climbed out of the ditch and set off across an unplanted field. The footing was dicey among clumps of dried soil, so she stopped and looked left and right. The full moon bathed the ground in a silvery sheen, accenting every cluster of earth with a visible shadow. To the right, the plowed field seemed to extend to the horizon. To the left she could make out a line of trees which suggested the presence of running water. She went that way and found a stream bed with a shallow current gurgling in the dark. Reasoning that following the descending current would lead her to lower ground, she located a well-worn deer trail beside the stream and walked in that direction. The trail was broad and smooth and free of obstacles, so she turned off her flashlight to preserve the battery. The shimmering moonlight was sufficient to light her way.

After forty minutes of easy walking, the stream bank flattened out and the trail vanished as she reached a meadow of tall grass. It was a warm night. Anne stopped at the edge of the meadow, removed her jacket, and stowed it in her daypack. Then she switched on her flashlight again and found what appeared to be a narrow path formed by a crease in the otherwise uniform grass. As she left the stream and entered the meadow, her flashlight began to flicker then went out altogether. Walking on in the dark, with crickets chirping on all sides, her thoughts turned inward. Her earlier trek across the unplanted field had triggered a memory and—though she tried to suppress the past—it came flooding back.

The fire which destroyed her family home and killed her father, had left Anne McDougal alone, yet feeling no remorse. Instead, she found herself wrapped in a kind of fatalistic numbness. Her mother had abandoned her, her father was gone, and she felt, not sad, but feral. Surrendering to her wildness, she was overcome by a craving for self-preservation. After the fire, to avoid the authorities, she adopted a false name and lived on the streets of Bisbee, keeping out of sight. She might have languished there and been absorbed into the ranks of the homeless, but one dark night she'd screwed up her courage and walked miles through newly plowed farm fields to reach the next county. She had no plan except to vanish, to be somewhere else, and become someone else. Exhausted, she slept beside a road, awoke to the sound of a school bus, and got on board.

"You're new," said the bus driver. She was a middle-aged woman with frizzy blonde hair and a welcoming smile. "What's your name, honey?"

"Anne...with an 'e.' Anne Scriptor...with an 'o.'"

"Well, Miss E and O, I'm Wilma with a 'W' and I think we're gonna get along just fine. And bein' as how you're my first customer this fine day, you just have yourself a seat and hold on. Our daily thrill ride around the loop, followed by our mornin' grind up and over the grade is next on our travelin' agenda."

That day, thirteen-year-old Anne entered into a world of deception which she'd have to keep juggling the rest of her life. As the school bus swayed around Miller's Loop and labored up Delano Grade, Anne rehearsed her story. She'd read the 'Scriptor' name in a book—she couldn't recall the title—but the author had said it was an ancient Roman name for scribe or writer. At the time she happened upon the name, Anne had been keeping a diary and, among the daydreams she recorded in her personal narrative was an aspiration to become a famous author. To the earnest girl, whose flights of fancy served to allay the harsh realities of an abusive family life, it'd seemed only natural to amplify her desires by secretly adopting Scriptor as her pen name. She would, she imagined, write children's books like Beatrix Potter. The idea was not so far-fetched, because Anne was a middling artist who was fond of sketching a version of Miss Potter's characters in the margins of her diary pages. She would merely have to work on her writing and her dream would be realized.

Her diary had been a gift from her favorite teacher. It was a treasured possession which she proudly showed to her mother, a timid woman who, fearing that Anne's father would disapprove, encouraged her daughter to keep the diary hidden.

"You have a talent," her mother whispered as the two of them huddled together on the porch steps, "but it's something your pa don't understand. Talent runs in the family but skipped your father and lit on you. Best keep this between us."

Anne's dream of authorship became a secret which she and her mother shared. One summer, the hopeful girl created an eight-page booklet featuring her own original writing and illustrations and pleaded with her mother to show it to a local artist who lived nearby. Weeks passed as Anne anticipated the woman's reply. At last she received a sealed letter and its contents wounded Anne's heart. She could still recite the words.

"Dearest Child," it began, "I must be honest with you. Your mother says that you seek a career in art and writing, but I must tell you that I cannot encourage this desire. Your drawings show little potential. Your writing is both labored and insubstantial. It will be best for you to seek other horizons. Please believe that I tell you these things only to save you from pursuing goals which will lead to regret."

Anne was ten and heartbroken. She crumbled the letter, ran to her room, and opened her dresser, searching feverishly for her diary, torn between a desire to destroy it as the trivial scribbling of a delusional child and an aching longing to pour her heart out onto its comforting pages. She found it at last, lying open on her bed with the lock broken and all her entries torn out. Nothing remained of her precious book except the defiled cover and a single sheet. On that final page, in her father's rough hand, was written the epitaph of Anne's creative aspirations: "No secrets in this house."

Think about something else.

Anne pulled herself back to the present, continued walking, then halted as she heard an unexpected sound. The faint noise was just discernable above the ongoing cricket-song which continued to permeate the meadow. Something was rustling in the tall grass ahead—probably deer. The crease she was following would likely lead to a herd that was either grazing or bedding down. No sense interrupting a deer family in the middle of the night. Coming between a mother and fawn would be an inexcusable error. A protective doe would be a challenging creature to meet in the dark and blundering onto a buck and his harem would be even worse. She was about to make a course correction when the omnipresent cricket chorus went suddenly silent and an unsettling scream pierced the night.

Chapter 27

The eerie sound was brief—a stifled noise reminiscent of a woman's shriek—chilling to hear in the dark and much too close for comfort. Anne recognized it instantly. A cougar was prowling the stream bed she'd left behind. The big cat would be conducting a midnight hunt, and, with luck, the searching animal would continue downstream. Or—Anne thought as she wetted a finger to test the breeze—it might catch the scent of deer in this meadow.

Anne remained motionless for five minutes and was about to make a cautious retreat when she heard something big tearing through the grass in front. Instinctively, she crouched down as sounds of frantic scuffling reached her. She heard the strangled bleat of a fawn, followed by a surge of primitive thrashing, then a low growl, then deafening silence. Kneeling there, Anne clutched her flashlight until her fingers ached. It was the only weapon she had, and it would have to do.

She might have remained there, tense and crouching, until dawn, but dark clouds obscured the moon and it began to rain hard. Drops fell heavily and a growing breeze stirred the tall grass until the meadow writhed like a restless whirlpool. The storm was soaking Anne to the skin, and, despite the proximity of a prowling carnivore, she needed to seek cover. The clamor of the storm might be sufficient to mask her movements. She'd have to take a chance.

Anne stood carefully and suppressed the urge to run. Running would invite the cougar to chase and, though she was fit, and her athletic strides would carry her swiftly away, a fleeing human would be unlikely to outrun a determined predator. She moved cautiously, sidestepping slowly until she was clear of the meadow grass. Continuing to resist an overpowering urge to sprint, she backed away, alternating glances behind to keep her footing and forward in case the cougar should charge out of the tall grass. Moving steadily, she inched up a gradual slope.

Time seemed to drag as she traveled warily uphill, climbing through the pouring rain, growing ever closer to a distant stand of cottonwood trees. She'd feel safe on higher ground and safer still with the trees between her and the big cat. As she moved, she continued to clutch her flashlight. Once safely among the trees, she'd search for a more substantial weapon. Topping the hill at last, Anne found the ground littered with downed branches. She set her flashlight aside, armed herself with a sturdy club, and pressed against the nearest cottonwood.

Peeking around the trunk, she looked back toward the tall grass. With a final rumble of distant thunder and a parting glimmer of sheet lightning, the rain abruptly ceased. In the sudden silence, she held her breath, listening intently. Hearing no sounds, she leaned her newly found club against the trunk, shed her packs, and climbed up into the cottonwood. Balancing on a branch, Anne ignored the meadow and looked south in the direction where she was certain she would find Delta City. From her elevated position, she scanned the far horizon and was pleased to detect the faint but unmistakable glow of urban lights. This confirmation caused her to smile. Once again, even in the dark, her inherent sense of direction had proven reliable. The city was out there and exactly where she expected it to be.

She judged the lights to be about twelve miles away. In daylight, on even ground, running and walking, she might be able to cover four miles in an hour. But sunrise would be a long time coming and, having tackled Old Goat Trail hours ago, she knew the land which lay between the tree and the city would be muddy and anything but flat. She studied the horizon a moment longer and then, since her lofty perch offered a commanding view of the meadow, she turned in that direction, taking in the entire span of tall grass from end to end.

It was a vivid sight.

Freed from its curtain of nocturnal clouds, the full moon was riding high again and every blade of grass in the meadow seemed to glisten with a luminous glaze of freshly fallen rain. Feeling secure in her tree, Anne studied the scene. There was no sign of movement. The deer herd and the cougar were long gone. At the right-hand edge of the meadow, she could see the beginning of the crease where, moments ago, she'd entered the tall grass. She could also observe how far she'd traveled before the cougar's cry had compelled her to halt. And she could pinpoint the place where she'd left the deer crease and cautiously carved out a new path by slipping sideways through the grass to reach the cottonwoods. A breeze stirred the grass and her eye panned left, following the direction of the wavering blades. Then she spotted it. Just ahead of the intersection of the two pathways she herself had etched into the meadow, she could make out a place where the grass was depressed in a wide and roughly circular indentation.

This must, her mind told her, *be the killing ground.*

There would be blood on the bent grass, and she was grateful that signs of it were muted by nighttime shadows. She wanted to look away, but her morbid curiosity got the better of her and, looking closer, she saw the rest. Radiating out from the deadly circle was yet another crease—a broad one which led away from the tall grass and back toward the stream. She was certain this marked the path the cougar had taken to ambush the herd, as well as the exit the predator used to carry the prey away in its lethal jaws. For the big cat, it'd been one way in and one way out.

"Efficient," she whispered aloud.

At the sound of her own voice, Anne shuddered, but she wasn't afraid. The cougar had given her a shock, but that distress had already vanished, as if washed away by the cascading rain. Within a few feet of her, a powerful carnivore had slaughtered a weaker creature and yet she knew that wasn't tragic. The cougar must eat, the fawn was less agile, so the result was only natural. It wasn't fear that made Anne tremble. She was shaking for other reasons. She trembled because she was soaked to the skin, because her hands were freezing, and because sitting high on a cottonwood branch in the chill night air was a bad idea. Plus, something far more pressing motivated her, a reason as primitive as fear and yet more urgent. She needed to pee.

"Here's yet another fine mess," she told herself. "Now, my dear, let's see if you can get yourself down without breaking an ankle, or your precious neck."

Despite the numbness in her hands, Anne slipped nimbly to the ground. Sheltering beneath the cottonwood's broad canopy, she found a likely spot. Facing downhill, she lowered her jeans, leaned her back against the trunk, spread her feet, and squatted to urinate. Sacrificing her handkerchief, she tore the fabric in half, pocketed one portion, and wiped herself with the remainder. Standing up to fasten her jeans, she used her heel to dig a shallow hole and buried the used fabric. Rinsing her fingers with a handful of wet leaves, she dried them on her pant legs, then bent down to open her daypack.

Guys have no idea how easy they have it in the bathroom department, she thought while she rummaged through the pack in search of dry clothing.

A fresh breeze was rising as she stripped off her soaked top and donned a dry sweater and sock-cap. She wrung out her blouse, draped it over the pack, and secured the garment in place by tying the sleeves together. Then she pulled on her jacket, wriggled into pack-straps, picked up everything else, and faced the far horizon. The glow from the lights of Delta City appeared fainter at ground level, but she was convinced the place was there and headed that direction.

As Anne walked, she realized she still carried her useless flashlight, so she reached back to slip the spent device into her daypack. It was awkward to keep going while she fumbled to unzip a side pocket, insert the flashlight, and pull the zipper home again, but she managed it. She had no intention of stopping and she could only spare one hand to put the flashlight away because—just in case—and although she wasn't afraid—she continued to clutch the cottonwood club in her other fist.

Part II: Clark's Dilemma

Chapter 28

July 14, Midnight
Tucson, Arizona

Late on July 14, several hours after he'd dispatched Anne Scriptor with instructions to hide the summer caches, and much later in the day than he expected, Clark received word that she was halfway through her assignment. He'd laid his plans with the idea that Anne's call would be his starter's pistol and, although the tardy girl was unaware of it, she'd cut things a bit too close for comfort.

Still, Clark could manage.

It was late, but his Tucson scheme was in motion and the resolute professor was in position, waiting in the dark and hiding in his closet as he rehearsed the night's agenda. First and foremost, he was 110% certain he knew the true assignment of the man whom the cartel had sent to, as they put it, *reexamine, and photograph the merchandise.* The big Russian's mission was far more sinister. No doubt the man was coming to murder him and seize the Clovis. Then, the instant Clark was dead, the Brotherhood's down payment, which had been marinating in the banking system, would be swiftly aborted. If the Russians had their way, he'd be robbed and killed and broke all at the same time.

But Clark had no intention of letting those things happen.

As for the down payment which the Russians hoped to recover, much of that money was already spent. Days ago, the calculating professor had alerted his bank to watch for the two million, with instructions to begin paying off his many creditors as soon as the money started trickling incrementally into his account. He knew that these initial efforts to settle his debts would mean money going out as quickly as it came in—like trying to fill an empty reservoir at one end while leaving the floodgates wide open at the other—like air deserting a punctured balloon. It irked him to fork out so much cash up front, but it was a prudent precaution, a necessary action taken to get a legion of collection agencies and lawyers off his case. Clark was about to disappear and the last thing he needed was a platoon of loan sharks nipping at his heels.

Once his outstanding debts were settled, he'd withdrawn a wad of traveling cash. After everyone, including himself, had a go at his account, the bank was under orders to instantly transfer the balance—five thousand dollars at a time—into a half-dozen off-shore accounts set up around the globe in Clark's name. Setting up the accounts had been deceptively easy. It'd taken him longer to track down a notary to certify his identity documents than the hour and a half he'd invested sitting at his office computer while opening accounts in Aruba, Zambia, and other points in between.

He calculated that this secondary slow leak of the principal amount could be accomplished before anyone noticed. With luck, by judiciously reducing his account to the tune of $5,000 in his pocket with the rest dispersed in all directions, he'd manage to siphon off a reasonable amount before someone, somewhere, got wise and pulled the plug. Meanwhile, despite making full use of the Brotherhood's down payment, there was absolutely, positively no way he was going to let the Russians have the Clovis—not with the Saudis waiting in the wings to pay him a cool eight million.

Naturally, he'd have to be alive to enjoy the money and he had every intention of doing that. Anne had done her job and reported in, which meant the Clovis was safely hidden. Now it was merely a matter of leaving Tucson undetected. To that end, Clark took up his post in the closet to wait for his Russian visitor. Just after midnight, his target arrived, and the professor sprang into the dark, with croquet mallets in both hands and malice in his heart.

Chapter 29

It only took a split-second for Clark's well-laid plan to come unraveled. As the waning moments of July 14 reached the midnight hour and drifted into July 15, he'd sprung from his closet, intent on knocking Fyodor senseless. His goal to ambush the Russian might have been conceived as a stroke of genius, but he'd been unable to control every variable, let alone a completely random one. Listening as the hall clock struck a quarter-past the hour, Clark stood in the dark in his study. He was motionless, caught up in a daze as he stared dejectedly down at the carpet. Both arms hung limply at his sides, each hand grasping a useless croquet mallet. Moments ago, he'd burst hot-blooded into the room, determined to waylay and switch places with a man his size, then escape undetected. Now his passion and his plans were dissolving away—like a fistful of insubstantial desert sand cascading through his open fingers.

"Unreliable Russians," he snarled.

Clark had specifically instructed his cartel customers to send the giant Fyodor, the big Cossack whose height and girth matched his own, making him the professor's ideal body double. Instead, they'd sent the huge Russian's younger brother, Dobry, a little weasel of a man and the cartel's most skittish member. With a heavy sigh, Clark considered the corpse. Although they'd never met in person, he recognized the small man from a photograph Fyodor had shown him when the two of them had shared drinks in Phoenix.

"You sure you're brothers?" Clark had asked as he examined the photograph showing the big Russian balancing his younger brother on his shoulder.

"Everyone asks that," Fyodor had responded. "And I tell them to ask my mother, which seems to settle the matter."

Unaware of the switch, Clark had been anxiously listening for the sounds of his victim's approach and, the instant little Dobry entered the study, the professor had bounded from the shadows, shouting bloody murder. The professor had rushed forward with a vengeance, ferociously endeavoring to subdue a far bigger man, but before he could strike a single blow, before either croquet mallet could be swung home, it was over. Cringing and yelping, the diminutive Dobry had clutched his heart and collapsed like a wet noodle, never to rise again.

Clark stood for a moment more, staring down at Dobry's lifeless body, and the fear etched on the small man's grotesquely distorted face, before turning away. Placing both mallets back into the closet, the disappointed professor crossed to the wet bar, poured himself a stiff drink, and returned to sit heavily down on the study's plush sofa. He was feeling angry and temporarily flummoxed. His escape plans called for a suitable body to be found when authorities searched through the charred wreckage of his ranch house. 'Homeowner slain in robbery gone wrong,' 'Spectacular fire claims life of university legend,' those were the headlines the professor was hoping for.

Obviously, Dobry's tiny corpse would not do, but it was too late to find another stiff, so Clark was forced to go with what he had. Determined to work things out as he went along, he finished his drink, left Dobry where the little fink had fallen, and proceeded to stage a counterfeit robbery. For fifteen frenetic minutes Clark calmed his troubled mind by dislodging books, overturning furniture, and rifling through what little remained of his once extensive collection of Native American artifacts. He hated to defile the few remaining pieces but, in his eyes, what had once been the collection of a lifetime was already greatly diminished.

For that indignity he had the United States government to thank.

After creating havoc in his once orderly house, Clark returned to his study and considered the tiny corpse lying there. How to make his plan work with the wrong body? Seeking inspiration, he scanned the room. His books would be of little use. His trophies were there: plaques commemorating this and that, a silver cup won as a wrestler at Cornell, a host of congratulatory certificates, but nothing to help with his present dilemma. Clark was losing hope, until he spied his medal. Thanks to his hasty rearrangement of the room, the medal's gilded frame was slightly askew. Hanging there next to his other awards, its slanted attitude seemed to be winking at him.

"Of course," he said aloud as his mind was transported back to events leading up to receiving the coveted award.

Years ago, the Archaeological Institute of America had called Clark a genius when they presented him with a gold medal for distinguished achievement. Everyone was all smiles and compliments on the night of the awards banquet. A cavalcade of well-wishers pumped his hand, all blissfully unaware of the behind-the-scenes controversy that nearly scuttled Clark's nomination. Few knew that, earlier that same year when the awards committee conducted a routine background check, the researchers had stumbled upon an astonishing result.

"Dr. Clark?" The committee chair had reported the problem to him with a long-distance telephone call. "Sir, I'm afraid I have some bad news."

"Go on," Clark replied. He'd expected something like this.

"Well, I don't quite know how to say this," the chairman continued. "Therefore, I'll just come to the point."

"Please do," said Clark.

"Well, you see, it's this way: our background check suggests that you have no fingerprints on file," the man emitted a nervous laugh. "That is, no fingerprints locally, none in the state system, none in the federal system, none with Interpol, in fact none anywhere at all."

"Ah, allow me to compliment you on conducting a thorough investigation which has resulted in an entirely factual finding," said Clark, his tone confident and matter of fact.

"But you have a passport and a driver's license and so on?"

"Naturally," Clark agreed.

"And yet you have never been fingerprinted?" The chairman sounded incredulous.

"Never," Clark confirmed.

"Well..."

"I guess you'll have to take my word for it that I am who I say I am," said Clark.

"Oh my, this is most irregular. Can I call you back?"

"Certainly, but please call soon, because I've already rented my tuxedo."

Clark never knew for certain whether his confident tone or his otherwise impeccable credentials, or a combination of his attitude and his resume, carried the day. Whatever worked, he got his medal.

Now, as a new plan to escape Tucson began to form in his mind, Clark held his hands to his face and stared appreciatively at his remarkably undocumented fingertips, until he was beaming with inspiration. Anxious to confirm that his revised idea would work, he knelt beside Dobry's body and hurriedly examined each of the little man's hands.

"Just as I thought," he said to himself.

In Clark, the Russians were dealing with a sophisticated partner. Many of the trappings of his doctorate in archaeology were useless, but one thing Clark had absolutely mastered was the art of conducting research. The questing professor had already completed a marathon investigation to confirm the value of his Clovis and, the instant the Russians contacted him with their offer to purchase it, Clark dug into the cartel as well. Warming to his work, he soon learned a great deal about his new customers. He learned that the Scarlet Brotherhood was a secretive society which operated independently of Moscow. Their mission was to advance the interests of an autonomous league of oligarchs who were ostensibly in the business of wholesaling heating oil and automobiles—in other words, operating shell companies through which the Brotherhood laundered rivers of illicit cash.

Scouring not only the public internet but also searching the secretive recesses of the dark web, Clark discovered the true nature of their enterprise. In addition to their outwardly legitimate businesses, the cartel dealt in drugs, prostitutes, and weapons, and, most importantly to Clark, they also bought and sold black market antiquities. The cartel operated primarily in third-world countries but as needed, they were active in North America, being especially eager to acquire pirated artifacts stolen from Native American tribes.

For organizational purposes, the cartel was structured along the lines of a Sicilian mob. Which meant that the clandestine corporation tended to attract fathers and sons, nephews and uncles, as well as brothers, of course. So far as Clark could determine, the Brotherhood was a strictly male organization, like an order of monks. Individual names were redacted from the documents uncovered by Clark's research, but that did nothing to mitigate the fact that three dozen members of the Brotherhood were listed on U.S. federal warrants as unindicted co-conspirators—thirty-six Russians, accused of extortion, trafficking in stolen goods, and murder.

Point taken: the cartel was dangerous, so he'd be careful. He'd keep the Russians at arm's length, trusting that, should the need arise, his military training would see him through. If push came to shove, he not only owned a pistol, he knew how to use it.

Tapping multiple sources to compile a profile of his Russian customers, the master researcher unearthed a jumble of information which was simultaneously tangled but also disjointed. Faced with the task of sifting through a mountain of disparate data, Clark approached the challenge systematically, just as he would in conducting an archaeological dig. Putting his head down, he dug deeper, looking for details about the inner workings of the cartel. Just as he'd done countless times, during hundreds of archaeological digs, the exacting professor carefully sifted through rough material, looking for the little things. Relishing the process of virtual digging and figurative sifting, he assumed he was operating in familiar territory. If it occurred to him that his internet sleuthing was leaving a trail, that fleeting thought had been insufficient to impede his efforts.

Buoyed by the challenge, Clark had forged on. Using his well-honed archaeological techniques to better understand his Russian customers, Clark spent weeks systematically narrowing his search, removing layers as he went, seeking the sublime, the subtle, and the intimate. He was intentionally looking for small details which other investigators might miss. Working on his computer, sometimes far into the night, he relentlessly shifted through the cartel's sordid background until he'd gained a handful of small but important insights.

Noted: the cartel's American field operatives wore identical suits and hats which made them easy to spot. Noted: despite the fact that the practice made them even more conspicuous, American operatives generally drove new black Bentley automobiles. Presumably they got them at a discount from their masters.

Noted—and most vital to his current situation—the cartel required that its field henchmen submit to the painful process of having their hands chemically charred to remove all traces of finger or palm prints. With this intimate fact in mind, Clark was not surprised when he knelt beside Dobry's mortal remains and examined the corpse's tiny hands. He found the fingers infused with a faint odor of hydrochloric acid, smooth as a baby's bottom, and completely and absolutely featureless.

"Okay, genius," Clark said aloud, "you have all you need. Now do your stuff."

So, Clark set to work on a fresh idea. He wouldn't set fire to the ranch house after all. Instead he would invent another story, one which would befuddle the authorities and the Russians or whoever else was watching. One which would cover his escape and buy him time to do what needed to be done. Moving swiftly and with deliberate determination, Clark stood up and retrieved his travel bag from the closet. Then he knelt on the study floor and removed Dobry's shoulder holster and weapon. Probably the holster was untraceable, and the weapon had no serial number, but why take chances? He stuffed the holster and pistol into his travel bag. Next, he reached into the dead man's pockets and grabbed the corpse's car keys and cell phone. Then he fished out the Russian's wallet and removed everything with Dobry's name, including a Texas driver's license.

Pausing, Clark examined the Texas license closely. It looked authentic, but it had to be a fake since the dead man would have needed fingerprints to acquire it. Somewhere Dobry would also have a fake passport. Fake IDs were something that the professor had coveted from an early age.

When he'd turned twelve, Clark had been obsessed with underground literature and he'd read a few too many leftist comic books, which led him to believe in the conspiracy theory that America was secretly controlled by sinister hidden forces. Owing to his suspicions, he resisted fingerprinting. And he'd been pleasantly surprised at fourteen to learn that he could obtain an Iowa learner's permit and commence driving without being fingerprinted. Later, at age twenty, the police had tried to ink his fingers when he was arrested for excessive speeding and, still later—when he was drafted—the military had tried it too. In both cases, a well-placed hundred-dollar bill had been sufficient to circumvent the procedures. As time passed, Clark had acquired his own set of bogus documents, but his fake IDs lacked the craftsmanship of Dobry's license. The Russian's license was a first-class thing of beauty, whereas Clark's forged documents were rather ordinary.

Thinking back, the professor recalled that he'd obtained a counterfeit driver's license, as well as his false passport, while stationed briefly in Texas—one of the few states then requiring drivers to be fingerprinted. All his fellow soldiers were traveling over the border to obtain forged documents in Mexico —not to avoid being fingerprinted, but rather to obtain a false birth date allowing them access to over-21 nightclubs. Clark had followed suit and he'd continued using Mexican sources to secure a string of updated documents. These had proven serviceable, but they were clearly inferior to Dobry's. And yet, his shoddy Mexican documents would soon be things of the past, because Clark now had a brand-new license and passport, both with a new face and pseudonym. These fresh documents were gifts from the Saudis and were of much higher quality. He suspected that, like most things, the Saudi gifts had been manufactured in China and, for a moment, he wondered if the Russians and the Saudis got their fake IDs from the same source.

One final look at Dobry's license and Clark stuffed the dead man's identifying documents and cell phone into his travel bag. The car keys he pocketed. He would dispose of everything else on his way to the airfield. Then he reached for his own wallet and transferred his documents to the corpse. He gave Dobry his social security card, university dining pass, credit cards, library card, grocery discount card, and anything else without a photo.

For a few seconds, Clark fingered his Arizona Bank debit card. He could keep the card and max it out at the nearest ATM. But soon after the cops were stretching crime scene tape around his ranch house, the bank card would be flagged and any use of it traced. Besides, he was rolling in cash. Thanks to his success in convincing the Russians to fork over a generous down payment, he was debt-free for the first time in decades and his travel bag was stuffed with greenbacks. An ample supply of money was there in all its spectacular glory, packed alongside his map, GPS, and a supply of burner phones courtesy of the Saudis. Nearby lay his duffle bag which contained everything else.

Armed with his escape supplies, generous gifts from the Saudis, and cold hard cash extorted from the Russians, he was more than prepared to walk away from the remaining contents of his local bank accounts. Better to leave those paltry sums undisturbed. What did he need with a few thousand dollars when he had an enormous payout waiting for him on the other side of the world? Without a second thought, he added his bank card and stuffed the wallet back inside the dead man's pocket. Clark stood up then and reached for one of the burner phones, prepared to dial 911, but he paused a moment to make certain he'd thought of everything.

Is this it? He quizzed himself as he crossed to the bar, poured one last drink, and studied his reflection in the glass. *Are you ready to do this? Can you pull it off?*

With his portly build, shock of white hair, and beard to match, he was a unique individual, even memorable, the type of person you'd recall meeting. But there were advantages to being a recluse and living several miles from the campus where he worked. There were perks associated with being anti-social by nature and having no near neighbors. The chief advantage was that, although he was a fixture on campus, a man whom most at the university recognized as the spitting image of Santa Claus, no one in the immediate area of his isolated ranch house knew what he looked like. That included the rural cops who were about to respond to his distress call. When the police arrived, they would find a disheveled house and a body with sufficient paperwork in his pockets to assume the dead man was Clark. By the time that got sorted out, the real Clark would be sipping tea on a balcony somewhere in the Muslim world, or at least well on his way to fulfilling that fantasy. For an instant, he wondered if he would appreciate Arab women and then immediately decided he would. Almond eyes, dark skin, and a submissive nature—he'd soon be ensconced in a country full of ideal women who apparently preferred plump lovers.

"Ah," he sighed as he allowed his loins to stir briefly before downing his drink and returning to his task.

Satisfied that he was prepared, he telephoned the local dispatcher, breathlessly reported that he'd discovered a burglary in progress, and declared he was going to confront the perpetrator. He hastily whispered his address and made a point of dramatically cutting off his call mid-sentence. Then he dropped the burner phone next to Dobry's body.

Good luck with my prints and his, he chuckled.

Finally, he picked up his travel bag, shouldered his duffle bag, and hid in shadows on the rear patio. He was leaving everything else—including his former life—behind.

Fifteen minutes later, two patrol cars arrived with lights flashing. While the cops rushed inside, Clark slipped around the chaos carrying his luggage. He had to presume the watchers were still there, so he used a screening hedge to obscure his movements until he was far down his driveway. When he reached Dobry's concealed Bentley, he got in and drove away.

Chapter 30

Clark had been right to assume the watchers were there. Had he been capable of turning back the clock and been granted the ability to observe those individuals assigned to spy on him, he'd have been amused to observe their confusion.

At 6 a.m. on July 14, Clark had been standing at the edge of The University of Arizona campus quad waving goodbye to Anne Scriptor whom he was dispatching to carry his summer geocaches to Colorado. As the little Volkswagen had driven out of sight and the professor turned away, two watchers observed the send-off from the top floor of the student union building.

"Well, there's another summer shot to pieces," said one watcher as he lowered his binoculars. He'd been shadowing the professor since the night before and he was thoroughly bored and more than ready to hand off his surveillance duties.

"Anything to report?" his relief asked.

"Same as last semester, same as last summer, same as last year, except this time the boxes are padlocked."

"Hmm. He doesn't trust somebody, I guess," said the relief. The padlocks seemed trivial, but nevertheless the relief man recorded the observation in their shared logbook.

"I don't blame him," said his comrade, as he added his initials to the logbook entry. "How many bicycles have I had stolen on campus so far?"

"Three, or so you tell me. Which is why I walk to work," said the relief.

They shared a chuckle and, when they'd watched Clark retrace his steps back to his departmental office, the night watcher and his relief man started downstairs.

"Binoculars," said the relief man.

"All yours. See you later this afternoon when the old fart's taxi arrives. Have a good day."

"Thanks. And, hey, good luck finding your bike," the relief man laughed.

"Screw you."

Later that same evening, following a routine shift change, the night watcher was back at his post outside the professor's desert home when he spotted a shadowy figure approaching the ranch house. The figure was small, no larger than a child. The night man spoke into his radio.

"Someone's lost," he said.

"Say vhat again?" asked the night manager on the other end, his thickly accented inquiry barely discernible over the remote connection.

"There's a kid out here. Lost, I guess. Probably asking directions."

"Kid? You mean goat or child? Do you see car?"

"No car. The kid—the child—is on foot. If there's a vehicle, it must be hidden down the driveway somewhere, because I don't see it."

"Vhat the hell? I call in."

"Okay."

"Let me know he comes out again. Or you are spotting car."

"Will do, out." *Dumb krauts*, he thought, *where'd this Bozo learn to speak English?*

The kid didn't come out and the night manager didn't call back. The night man waited another hour. Then he started down toward the ranch house, leaving for the first time the hillock where he'd manned his observation post every other night for the past eighteen months. This break in Clark's routine made him nervous so, as he descended the hill, he unsnapped the keeper on his holster. He hadn't drawn a revolver since retiring from the San Diego P.D. He'd use the gun if he had to, but he never got the chance because he saw flashing lights coming up the long rural driveway, which caused him to duck into the shadows and rush back to his post.

"Hell! The law is here," he reported into the radio.

"Vhat law?"

"Local police. Two local patrol cars."

"They see you?"

"Negative."

"Any sign of professor?"

"Negative."

"Get now your ass out!"

"Understood," the night man growled and under his breath he muttered, "Dumb krauts."

Chapter 31

Five miles from his ranch house, Clark stopped the purloined Bentley beneath the full moon and glanced at his watch. It was early, not yet two in the morning, but he was running behind schedule. Moving quickly, he stuffed the dead man's identification papers and cell phone into one of his own spare socks. Then he stepped onto the dark roadway, added stones, knotted the top, and pitched the weighted sock far out into a roadside pond. When he was certain the sock was underwater, he selected another spot in the pond and tossed in Dobry's pistol and holster.

Thirty minutes later, he reached an isolated airstrip in the desert hills where he left the conspicuous Bentley behind and boarded a private jet—a deluxe conveyance arranged by the Saudis. The professor's carryon luggage consisted of a travel bag stuffed with a change of clothes along with lots of cash, his map and GPS device, prepaid burner phones, and new identity papers. In the cargo hold was his duffle bag containing a plastic pistol with synthetic ammunition, a change of clothing, two saddle blankets, two empty toolboxes, and two combination padlocks. On his lap, he carried a candy box containing several wafers of a green substance which his naïve pilot noted had the distinct aroma of almonds.

"A gift for the tribe," Clark lied as he chatted with the young pilot before takeoff.

"Smells delicious," the pilot said, and he grinned expectantly.

"I'd offer you a piece," Clark said, "but you know how it is."

"Don't I ever," agreed the pilot. "You all set for takeoff?'

"I am if you are," Clark answered.

Moments later the jet was aloft and winging its way northward. Clark's escape plans for the wee hours of July 15 had called for him to leave behind a suitable corpse in his Tucson ranch house—a body-double to be discovered and mistaken for him. Instead, he'd been stuck with a diminutive substitute and yet he'd made the best of things. He'd telephoned the police to report a robbery in progress, implied that his life was in danger, whispered the address of his remote ranch house, and hung up. When law enforcement arrived, Clark had slipped away and was soon aloft in a private jet on his way to a northern Arizona airstrip. The Saudis had supplied the jet and Clark had brought the rest.

Cruising through the night sky, Clark glanced out the window. The passing clouds reflected the pulsating glow of the jet's wing-tip lights—red on the left and green on the right, holiday colors in mid-July. He looked below at the landscape which was partially illuminated by the full moon. In time, the sun would rise and Anne, his faithful graduate student, would be down there somewhere, although much farther north. She'd be hard at work, continuing to fulfill her assignment, driving her route, blissfully unaware of her true mission, and out of danger. He presumed she'd be safe, hoped she was. Pulling his map and his GPS from his travel bag, he arranged them on the seat beside him. Then he extracted one of his Saudi burner phones and punched in the accustomed number.

It was time to call the Russians and he'd decided not to risk using his smartphone. The Brotherhood would be able to use that familiar device to pinpoint his location. Better to do the unexpected, to use a burner, and keep them guessing. The Russian who answered identified himself as Sasha. Yet another player, Clark thought, and before the man could ask why the professor was calling from an unfamiliar number, Clark interrupted.

"There has been a terrible incident," Clark lied. "Your man was intercepted by someone and wounded. He managed to reach my house before he died. What was I to do? I panicked, traded places with your man, and fled."

There was silence on the other end of the line, then a voice, barely recognizable as human, crackled through space. The insubstantial voice waffled in the air, like a lost echo, sounding distant and desperate. The fleeing professor found the sound reassuring and smiled as he lounged contentedly in the jet's comfortable, over-stuffed cabin seat.

"You are telling—[static]—that you exchanged places with Comrade Dobry?" The voice sounded doubtful.

"Exactly," said Clark.

"Something appears to be wrong with our connection," said the voice—presumably it was still Sasha. "How is this possible?" More static, followed by a bewildered tone and more questions. "Are you—[static]—How can—[static]—I am—[static]—not authorized to—[static]—."

"I've lost you I'm afraid," said Clark and he ended the call. Let them stew a bit. Besides, no sense giving them extra minutes to trace his location. Clark took a sip of coffee, looked out the window at the passing night, and casually redialed the Russians.

"[Static]—your location—?" asked Sasha.

Clark understood that snippet of conversation and he had no intention of telling this latest in a long line of Russian handlers how to find him.

"Look," the professor said, "I'm rattled, see? You know what I mean by 'rattled, comrade?' It's an American idiom meaning I've had the bejeebers scared out of me. I'm not used to having people die on my carpet, so at the moment, I'm on the run."

Suddenly the connection deteriorated into a strident scramble of pops and crackles. Clark had heard something like it before, when he was being interviewed at the campus public radio station. He remembered the engineer referring to the tumultuous static as 'frying bacon.' The noise was irritating and so loud that Clark held the receiver away from his ear and waited. At last the voice returned and, as if by magic, the transmission came in loud and clear.

"Dr. Clark? Are you there?"

"Yes," Clark responded. "Is that you, Sasha, and did you understand what I said?"

"You are fearful," said Sasha. "That much we understand. We will assist you. Give us your location and we will send assistance."

I'll just bet you will, thought Clark.

"Sorry, no dice, comrade, because I no longer know who to trust," said Clark.

"But the treasure..." the Russian's voice trailed off.

"The treasure is safe," said Clark truthfully. "And I have it in hand," which was technically a lie, although he'd have it soon enough.

"I see," Sasha responded. "And now I suppose that you wish to make to us a new proposal."

Clark could imagine the 'us' that Sasha referred to. There was probably a committee of mobsters listening in on their conversation. The professor seemed to detect a reverberation on the line, and he could almost hear the others breathing in the background. He was dealing with a party line, which probably contributed to the difficulty of maintaining a clear connection.

"Indeed, I do have a new proposal," said Clark. He was pleased that, despite all the participants in this conversation, real and imagined on his part, it was he and only he who was in control. "You must all realize that things have gotten too risky for a simple transaction. You need the merchandise and I require the rest of my money. Now, I'm willing to hold up my end of the bargain. But people are dying, so I'm going to divest myself of the treasure in a way that gives me confidence that I won't be next."

"Go on," prompted Sasha. "Please give us all the details."

"Well, my friends, I'm sure asking for 'all the details' is your way of trying to stretch things out in order to discover my location. But you needn't bother because I'll end this call in a moment and my watch tells me that you won't have nearly enough time to pinpoint me. So, listen carefully, comrades, because I'm only going to say this once."

In a brief monologue Clark informed Sasha that, given the current circumstances, he had no intention of delivering the treasure face-to-face. Instead, he'd hide it in a remote spot somewhere in the Four Corners area where the borders of Arizona, Utah, Colorado, and New Mexico come together. In a day or two, once the treasure was securely hidden and he felt safe, Clark promised to reveal the coordinates by telephoning again, using his familiar smartphone. Having imparted that load of vague information, the professor gleefully pictured gangs of identically dressed Russian toughs riding around in black Bentleys—conspicuous foreigners roaming rural western byways in anticipation of receiving word of the promised location.

When it was clear that Clark had finished, Sasha made one final attempt to voice objections. But the professor assuaged the man's reservations by adding that he would naturally forego his final two-million-dollar payment until the Brotherhood had retrieved the treasure and verified its authenticity. In response to this announcement, the professor seemed to detect a collective sigh of relief from the eavesdropping crowd. Then he ended the call, broke the burner in two, and tossed the pieces into his travel bag. With the Russians handled, Clark turned his attention to his map and notes. He studied these references for fifteen minutes until he grew drowsy. It'd already been a long night and the new day was just beginning. Switching off the overhead light, he reclined his seat and closed his eyes.

Chapter 32

While he slept, Clark dreamt of the past as his unconscious mind mused about the motives which had driven him to commit archaeological heresy. How, after a decade of frustration, a distinguished professor had slipped from the noble ranks of pure science. How a once untouchable professional had descended into the unforgivable sin of viewing a particular artifact, not as a cultural treasure to be studied and preserved, but as a commodity to be sold to the highest bidder.

It'd all begun a decade ago with the rape of his personal collection.

In ten short years, every one of Clark's most precious artifacts had been taken from him. The outrage was perpetrated by what he condemned as a series of federally sanctioned thefts, all carried out under the banner of the Native American Graves Protection and Repatriation Act. Publicly, as a respected scholar at a major university, Clark was obliged to accept NAGPRA rulings. In private, he despised the politically correct legislation which had inspired certain misguided federal activists to overreach their authority by targeting his personal collection.

The simple fact was that the artifacts which he'd lovingly accumulated during his long and distinguished career, the prehistoric treasures he'd enshrined in his home, included no human remains. And yet the Feds had come after him with pitchforks and torches. He'd been harassed like a common criminal and vilified by zealots who used the Act as justification to seize his collection. Exploiting a technicality, they'd proclaimed his pieces to be funeral objects and sacred relics and confiscated them with the flimsy excuse that each seized artifact 'might' have been associated with prehistoric burial rituals.

Nonsense! He'd fumed. *Using that logic, why not seize the dark suit, plain necktie, black socks, and patent leather shoes I wore to my grandmother's funeral? Why not go after the other pallbearers? Why not impound the hearse? Why not confiscate the flowers and seize the casket?*

Suppressing a secret resentment that festered and expanded each time an object in his ever-dwindling collection was usurped by the government, Clark was compelled to endure the pain of surrendering item after item. To observers, he appeared to cooperate with an outward show of what they mistakenly interpreted as grace and humility. Though he seemed resigned to the situation, he inwardly cursed the process as nothing short of legally sanctioned highway robbery.

Throughout his decades as a field archaeologist, Clark had specialized in small objects and his personal collection of tiny bird-points and effigy stones had been unrivaled. But after NAGPRA was finished with him, the world's finest assortment of miniature prehistoric artifacts was reduced to a sad legacy of four hundred empty glass vials. The treasures he'd so painstakingly unearthed and so expertly preserved were suddenly gone. Everything he'd once cared for was taken from him, all of it claimed by tribal interests and returned to the ground.

In short order these relentless assaults on his ego caused Clark to hit rock bottom.

Deprived of the tangible manifestations of his life's work, the once renowned scholar began to lose interest in his profession and his teaching. For a time, he managed to put on a brave face and neither his faculty colleagues nor his students suspected the depths to which he was inexorably sinking. Even Anne Scriptor, who was more perceptive than most, had failed to see beyond the shell of a man whom Clark had become. So convincingly had he played the part of the revered scholar that, despite his troubles, he'd managed to become Anne's trusted mentor and—dare he say it—her hero.

And yet, though he hid it well, Clark—as a scholar and as a man—was beginning to evaporate. As his professional star began to fade, his personal life also unraveled. His finances faded and—deprived of her meal ticket—his young lover left. His world crumbled and his campus and professional colleagues began to suspect something was amiss. It was then that the dean called him in for a chat and the sinking professor managed to maintain a shred of dignity by accepting his department's insistence to either resign or take a long-delayed sabbatical. Leaving the university, even temporarily, was a hard compromise for a man who had lived and breathed academia for four decades. Being barred from his campus amounted to a death sentence. Clark retreated to his isolated ranch house, became a hermit, and continued drinking. He might have expired there, alone, and despondent, if it hadn't been for one momentous night two years ago.

It was a chilly December evening and the exiled professor had wasted that bleak day, as he wasted most days, sleeping late, lamenting his lost collection, cursing his fickle lover, and drinking heavily while randomly surfing the internet. Around midnight, after tiring of adorable cat videos and gratuitous porn, he pulled his credit card from his wallet and purchased, from an arbitrary eBay dealer, a miscellaneous lot of Native American artifacts. Indifferent to the process, he pressed 'add to cart' and 'purchase' without bothering to look at the illustration.

Drunk as he was, he forgot about the acquisition until a week later when a nondescript package arrived in the mail. He sat the box on the kitchen table and left it unopened for several hours. Finally, as his hall clock struck midnight, he savaged the package with a butter knife and ripped it open to find a small wooden box filled with half-finished flints and a handful of pottery sherds—all complete junk. He spread the contents out on the table and poured himself another drink.

"Rubbish," he said as he examined his impulsive purchase and the enclosed receipt. "One-hundred-and-forty-two dollars' worth of un-be-frigging-lievable garbage!"

Clark growled, cursed himself for a fool, downed the drink, and was about to pitch the box and its contents into the trash when something caught his eye. He turned on the overhead kitchen light, sat down, put on his spectacles, and pushed the rough chips of flint and useless sherds aside. Then he stared. Staggering to his feet and rummaging in a desk drawer until he unearthed a magnifying glass, he returned to the table and stared some more until he was certain.

"I'll be darned!" he exclaimed.

There in the middle of the jumbled junk was something curious. It appeared to be a bit of hardened earth about as long as a finger but rounded in the middle and tapered at either end. At first glance it resembled a cocoon. Clark picked it up, placed it in his palm, and closed his fist.

It fit perfectly.

Clark felt a thrill. This was not a natural object. It was man-made—fashioned from wet clay and probably hardened in the coals of an ancient fire pit. How long ago? To find out, he'd have to date the thing. What would that take? He hurriedly did a mental inventory of equipment on hand. His garage was filled with the tools of his trade, including a brand-new X-ray fluorescence spectrometer. He'd received the prototype device years ago—a free sample sent by an optimistic manufacturer in hopes that the famous professor would use it and pen a glowing endorsement. He'd accepted the gift, but he'd written no endorsement. He hadn't even bothered to take it out of the box. He'd find the mechanism in the garage and give it a try.

Clark put the cocoon in his pajama pocket, opened the pantry door, passed through to the garage, and flicked a wall switch. While row after row of dazzling lights illuminated, he lingered in the doorway for a moment, remembering the naïve enthusiasm which had seized him years ago when he'd lovingly converted this sizable space into a state-of-the-art laboratory. He'd sold most of his luxury vehicles and used the money to purchase all the latest technology for analyzing artifacts. If he cared to, he could fire up his machinery of science and subject his mysterious little cocoon to a CT scan, or carve a microscopic slice from it and evaluate the sliver under an electron microscope. Or he could scrape a bit of material off the surface and carbon-date the tiny organisms he knew that any mud—even certain prehistoric mud—would contain. If he was very fortunate, there would be a sliver of organic matter inside. A seed pod or blade of grass would surely be too much to ask, but he was suddenly—and for the first time in years—hopeful.

He strode into the garage and, when his bare feet encountered the cold concrete floor, he felt an abrupt thrill as his dormant sense of curiosity came flooding back. It was freezing in the garage, but his mind was on fire. He was experiencing a reawakening of the boyhood passion that had first compelled him to search out and unravel the mysteries of the past. As he turned up the thermostat, he thought of his mother's discarded egg cartons, a score of which he'd filled to overflowing with tiny rocks and bones collected on the family farm in rural Iowa. He thought of school science fairs he'd taken by storm. He thought of his heady undergraduate days at Cornell and all the rest of his training and field work. For the first time since his breakdown, Clark was beginning to think like an archaeologist again. He had a mystery on his hands, and he would approach this cocoon challenge systematically. Keeping the object intact, he would conduct his exploration methodically, using the least-invasive analysis, and he would begin by determining how old the object was.

Clark removed the tarp that covered his workbench. The box containing the X-ray device would be on the opposite side of the garage, exactly where he'd left it long ago. But first things first. It would take a moment to organize things before he fired up the analyzer. He'd need a field notebook and gloves and room to operate. The bench was cluttered with an array of ancient hammer stones he'd been in the process of categorizing in those happy days before his present fall. The nondescript stone tools, which looked like ordinary rocks to the uninformed eye, were ovular and just the right size to be held in one hand in order to chip and shape an ingot of raw flint. At the moment, however, they were in the way, so he cleared a space, retrieved the cocoon from his pocket, and placed it on the workbench. He was about to initiate an orderly research procedure when he spontaneously picked up the nearest hammer stone.

Had it really come to this?

Was he going to behave like an uninitiated freshman, impatiently using a mallet instead of a scalpel to see what was inside the cocoon? Surrounded by the exacting tools of his trade, would he violate every tenet of research and simply smash the thing? Clark sighed and lowered the stone for an instant. Then he raised it again and impulsively shattered the cocoon.

Chapter 33

Clark's rash behavior had two immediate effects. First, he completely obliterated the cocoon's hardened shell. Second, because he'd acted like a foolish novice and failed to don safety goggles, the exploding fragments peppered his face, causing him to reel back from the workbench, cursing and clutching his eyes. Dropping the stone, he missed his bare foot by inches and stumbled to the utility sink where he splashed water until he cleared his vision. Then he toweled off and returned to the workbench, still muttering under his breath.

Pieces of the cocoon lay scattered across the bench.

"Humph," Clark exhaled the unhappy syllable. His shoulders slumping with resignation, he was about to admit failure and sweep up the remnants of the disaster when he noticed something black amid the dun-colored debris. Brushing fragments aside, he beheld a miniature projectile point—a single piece of obsidian. One glance of his practiced eye confirmed that the volcanic glass had been painstakingly worked on both edges, with a distinctive and instantly recognizable pattern of fluted grooves at the base.

It was by such a stroke of fortune that a completely singular, amazing, and extraordinary miniature Clovis projectile point came into Clark's possession. A lay person might mistakenly label the thing an 'arrowhead,' but he knew better. This was no dime-store knickknack, no curio from a roadside stand. This was the genuine article. It was, as his old dad used to say, *the real McCoy*.

Seeking a closer look, he reached for the fluorescent magnifying lamp which hovered near the workbench. The lamp's angular armature gave the apparatus a bird-like appearance—its hinged joint resembling the bowed neck of a sandhill crane. Swiveling the viewing device into position, the intrigued professor toggled the switch and centered the luminous halo to shine directly on the artifact.

"Eureka!" Clark shouted and a thrill coursed through him, while echoes of his booming voice reverberated in the spacious garage.

Tingling with joy, he opened a locker, took off his pajamas, donned a flannel shirt and cargo pants, and encased his cold feet in warm slippers. Glancing out one of the garage's constricted windows, he studied the cold December desert for an instant. Then he warmed his hands at the register, slipped on a pair of vinyl gloves, and pulled his bench stool closer. Staring intently through the magnifying lens, he reached out with a pair of nylon-tipped sorting tweezers. The object was compact—possibly a diminutive bird-point used to kill small game—but it was far from delicate. Still, it would be prudent to handle it carefully. Gently grasping the projectile point, he turned it over, pivoting the artifact so the sharp tip faced left and the concave base, with its fluted groove, was nearest his right hand.

"Better and better," he whispered as he beheld a rose-colored vein running the length of the dark surface. Compared to the shiny black obsidian, the rosy vein was muted in appearance. It was almost as if the maker had positioned the artifact vertically and guided a trickle of red wax down its length from point to base. And yet the red vein was not inlaid or otherwise superficial, it was an integral part of the stone. Obviously chosen for its esthetic value, the preformed rock made the Clovis more than a piece of craftsmanship. The maker had created not just a practical tool but a work of art. As he stared at the artifact, the professor's mind was already racing ahead, contemplating his next step. The obsidian was inorganic, but he could still conduct a geochemical analysis of the stone to determine its geological origin. Steadying the Clovis with his tweezers, he took up a scalpel, intent on gently carving a sliver of rock from the object, when his attention was arrested.

"Man, oh man," he exclaimed. "Don't tell me I can be that lucky!"

He'd been looking along the narrow band of red from point to base, searching for the least invasive location to extract his analytic sample, when he seemed to see something more. He put the tools aside and reached out a tentative gloved finger to ensure that his eyes had not deceived him. He was not mistaken. There was something there. He could feel it. The artifact's sleek surface contained not only razor-sharp edges and a decorative stripe but also, at its base, was a delicious flaw. Clark had been thrilled to discover the Clovis was a blend of red and black obsidian. He was certain this duality would allow him to trace the origin of the preformed stone. But his joy at the artifact's bi-colored composition had instantly redoubled when his touch confirmed that he'd found a pathway to tracing the artifact's age.

Clark envisioned what must have happened.

Like most prehistoric points, this Clovis had once been attached to a shaft of wood or bone by means of a leather tie. The fluted groove at the base facilitated this juncture. In this instance, the handle, or haft, had been removed and the binding material unwound prior to encasing the projectile point in clay. But that separation process had left behind a fractional remnant of leather. Trapped in a slice no broader than an eyelash, the weathered material had lodged in a nearly imperceptible nick in the Clovis' base.

An opportunity to test organic matter, even a tiny fragment, was a tremendous advantage. The snippet of leather could be carbon-dated and knowing the age of the leather would complement other information Clark was certain he could glean from the rock itself. It was tempting to test the leather first, but that would require a fieldtrip. He'd do his homework first. His garage contained everything he needed to analyze the obsidian, so he'd begin with the rock.

Discovering the source of obsidian was relatively straightforward. A form of natural glass, obsidian is born when molten lava cools rapidly and fails to crystalize. Clark was well aware that every piece of obsidian is endowed with a unique geochemical composition, as individual as a human fingerprint, which ties it to a particular volcano. Of course, knowing the birthplace of a bit of obsidian and even the date of the eruption which formed it, doesn't explain when the preformed rock came into the hands of the ancient crafter who fashioned it into a Clovis point.

Which is why the leather was important.

The act of carbon-dating the leather, when united with obtaining the geochemical signature of the preformed stone, would give Clark two ways to define his Clovis, a pair of data points which intersect to form crosshairs.

Windage and elevation, he thought.

Zeroing in on his Clovis would be like the old days when Clark was in military harness, sighting through his sniper scope to pick off a distant adversary. With well-remembered images of rifle and target on his mind, Clark formed his gloved hand into a child's pretend pistol and pointed the barrel of his index finger at the tiny Clovis point.

"Bang," he said aloud. "I got'cha."

With diligent work in the analytic trenches, Clark had every confidence that he'd learn not only *where* the obsidian had come from, but also *when* it had been fashioned into the Clovis. Grinning with anticipation, he looked once again at the magnified view of his unexpected find, marveling at its durability as a geologic material and relishing its symbolic worth as a testi mony to humankind's ingenuity. Researching the divinity of the Clovis would take time, but time was something the professor had in abundance.

"Here we go," Clark told himself.

There was physical work to be done but not without a systematic plan. Seeking to organize his thoughts, he tossed his gloves and searched one of his daypacks until he found an unused field notebook. Pencil in hand, he began making notes. At the top of the first page, he printed the question 'Chain of Custody?' Then he paused.

What, if anything, could he write under such an important heading?

His first thought was to contact the seller. Surely that individual would have information about the custody chain. Any clue would be helpful, such as where and when the seller obtained the artifact, who had it before, and where and when that party came into possession, and so forth, as far back as possible. But neither the package containing the Clovis, nor the transaction receipt, included a return address, so there was no obvious paper trail. Even the postmark was smudged.

Was there an electronic record?

Clark glanced at the garage's recycle bin which overflowed with liquor bottles. A week ago, when he made the purchase, Clark had been drinking heavily and he retained no memory of the seller's name or location. Opening the laptop on his workbench, he reviewed his web browsing history, but was unable to activate the original eBay link. The seller's contact information, along with all traces of the online store and any record of the transaction, had vanished.

A few more keystrokes and an examination of his credit card statement also led to a dead-end. There was no record of the purchase other than the amount paid and, next to that dollar figure, instead of a clue to the seller's identity, the disappointed professor discovered nothing but a cryptic set of nonsense characters and random numbers. Disheartened, Clark closed his computer and penciled a big fat zero in his notebook. Then he stared at the unhelpful page, disappointed and yet thinking the goose-egg shape reminded him of something. He'd written the zero as a mocking answer to his custody question, but the figure seemed somehow relevant. Striving to make a connection, he continued staring at the oval shape until inspiration struck him.

"Cocoon," he said aloud as he used his pencil to write a 'C' to the left of the zero, then added the remaining letters to spell out the vital word. "Cocoon."

Thankfully, the wreckage of the clay still littered his workbench. Shifting the magnifier to focus on the debris and using his tweezers to search through the fragments, it only took a moment for Clark to discover not one, not two, but four tiny seeds. Feeling a surge of excitement, he corralled these treasures one-by-one and gently rolled them onto a ceramic tray. Then he picked out a half dozen bits of clay and placed them on a separate tray. Dealing with the remaining rubble, he donned safety goggles and a dust mask, swept the excess clay into a plastic bin, and sealed the lid.

"To keep from having to back up, always keep a back-up." He said aloud, repeating the mantra which he'd tried to drill into his students every term. The advice represented his often-futile attempt to convince careless youngsters that the best way to keep a research project moving forward was by collecting and retaining redundant samples, even when those samples seemed rather ordinary. "There are no small samples," he told his students. "Only small imaginations."

Lacking even the remotest anecdotal hint regarding the artifact's custody, Clark was obliged to examine the evidence on hand. With the addition of the seeds and clay, that body of evidence had increased exponentially. Now, he could not only analyze the Clovis itself and the leather, he could also evaluate bits of the artifact's mud cocoon and a bountiful handful of seeds.

"Hi ho, hi ho," Clark sang. "It's off to work I go."

Embarking upon a well-remembered routine, the professor began the exacting process of preparing specimens for analysis. Opening a wooden cabinet, he used both hands to carefully extract an ultraviolet sanitizing glove box. The glass-walled box was somewhat larger than a home aquarium, but, unlike a common fish tank, this chamber had two large holes in its wider side. A rubber iris was embedded in each hole, a precaution which allowed a researcher to reach inside the box by threading both hands through the irises and into a pair of built-in gauntlets. Using the flexible elbow-high gauntlets, Clark could manipulate the contents of the glove box without breaking its airtight seal.

Leaving the box unplugged, he centered it on the cleared workbench, opened the hinged lid, and placed the Clovis point, clay sherds, and seeds inside. Next, he added a collection of tools including a square-tipped scalpel, his trusty tweezers, rubber sealing corks, and glass test tubes with each tube numbered and mounted vertically in a ceramic rack. Donning safety glasses, he sealed the lid, plugged the unit in, and sterilized the glove box by flicking a switch to activate a set of internal UV lights. Fifteen minutes later, when the lights extinguished, he maintained the seal by reaching into the irises. Threading his hands into the gauntlets, he flipped things over for a second treatment. When the second sterilization was complete, he manipulated the dexterous gauntlets to grasp his tweezers. Picking up the seeds, he deposited one each in the first four test tubes and sealed each tube with a rubber stopper. He followed the same process to create a pair of tubes containing clay fragments.

Then he began his surgery.

Guiding the scalpel, he applied gentle pressure to the base of the Clovis and flaked off a few tiny pieces, being certain to create fragments which included red and black stone. Dividing the stone slices into two piles, he tweezered each grouping into a separate test tube and worked methodically to cork each tube. Next, he carefully sliced the fragment of leather, leaving most of it attached to the Clovis while peeling away two sets of slivers which he dropped into the remaining tubes, corking both as he finished. Mask and safety goggles in place, he pulled his hands from the gauntlets, donned a pair of vinyl gloves, and opened the box. Carefully retrieving the portable rack with its corked test tubes, Clark carried the specimens across the garage floor in the direction of his machine array. The prodigious assortment of equipment ran the full length of the opposite wall. Many of the pieces were manufacturer's samples which he'd received without cost, but a dozen of the indispensable devices were his own purchases. They were costly items, a reality which irked his former lover.

"We need money so bad," she'd taunted when he announced they were dead-broke, "why don't you sell off some of that junk in our garage?" She was standing in the doorway, hands on hips, and scowling defiantly at Clark, her overweight sugar daddy who slumped at the kitchen table, nursing a beer.

"The only junk associated with *my* garage is your useless Peugeot," Clark growled as he took another drink and tossed the keys in her general direction. "Why don't you do us both a gigantic favor and pack-up all your junk and take that idiotic Frenchie car and disappear?"

"*C'est ta perte, idiot,*" Bridgette shrugged, declaring, in French, that it was his loss and insulting him with a final impertinence which needed no translation.

"*Ne laissez pas la porte...*" Clark began, but Bridgette was out of earshot before his muddled mind could work out how to tell her not to let the door hit her on the way out.

His suggestion that she get lost, permanently, turned out to be the one and only directive which, in their two stormy years together, the troublesome blonde had followed to perfection. In less than twenty minutes, the mercurial

Bridgette was gone. But so was her attitude, her crap, and the Peugeot, and good riddance because Clark had no intention of selling a single scrap of his equipment.

"You never know," he'd told himself.

Now he knew. Taken together, the donated equipment, combined with apparatuses dearly purchased, made for an impressive collection of scientific devices. He was thankful he'd accumulated so much and grateful for the opportunity to make use of the stuff. Despite Bridgette's wheedling objections, he'd gotten rid of his stable of automobiles and transformed his roomy garage into a well-stocked high-tech laboratory, retaining only the vintage Peugeot, which he relegated to a cramped corner of the sprawling space. The result was a state-of-the-art facility containing much of what was needed to deal with his specimens. The well-stocked garage held everything necessary to prepare the material and half of the equipment needed to perform the analysis itself. What was missing, of course, was a costly and enormous accelerator mass spectrometer, but that essential machine was only a taxi ride away.

Clark glanced at the wall clock. Plenty of time left. No need to rush to campus.

For the time being, his destination was only a few steps away where a second sterilizing glove box waited. It was an oversized model, large enough to accommodate a broad internal work surface and an abundance of tools. Inside, arranged in precise order, he'd find everything needed to reduce diverse specimens to uniform pellets.

Chief among the tools of the professor's trade was an array of stainless-steel compactor cylinders, each with its own nesting segments, inlaid filtering sieve, and efficient plunger. His goal was to systematically load the contents of each test tube into a separate compactor and crush each into dust. Then he'd pack the dust into pellets and insert the pellets into analyzing machines.

Once the pellets were formed, he could evaluate the inorganics—the pulverized obsidian and clay—right there in the garage. The organic pellets—seeds and leather—he'd have to transport to the university's Accelerator Mass

Spectrometry Lab. Using the huge AMS machinery without permission would be a challenge, but Clark was certain he could pull it off.

Meanwhile, he had homework to do.

In addition to the compactor cylinders, the oversized glove box contained several pellet molds—the smallest he could find—no larger than a standard automobile lug nut. Each mold was numbered to correspond with its matching test tube. Placing the rack of tubes inside the glove box, Clark positioned the pellet molds methodically, arranging them one-by-one, making certain their placement aligned with the correct test tube. After the test tube material was reduced to dust, one specimen would look much the same as any other and it wouldn't do to mix them up.

With everything in place, the exacting professor sealed the roomy glove box and proceeded to sterilize the contents. As the UV process commenced, emitting an audible hum, Clark removed his vinyl gloves, rinsed and dried his fingers in the utility sink, and took advantage of the delay to consider the fragments he was about to analyze.

The Clovis presented Clark with a puzzle which he had every intention of solving. It was primarily a question of when and where.

To address the *when* of his puzzle, he'd make use of the leather and seeds, which were ideal candidates for radiocarbon dating. He'd pulverize these organic materials, trundle the compacted pellets to campus, and run them through the university's exacting machinery.

To address the *where*, he'd turn to the clay and obsidian. Once these were reduced to dust, he could analyze both at home. Of these two inorganic materials, he'd rely most heavily on the obsidian. The clay was an interesting wrinkle, but no more than that. The obsidian and the clay might share a geographic location, but the latter amounted to an ambiguous shell which would be of marginal use when it came to pinpointing an origin. Dirt was dirt and, based on Clark's experience, in all but a few rare instances, there was—geochemically speaking—hardly a nickel's worth of difference between the soils of many nations.

Obsidian was another matter entirely. If clay is a meandering dirt path which may or may not lead to a tangible destination, obsidian is a broad, dependable turnpike complete with landmarks and road signs. Obsidian, Clark knew, was a specialized material which originated in a relative handful of locations—namely in the immediate neighborhood of a particular type of dormant or active volcano. By analyzing the trace element composition of his obsidian dust, he would learn the first link in the Clovis' chain of custody. He would, at least, know the origin of the preformed rock. Where the obsidian had been between the site of its creation and its unexpected arrival on Clark's doorstep would be harder to determine.

Knowing its birthplace would be a start, but only that.

Despite being geologically limited, obsidian tended to get around. The glossy rock had been widely used by prehistoric peoples. As a result, a dizzying array of stone tools had been unearthed around the globe. For centuries, archaeologists had been finding obsidian in countless digs from Iowa to Okinawa. The rock was literally everywhere, even though a great many of the sites of discovery were devoid of volcanic activity.

The solution to this conundrum of limited origin sites versus wide distribution was simple. The broad dispersal of obsidian beyond the expected bounds of its birthing volcano was a product of portability and trade. Thus, a bit of obsidian spawned by a coastal volcano might be broken free and picked up by sentient hands and carried inland. Whereas obsidian born in rugged mountains was transported to the seashore, and so forth. For eons, until the utilitarian rock was supplanted by bronze and iron, obsidian was carried by living individuals as they traveled across vast tracts of land, traversing all manner of topography, even spanning continents. It was these so-called down-the-line transactions which conveyed obsidian from a given point of origin to faraway lands.

How far, the professor wondered, *has this unique Clovis point journeyed from its birthing place? Time will tell.*

Clark's musing was interrupted by a buzzer. The fading ultraviolet light told him that the sterilization was complete. He took a seat on a raised stool and threaded his bare hands into the box's gauntlets. Since his specimens were suspended vertically in their glass tubes and the tools were all in upright positions, there was no need for a second sterilization procedure. The professor took a deep breath and began the compacting process. Starting with the organic fragments, he carefully unstopped the first test tube and tilted the glass container to drop a seed into the first pulverizing canister. He used the first compactor to manually crush and sift the seed until the material was reduced to a gray amorphous dust. With infinite care, he filled the first pellet form, gently compacted the seed dust, and sealed the pellet. Then he rolled the used compactor aside and left his remaining seeds uncrushed to create a vital back-up in case something went wrong.

Keeping each specimen separate, the thorough professor used a fresh compactor to create each new pellet. After forming a pellet, he dexterously poured surplus dust back into its test tube and pushed the cork in place to preserve spare material should it be needed. He worked steadily and cautiously, compacting in turn a pellet of leather and clay, until he came at last to the obsidian fragments. Contemplating the finality of what he was about to do, Clark pivoted on his stool and glanced over his shoulder. Once reduced to dust, the red and black fragments of obsidian could never again be reconstituted as part of the Clovis. Pulverizing seeds and clay and leather was one thing. Reducing the obsidian to powder would be like erasing history. Looking across the room, he could just make out the shape of the tiny projectile point, an inorganic black speck, still encased in its sterile glove box.

Maybe it would prove to be an ordinary garden-variety artifact and yet it could as likely be an irreplaceable treasure. Seeing the Clovis there and contemplating its potential, Clark was momentarily overwhelmed by sentimental memories of his teaching days. Sitting on his stool, he sighed and allowed himself to reminisce regarding his favorite topic which he expounded in a special, well-rehearsed lecture. It was a gem of a presentation which, over the years, he proudly trotted out whenever outsiders dropped by to observe his classroom.

"A command performance under the microscope," he said aloud as he conjured up an image of those memorable days when, as an accomplished lecturer, he'd been pleased to sing for his supper. It was no secret that the dean and certain of Clark's faculty colleagues were envious of his accomplishments. Throughout his impressive academic career, the act of checking up on the department's famous professor had become something of an obsession with the university. For forty years, once every term, he'd endured the scrutiny of a host of campus curiosity seekers. A few came to observe his teaching under the guise of administrative scrutiny, but most were simply curious. Whatever their motives, the well-connected professor always knew in advance of their coming and he was only too happy to perform the same tried-and-true lecture as many times as visitors cared to witness it. Meanwhile, his students never tired of Clark's performance and he was convinced that even the most jaded interloper was equally impressed.

Modestly billed as his 'Handy-Dandy Intrepid Clovis-Knapping Lecture,' the presentation was a pleasing combination of theoretical content, practical demonstration, and carnival showmanship. Over the years he'd honed the memorized piece to perfection, adding just enough drama and new detail with each re-telling to enhance his reputation, while also keeping the interest of each succeeding crop of students. As a spellbinding lecturer, Professor Clark had no equal. He'd begin his jewel of a talk with a modest introduction. He could almost hear himself at the zenith of his power, holding forth in a packed lecture hall.

"Named for excavations conducted in 1933 near Clovis, New Mexico," he would tell his rapt audience, "Clovis projectile points were once state-of-the-art technology. Eons ago, ancient artisans applied fracturing and pressure techniques to fashion an array of practical stone tools. It took skill to convert naked rock into something more useful. The maker had to master a host of techniques, including the fine art of striking a stone just so—an efficient, yet subtle, process we now classify as 'knapping.' Not every soul could master the process, but, to a skilled prehistoric fabricator, with an unlimited supply of rocks and an infinity of time to work," he boasted, "the process soon became second-nature, as you'll observe."

With this, the renowned professor would don a leather work apron, push his lectern aside, and use a stool to climb onto his specimen table. He'd then proceed to sit cross-legged, in full view of every corner of the university's vast auditorium-style lecture hall, as he manufactured a Clovis point in real time. Using a striking stone to separate a likely segment from a sizable slab of obsidian, he'd begin with a sure-handed knapping technique. With precise blows, he'd strike at just the right angle, then pull the fractured piece free. Obtaining a fist-sized chunk, he'd halve it and halve it again until he'd achieved the desired preform. Eventually, as he continued to work the material, he'd employ wood and bone tools to refine his efforts with the goal of expertly manufacturing a passable Clovis in a half-hour or less.

His personal best was twenty minutes.

Continuing to lecture as he worked, Clark would declare that the versatile points were once so ubiquitous that they literally changed the face of the planet. He would point out that most experts cite the Clovis as having significant and irreversible impacts on the prehistoric world. In particular, the widespread use of Clovis points led inextricably to the extinction, by hunting, of North America's megafauna, including the gigantic mastodon, a distant relative of today's elephants.

"A powerful weapon shaped somewhat like a typical arrowhead, but sleeker and bifurcated with sharp edges on both sides and a fluted base, a standard Clovis is a unique tool," Clark explained, showing his work at regular intervals. "It has a tapered point at its head with a half-moon indentation at its base. The base is purposely dulled to allow the maker to work with the preformed blade without the hazard of slicing his own hand. A well-formed base also includes a fluted groove which allows the maker to add a handle by attaching a haft of wood or bone to the finished product. With a practiced eye, a skilled worker could readily select an ideal stone—usually flint, jasper, or obsidian—and be confident that it would fracture in an expected way. With so much uncertainty in prehistoric times, it must have been a blessing to know that certain stones would behave predictably...and voila!"

Holding his finished Clovis point aloft to classroom applause, Clark would conclude his lecture by noting that the tool was utilitarian, but also elegant, and so omnipresent during its ancient hey-day that thousands have been discovered around the globe.

"Thus," he concluded, "Clovis points can currently be found in museums throughout the world, where even the most casual visitor can appreciate the skill and ingenuity required to produce them."

Recalling his well-remembered lecture, Clark smiled as he admired the dark treasure lying a few steps away. He himself had unearthed thousands of the points, and yet he had an irrepressible feeling that this particular find was not just any Clovis. So strong was that feeling that he was inspired to take another look at his treasure. Standing up, he crossed the room, placed both hands on his workbench, and leaned forward to regard the miniature artifact with reverence.

Eons ago some ancient being had meticulously created this tiny bird-point. It couldn't have been easy to make one so small and it must have taken several tries and infinite patience. Once the thing was perfected, with its distinctive red stripe bisecting one side, that enterprising prehistoric soul had entwined a cord of leather around its base. One day, for whatever reason, the artisan had removed the cord, covered the point with clay, and flexed his palm to seal it in. Then the anonymous craftsman would have thrust the clay into the scorching embers of an ancient fire in order to harden it and create a protective shell.

Thinking it over, Clark decided that the maker hadn't intended to use the point for hunting. Maybe this perfect point had served as a prototype. Something to show to apprentices, an ideal model to be emulated. Perhaps it had been a talisman, a good luck charm. Probably it held such power that the maker would have carried it to his grave. In earlier days, Clark would have been on the phone trumpeting his discovery, inviting colleagues to share in his revelry, and making notes for a scholarly article.

As it was, he remained absolutely silent.

Chapter 34

For a decade, activists had been able to plunder Clark's collection for one reason and one reason only: because he'd fastidiously published the details of all his prior acquisitions. To rob him, all those thieving bastards in Washington had to do was surf the internet and they had a shopping list.

Not this time.

Instead of advertising that he possessed an extraordinary Clovis birdpoint, he kept its existence a secret. This particular point might prove to be the smallest and oldest prehistoric tool known to the New World, a possibility which would make it not only extremely rare but also tremendously valuable. Clark shook his head and repositioned his mask and goggles, trying to refocus his energy on the task at hand. No sense fantasizing about the thing's nature or worth until the test results were known. Resisting further distractions, he returned to work, reducing the obsidian specimens to compacted pellets and back-up material. When finished, he pulled his hands out of the gauntlets, dried his fingers, and donned a fresh pair of vinyl gloves. Opening the lid, he carefully removed the organic pellets. He left the inorganic pellets and the back-up test tubes inside the glove box, sealed the lid, and checked the time.

Right on schedule.

An aluminum specimen case sat on the worktable. The professor opened the lid and carefully inserted the seed and leather pellets, nesting each into a separate, snuggly fitting compartment. There was room in the large case for many more specimens, but the two organics were all he needed. Double-checking the specimen numbers to make certain he had a pellet containing leather dust and another holding pulverized seed particles, he closed the case and latched the lid. He'd take the case along when he went to campus. In the meantime, the padded case was the most prudent place for the organic pellets.

It would be hours before Clark would risk entering the university's accelerator laboratory. He'd wait for the cover of darkness to be sure he was alone in the secure lab and unobserved. Fortunately, the university's students and faculty were on Christmas break. Clark was counting on the main campus being virtually deserted, with only a few security vehicles making sporadic rounds. He was on a first-name basis with all the guards who wouldn't find anything unusual about the eccentric and well-known professor traipsing around the university grounds at odd hours. It would not be the first time Clark had been spotted on campus at midnight or three in the morning on his way to or from some esoteric academic chore.

"How-do, professor. You have yourself a good evening," would undoubtedly be the extent of his interaction with security.

There were advantages to being a tenured professor with decades of institutional experience and a reputation as a colorful but apparently harmless lone wolf. One of the chief benefits was the privilege of having the run of his home campus with door keys, entry codes, and passwords galore in his possession. With luck, he'd be through the campus and in and out of the lab before anyone noticed. It would be an extravagance of course, the idea of processing his pair of tiny pellets through a machine which was designed to handle forty samples at a time. It would be an unconscionable use of the multi-million-dollar accelerator mass spectrometer and one he'd rather not answer for.

Meanwhile, it had taken most of the morning to prepare his pellets and it was nearly noon. Time for a sandwich, he decided. Returning to the house, he paused in the hallway to make certain the grandfather clock was keeping good time, then he made his way to the kitchen. As Clark ate, he mapped a schedule in his head. After lunch he'd spend the early afternoon back in the garage analyzing the Clovis dust and the clay particles, a task which amounted to scanning and graphing the inorganic material. Sometime around three o'clock in the afternoon, he'd call for a taxi and head to campus, carrying the case containing the organic specimens. He'd arrive on campus with time to spare, have another bite to eat somewhere, and wait for sundown before sauntering to the AMS lab to run his organic tests. He downed a glass of milk, loaded the dishwasher, and returned to the garage.

Opening the box marked 'XRF,' he extracted the brand-spanking new handheld X-ray fluorescence spectrometer—the one he'd yet to use—and took a moment to review the instructions. He had a vintage field model in his office at the university, but this one was much nicer.

"New project, new tool," he told himself.

This unsullied device was also a field model. It was light, compact, accurate, and perfectly suited for the homemade investigation he had in mind. To the uninitiated, it looked like an ordinary power drill with a trigger mounted in the handle and a tapered nose. The only hints that it might be something fundamentally different was the device's high-resolution viewing screen, a handful of extra cords, and a conspicuous yellow-and-black sticker warning of radiation danger. Definitely a tool which, along with a power drill, you wouldn't want someone to stick in your face.

Plugging in the analyzer, he frowned at the inorganic pellets waiting side by side in the glove box, wishing they were larger. But he quickly decided they'd do. He typically used an XRF to determine the geochemical composition of small artifacts, which meant he often worked with tiny, sometimes nearly microscopic material. To accommodate small specimens, he'd designed a donut-shaped receptacle which allowed him to center a small pellet inside what amounted to the donut hole. The donut also allowed him to press the XRF's nose against the pellet without mashing the compacted dust. He checked to make certain the XRF was properly connected to his printer, then he plugged the device in, turned it on, and did a test run using the tabletop as his subject. The display screen and the printer worked perfectly. With the XRF primed and ready, he began with the most redundant material, saving the precious obsidian pellet for last. Having left the compacted inorganic dust side-by-side in their ceramic molds, he put on a fresh pair of vinyl gloves, opened the glove box, and secured the clay pellet. Inverting the pellet mold, he lightly tapped the ceramic casing and was pleased to watch the pellet itself slide neatly into the donut hole.

"Sweet," he said aloud as he positioned the XRF and prepared to lightly press its nose against the compacted pellet. Then he paused, feeling suddenly light-headed. He put the XRF aside, yawned, and stretched luxuriously. It had been a long day. His vision was cloudy. With the clay pellet in place, Clark carefully covered the sample, switched the machine off, and squinted in the direction of the lab's comfortable sofa. Seemingly out of place in his otherwise shiny steel and glass laboratory, the funky over-stuffed sofa had been installed in the garage years ago when a particular experiment had required a prolonged waiting period.

It looked inviting.

The XRF process wouldn't take long. The results would be almost instantaneous. It'd taken him hours to obtain specimens and prepare the dust pellets. That'd been slow and exacting work. The XRF analysis, on the other hand, would be a cinch. He could complete it in a matter of moments, but he just couldn't stay awake. A brief nap was all he needed. He stretched out on the sofa, pulled a warm blanket up to his chin, and closed his eyes.

As he slept, his relaxing mind composed a dream which magically transported him to a fanciful and impossibly small location. He imagined himself *inside* the XRF machine, miraculously reduced to the size of a miniature observer. Looking closely, he saw silent X-rays bombarding a specimen, traumatizing, and unbalancing the material. Blessed with the ability to experience the process unfolding at the molecular level, the sleeping professor stepped aside as frantic electrons hustled past, rushing to bring a disturbed atom back into balance. Their abrupt movements emitted fluorescent rays which were detected and analyzed by the device's internal computer. All this, he viewed objectively, following the motions of electrons as they whizzed back and forth, turning his head one way and then the other, like a diminutive spectator watching a miniature tennis match. Seeing the process as a dreamer,

Clark was reminded of the ricocheting antics of a vintage pinball machine. His fertile imagination even conjured up the clacking of steel balls and the tinkling of celebratory bells.

Surrounded by pulsating images, Clark was mesmerized until the XRF began to print its results, whereupon his fanciful dream seemed to convey him from a microscopic environment to the cavernous pit of his university lecture hall, where he observed himself attempting to explain the X-ray process to his confused students. To clarify things, he was providing an example from his own experience as a marksman.

"Think of the phenomenon this way," he told his imaginary class. "It's like shooting a bullet at a rock but ignoring the target and looking instead for the wayward ricochet. The XRF's internal detector analyzes the ricocheting fluorescent rays. That analysis creates a unique geochemical fingerprint in the form of a graph which summarizes the specimen's trace element composition. In your text you can see how a fluctuating line indicates the relative abundance of each element, giving the graph the appearance of a stylized mountain range."

Absorbing these concrete images, the students seemed to utter a collective sigh of comprehension. God, how he loved those teachable moments! The next challenge, he knew, would be helping students grasp the details. The XRF process was so familiar to Clark that he could literally run an analysis in his sleep. And yet, the procedure consistently baffled his students, inspiring him to create a practical application to help them understand.

"Suppose we test the elemental composition of something recognizable," the dreaming professor saw himself telling his earnest but confused students. "Thanks to the magic of projection science, the results of our analysis will be shown in graph form on the screen behind me. Today we're going to analyze a recent historic artifact: a coin produced during World War II. In 1942, when key metals were needed to produce armor plating, nickel itself was a rationed commodity and the U.S. Mint was ordered to stop using it. Consequently, American five-cent pieces minted from 1942 to 1945 contained absolutely no nickel. Instead, thousands of so-called 'War Nickels' were minted using an alloy of copper, silver, and manganese. Much experimentation was required to get the weight correct so the new coins would function in vending machines and pay-telephones."

When his audience began to titter, Clark had to restore order by explaining, "Yes, my young friends, there were once such devices as payphones. Now let's focus, people. Eventually, the modified coins were redesigned to contain 56% copper, 35% silver, and 9% manganese. Remember those proportions. I hold in my hand a 1943 War Nickel which my banker tells me is rare enough to be worth a cool thousand bucks. So, lights and drumroll please—let's check the fingerprint!"

Placing the 1943 Jefferson-head nickel in the university's XRF analyzer produced a projected image of a graph. The graph showed strong peaks labeled Cu (copper) and Ag (silver) with several blips identifying other elements but nothing for Mn (manganese).

"Thoughts?" Clark asked. "Where, for example, is our manganese?"

Invariably, a bright student—such as his prize pupil, the irrepressible Anne Scriptor—would explain the lack of manganese in the War Nickel fingerprint by pointing out that only the surface of the coin was analyzed. As a result, the heavier elements of copper and silver kept X-rays from penetrating beyond the coin's superficial coating, thus making the internal manganese all but invisible for XRF analysis purposes. As for the numerous blips indicating the presence of other material, Anne would conjecture correctly that this was evidence of contamination by such factors as human handling, mingling in cash registers with other money, spilled beer, and any number of other events in the life of a pocket coin.

The dozing professor could just hear Anne rattling off the accurate answers and he pictured her in his mind's eye, a precocious learner, always doing her homework and always one step ahead of her classmates. That girl was a pistol! If anyone deserved a supporting role in his self-aggrandizing dream, it was the indomitable Anne. Building on her insights, Clark dreamt on, guiding the class to the notion that a truer geochemical fingerprint could be obtained by sterilizing the process, crushing the coin down to a fine powder, and rerunning the test.

"Should I pulverize this thousand-dollar nickel?" he imagined himself asking the rhetorical question. "Not on your life! But, earlier today, I secured a less-rare 1945 nickel which is worth about a dollar to the average collector. Then, in order to prove that pulverizing and sterilizing produces a more accurate graph, I crushed it into a pellet of dust and voila!"

The projected image of the new graph showed two soaring peaks for copper and silver, a blip for manganese, and nothing at all for other trace contaminants. So impressive was this demonstration that the pedagogy was written up in several journals, giving praiseworthy credit to Clark, thereby further embellishing his reputation as a teacher and scientist. Recalling his successful nickel experiments as his dream wandered on, Clark had to admit to himself that an examination of his Clovis' surface would be insufficient to tie the obsidian to its birthplace. Only a geochemical analysis of the pulverized stone could accomplish that end and, even then, a match could only be made if a researcher was able to cross-check a specimen's fingerprint against a master file which included XRF graphs of all the world's volcanoes.

Fat chance, he mumbled in his sleep.

Such a reference did not exist. For decades following the introduction of XRF technology, practitioners have advocated for the compilation of such a file. Not counting vents in the depths of oceans, Planet Earth hosts a limited number of volcanic sites, so it would not be an insurmountable task to chart and catalog them all. Piecemeal attempts had been made, but the archaeological world did not yet possess a complete encyclopedia of volcanic fingerprints. Even when Clark had printed out his graph, the chances of matching it with a site were slim. But, at the moment, he was on a mission and not to be deterred by such an inconvenient problem... problem...

Awakening from his nap with a start, Clark glanced at his wristwatch as echoes of his inner thoughts swirled in his emerging consciousness. Though his dream had carried him on what he imagined to be a lengthy journey, he'd only been napping for forty minutes.

"Up and atom," he commanded himself as he lurched to his feet to resume his work.

Rapidly processing the clay pellet, Clark decided that a cursory analysis would suffice. After conducting a minimum exposure, he merely glanced at the graph on the XRF's display screen before sending the image to the printer. He'd study the clay printout later. He had an abundance of clay and he could prepare and process another pellet if necessary. But the obsidian was more precious. There was only so much of the Clovis to go around, a reality which made the cautious professor reluctant to risk carving more slices from the tiny bird-point. Too much surgery risked fracturing the piece. He'd go with the Clovis dust he had, and he'd be more thorough. He'd prolong the X-ray exposure and take time to preview the results on the XRF screen before printing the graph.

As the sound of the printer began to crank out the clay graph, Clark turned his attention to the obsidian pellet. Nesting the Clovis dust in place, he activated the XRF. After a few minutes, the viewing screen flickered, and the obsidian graph drifted into view. The image was clear as a bell. Soon he'd set the printer stylus working back and forth to etch out the obsidian fingerprint. For the moment, he was content to study the screen.

At first glance, there were no surprises.

Obsidian—like everything else in the universe—is composed of a mixture of elements and each element is composed of atoms. When disrupted by X-ray bombardment, atoms are unbalanced. The XRF operates on the principle that any molecular imbalance is instantly resolved by Nature. When the device's X-ray beam penetrates to within a whisker of an atom's center, it dislodges a circling electron, causing an imbalance. A fellow electron rushes to restore equilibrium by replacing the missing particle and the amount of energy released by that motion is unique to a particular element. The expended energy takes the form of fluorescent radiation which the XRF interprets to create a line graph. An XRF graph records the trace element composition of a specimen as well as each element's intensity or abundance. Just like the image of an auditory soundtrack, the higher the graph line peaks, the greater the volume. The primary expected characteristic of obsidian, which graphs as a towering peak, is instantly recognizable.

And there it is, Clark told himself.

Obsidian forms when super-heated lava meets cool air and hardens rapidly. Studying the graph on his screen, Clark saw precisely what he expected. The graph was dominated by a vertical spike labeled $SiO2$—the scientific notation for silicon dioxide, a chemical compound of two of Earth's most common elements, namely sand and oxygen. In other words, volcanic glass.

Want to make a bunch of volcanic glass? Clark thought. *No problem. Simulate the inferno of a volcano by heating California's sandy coastline to 3,000 degrees, supercool the result, and, presto, you've created a glassy seashore composed of hundreds of miles of slippery, transparent, and extremely breakable beachfront property.*

Clark knew that every scrap of obsidian, no matter its origin, will register silicon dioxide of at least 40% on an XRF graph and readings of 70% or higher are not uncommon. His Clovis dust graphed at 67%. Although this expected peak will dominate the graph, other elements in the tested stone are also visible. Displayed together, these create the geochemical fingerprint which ties a particular piece of obsidian to a specific volcano.

Anxious to examine his obsidian graph in detail, but wishing to test himself, the confident professor suppressed his curiosity. Relishing the challenge, he turned off the viewing screen and printed his obsidian graph. Retrieving his printouts, he separated the two graphs. Electing to review the clay graph later, he folded the paper and placed it in his shirt pocket. Then he took up the obsidian printout and strategically creased the paper so that only the $SiO2$ peak showed. Based on the physical appearance of the Clovis and knowing its formation to be primarily a product of sand and oxygen, Clark would see if he was capable of guessing the remaining elements which formed his obsidian.

"Our waxy red stripe is the key," he said aloud. "That must be pitchstone...which chemically is..."

Wracking his brain, he pictured himself in the throes of his undergraduate degree, trading intellectual punches with Ezra Plough, his irascible chemistry professor. Dr. Plough was a stickler who'd insisted that his students memorize the periodic table of elements. He could see the demanding instructor's scowl, visualizing the impatient expression that frequently animated Plough's wrinkled face. It was a powerful image and the answers popped unbidden into Clark's questing mind.

"Fe, iron," he said with assurance. "Zr, zirconium. Al, aluminum...and some other 'ums' I can't recall." Exhausting his guesses, he surrendered and peeked at the printout. "Calcium! Sodium! Potassium! And...traces...traces of hydration suggesting water, of course!"

It may not be possible to get blood from a stone, Clark told himself, *but water? Yes.*

He smiled broadly, recalling that the fundamental difference between shiny black obsidian and waxy red pitchstone was the latter's water content. Tracing his questing fingers along the graph, he noted the peaks and valleys of the Clovis' XRF geochemical fingerprint as the meandering line marched across the unfolded paper. It was an unmistakable pattern and one which Clark was certain he'd encountered before. But where?

"Brodeur, Brodeur, Brodeur," he told himself. "Where the fu...?"

Firing up his laptop, he typed the search terms 'Brodeur' 'Volcano' and waited while the unseen CPU churned. Almost instantly, two publications popped up: 'Brodeur's Magazine, Volume V, 1853, Volcanoes of Central France' and 'Antiquities Quarterly, Spring 2003, Apperson, *The Italian Question.*'

The first citation led him to the nineteenth-century magazine, published a hundred years before Clark was born. To his delight, he found a copy of the vintage periodical faithfully and legibly reproduced in its entirety. Unfortunately, the same could not be said of the more recent reference. Following links to the Apperson article, Clark discovered a hazy and nearly unreadable copy. He printed off a true copy of the 1853 volcano article but could only manage a fuzzy and highly pixelated image of the 2003 publication. He recalled having read the text in its original form and he was especially disappointed with the reproduction of Apperson's XRF graph.

Clark had first discovered Brodeur during his undergraduate studies and had read his works with enthusiasm as his youthful imagination was captured by the exploits of the nineteenth-century archaeologist and the man's vivid descriptions of French volcanoes. As for Apperson, he too had read Brodeur and, armed with technology undreamt of by the Frenchman, the modern explorer had expended considerable time and resources tracing the steps of his long-dead predecessor. Sparing no expense, Apperson had applied XRF techniques to analyze certain volcanic rocks littering the French countryside. But the modern author's work was of no help to Clark because Apperson had failed to populate the internet with a decent copy of his findings. Whatever Apperson's excuses—copyright concerns, lack of technical aplomb, or just plain indifference—Clark's efforts to locate a clear copy proved fruitless.

"Sloppy," was Clark's verdict as he tried to compare his crisply printed XRF graph to the washed-out Apperson version. In desperation he overlapped the two sheets and pressed them against the nearest windowpane. Squinting, he tried to imagine that the two graphs were identical, but there was only one way to be certain.

"Need confirmation," he decided and that meant he'd have to enlarge the mission of his campus visit to add a stop at The University of Arizona Mineral Museum. Given Clark's desire to clarify the importance of Brodeur's observations and Apperson's subsequent findings, a tour of the museum's dusty library became just as vital as his proposed late-night visit to the accelerator lab. Surely the museum's collection would include a better, clearer copy of Apperson's graph. He'd know the answer soon enough, but in the meantime, he'd consult his own homegrown references.

Glancing at his wristwatch, Clark realized he'd have to get a move on. Proceeding with a sense of urgency, the resourceful professor clutched the obsidian graph in his hand as he rushed back to the house and into his study. Standing at the huge world map which stretched across the western wall, he used his free hand to trace a horizontal line along the 45th parallel north— the latitude which figured so prominently in Brodeur's writing. Beginning with the east-west line which roughly marks the border between Montana and Wyoming, he continued eastward, crossing over the symbolic demarcation which separates Vermont and Upstate New York from Canada. Walking steadily to his right, his finger moved over the Atlantic until he reached France. Tapping a spot near the center of the faraway country, he left the wall map to search out a more detailed scale.

Digging through his collection of world atlases, Clark unearthed a broad map of contemporary France which stretched across two sizable pages. Unable to find adequate table space, he placed the oversized book on the floor. Kneeling there on the carpet, he was about to commence his research, and yet he felt he was not quite ready. Sensing that something else was needed, he made a mental inventory of the reference materials contained in his rambling ranch house.

"More," he told himself as he struggled laboriously to his feet. "I need more!" he shouted as he rushed from the study and scrambled down a broad hall in the direction of a narrow doorway. Pulling on the knob, he burst into the cramped room and fumbled for the light switch. "Nuts!" he blurted.

He'd come to this little-used alcove to search through his large-format archaeological maps, but to reach them he'd be obliged to dig through the strange confusion of the jumbled storeroom.

Strange confusion, he thought to himself, *what gives? Where in the blessed world is that phrase coming from? The last thing I need is some odd-ball notion rattling around in my head. Strange confusion... strange confusion?*

All at once he found he couldn't get the two words out of his head. Strange confusion—the phrase echoed in his mind. Repeating relentlessly like a persistent earworm, the words crystalized into a recurring tune which he couldn't dislodge from his brain. Moving storage boxes aside while the words drummed in his subconscious, he cleared a path to reach a floor-to-ceiling stack of wide-format file drawers. Muttering, he climbed on a stepladder and, skinning his knuckles as he pawed at the metal handles, began rifling through his collection of over-sized cartographic masterpieces. Over the years, he'd stored dozens of reference maps in the stacked drawers. With a growing feeling of exhilaration, tempered by frustration, he searched feverishly to locate a half-remembered survey chart of France.

Talk about your archaeological digs!

Clark had been meaning to reorganize this rambling collection, planning to put the haphazardly filed maps into some semblance of logical order. As it was, in the wake of decades of ad hoc research and last-minute class preparations, he'd left them in a hopeless jumble.

"Come on," he admonished himself. "Come on..."

Heedless of the mess he was making, the persistent professor pulled sheet after oversized sheet from the drawers until the tiled floor was covered with discarded maps. At last, he located the desired chart. Gripping it tightly, he descended the ladder then scrambled through the dislodged paper—nearly losing his balance as he struggled through the chaotic pile, trying to gain traction like a frantic winter hiker schlepping through knee-deep snow.

Leaving the disheveled mess behind, he rushed from the storeroom, hustled back down the hallway, and returned to the den where he fell once again upon his knees. Placing the geographic and archaeological maps side by side, he gathered up his plotting tools. With his field notebook, mechanical pencil, and magnifying glass in hand, he sprawled beside the open maps like an enthralled schoolboy caught up in the thrill of learning. With everything in readiness, he opened his notebook to a gridded page and began. Peering through the magnifying glass, the questing professor studied the contours of central France, searching for place-names included in the 1853 article.

"Puy...puy...puy," he said aloud, articulating the prefix that permeated Brodeur's article. Living up to his surname which translated as *embroiderer*, Clark's long-dead informant—the European author and amateur archaeologist, Jean Brodeur—had constructed his article using flowery prose, especially the prefix *puy*, which—in vernacular French—translated to *isolated hills*. Clark had to admit the word was an apt way of describing the cone of a dormant volcano.

"Puy...puy...puy," he repeated until, at last, he saw them.

In central France, precisely where the professor hoped to find them, his maps showed a cluster of elevations. Here were the landmarks Brodeur had chronicled: *Le Mont-Dore* and *Puy de la Crotz*. The highest points in central France, their exotic names translating, in the dialect of the region, to Gold Mountain and The Mount of the Cross.

Who'd have thought, Clark pondered as he breezed through the translations, *that young Bridgette's obsession with all-things-French would bear practical fruit? How could I have foreseen that her heavy-handed and impatient efforts to teach me, her dullard lover, the rudiments of the romance language would pay such dividends long after her unceremonious departure?*

Lying in Bridgette's loving arms and enduring her many tantrums, he'd learned enough French to be dangerous. Feeling his loins stir, Clark sighed and refocused on his work. Pushing the comely Bridgette from his mind, he noted pertinent latitudes and longitudes and plotted the intersections on his grid. Creating context, he located surrounding features and used his little finger to approximate relative positions as he sketched in these complementary points. As he worked, he also added corresponding place names, achieving rough translations by recalling the rudiments of his lover's tutelage supplemented by his half-remembered secondary school language lessons.

He cross-referenced the geographic and archaeological maps, feverishly plotting additional points in his notebook. He was locked into his task with the phrase *strange confusion* continuing to pulsate through his head while images of the past and present swirled about him. Brodeur and Apperson, the flaxen-haired Bridgette and Gold Mountain, the Cross and the Clovis, the concepts encircled him like orbiting planets. For a fleeting instant, he imagined that giving-in to such a churning cauldron of mental confusion must be what it was like to go insane. Only the hall clock striking two-thirty snatched him from his trance and brought him crashing back to the present.

"You're a dangerously inquisitive critter," he said, both admonishing and praising his almost maniacal efforts to nail-down the lineage of his Clovis. "And it seems your snooping has landed you squarely in France, of all places. Your digging has led you to the neighborhood, at least. Now it's time to take your campus fieldtrip!"

After telephoning for a taxi, Clark sat in front of his ranch house fidgeting with his specimen case while he waited impatiently. It was cold on the porch and he was glad for his topcoat and scarf. December in the desert was no picnic. He'd resisted trading in his reliable but stodgy greatcoat for one of the more fashionable and modern pleated jackets. He'd tried one of the puffy garments on at the Eddie Bauer Outlet Store, but his mirror image told him he looked less like a contemporary millennial and more like an orange Michelin Tire Man.

He should have waited inside, but he was anxious to get going. Sitting there as the December chill began creeping up his pant legs, he nervously patted his suit jacket and overcoat to make certain his field notebook, his XRF graphs, and his copies of the Brodeur and Apperson articles were in his pockets. He couldn't squeeze anything more into his tightly fitting specimen case, not so much as a scrap of paper. He might have crammed the extras into a daypack, but it would be challenging enough to cart the awkward case around campus without adding more luggage.

Clark stared down his long sloping driveway, willing his ride to appear. He checked his smartphone—no alert—where was the buzzard?

Having to rely on taxis was a nuisance, but, after his second DUI in five years, the Arizona cops had flagged the imbibing professor's license. So, it was Clark's own fault that he had to depend on others for transportation. Even if he'd managed to stay sober, he had nothing to drive. Shortly after the authorities had revoked his driving privileges, the ranch's last remaining vehicle had rocketed out of his life with Bridgette at the wheel. When his lover left, he'd been tempted to sell his sprawling split-level home, abandon the desert environs of rural Marana, and move into Tucson proper. But, if he was going to live in the city, he wanted to be within walking distance of the campus and the urban houses bordering the university were tiny structures with dinky garages, so where would he put all his stuff? Besides, he preferred the privacy of his isolated acreage. He liked playing gentleman-cowboy and even imagined he might get a horse someday. All of which meant that he was destined to stay put and that every trip into the city would mean an adventure in sitting and waiting on one end or the other.

The taxi honked twice as it started up the long driveway and Clark scrambled to his feet.

Chapter 35

The drive from Clark's acreage to The University of Arizona campus in Tucson should have taken twenty minutes, but it took nearly four times that long. The taxi made slow-and-go progress as it wallowed through a sluggish tide of automobiles, trucks, and buses. Its inertia reminded the professor of the chief reason he'd decided against moving to the city. The perils of urban traffic were enough to, literally, drive a person insane. Even with the university on holiday break, the freeway was packed with vehicles and Clark began to wonder if he'd make it to campus before the Mineral Museum closed.

He rechecked his smartphone and confirmed that the science center, a complex which included not only the museum but also the university's planetarium, was indeed accessible during holiday break and would remain open until 6 p.m. He'd been putting-off his trip to campus because his original goal had been to wait for sundown to complete a single errand. Suddenly, he not only had an extra errand to run, he also had a new and much earlier deadline. The museum would be closing soon, and he'd rather not burglarize the place. In checking his assortment of entry devices, he'd discovered a key to enter the upper story of the science center, but no key or access code for the lower floors which housed the museum and its cavernous library. As the taxi limped on, he tried to remember the last time he'd been downstairs, but all he recollected was that it'd been an unpleasant experience. He tried to recall if the library had a security system, telling himself that, if it came to that, he might have to force a lock or two.

And it might well come to that.

His research had reached a perilous juncture—a tipping point where a visit to the museum's library was absolutely essential. Clark could do nothing with the rotten facsimile of Apperson's XRF graph. He needed a true copy to confirm the importance of that critical reference. With luck, he'd be able to complete his two-pronged mission of gaining access to the mineral library as well as satisfying his desire to sneak into the AMS lab and fire-up the university's spectrometer.

Two birds, one stone, the professor thought to himself as the taxi reached campus at last. "Turn here," he instructed the driver who, unimpeded, would have taken Clark to the wrong building. Redirecting the confused man, the professor steered him through the campus and guided the taxi to a stop in front of Flandrau Planetarium.

"Kind'a early to be checkin' out the stars ain't it, Doc?" asked the driver.

The man had been Clark's regular chauffeur for a year and, from time to time, the chatty jackass had literally talked the professor's ear off, probing his captive passenger with asinine questions which Clark answered obliquely with terse replies. Like most lay people, the driver assumed that, since Clark was a scientist, the learned man would know the answer to every nonsensical technical question that popped into his uneducated head. Unconcerned that Clark's expertise lay in the focused areas of archaeology, geology, and cultural anthropology, the man persistently asked his passenger to explain the antics of wild javelina, the vagaries of the weather, or the celestial whims of the planets. To make matters worse, the driver apparently considered his informal acquaintance with the taciturn professor sufficiently close to address his fare as 'Doc,' a liberty which Clark detested.

"Going to the Mineral library, in the basement," Clark mumbled as he paid the driver. He resented the notion that where he went and what he did on campus was any of the man's business. Still he needed a ride home, so he hastily added, "I'll phone for a return trip. It'll be late—uh..." Clark was going to say 'Larry,' but he hesitated, realizing that, despite riding in the man's taxi for months, he wasn't sure he remembered the man's name.

"Right you are, Doc," the driver agreed.

Clark cringed and hurried toward the main door, lugging his specimen case in one hand and his smartphone in the other. As he approached the entrance, he was obliged to step across the face of the building's 'Sidewalk Sundial.' Decorative as well as functional, the stylized sundial was a feature of the entryway sidewalk. As the agitated professor passed over the embedded art piece, his shadow fell across the dial, momentarily demarcating the lateness of the hour. Spurred on by this reminder that the December day was fleeting, Clark rushed inside and hurried downstairs, wondering if he'd have time to accomplish his library errand.

Talk about locating a proverbial needle in a haystack the size of Europe, he thought as he descended, *finding Apperson's graph and his source map of central France will be no easy task. Over the decades, French volcanoes have been overlooked. Instead, researchers seeking obsidian sources have concentrated their efforts further south, focusing on Italy and various Mediterranean islands, and with good reason since that's where the pertinent volcanoes are. France on the other hand...*

Clark's thoughts were interrupted as he reached the bottom of the stairwell and gazed down the narrow hallway stretching before him. At the far end, blocking the library entrance, was a lone desk and at that desk sat the last man in the world Clark wanted to see. Suddenly he recalled why his last visit to the museum's library had been so disagreeable. Shaking his head in disbelief, the flummoxed professor started down the hall. Just when it seemed his luck was changing, there in the flesh sat Leslie Munger, the campus curmudgeon and sworn enemy of, as the officious man was fond of phrasing it, the *soft sciences.* To Leslie, astronomy, chemistry, math, physics, geology, and biology were hard sciences, solid disciplines where facts ruled. Whereas anthropology, sociology, philosophy, and—God forbid—archaeology were soft areas of study where opinion and conjecture reigned.

Arriving at the entrance, the out-of-shape professor asked for a French obsidian source map, a breathless request which caused the librarian to raise an eyebrow.

"A source map in French do you mean?" the petulant librarian asked with an uncooperative frown. The spindly man was several years older than Clark,

a crabby campus denizen who teetered on the brink of retirement yet continued to cling—like a land-locked barnacle—to his post as petty gatekeeper. A
puny specimen whose arms jutted out of his short-sleeved shirt like unsub-
stantial strands of linguine, the ancient guardian of the museum's reference
library had an oversized head of stark white hair, cut impossibly short, and a
wispy moustache. His name badge broadcast his feminine-sounding name in
18-point type, and, for a moment, Clark imagined the unfashionable bow tie
which hovered at the base of Leslie's skinny neck was about to start spinning
like a cartoon pinwheel.

"Not quite," Clark managed to say as he strove to keep the edge off his
voice. "What I'm seeking is a source map showing a specific location and
XRF—that is the X-ray fluorescence spectrometer—analysis. It's all explained on the request form which I emailed an hour ago. I'm particularly
interested in a 2003 work by Apperson relating to obsidian deposits within
the central region of *l'Hexagone*."

Clad in a stiff white shirt with miniature American flags on both collars
and a "don't tread on me" campaign button on his shallow chest, Leslie was
silent for several moments. Though he didn't say a word, his eyes spoke vol-
umes as he glared, in turn and with equal hostility, at Clark's conspicuous
specimen case and his copy of the professor's paperwork.

So, thought Clark, *the intractable Leslie has my request form. Which means
he knew I was coming and still he's choosing to stall. Much good it did to send
the paperwork in advance. This is my punishment for doing things by the book.
From the old crank's pained expression and his patriotic outfit, he must think my
legitimate request to view the vintage article is a communist plot and he probably
suspects that my case is crammed full of unpatriotic handbills. I've got no time
for...*

"I recognize you as our local smart aleck from across the quad," Leslie
snarled. "The eminent Dr. Clark, flouting his vast knowledge. Come to visit
his inferiors here in the bowels of our little museum. Come to bamboozle us
by throwing his vocabulary in our faces. I suppose you think I don't know
that France, due to its unique shape, is sometimes referred to as The Hexa-
gon. And by the same token, you appear to be unaware that I understand the
meaning of the abbreviation XRF."

"Help me out here, Leslie," Clark crooned. "I know you're a busy man. If you could just point me in the direction of French geological surveys, I..."

"Lower Level, Aisle 17-B, tier 4, box 8" the librarian interrupted as he noisily hand-stamped Clark's request form. "I ought to make you leave your suitcase here, but I'd rather treasure the image of you struggling to lug the thing down and back up our vintage spiral staircase. Not responsible for accidents. We close in thirty minutes."

Thanks to Leslie's remarkable memory, it took no time at all to locate the Apperson article in the March 2003 issue of *Antiquity Quarterly*, but it took Clark fifteen minutes to maneuver his smartphone into position to take an in-focus picture of the pertinent graph. Try as he might, he couldn't get the bloody closeup right until he put the periodical on the floor and loomed over it, striving to keep his balance, like a giant turkey buzzard riding a desert thermal. He took multiple pictures, dividing the wide graph into three segments.

Satisfied with his photos at last, he popped the magazine into its archival box and hurried up the narrow winding staircase, lugging his specimen case behind him like a man dragging an oversized badger to the top of a church steeple. He'd managed to get what he needed, but he'd cut the timing close. Stumbling back to Leslie's desk, the fatigued professor found the bureaucrat waiting impatiently with one eye on the hallway clock and both hands on the sliding metal gate.

"You wouldn't have locked me in down there, would you?" Clark asked.

"Just try me," replied his would-be jailer.

Emerging from the museum as the winter sun neared the horizon, Clark cursed the troublesome Leslie, turned up his coat collar, and walked off campus for supper. Sticking with his original plan, he'd wait until full dark before risking a visit to the accelerator lab.

Better safe than sorry.

There were several restaurants within walking distance, but only one, a burger joint called 'The Wildcat Burger Barn,' was open. Clark trundled inside, placed his order, and cleared a space at one of the bistro's empty tables. Balancing on an uncomfortable stool, he ate a lukewarm sandwich and sampled a cluster of unappealing fries while striving to view Apperson's chart on the constricted screen of his smartphone. Comprehending the disjointed chart in the dim light of the Burger Barn was a bit like trying to assemble a jigsaw puzzle while looking through a drinking straw and wearing mittens, but the persistent professor managed it.

Despite the shortcomings of his piecemeal images, there was no question that his homemade XRF findings matched Apperson's graph exactly. The elements were identical, from the soaring spike of silicon dioxide to the complementary ridges of iron, zirconium, aluminum, and all the rest. No question that Clark's Clovis had been shaped from obsidian that originated in central France's cauldrons of prehistoric fire and brimstone. As far as Clark was concerned, the match conclusively resolved Apperson's 'Italian Question' which, he knew, was really a two-part inquiry: *Were Mediterranean islands near Italy the exclusive source of obsidian used to fashion prehistoric French artifacts, or did the volcanoes of southern France produce their own volcanic glass?*

Clark had been taught that the answers were, respectively, 'yes' and 'no.' Brodeur and Apperson had disagreed and now Clark joined them in adhering to the reverse. *No*, all French obsidian *did not* originate in the Mediterranean and, *yes*, local volcanoes produced their own.

Writing 150 years apart, the two authors overturned the conventional wisdom that islands in the Mediterranean Sea were the source, through trade, of obsidian fragments and tools which made their way to France. Aware that ancient volcanoes abound in the region, Apperson had followed Brodeur's 1853 directions to conduct a fresh examination of French topography overlooked by others. In 2003, Apperson launched an expedition, rediscovered a lava flow described by Brodeur, and conducted an XRF analysis which confirmed the presence of native obsidian in central France. Following different leads and working years apart, the two men had achieved results which pointed to *Le-Dore* and *de la Crotz* as origin sources for a unique brand of obsidian. Building on their conclusions, Clark confirmed that his Clovis was unquestionably born in France.

"Huh," Clark said aloud, feeling a bit disappointed that he was unable to conjure up a more enthusiastic response. "Tired," he added, recognizing his exhaustion. He'd been awake and working feverishly since late last night and the fact that his exertions had been more mental than physical only served to increase his profound feeling of weariness. "Don't quit on me," he told himself, understanding there was still much to be done. Seeking to refocus his diminishing energy, he reached into his suit pocket, pulled out his photocopy, and read aloud, in a sotto voce whisper, Brodeur's words:

"From the Puy de Crotz, as a central point of observation, is a deep ravine," the long-dead author proclaimed in his 1853 narrative. "Running betwixt de Crotz and Mount La-Dore in the near distance, the ravine is strewed with colossal ruins from the rocks above, which consist of conglomerate, enveloping currents of trachyte and basalt, mingled in strange confusion."

Clark paused as he recognized at last the source of the troublesome earworm that had assaulted him in his map room. "Strange confusion," he repeated. Then he continued reading aloud, with feeling, his voice rising with each word until he was literally shouting the final syllables.

"Among the blocks lying in the ravine, are many of a trachyte approaching to obsidian, with resinous luster and fracture, and black in color; also, a rarer variety, compact, hard, and of a brick-red color, with something of the gloss of pitch-stone. A trove of preform rock, in a jumbled ravine, within sight of Roche de Solutre, a limestone escarpment of prodigious...of..."

"Eureka!" Clark bellowed.

"Problem?" the cook shouted from his post at the stove.

"Nothing," said Clark. "Never mind. Something from the late nineteenth century just struck me right between the eyes."

"You're sayin' we got some kind of old rats in here?" the cook asked. Alarmed by Clark's outburst and the rotund professor's physical antics, the concerned proprietor appeared in the dining area wearing a stained apron. He held a rolling pin in one hand.

Seeing the anxious and disheveled man, Clark realized he'd been making a spectacle of himself. While reading the Brodeur passage and digesting the revealing words written over a century and a half ago, the increasingly stimulated professor had been on his feet and pacing as he pictured the French ravine with its rocks 'mingled in strange confusion.' Inspired by Brodeur's words, Clark had conjured up an image of his prehistoric Clovis maker. He saw an earnest human, searching through rubble, kneeling to marvel at a lustrous stone of black and red, and popping the unique rock into his leather pouch. Then he imagined the man turning to face the northeast, gazing upon the distant outline of the Rock of Solutre, and gauging the walking distance to return to what—his hunting camp?

His hearth and home?

It was at this point that Clark's spoken recitation of Brodeur's treatise collided with his internal thoughts and the animated professor had shouted 'Eureka!' at the top of his lungs.

As the cook eyed him warily, Clark's mind continued to race. Two scientists, more than a century apart, had reported, and Clark had confirmed, that the obsidian which formed his Clovis had originated in a ravine between *La-Dore* and *Puy de la Crotz*, between the gold and the cross. That in itself was interesting, but not quite enough to compel the professor to cavort and swear in public.

So, the preform rock had been born in France? So what?

It wasn't merely the Clovis' birthplace that had triggered the professor's passion. Something else had set Clark off. Something about the general location commanded his attention. Something beyond the ravine with its rocks of strange confusion and beyond its surrounding volcanoes—something which Clark had nearly missed.

"A moment," he told the startled cook. "I just need a moment to..."

Rushing back to his table, the agitated professor whispered urgent voice commands until his smartphone displayed a contemporary map of France. With trembling fingers and barely able to stand, he manipulated the image so he could look north and east of *The Mount of the Cross*...and...there it was! The something which had set him off and, seeing it, he held the smartphone close and stared until both eyes lost their focus and the hairs on the back of his neck began to tingle, then stand to attention. He nearly swooned, recovered his balance, sat abruptly down, and closed his eyes.

"Solutrean," he whispered. "Solutrean," he repeated as he looked toward the cook, then stared at the ceiling with both arms outstretched, transfixed like a prophet of old beholding a divine parting of clouds. All at once, the disparate pieces of his marathon of research began to conglomerate in his imagination. The pieces were literally swirling around his head in a clockwise direction. He gazed upward as the images seemed to accumulate into a cohesive whole, like the frame of a film coming into sharp focus.

"Bingo! It's a Bingo!" he told himself.

"Closing up, mac," the cook responded with an uncertain tone. He backed away, side-stepping toward the kitchen, keeping chairs and tables between himself and his odd customer. The unnerved man had been watching Clark's antics and listening to his gibberish with one eye on the clock and the other on his wall-mounted telephone. Another fifteen minutes of this nonsense and he'd have called the cops. It was closing time and, if needed, he'd summon the law to come and force this goofy diner to move along. He needed this nut-job to take it outside, with his white beard and wild hair, too well dressed to be a transient, but too loud and ludicrous to be anything but crazy. He had no intention of being stuck with an obese mental patient who looked like a misbegotten Santa Claus.

Merry Friggin-Christmas! Why do all the weirdos come to my place after dark? he asked himself. *Does my open sign include a footnote inviting space aliens and wackos of all stripes to come in and order a burger? How can I get this crazy kook to leave? Maybe if I point toward the door?*

"Let's go, pal," said the cook, screwing up his courage now that the wall phone was in easy reach. "Take your dang suitcase and your nineteenth century and your Bingo game outside."

Accepting the abuse, Clark gathered up his things. The man had every right to be upset. Caught up in visualizing plausible solutions to his Clovis puzzle, Clark had been forging a chain of custody, link by fantastic link, as he steadily sought to connect his treasure to France's ancient Solutrean Culture. His mental gymnastics had been moving him ever closer to a collision with the past until at last his emotions had boiled over like a ripe volcano and he'd instinctively shouted not only 'Eureka' but also 'Bingo' at the top of his lungs.

What the cook made of his unprompted declarations, the professor hadn't time to consider. Picking up his smartphone, his papers, and his specimen case, Clark ate one more French-fry, left a generous tip, and strode into the Tucson night. Walking with a purpose, the specimen case seeming suddenly lighter, his lively steps the tread of a much younger man, the optimistic professor was bound for the AMS lab and what he hoped would be a rendezvous with destiny. As he ambled back toward the deserted campus, his teeming imagination helped him envision a preview of the map-matching exercise he planned to complete when he returned home later that evening. He was certain that, when he looked more closely at the maps lying on his study floor, reviewing everything through a Solutrean lens, he'd be able to consolidate all the evidence he was steadily accumulating. Enhancing those proofs with the results of tonight's AMS analysis, he'd place everything inside a coherent box and wrap his solution up with a big black and red bow.

He was absolutely sure that the ring of French volcanoes which included the Gold and the Cross would overlap precisely with an amoeba-shaped swath of principal archaeological sites attributed to the prehistoric Solutrean Culture. Chances were excellent that his Clovis was a Solutrean artifact shaped from obsidian which originated in the Culture's neighborhood. That marked an intriguing starting point and might have been a sufficient finding for an ordinary man. But Clark was far from ordinary and he was beginning to think that the charmed life he had once lived, and which had so nearly deserted him, was about to be revived. The obsidian and the artifact were Solutrean and that was astounding. But, in Clark's mind, that finding was not an end in itself because it begged the larger question.

"How in the blessed world" he asked aloud, "did my little old French projectile point end up all the way over here in North America?"

As he reached the edge of the main campus quadrangle and started across, he considered the larger question which he'd just posed to himself. *Not exactly an elegant research question,* he told himself. How long had it been since he'd been all the way through the research drill? It was one thing to expect his students to parse out the research process by proceeding through the steps of identifying the variables, stating the problem, and formulating a hypothesis. *What are you working with? What do you propose to do to it? What do you predict will be the outcome?*

"This study is to determine the chain-of-custody of a singular Clovis bird-point as compared to..." he paused realizing his obsidian treasure defied comparison. Even if he wanted to set up another similar Clovis point as a control, the Feds had left him nothing to work with. "Compared to zero," he decided.

He defined his variables as time and space: the age of the artifact, the age of the obsidian, the source of the artifact, and the source of the obsidian. His hypothesis, his guess of the outcome, was already tainted because he was well down the road with his methodology, but he'd give it a shot. He decided to try and take himself back to the moment he first spotted the remarkable Clovis lying amid the debris on his worktable. His initial impression would inform his hypothesis.

"The age of the Clovis won't exceed 13,000 years before-present," he predicted using the upper range of the presumed New World Clovis Culture. *"Not,"* he quickly added.

Caught up in the grip of his belief that the Clovis' underlying obsidian was traceable to prehistoric France, he revised his hypothesis. "Let's try this: The age of the Clovis will be no less than 20,000 years before-present. This will account for its hypothetical Solutrean birthplace and—"

Clark shuddered and suddenly realized he had an urgent need to urinate, so he picked up his pace. A brisk walk across The University of Arizona quad in the chilly December air, a refreshing leak in a university restroom, and Clark would be able to pursue another piece of his Clovis puzzle. But he'd only be able to launch that pursuit after he'd emptied his bladder.

Arriving at the Physics Building in a state of—as a scientist would put it—unresolved elimination, he rapidly entered his access code and slipped inside, nearly forgetting to suppress the alarm. Temporarily unable to locate the men's room, he found himself in a nondescript hallway and had to back-track. Bursting through the restroom door, he placed his specimen case beneath the nearest sink and sprinted to the urinals. He was nearly halfway finished when his thoughts raced ahead to his mission in the AMS lab. From the instant he smashed the cocoon in his garage-laboratory to this moment, here at the urinal, the evidence he'd been assembling had led Clark in an inevitable direction.

As surely as my liquid by-product splashes into this drain trap and seeks the waste pipe below, Clark told himself, *my work has led me toward an amazing possibility. A possibility which, within the coming hour, will be conclusively tested. A possibility which...*

Abruptly the professor paused. Threading his zipper home, he hurriedly washed his hands. As soon as his fingers were dry, he patted his pockets, not frantically, but purposefully, as if he'd planned all along to stop short of entering the AMS lab to engage in one final ounce of preparation. In all the excitement prior to leaving home and since, he'd entirely forgotten to examine the XRF graph produced by the pulverized clay. Instead, he'd folded up the elongated printout and stuffed it into his shirt pocket. The confined environment of this institutional restroom, mere steps from his destination, was not conducive to a thorough examination, but it would be something to study while he sat in the lab and waited for the AMS to work its magic. He was relieved to find the folded paper right where he'd put it. He peeked at the graph but left it where it was. It would keep until his AMS analysis was underway. Picking up his specimen case, he elbowed his way out of the restroom and headed down the hallway.

Regardless of when he got around to reading the clay graph, Clark was certain its geochemistry would complement the rest of his data. The rock, the leather, the clay, the seeds, and the maker—all had congregated in central France in the dim past to inhabit a moment of creation and conservation. A unique Clovis had been manufactured and lovingly preserved. Using the AMS to quantify the age of his organic markers, the fortuitous seeds and leather, Clark would nail-down the details of this prehistoric event.

Reaching the lab's secure door, he punched in the code, suppressed the internal alarm, and made himself at home. He'd reverse the input to erase his codes on the way out, leaving no breadcrumb trail for administrators to trace back to their favorite wandering professor. The spacious laboratory was a well-ordered collection of stainless-steel pipes and valves, as antiseptic as the inside of a pasteurizing machine, and sparsely illuminated by low-intensity ambient lighting. A bit dim for scientific work, but Clark knew his way around, so he decided not to ignite the main lights.

No sense attracting attention by making the place literally glow in the dark.
As for noise, the room was far from silent. The sound of a 24/7 vacuum pump filled the cavernous lab with a constant vibration. The ambient sound was so pervasive that, even when the professor finally activated the spectrometer, the pump's modulated hum would most certainly mask the subtle noise of the machine in action. Loading his two pellets into the circular specimen receptacle, he felt momentarily guilty for wasting the other thirty-eight positions. But he comforted himself with the knowledge that processing fewer specimens meant spending less time in the lab. No sense hanging around to have his clandestine outing discovered.

Programming the computer to receive the accelerator's results, Clark took up the lab's clipboard and reviewed the procedural checklist. This wasn't his first AMS rodeo, but he needed the procedure to go off without a hitch and it never hurt to confirm the protocols. Convinced that all was in readiness, he pulled out his unread XRF graph, spread it out on the nearest table, and flipped the AMS switch.

Chapter 36

Sitting in the taxi on his return trip home, Clark could hardly contain his excitement. The driver, Larry—or whatever his name was—chatted blithefully away in the front seat while Clark sat in back, with his specimen case at his feet, one hand clutching his AMS printout and the other holding his belatedly studied XRF graph. He was rocking in his seat and about to burst—literally burst.

"Pull over here, will you?" Clark implored.

"You sure, Doc?" the driver asked as he stared dubiously at the dark patch of Arizona desert stretching beyond the roadside.

"I need to take a leak," Clark lied.

"Okay then," said the driver, his voice filled with compassion. "Take your time, Doc. I'll shut the meter down."

"Thanks," said Clark.

Emerging into the chilly night air, Clark turned up his coat collar and picked his way through the tundra, hoping he wouldn't encounter a nest of jumping cholla or a moonlighting javelina, but even the risk of running afoul of a clinging cactus or wild pig couldn't dampen his spirits. The sky overhead was a festival of stars. The moon was riding high and the giddy professor could see just enough of the desert floor to make his way. He walked swiftly but carefully, trying not to stumble, but wanting to put considerable distance between himself and the idling taxicab. He needed a cushion of space. Not for modesty, because his bladder was fine, but to accomplish an even more pressing task. Clark hadn't made the driver stop in the middle of the night, in the middle of nowhere, to relieve himself. He had a far more pressing reason for trundling alone out into the Arizona darkness. When at last he'd managed to place a small hillock between himself and the taxi, the exhilarated professor stood in a clearing, raised both hands above his head, and danced in a circle, celebrating at the top of his voice.

"So-lu-tre-an! So-lu-tre-an! Give me an 'S!" Give me an 'O!" Give me an 'L!' Give me a...oh, never mind! I'm gonna be rich! I'm gonna be rich! I'm gonna be rich!"

As he danced in the desert, Clark's reeling brain added up all the delicious evidence he'd accumulated. Then he added it up again, and again, and once more, and each time the answer came out the same. It was the clay that completed the puzzle. It had been the clay all along.

An hour ago, sitting in the AMS lab, casually reviewing the geochemical fingerprint of his clay specimen, the revelation had struck Clark. The sensation didn't resemble a thunderbolt. It was more like the distant sun breaking through to brighten a cloudy day. It was warmth and light, but mostly it was vision. The moment Clark saw the clay graph, he recognized the pattern. His photographic memory was a burden at times, filling his head with a boatload of trivia, but occasionally, it served him well.

Even a blind pig finds an acorn now and then, he told himself.

Seeing the graph and recalling the pattern, he knew what he had, and it was fortunate that his presence in the lab afforded him the opportunity to instantly confirm his belief. The reinforcing documentation he needed was at his fingertips, literally within reach. With trembling hands, he positioned his clay graph next to the keyboard, sliding it on top of the procedural checklist and securing it in place with an alligator clip. Entering his password, Clark searched the AMS' comprehensive database, confident the relevant record would be there.

Moments later, he had his confirmation.

As Clark danced in the desert, he celebrated the convergence of so many coincidences: the clay cocoon, the revealed Clovis, the seeds, the leather, the eloquent Brodeur, the sloppy Apperson, and finally full circle back to the clay.

"Take your place on the great Mandala," Clark recited the Peter, Paul, and Mary classic to himself, "as it moves through your brief moment of time," the words came flooding back to him. "Win or lose now, you must choose now, and if you lose..." he forgot the rest, but the implications were clear. The wheel of life was cycling back, and Clark was being presented with a second chance to climb on board.

"I'm gonna be rich," he repeated.

If he hadn't freed the Clovis from its cocoon, if he hadn't consulted his maps and run his homegrown analysis, if he hadn't remembered the Brodeur article and if the Frenchman hadn't inspired Apperson and if Clark hadn't run the Leslie gauntlet to obtain a clear copy of Apperson's XRF graph and if he hadn't been sitting in the AMS lab...

But all those things had happened and here he was, dancing on the cusp of his personal resurrection.

Figuring Larry could wait a bit longer, Clark cleared a space on the desert floor and sat down. *God, bless me,* he thought and then, enraptured in the dark, he invoked the childhood prayer he'd recited every night growing up and the same prayer he'd said all through his harrowing days in Vietnam. *And God bless Mama and Daddy and Sissy and Bingo and Rex and all the people and all the pets in the whole wide world.* He paused then, a bit reluctant to tempt fate by altering his solemn childhood blessing, but he did it anyway by adding aloud, "And God bless the AMS! Amen!"

If not for the university's accelerator mass spectrometer lab and their generous cooperation with researchers small and large, the rejuvenated professor wouldn't be sitting in the desert, wrapped in prayer, and about to reclaim his life. The AMS lab regularly assisted off-campus scientists and scholars with specimen analysis. Over the years, the lab had conducted more than 100,000 radiocarbon measurements as well as complementary XRF analyses, evaluating a host of diverse material, everything from a fragment of the Shroud of Turin to encrusted doubloons from a Caribbean shipwreck. During his decades on campus, Clark had been called in several times to consult, especially when the lab was processing material that touched on Native American objects. Three years ago, a sealed canister had arrived and the lab immediately telephoned Clark.

"Right up your alley," the technician assured him. "Presuming your alley runs through America's Heartland."

"Tell me more," Clark said, intrigued that his pride in his midwestern roots was literally tingling with anticipation.

Hearing the details, Clark cancelled his afternoon class and headed for the AMS lab. He arrived to find the place bustling with activity. It was a typical mid-semester weekday and, after exchanging greetings with half a dozen colleagues, he found Marsh Henderson at the lab's elaborate XRF computer terminal.

"Just coming up now," Marsh informed the curious professor. "Didn't expect you so soon."

"Not every day Iowa comes to the desert," Clark observed as he took a chair and waited for the data to materialize.

"You got that right," said Marsh. He was a personable young man with red hair, a new doctoral degree, and a new wife. "So, like I told you on the phone, the canister contains two pottery samples. One from northeast Iowa—from one of those bear-shaped effigy mounds overlooking the river. And the other one's from northwest Iowa, your old stomping ground. Three hundred miles apart. Already finished with the bear site. That folder contains your XRF printout."

"My copy?" Clark smiled.

"Yes, sir."

"Why are you so good to me?" Clark joked.

"Other than the fact that you chaired my doctoral committee and you're my favorite teacher of all time and you were best man at my wedding?" Marsh inquired.

"Yeah," said Clark, "aside from those things."

"Well," the tech bantered, "it was either this or name our first-born after you."

"Wise choice," said Clark. "To go with the folder, I mean." Clark opened the file and studied the contents. "No surprises here," he frowned.

"Nope," agreed Marsh. "Standard stuff. We pegged the bear pottery at 950 before present and we double-checked their XRF analysis which confirms that the trace element composition of the bear clay is unique to the Effigy Mounds of extreme northeast Iowa. It's a vintage artifact of the region, Late Woodland Culture, about a thousand years old with just what you'd expect in a geochemical fingerprint, lots of iron, right?"

"Right," Clark agreed. His tone was dubious as he studied the rather ordinary graph. "So, what's the anomaly you were going on about?"

"Our Iowa partners—as I said, a sophomore anthro class at your old alma mater, Droxit College—have a problem statement. It concerns the Woodland Culture, native to the eastern corner of the state and builders of all those cool earthen mounds shaped like bears and eagles and snakes and such...like you need a lecture on the mounds... Anyway, the Droxit theory is that the eastern Iowa Woodlanders established active trade with the contemporary Mill Creek Culture in the far west. Reasoning the trade route would move westward, they submitted two nearly identical pottery sherds for analysis— one unearthed in the east and one in the west. They're asking us to confirm their hypothesis that the primary element in both fragments will be Effigy Mound iron and other trace elements which'll match right down the line."

"I'm going to go out on a limb here and guess the XRF graphs don't match." Clark speculated.

"Nope," Marsh responded. "Not even close. And here comes our anomaly." He tapped the computer screen. "After I called you, I ran it again, just to make certain. I'll print it out and you'll see."

Marsh collected the hard copies and handed them to Clark.

"Same age...a thousand years old, plus or minus..." said Clark as he examined the paperwork. "and...ah..."

"Yeah. *Ah*," Marsh agreed.

"A huge spike of Praseodymium in the far west sample and only a trace of iron," Clark announced as he studied the graph and fondly recalled his undergraduate field-school days spent laboring and sweating in the humidity of an Iowa summer. The best part, he remembered, was the revealing bikini tops and skimpy shorts worn by his coed classmates. He was a virile grunt then, clean-shaven with a tan and a flat belly, laying out grids, digging working holes, and using a trowel to square-off distinct edges. He'd also sifted tons of excavated Mill Creek dirt, unaware that Praseodymium was present. He hadn't encountered the rare earth mineral then, and now he couldn't help wondering what else he might have missed in those erstwhile days before the advent of X-ray fluorescence analysis.

"Yeah. Praseodymium. Good old 'Pr,' Marsh continued, adding his infectious grin to his already animated face. "Atomic number 59, aka the least-rare of rare earth minerals and the primary ingredient in volcanic minestrone."

Clark grinned back at his likeable colleague. Marsh had been a precocious undergraduate and a lucid grad student with a knack for cutting through the scientific bullshit to hit upon the nub of a matter. Among its other attributes, Marsh's 'good old Praseodymium' had a reputation of providing chemical nutrition to an obscure organism which, against all odds, lived in the sweltering confines of a volcanic mud-pool. Praseodymium makes a harsh environment not only tolerable, but also nutritious, if you happen to be a supple living bacterium which resembles an undulating cat's whisker. Hence, in Marsh's whimsical opinion, the enabling Pr mineral provided the hungry bacterium with what amounted to volcanic soup.

As a result of numerous digs Clark had experienced in the wilds of western Iowa, he knew the Mill Creek Culture once inhabited a region along the Missouri River. It was fertile land and also adjacent to one of the American Heartland's few volcanic fields. Given this unique location, it now made perfect sense that clay used to form Mill Creek pottery would be infused with Praseodymium. That word was a mouthful which tended to trip-up young geology majors. *Praise-ee-oh-dim-ee-um*...Clark preferred to call it 'Praise.'

"Other samples might support the premise that trade existed between eastern and western Iowa," Marsh noted and Clark suspected the compassionate technician was rehearsing a way to word a report which would let the hopeful second-year Droxit students down easy. "But the idea isn't supported by these particular pottery samples."

"Too bad," said Clark, "but science ain't for sissies."

"Yeah-boy," Marsh agreed. "Anyway, that chart is still something. Did you ever see an XRF spike like that one?"

"Nope," said Clark as he studied the Mill Creek graph with its towering 'Pr' peak, the vertical line rising so dramatically that it ran off the top of the page. It was an unforgettable sight and one which had been etched in the professor's memory that day. So much so that, moments ago when Clark encountered the singularity a second time, he'd instantly recognized the pattern.

Using the AMS computer to locate and display the archival image of Marsh's XRF graph, Clark had copied it from the lab's virtual files and printed it out. It matched exactly with his own X-ray analysis of the ancient clay which had encased the Clovis. Adding the printout of Marsh's graph to his documentation, he closed the archival file. Seconds later, the results of the evening's radiocarbon dating exercise flashed onto the AMS computer screen. Clark printed out the findings. Having thus determined the age of the seeds and the leather, he grinned like a fortunate child who has reached into an apparently empty kitchen jar, only to discover an oversized chocolate chip cookie, and his contentment was complete.

"Touching down, Houston," Clark said aloud as he'd shut everything off and gathered up his things.

Five minutes after locking up, Clark's hands had been shaking as he sat on a commode in the men's room and recorded the new evidence in his field notebook. The off-campus burger wasn't sitting well, or maybe it was excitement that stimulated the professor's bowels. Either way, he'd needed a bathroom break before summoning his taxi for the trip home and the respite afforded him the opportunity to sit and examine his new data.

His freshly obtained AMS spectrograph of his seed pellet had confirmed that the clay cocoon was only 1,000 years old—far younger than he expected. His homemade XRF graph, when cross-checked with the archival copy of Marsh's Mill Creek data, confirmed that the clay itself was native to Iowa—a finding which placed it in the correct hemisphere but at the wrong time and on the wrong continent. After noting these unforeseen outcomes, Clark had penciled in the evening's bombshell. In a succinct note, he'd recorded the surprising news that the spectrograph of the leather, and by association the Clovis itself, dated to an astonishing *17,000 years old!* Not content with the exclamation point, Clark underlined the finding and summarized his conclusions:

The 1,000-year-old clay traces to Iowa, whereas the obsidian traces to France, and the 17,000-year-old leather pinned to the base of the Clovis makes the artifact, by association, much older than its clay cocoon. Quite simply, an artifact far older than any known North American Clovis Culture and created 4,500 miles away, somehow reached the western fringes of Iowa to be preserved, and quite possibly revered, a mere thousand years ago by the Mill Creek Culture. This accumulation of evidence leads me to an unshakable conclusion. Namely, that at least one fragment of Old-World obsidian technology has spread to the New World and much further westward and significantly earlier than leading experts in my discipline, and indeed I myself, supposed.

Alone in the dark desert, Clark tilted his head back and looked at the stars, wishing he could harvest the testimony of those celestial witnesses who were undoubtedly on the job all those eons ago. The wind stirred and, feeling the chill of the growing breeze, Clark ended his reflections and decided to call it a night.

"I'm gonna be rich," the bubbling professor repeated under his breath as he made his way back to the taxi. It was nearly 2 a.m. and the exhausted driver, who had dozed off, awakened with a start when his wayward passenger opened and slammed the rear door. "Home, James," Clark commanded with an air of jocularity.

Arriving at his ranch house, the professor bounded out of the idling vehicle and handed the driver a hundred-dollar-bill. "Keep the change," he laughed.

"Thanks, Doc," said the driver. "You're a pal. And by the way, let's have none of this 'James' stuff. It's okay for you to call me Jimmy."

Clark rushed inside and hurried straight to his study where a rapid review of the maps on his carpet reinforced his joy. Leaving the maps where they lay, he consulted his extensive library. Unlike his disordered map room, his collection of archaeological reference texts was impeccably cataloged. It only took a moment to locate the books he was seeking. Pouring himself a drink, he built a roaring blaze in the study's broad fireplace, wrapped a comforter around his knees, and sat on the cozy room's overstuffed sofa. He patted the covers of five vintage books, admiring the superb bindings, trying to recall the last time he'd opened them. Building on a sheaf of accumulating facts, it only took the diligent professor a few hours more among his antiquated books to absolutely authenticate the truly astonishing worth of his Clovis.

And such a worth!

Although found in America, his miniature Clovis compared favorably to documented sets of comparable—though larger—points unearthed in distant France. Moreover, Clark pored over one of his more obscure reference works until he added the final threads to the tapestry of conjecture he was steadily weaving. In the wee hours of the morning, on the twenty-eighth day of his research marathon, a little-consulted book, centuries old and written in French, yielded the final kernel of data he was searching for.

He rediscovered the revelation in a half-remembered passage. Summarized in a few succinct sentences, the French scientist, L.W. Laurent had postulated a critical notion. Laurent believed that prehistoric humans associated with the Solutrean Culture were transitioning from the production of utilitarian tools to the creation of purely decorative items. Stripped to its essence, the Frenchman's theme was simple but profound. Around the time Clark's singular Clovis had been fashioned, modern Europe's Ice Age ancestors were experimenting with aspects of artistic expression.

In France this emerging human affection for art manifested itself in numerous cave paintings and relief sculptures. A tendency toward art in general, and individual adornment in particular, was also evident, the long-dead author maintained, in the appearance of miniature versions of everyday tools, *including Clovis points.*

Finally, and most relevant to Clark's research, not only were prehistoric individuals miniaturizing everyday objects, they were also engaging in the peculiar practice of encasing such representational items in clay. Where miniature points and blades were concerned, Laurent speculated that this action was an attempt to preserve hunting magic. If the author's surmises were correct, ancient humans associated with the Solutrean Culture were engaged in more than hunting and gathering and trying to stay alive in a world engulfed in ice. They were also immersed in a rudimentary attempt to create talismans which symbolized the maker's concept of luck or good fortune.

It was a radical notion and well ahead of its time.

Not surprisingly, the author reported that his conservative colleagues, including a number of churchmen, were skeptical of his speculative conclusions. And yet, Clark was convinced that Laurent had been on to something. As every thoughtful researcher who delves into human prehistory must acknowledge, art is significantly older than the Johnny-come-lately disciplines of mathematics and science.

Laurent, the quixotic Frenchman, might have been a dreamer whose deductions ran counter to the scientific and religious norms of his era, but Clark was impressed by the man's suppositions. Inspired by Laurent's premise, Clark gained a new respect for the Clovis. He began to think of it as not merely an efficient tool and work of art, but also as an object forming a magical link between the Old World and the New—a link which exponentially amplified the artifact's value.

Returning to his garage laboratory, Clark turned on the lights and opened the sterilizing glove box. Carefully avoiding the sharp point and edges by picking up the tiny Clovis by its base, he gently placed the point on his palm and balanced it there, like a man trying to guess the value of a foreign coin by estimating its raw weight.

"Okay," he told himself. "Say it...you know it's true...say it already."

He had no doubt that this miniature point was far older than a typical North American Clovis. Instead it was much closer in age to Old-World tools.

"Say it..." he prodded himself.

Buoyed by his findings, Clark knew he would stake his reputation on his astounding conclusion. By pure chance he'd discovered what amounted to an archaeological Rosetta Stone. Just like that vital fragment of rock which enabled scholars to translate ancient hieroglyphics, Clark was convinced that this tiny artifact was the conduit to verifying something of equal importance.

He had only to hold the Clovis for a moment more before he was certain that the treasure which he held in his hand was the key to nothing less than the controversial Solutrean Hypothesis. On the strength of this single object of exquisitely worked obsidian, Clark was convinced he could substantiate the Solutrean. With this unique Clovis he could confirm and resurrect the boldly postulated and often maligned scientific theory that America's original inhabitants migrated to this continent from Europe. Not overland from Asia, or up from some mythical underworld, but from the east, traversing the fringes of once-frozen oceans to arrive from the Old World.

It was a notion confirmed by his Clovis' fantastic journey from east to west.

Substantiated by Clark's discovery, the often-discredited hypothesis would gain traction, relegating native peoples to late-comers and confirming the contentious notion that prehistoric Europeans first populated the Americas. Clark's conclusion was inescapable. The evidence was irrefutable.

The Clovis' existence conclusively proved that ancient members of the Caucasian race were first to reach the New World, not the distant forerunners of Navajo or Hopi or Ojibwa or any other tribe, but the ancestors of ordinary, everyday prehistoric white people. Certain interpretations of the Solutrean Hypothesis were wildly popular with white nationalists, neo-Nazis, and other master-race advocates.

Because Clark's newly discovered Clovis was most certainly the elusive key to proving an otherwise provocative idea, whoever possessed this artifact—providing he marketed it to the right people—could name his price.

So, Clark did.

Chapter 37

Dr. C. Arnold Clark—once a discerning collector of Native American artifacts—curbed a scholarly desire to merely accumulate and study extraordinary objects. Instead he turned to the dark web to proclaim that he possessed, and was willing to sell, the key to the Solutrean Hypothesis. Making his scheme known through black market contacts, he offered the fantastic treasure for sale to the highest bidder. Then he did something which only a madman, or an extremely confident expert would do.

He set the starting bid at six million dollars.

At first, Clark received no response. Then an anonymous bidder offered a few thousand dollars and the professor was beginning to despair when the Scarlet Brotherhood, a ruthless Russian cartel, sent an encrypted email containing an offer of three million. Final negotiations were conducted through a year's worth of relentless email exchanges, during which Clark managed to convince the frugal Russians to raise their bid to four million. As a result, the professor had been all set to deliver the Clovis to the cartel, until a month ago when he tried to pressure the Brotherhood into advancing half the sum as a down payment. It was a bold ask, but the impoverished professor needed the money to cover bad investments, gambling debts, and other unfortunate byproducts of his wastrel lifestyle. Feeling pinched for cash, Clark demanded his customers pay half up-front and fork over the balance on delivery. He told them he needed the money right away and set a deadline. Faced with the professor's ultimatum, the cartel promised to pay but missed Clark's deadline and then seemed to lose interest. Just when the Russian deal seemed about to fall through, a Saudi operative approached him with a far better offer—200% better to be exact—whereupon Clark switched buyers.

He didn't tell the Russians of course. His decision to change customers had been a tough call because Clark was very far down the road with the Russian deal. The cartel hadn't sent the promised down payment, but what if they did? The Russian dithering and the Saudi offer made things complicated—so complicated that Clark began looking for a way out. A week ago, that exit seemed to materialize when the Russian's missed yet another down payment deadline. When those promised funds did not materialize, the professor momentarily considered backing completely out of the Russian transaction. That would have been the safe thing to do, the smart thing to do. He should have told the Russians to keep their dang money. He should have told them the deal was off and gone with the Saudis.

But it was too late to be either safe or smart. Clark desperately needed the upfront cash and the Saudis had already nixed the idea of a down payment, so that was that. Like it or not he'd have to keep the Scarlet Brotherhood in play. He'd have to convince the Brothers to fork over the two million, then risk pulling off a double-cross by switching buyers. The die was cast, no turning back. Instead of cancelling the Russian deal, the professor doubled down. The Russians had given him a contact phone number with strict instructions to call only in case of emergency and Clark decided that their repeated failures to pony up the two million met those criteria. Taking a deep breath, he boldly used his smartphone to contact the Russians and demand the missing down payment.

"Well, what about it, comrade?" Clark insisted after he'd given the man who answered the phone an earful.

"We are aware of the agreement, but there has been an unexpected delay," the Russian told him.

"Pardon me, but which one are you again?" Clark asked.

In two years of tense negotiations, Clark had spoken by telephone with as many as a dozen so-called 'handlers,' none of whom he'd ever met in person, and he was growing weary of trying to keep them straight on the basis of their voices alone. To him they'd all begun to sound like identical versions of the same omnibus foreigner, although he had to admit that this one had pretty good English.

"You will remember me as Magar," said the Russian and he sounded annoyed.

"Well, Comrade Magar. If you are, as you say, 'aware of the agreement,'" Clark insisted, "then where the hell is my money?"

The silence on the other end of the line suggested that this particular Russian was having second thoughts. Time to bluff, thought Clark.

"Are you there, comrade?"

Clark heard an audible sigh on the other end of the line, and he took this as a sign that the Russian was struggling to resolve some internal dilemma.

"This is a complicated situation," Magar said.

"Complicated? In what way, I wonder?" Clark asked.

"The thing is, Dr. Clark," Magar said, his tone turning icy, "you are asking us to provide you with a considerable amount of money—this so-called 'down payment'—with no guarantee that we will receive the promised treasure."

Treasure, Clark thought, *that's the code word these pathetic underlings are using for my Clovis. Probably this Magar character and all the other inhabitants of the cartel's lower echelons have no idea what I'm offering for sale.*

"Listen," said Clark aloud, "I'll make this simple for you. Either I get my frigging down payment today or the deal is off. Do you understand what I'm saying, comrade?"

"Ah."

Silence again. Was this some sort of Russian tactic?

"Well?" asked Clark.

"Dr. Clark," said Magar, "may I offer you some friendly advice?"

"Please do, I'm all ears," said Clark and he hoped that Magar's command of English included the ability to comprehend a sarcastic tone of voice when he heard one.

"First allow me to tell you directly, with all due respect, that I find your vulgar profanities and your use of the term 'comrade' offensive. Your use of this term implies a caricature of a Russian personage and it presumes a bond between the two of us which does not exist, because you, sir, have not earned the right to consider me a brother-in-arms. And let me tell you plainly, Dr. Clark, that you are nothing to me but a craven capitalist who sells trinkets for personal gain. Have I been unclear in any of my statements?"

"No indeed," said Clark. "Your candor is quite refreshing, and your English is impeccable. So, let me see if I have this straight. Apparently, you object to my language and you consider me a barbarian, which is fine with me. You believe I crave money and you are correct. I not only crave cash, I worship it. So, you can rest-assured that, if you honor our agreement and send me the promised down payment, I will do my part to earn the additional two million. So, here's what I need from you, sir. I need you to stop jerking me around and I need you to send me my money. I'm going to hang up in a second and log onto my account. And, if I don't see a two million down payment—that's a two-and-six-zeros—being posted there by..." Clark glanced at his watch. "By 3:30, you and your precious cartel can kiss our deal goodbye."

Clark ended the call, turned on his computer and waited. He'd already accepted the Saudi's more generous offer. Forcing the Russians to cough up the down payment would be a mixed blessing, solving his immediate cash-flow problem but spawning a future dilemma. A lot might happen in the coming days, but the professor could envision no scenario in which the Russians and the Arabs would agree to share a single Clovis.

"I'll cross that bridge when I come to it," he decided.

He stared at the computer screen. The hall clock struck the quarter hour. Then, like a final buzzer-beating lob from mid-court, the money began blinking into his account at 3:25. As the professor had instructed, each installment was a $5,000 increment. A deposit of ten thousand or more would compel the bank to notify the Feds and the last thing Clark wanted was Federal scrutiny. Seeing the money trickling in, he made another call and Magar answered on the first ring. He thanked the Russian and then he told him the bad news.

"I'm being watched," said Clark. "So, I'll need a bit more time to make arrangements to deliver the treasure. This is for your protection as well as mine."

"How much time?" The Russian sounded dubious.

"A week at least," said Clark, fully aware that asking for seven days was a request the Russians would be unlikely to honor, which was fine with him—he really didn't need a week.

"We will allow you forty-eight hours," said Magar. "And before that time has passed, our representative will contact you to make arrangements to reexamine and photograph the merchandise. Therefore, sir, have a care because you have tried our patience for the final time. We will not tolerate failure and there will be no further payment until the treasure is in our hands."

"No problem," Clark said. "Absolutely no problem."

Clark hung up and resumed his routine. He went to the campus as usual, taught his morning class, held office hours, and hosted his afternoon seminar. Then he went home, started packing, and grudgingly fielded a late-night Russian call to schedule the reexamination. The very next day, on July 14, he met with his reliable graduate assistant to organize the closing details of a typical GPS navigation assignment, the same caching project he'd sponsored every college term for decades. Early that morning, he and Anne Scriptor had loaded a set of ordinary toolboxes into her Volkswagen Bug. Then, at exactly 6 a.m., he'd dispatched her with instructions to cache the boxes at remote locations in western Colorado.

With Anne on her way, Clark had continued with his usual routine and his watchers also settled into their habitual surveillance. The Russians had given him a deadline and the clock was ticking, but Clark was unperturbed. There would be time enough. Anne was playing her unwitting part by dutifully distributing the caches, the Russians were simultaneously fuming and cooling their heels, and his watchers, who believed they had Clark on a leash, were about to realize the tether was the other way around.

Because, shortly after Anne left Tucson, Clark dealt with his Russian inspector and vanished.

Chapter 38

Dawn remained far away as the jet—a conveyance generously supplied by Clark's Saudi customers—drew closer to his destination, a remote airstrip on the outskirts of the northern Arizona town of Page. Just before two in the morning of July 15, the pilot's voice on the intercom interrupted the professor's nap.

"We'll be on the ground in fifteen minutes," he assured his passenger.

Clark opened his eyes and sat in the dark for a moment while lingering images from his extended dreams continued to echo in his mind. He'd been reliving the past. Time to face the future.

This Is Your Life, he told himself, invoking the title of a vintage television program which used to invite viewers to witness the life story of a celebrity as told by voices and images from the subject's past. When Clark was a boy, he and his parents had watched the program together. Only years later, when he'd grown to maturity, did Clark recognize the bittersweet aspect of the now-defunct program. Only then did he appreciate the predicament of the fading icon, in the twilight of his or her career, sitting in an armchair while memories played out on camera. The subject's life was ending. The man or woman of the hour was in the undesirable position of doing fewer things for the first time, and a truck-load of things for the last time. His dreaming mind had taken him on a similar journey which led him to his one-Clovis-two-customers dilemma, and yet...

"That *was* your life," he corrected himself. "High time to chart another." He declared as he turned on the jet's fashionably recessed overhead lights, gathered his things, and prepared to deplane.

When the jet landed in what appeared to be the middle of nowhere, Clark could tell that the young pilot was impressed to see that a Navajo police vehicle—a fully-appointed Jeep Rubicon no less—was waiting on the rustic tarmac. Although Clark didn't bother to observe the pilot's reaction, the young man was probably even more impressed when his mysterious passenger got into the Rubicon, started it up, and drove away with the rooftop light-bar flashing. Clark was feeling his oats. The only reason he didn't sound the siren was he wasn't certain he knew how to turn it off again.

Part III: Diak and the Pilot

Chapter 39

July 15, 2:15 a.m.
Northern Arizona

The young pilot was impressed all right—so impressed that he jotted down the Rubicon's description and license plate number. In a moment he'd call his Saudi contact and report. Once that call was completed, he planned to place the phone on the ground. Next, to thoroughly destroy the device, he'd stomp it into tiny fragments and grind those bits under his boot. He would do these pedantic things as instructed and not because anyone could possibly be watching in this remote location. He would follow orders because the phone was evidence and the Saudis had cautioned him to leave no traces.

He'd make the required call, obliterate the phone, and then wait for dawn to take off again. When the sun rose, he'd fly back to Tucson where he'd receive a cash bonus and a new phone from his Saudi benefactors. Eventually, he'd be instructed to return and pick up his furtive passenger. By then, the arid climate and high desert winds would have already begun to erode the fragile wreckage of the discarded phone. In time, the wind and shifting soil would gnaw at the pieces and its marvelous components would be reduced to particles so fine as to be virtually indistinguishable from the hard-packed sand that formed this remote runway.

Thinking of the runway, the pilot remembered that he'd have to pull up the tarps and scatter the rocks to obscure the boundaries of this isolated landing strip. The spot itself was naturally level and free of stones, so it had taken only minimum preparation to make it a suitable surface.

He'd scouted the place by car and prepared the spot meticulously before relocating it from the air, then practicing landings and take-offs. The temporary markers he'd assembled were essential for a night landing. But he'd be returning in daylight and he'd flown enough trial runs to manage a day landing and takeoff without the aid of ground references. He'd make his call in a moment, then take care of the markers. For the present he was content to contemplate his surroundings.

The young man stood in the enveloping darkness, straddling the primitive runway. Above him sailed the bright distant moon while the overarching night sky overflowed with stars from horizon to horizon. As he looked aloft, he involuntarily fingered the metallic wings pinned to his lapel. Never mind that they were unofficial insignia—a prize extracted from a cereal box when he was nine years old. He'd treasured those wings throughout childhood, and he treasured them still.

The pin was a token of his boyhood aspirations and the endless sky above him seemed to manifest those dreams by forming a bridge between his hopeful past and his promising future. Like most pilots, he considered himself a creature of the air. The places he touched down were merely temporary ports-of-call to which he was periodically tethered. He tolerated the ground, but it was for his journeys aloft in the unfettered sky that he lived. He'd become a pilot to chase his dreams and, just when it had seemed that those dreams might not materialize, money had suddenly come his way to make them possible.

"Money," he said aloud.

In return for a few hours of ordinary flying, he'd already received substantial sums from the Saudis, not to mention an unexpected bonus from an anonymous benefactor.

Apparently, more than one well-heeled angel had taken an interest in his portly passenger. The additional thousands he would pocket when he next retrieved his professor would be enough to finance the optimistic pilot's plan to retire young and spend his life flying to every corner of the globe.

With money he could purchase his own aircraft and set his own schedule. No longer would he slavishly adhere to the wishes of others, ferrying the rich and famous here and there in their expensive aircraft. He'd buy his own jet and travel the world alone, spending as much time in the air as possible. In his vision of the future he would dwell among the clouds and only return to earth to sleep, to fornicate, and eat, and eventually, on some far-off day, to die.

But his death was a distant idea and far from his mind. For the present, for this moment in the dark, it was good to be alive, good to be young and unexpectedly wealthy, and blessed to have a bright future spreading out before him. He inhaled the clear night air and continued to study the sky until he decided it was time to call the Saudis. He reached into his jacket pocket but, before his fingers could retrieve the phone, he heard a rustle of fabric behind him and felt a sharp pain at the base of his neck.

Chapter 40

Diak paused on the remote runway. Wiping his knife on his trouser leg, he re-sheathed the blade, then rolled the body over and knelt to check for a pulse. The pilot's wristwatch blinked from 2:39 to 2:40 a.m.—a mocking chronology which reminded the German that he'd arrived too late. Having failed to intercept the elusive Clark, he might have spared the pilot. But he was angry with himself for missing the professor and, in the grip of that anger, he'd acted impulsively.

If the German felt any regret, the emotion was fleeting because, although he had a great need for the jet, he had no need for the pilot. Besides, the man had failed to fulfill their agreement. He'd failed to report the timing of Clark's bid to escape from Tucson and that failure had caused Diak to get a tardy start. Perhaps the enterprising pilot, who seemed to have been working both sides of the equation, deserved to die.

A would-be traitor played a risky game.

Diak knew this well because he himself was walking a dangerous tightrope as he sought to juggle allegiances. He'd begun his quest for the priceless Clovis by briefly prodding the professor and then presenting himself to the Russians as an ally, pretending to aid them while secretly siphoning off their intelligence to further his own purposes. Even now, the German hoped to exploit the Brotherhood's belief that he was working with them. If he met any Russians in the field, they might take him to be a comrade and Diak would nurture that illusion as long as it suited him. But, if things came to a head, he wouldn't hesitate to eliminate the men who were, in reality, his competitors.

The German had no love for the Russians who, in the closing months of World War II, had grappled with the Nazis in a bloody campaign to 'liberate' Poland. For weeks, both sides had rained artillery rounds and dropped bombs, indiscriminately killing scores of hapless civilians caught between the ambitions of competing ideologies. 'Collateral damage' the warmongers had called it. His Polish ancestors had been part of that unlucky collateral and his mother had been peripheral damage as the victorious Russians first orphaned her, then ignored her, and finally banished her to East Berlin where she walked the streets, birthed her only son, and died a forgotten whore.

"Bastarde," he said aloud, condemning all Russians as he sought to steer his thoughts away from painful memories.

He blamed the Russians for his mother's fate. He also hated them for disfiguring his face and mutilating his loins. That compounded hatred would guide his actions. The thought of having, as needed, to destroy a Russian or two would present absolutely no problem for the German. In the meantime, double-crossing them not only fed his vengeance, it was also great sport and so incredibly easy.

As for the Saudis, as soon as the Clovis was in his possession and the time came to bargain for it, Diak was more than prepared to negotiate with the renegade prince who sought to purchase the artifact by outbidding the Russian cartel. The prince may or may not possess the millions needed to purchase the Clovis, but the German would soon plumb the depths of the Arab's solvency. He would negotiate, yes, but there would be no haggling. *Zählen meinen Preis oder gehen weg,* he thought—*pay my price or walk away.*

Finding no pulse as he knelt next to the pilot's body, Diak searched the dead man's pockets, found a handwritten note, and retrieved a cell phone. The note described Clark's vehicle, information which would come in handy.

As for the phone, the emblem of two crossed swords and a palm tree on the obverse of the device's protective case left no doubt as to its ownership. At some point, the Saudis would be wondering why their man didn't report in. Let them wonder. If they got nervous and telephoned their pilot, Diak would answer with a noncommittal grunt and he might be fortunate enough to trick the caller into revealing Clark's whereabouts—assuming the Arabs knew his location which, given the unpredictable professor, was a big assumption. Nevertheless, the German would add the cell phone to his arsenal.

He'd already linked himself to the professor's smartphone and, through that instrument, to the Scarlet Brotherhood's communication network. This newly confiscated phone might create an opportunity to infiltrate the Saudis as well. By establishing clandestine connections to both camps, the German would place himself squarely at the center of the current treasure hunt and become the concealed hub around which all actions revolved. As he'd done in facilitating past schemes, he would insinuate himself into what others falsely believed was a closed system.

Pocketing the Saudi phone, Diak stood up and took a moment to scan the runway. He could see that someone—probably the dead pilot—had taken pains to demarcate the remote patch of ground. Someone had meticulously gathered stones, painted them white, and lined them up to form a crude runway. White tarps had been stretched out and anchored down at opposite ends of the runway to mark approach and takeoff boundaries. He knelt down again and took up a handful of soil. The ground seemed to be composed of ancient volcanic dust, hard packed over the centuries and sanded smooth by wind erosion, creating an almost perfect surface for an ad hoc airfield. All the extra preparations—the tarps and white rocks—had been added to facilitate takeoffs and landings. Providing a pilot knew where to look, these artificial additions would be visible from the air, even at night. But this isolated plateau had been carefully chosen and, lying as it did between a pair of featureless gray hills, it was unlikely to be noticed by other passing flyers. Even with the jet sitting on this improvised landing strip, the place would be hard to spot and, once the jet was gone, the site would be nearly invisible. It might be a risk, but he'd leave the markers in place in case he needed to return here.

Diak took a moment to consider the length of the runway. It was a short field and he imagined the pilot must have practiced taking off and landing here in the daylight in order to manage the task at night. He himself had no time to practice and no luxury of waiting for dawn. He'd missed the professor and must press on, even though the prognosis for a successful pursuit was doubtful.

The facts were bleak.

Thanks to the pilot's failure to report the professor's sudden departure, Clark was gone, probably driving north. Diak had come too late to catch the elusive man at the airfield and there was little hope of following him in the trackless expanses of northern Arizona. The German's only option was to get ahead of the wandering professor—far enough ahead that he could wait for Clark's next move; locate the girl who was apparently assisting him; or do both. To this end he'd abandon his earth-bound sedan and commandeer the jet.

He might fly back later to retrieve the sedan or have one of his contractors pick it up. Its fate was inconsequential. Like the pilot, the vehicle was expendable. If necessary, he'd submit the sedan to the elements. The plates and registration were phony, so whoever found the vehicle—if indeed it was ever found—would be unable to connect it to the German or anyone in his organization. Diak would leave the car behind and the unlucky pilot too, but not the sedan's cargo.

Recognizing that he needed to be on his way, the German hurried back to his vehicle and gathered his supplies. Returning to the jet, he quickly inspected the aircraft's cargo areas and, finding both the main and forward holds empty, stowed his gear inside. Then he secured the outer cargo hatches and took one final look around the airstrip.

Beneath the full moon, the pilot's body was reduced to a dim lump—a featureless wrinkle in an immense sweep of primitive topography, a fragile human shell, impermanent, small, and already cold. Ignoring the corpse, the German passed beneath the wings and stood at the base of the jet's exterior staircase taking a moment, before he ascended, to drink in the absolute silence of the remote plateau.

This vast and sweeping America, he thought, *such a country!*

Once inside the jet, he toggled a switch to retract the stairs, which he locked in place. Sealing the exit door, he assured that nothing was out of place by inspecting the passenger compartment where, in flight, even an unsecured ceramic cup could be a hazard. Then he made his way to the cockpit, strapped himself in, started the turbines spinning, and ignited the engines. Diak hadn't flown in years, but he felt comfortable with the high-tech layout. Everything was familiar and the enhanced instrumentation held no challenge. He turned the jet and pointed it toward the far end of the strip. Eyeballing the distance, he decided to trust that it encompassed the 3,000-plus feet needed for a successful take-off. He throttled-up and was in the air in seconds.

It was a sweet ride.

The Saudis hadn't skimped in chartering this Cessna Citation Mustang. Diak had read a technical article expounding the virtues of the sleek aircraft and he knew it to be a multi-million-dollar machine with a reputation as a versatile micro-jet. It was not only swift, he recalled, but also extremely light-weight, a characteristic that allowed it to access smaller and more primitive airfields.

Aloft in the clear night air, Diak could see the Page tower lights in the distance. The German was reasonably certain that the dead pilot would not have filed a flight plan for the Mustang. But, just in case, he would avoid complications by flying low until he was clear of the airport terminal. No sense attracting attention by violating the small airfield's altitude restriction. He passed the Page perimeter marker and continued his conscious effort to appear conventional as he steadily climbed to 8,200 feet and settled into the aerial vector reserved for light civilian aircraft. On radar, with his transponder activated, the jet would be an ordinary blip, moving predictably through the night sky, displaying no fancy maneuvers or aerial acrobatics to raise alarms. His trajectory, his speed, and his altitude would appear unremarkable, just an ordinary commuter aircraft, cruising safely at less than 300 knots and adhering to his vector. For all anyone knew, or cared, the Mustang would seem to be a small corporate jet, transporting ordinary passengers to an ordinary business meeting.

It was a clear night, so there was no need to rely on instrumentation as he winged northward. Visual flight rules applied, and this was yet another reason that the jet was unlikely to be noticed. Even if somebody happened to be awake at one of the sleepy spots he overflew, chances were no one would pay him the slightest attention, let alone hassle him about a missing and completely voluntary flight plan.

Diak studied the landscape which stretched out before him. In the vivid light of the full moon, ground features were discernible. Far below he could distinguish the gleaming outline of Lake Powell. As he passed overhead, the sprawling reservoir seemed to slide beneath the speeding jet, like a luminous branching tree, its countless side canyons radiating from the main channel like glistening twigs searching a dark sky. The vivid scene reminded him how much he loved flying.

For a time, the German followed the serpentine lake until it narrowed and then disappeared entirely in the primitive topography. After that, he flew for miles with nothing visible below and only the stars and moon above. The digital cockpit clock showed 0315 hours—3:15 a.m. Where would he be when the sun set on this busy day?

Time would tell.

For the present there was still much to be done. When he was clear of eavesdropping towers, he used his radio to relay a coded message intended for his contractor in Grand Junction.

"Repeat message, over," Diak instructed the Salt Lake dispatcher.

"Mother flies the prison road and rolls with number four, over," repeated the dispatcher in a dubious tone.

"Send it just like that please, over."

"Your nickel," said the dispatcher. "Out."

"Out," said Diak.

As instructed, the oblivious dispatcher passed the message on to Conroy14, Diak's efficient contractor who served the German's interests in the Colorado Grand Valley and the eastern fringes of Utah. Far away in Grand Junction, Conroy14 was awakened by his cell phone which chimed to alert him of an important text message.

Conroy14 had been employed for two years, living in the western Colorado city of Grand Junction, and providing logistical support for what he believed was a company of wildcat energy prospectors. A veteran of the region's oil shale boom and bust, no one had to remind Conroy14 of the need for codes and secrecy. In his time with the company, he hadn't asked a single unprompted question, nor had he blinked at being asked to be on-call at all hours to transport vehicles or cargo or people to and from a variety of assigned coordinates. Complying with this early morning request would be no exception.

In possession of the German's message, Conroy14 put the coffee on, yawned broadly, and sat down in his underwear to pull up the 'Mother' file on his computer. He typed in 'flies the prison road,' and was redirected to a detailed map of Colorado Highway 50. A highlighted arrow pointed to an obscure airfield situated in a lonely spot between the tiny town of White-water and the larger municipality of Delta City. The highway ran roughly south, connecting the metropolis of Grand Junction to the two smaller communities. The isolated four-lane traversed mostly desolate country and passed close to the Delta Correctional Center—which accounted for its code name.

There's your prison road, Conroy14 confirmed to himself.

The location was clear, as was the need. Someone important would be arriving early at the rural airfield and, once on the ground, they would need transport. The latter part of the message contained the code which told Conroy14 what to deliver. He didn't know or care to know why someone would be flying in the dark, or who was coming, and there was never any question of when. Every request from his well-paying clients came with an explicitly implied ASAP. The only question was the precise nature of the item to be delivered.

'Rolls with number four,' the message said—a code which called for a specific vehicle.

Conroy14 stood up, unlocked his key cabinet, searched for R-4, and was only mildly surprised to see the key-fob for a brand-new Toyota 4Runner hanging there. This was great because, ever since it had become part of the stable of vehicles he was charged with managing, he'd been longing to fire up the fine-looking heavy-duty camo-colored beast of an SUV.

Clearly understanding his assignment, Conroy14 put on his cargo pants and boots and shoulder holster, then added a sweater, jacket, and ball cap. He glanced at the clock, called to wake up his wingman, gave the cursing sleepyhead directions, and headed for the company garage. The obedient contractor would rush the Toyota down to the airfield right away and make certain the runway boundaries and the threshold and run-out points were illuminated. Then he'd walk away and wait as long as necessary beside the isolated highway for the wingman to show with his ride back. He wouldn't greet the arriving individual. That was never part of the deal. He just delivered the rides. Sometimes he'd get the vehicle back, sometimes not. In any event, it would be chilly out there among the lonely dirt hills which paralleled the pavement, but Conroy14 was sure to earn a generous fee for this little shuttle service, so he was more than willing to wait.

Meanwhile, convinced that his instructions would be carried out by the time he landed, the German consulted his charts and heading. Then he double-checked his speed. It was roughly 300 nautical miles from Page, Arizona, to Delta City, Colorado. If he pushed his speed to the max, it would take less than an hour to reach his destination, but he wanted to conserve fuel and he needed sleep, so he throttled back, put the jet on auto, and settled in. He was tired. He would close his eyes at least.

Chapter 41

The jet hummed smoothly northward through the early morning hours of July 15, encasing Diak in a cocoon of ambient noise. Gliding through the predawn darkness, he kept his eyes closed while images of the past flickered in his pacified mind.

For nearly two years, Diak had been aware that Dr. C. Arnold Clark, professor of archaeology at The University of Arizona, had been striving to market a rare treasure of some kind. The professor's inquiries on the dark web had caught the German's attention. Although Diak was not at first quite certain what the professor was peddling, he'd nevertheless posed as a customer and submitted a monetary bid. For his trouble, he'd received an insulting reply. The German had been on the point of moving on to a more profitable project until he detected that his frequent competitors, and occasionally reluctant allies, the Scarlet Brotherhood, had entered the contest with a multi-million-dollar offer. With millions on the table, Diak's interest was instantly rekindled and he'd mobilized his network of contractors to watch and wait while he himself hatched a scheme to hijack the enterprise, whatever it might prove to be.

Diak continued to spy on the professor and, for a time, the scheme seemed to lose traction. Clark had demanded a down payment and the Russians were balking. Fearful that his opportunity to steal the treasure was slipping away, the German contacted the Brotherhood and offered to broker a compromise. He'd nearly succeeded in convincing the Russians to pay a few hundred-thousand up front when—to his complete surprise—Clark cajoled the Brotherhood into forking over the entire $2 million. It was at that point that Diak presumed Clark wouldn't live to see another sunrise.

But Clark wasn't murdered, at least not yet, and then, a week ago, Diak's watchers reported a break in the professor's routine. In the afternoon, instead of catching a taxi to take him home, as was his custom, the professor remained on campus, presumably working late. Then Clark walked across campus to the student union and sat at a seemingly random table with three young people. There was no conversation, but the professor shared an extended side-long glance with the young man sitting diagonally from him. Moments later, the two of them got up in sequence and followed one another to the tray return. While waiting in line, the professor and the young man were observed exchanging envelopes. When the two left the student commons and headed in opposite directions, the watcher assigned to the professor was faced with a dilemma. It could mean the watcher's job to leave the professor unobserved and it would go equally hard on him to let the young man disappear.

The watcher had taken a gamble and followed the younger subject and he chose correctly.

The German remembered how nervous the contractor had sounded when he telephoned to account for his actions. The anxiety was evident in the underling's quavering voice. Diak kept his own voice patient and even. He seldom encouraged initiative in his contractors, but he had to admire the decisive nature of this watcher's decisions and he said so.

"I've read your statement," said Diak. "Now tell me—in your own words—what happened."

The watcher, whose contractor designation was Vincent23, reported that he'd left the professor and followed the young man until he observed his new target claiming a vehicle from a campus parking structure. Then he'd tailed the subject by car to the South Nogales Highway. For a moment, Vincent23 had believed that the target, who appeared to be Hispanic, was heading for Mexico and so he'd called in a request for assistance at the border. But he'd rescinded that request moments later when the old Ford pickup he was following changed directions and headed toward the Tucson International Airport. The truck skirted the main airfield, turned at Aero Park Boulevard, and entered the parking lot of the Flight Learning Center. The young man parked and went inside. Vincent23 also stopped. Then, after waiting to make certain he was unobserved, the contractor got out and inspected the truck. Vincent23 had used his cell phone camera to capture the license plate and four stickers on the front windshield. The stickers included a UA student parking pass, a downtown Tucson parking sticker, a Cactus League baseball parking medallion, and, most importantly, a bright red and yellow decal allowing the driver access to a secure parking area—a specialized lot reserved for a local commercial aircraft group known as Bombsight Services.

Vincent23's suspicions had been aroused and so, acting on yet another hunch, the curious contractor walked to the far edge of the learning center parking lot and stood behind the broad trunk of a shading sycamore. From this concealed position, he looked out across a desolate stretch of desert tundra toward a cluster of buildings that lay beyond. In the distance he could see the hangars and tarmac of Bombsight's commercial complex.

The contractor had waited there for fifteen minutes as the cicada bugs began to sing in the branches above him. When dusk arrived, Vincent23 saw what he was hoping for. A side door opened, and his young man emerged from the learning center. The subject stood motionless for a moment, then quickly sidled along the building to a corner, where he stopped and glanced left and right. Abandoning the learning center, the young man walked briskly across the open ground. Each step dislodged a russet cloud of fine desert dust as the honey-colored light of the slanting sun marked his path toward the distant Bombsight complex.

"It was a dang good cover," Vincent23 had recorded in his written statement. "This boy, he parks at the learning center in case he's followed and—while his tail searches inside—the quarry beats it out another door and scurries, quick as a bunny, to his real destination."

Asked what had made him decide to watch outside rather than going in, Vincent23 explained that the truck's conspicuous stickers were the catalyst.

"Appeared to me that this hombre has got no connection to the trainin' center—fact is it was the one place he don't have no parkin' decal for. And, from all his stickers, seems to me he's got a hard-on for handy parkin'. Seems like a case of all hat and no cattle. Why display all them stickers then leave his truck somewheres he's got no sticker for and walk a country-mile to a lot where he does? Why hike all that way around to risk a parkin' ticket?"

The German smiled as he listened to Vincent23's drawl. When the Texan rang off, Diak immediately phoned the contractor's supervisor with instructions to continue shadowing the young man. Vincent23 was thorough and additional reports began flowing in. The new target turned out to be Jesus Santo, a commercial shuttle pilot who ferried aircraft of the rich and famous from place-to-place. He was a journeyman flyer whose fortunes had taken an abrupt turn for the better. Overnight, Santo had blossomed from a perennially underemployed twenty-something to a well-heeled man about town. In a matter of days, gone was his old red Ford pickup, the shoddy vehicle that Vincent23 had tailed to the Tucson airport. In its place was a shiny new Aston Martin which had no parking stickers to mar the fine lines of the luxury vehicle's very sleek and very proper British windshield.

The reports were so compelling that the German left his Flagstaff headquarters to come and see for himself. On the day the German had arrived in Tucson to inspect the pilot's new wheels, Diak waited until midnight and then he drove to the learning center lot. He telephoned Vincent23 to thank him again for his excellent surveillance work and the eager contractor had wanted to join his boss, but Diak insisted on continuing alone.

"Nothing personal," he assured the disappointed contractor.

"Understood," was the expected reply.

Diak was reinforcing, and Vincent23 was acknowledging, the German's legendary obsession with anonymity. The policy was strictly enforced. The fewer people who saw the distinctive face of their mysterious leader, the better.

After ending his conversation with Vincent23, Diak remained in the parking lot, taking a moment to examine the young man's new convertible. Since coming under Vincent23's scrutiny, Santo had continued his practice of parking off-site and walking across the desert to reach the Bombsight

property. Vincent23's inquiries had revealed that the young pilot was training on a new jet that evening and was, at the moment, far from Tucson, flying
night maneuvers.

It was late and there were no other cars in the learning center lot and no
lights in the building. A gentle Arizona rain was falling, and the car's lustrous
silver finish was protected by a custom-fitting car cover. Diak lifted the cover
and ducked underneath. The convertible's hardtop was in place, but he expertly jimmied the door lock. A rapid search of the Aston Martin's glovebox revealed a nest of parking violations along with a cluster of individually
packaged condoms and a fistful of upscale clothing receipts. The lack of current parking stickers and his accumulation of unpaid tickets suggested that
young Santo could no longer be bothered to park by the rules. The condoms
and clothing spoke for themselves. In short order, a young law-abiding mini-
mum-wage earner had been transformed into a fearless scofflaw and budding
libertine who was taking Tucson by storm with a consumptive and conspicuous spending spree.

Faced with these dramatic changes in Santo's behavior, the German had
three questions. *Where did the money come from? What was the young scamp
being paid for? And what else could be bought?*

To complement Vincent23's insightful field work, the German left the
desert behind and drove back to Flagstaff where he began an online search of
Santo's finances. It was an effort which proved to be no challenge. Like many
of his millennial generation, the young pilot was not only obsessed with technology but also criminally careless with his passwords. As a result, it took
less than twenty minutes to access the target's bank accounts and credit card
record. His $3,500 American Express debt had been recently paid in full. As
for the source of those funds, his savings remained at the five-dollar minimum, but his checking account had recently increased by $63,000—a verita-
ble fortune for a lad of twenty-five.

The total amount was less significant than how it had been accumulated.
Any deposit over 10k would require the credit union to notify the Internal
Revenue Service. Involving the IRS would be the last thing an anonymous
funding source would desire. If, as Diak suspected, the money was dirty, it

had doubtless been deposited in incremental stages, with no one deposit exceeding the $10,000 threshold. On his first pass, the German could only view the most recent transactions and ending balances, but he did a quick calculation and went looking for figures that matched his suspicions. Pinpointing the source of the pilot's bonanza had taken another day of sleuthing. The German labored online, relentlessly bushwhacking through a labyrinth of fund manipulations and tracing along a twisting trail of indirect transactions. Eventually he'd identified seven separate $9,500 cash transfers, launched from a pair of offshore banks, and steered circuitously into Santo's credit union account. Diak smiled contentedly. Not for nothing had he earned the appellation, 'Detective.'

Continuing to monitor the pilot's account, he observed that, the instant the money arrived, the young man began spending it. Marveling at the pilot's behavior, Diak whistled through his teeth. Impressed by the amount of the sudden windfall, he was even more amazed to see that the young cavalier only took a few days to burn through half of it. Anxious to see what his contractor would make of the source of the pilot's sudden income, he picked up the phone and shared his findings with his newly minted protégée.

"Jersey boys," Vincent23 had guessed.

The German had smiled approvingly at his young Texan's insight. "Yes, the Channel Islands," Diak confirmed. "As we both know, the Isles of Guernsey and Jersey are the favored banking repositories of clandestine Saudi Arabian funds. Something is definitely in the wind if both the Russians and the Saudis are involved and substantial sums are on the table. What is your conclusion?"

Vincent23 had apparently been giving the matter considerable thought because his response was instantaneous and succinct. "Treasure," Vincent23 said.

"Indeed," said the German. "Our slippery professor obviously has something of considerable value. Something he is shopping to some rather well-heeled and extremely dangerous people. Perhaps we should lend a hand."

Not wishing to approach the pilot in person, the German had dictated the contents of a note which Vincent23 delivered to the young man. The note promised a generous payment for discreet information and invited the pilot to a secluded place to receive the money and instructions. The possibility of more cash had apparently been irresistible, and the naïve pilot had come, answered several questions, and received instructions. The transaction had lasted less than twenty minutes, and it seemed to be profitable for all concerned. With the pilot on his payroll, the German had conferred once again with his Tucson contractor.

"Now that we comprehend the pilot's role, I will look deeper into the professor's online activities in order to discover the nature of this treasure he is so eager to sell," the German told Vincent23. "And you, my efficient watcher, will remain in Tucson and take immediate charge of the physical surveillance of Dr. Clark and his pilot. I will inform the others so there will be no question of your authority. Consider this a well-earned field promotion which will require you to quickly become an expert in all things Clark and Santo."

"Yes, sir," said Vincent23.

"For certain, I want you to get up to speed on the professor. We have gathered nearly two years of intelligence on Dr. Clark and I want you to carefully reexamine every scrap of it."

"What am I lookin' for?" Vincent23 asked.

"Wrinkles," said the German. "And I have every confidence that you will know them when you see them."

Chapter 42

Early on the morning of July 15, while Clark was organizing his escape, and several hours before Anne Scriptor would be wrestling with her muddy Colorado hill, Vincent23 abruptly sat up in bed in Tucson and rubbed his eyes. Moving haphazardly before he was fully awake, he fumbled in the dark until he located his reading glasses on the bedside table. He threaded the glasses onto his ears and glanced at the clock. It was just past midnight. He stood unsteadily up, aimed his chilled feet into his slippers, and turned on a light.

The nervous contractor stumbled to his work desk and consulted the master calendar he'd devised. It took a moment for his sleepy vision to clear. Vincent23 had been studying background materials on Dr. C. Arnold Clark for two days straight and recording his observations on large sheets of butcher paper which covered one wall of his home office. After nearly two years of surveillance, there was much to review, and the field agents hadn't made things easy for him. The other watchers had reluctantly surrendered their logbooks and Vincent23 knew what they were saying behind his back. They were grumbling that a young and relatively inexperienced Texas-transplant had somehow leapfrogged over more senior contractors to reach a coveted management position in the German's organization.

"What the hell?" became the question of the day and "why?" was running a close second.

Why was the Tucson team—an uneasy combination of German and American contractors—wasting so much time monitoring the mundane activities of an obscure university professor? Why were so many contractors stuck in the desert shadowing an unremarkable man whose actions never varied? Why had this upstart Texan been assigned to supervise their efforts, including the confiscation and re-reading of their notes? Why did the boss care? Why did Vincent23 care?

Vincent23 didn't know the answer to every question posed by this assignment, but he knew the answer to the last one. Vincent23 cared because the boss cared, end of story.

So, the diligent contractor had spent nearly forty hours reexamining everything the surveillance teams had compiled on Dr. Clark. He'd worked for long stretches with only a smattering of sleep and had soon discovered that the grumbling field agents were right about one thing. Taken together, the reports were undeniably the most mind-numbing chronicles of redundancy he'd ever encountered. Which was saying a mouthful, because last year he'd worked as a classroom aide in West Texas. Fighting a losing battle in his efforts to teach English composition to rural high school freshmen, he'd slogged through tepid attempts at prose which left much to be desired.

Hormones with legs, his supervising teacher had called them. *If only these lusty teens could harness their adolescent libidos and channel all that passion onto the written page.*

Reading reams of repetitive reports on Dr. Clark's boring activities had dredged up unhappy memories of Vincent23's days as an under-paid aide to a high school English teacher. And yet—just as he'd done in his previous job of reading a seemingly never-ending cascade of indifferent freshman essays—Vincent23 had waded through the Clark dossier. He'd read the thing from cover-to-cover until he reached the most recent entry, a field report submitted by a surveillance team assigned to The University of Arizona campus. Dated July 14—less than twenty-four hours ago—it described the professor's well-established procedure of dispatching a graduate assistant to implement the term's geocaching exercise. The sleepy contractor had reviewed the tedious report through drooping eyelids. Then, as his hall clock struck eleven, he'd called it a night. He'd been instructed to report his findings to the Ger-man in a morning conference call and he wanted to be sufficiently rested to make an intelligent, if inconclusive, statement.

"No wrinkles," was what he planned to say.

Vincent23 had gone to bed with the details of Dr. Clark's recent campus activity buzzing in his head and a faint notion that he'd somehow missed something. He'd fallen asleep vowing to reexamine the material with fresh eyes first thing in the morning but without a firm idea of what was troubling him.

Only later did he awaken with a sense of urgency.

Stumbling to his desk, he squirmed in his chair, half hoping to dismiss his fears, but a few moments spent reviewing his notes and he was certain of his mistake. His research had been diligent and yet he'd failed.

"Dad gum it!" He shouted as he struggled to his feet, rushed to the wall, and scanned his calendar entries. Breathless, he searched for the correspond-ing weeks of each prior term: *Summer Session 2016...Fall Semester 2016... Spring Semester 2017...Summer 2017...Fall 2017...Spring 2018...*

It was just as he feared.

He turned from the wall, collapsed back into his desk chair, and skimmed rapidly through yesterday's campus logbook until he found what he was look-ing for. It was a brief entry of two succinct lines which contained a single detail that the campus surveillance team had failed to highlight. It was, to put it mildly, a wrinkle—an anomaly that distinguished this session's geo-caching assignment from all others the watchers had observed. Simply put, the team had erred in failing to attach significance to the fact that Dr. Clark was dispatching cache boxes which were *padlocked*. The boxes had never be-fore been locked, and yet the observers did not stress this variance. Their oversight was careless, but Vincent23 blamed himself as well. The field re-ports he'd been reviewing had grown so banal and predictable that he'd fallen into the habit of failing to read them closely. Consequently, he'd missed the irregularity and a fitful hour had passed before the dreaming contractor was struck with the significance of the padlocks.

"Shoot," he sassed himself for his blunder. "I ought to have the hound knocked out of me."

Wide awake now and intent on redeeming himself, the flummoxed Texan was about to pick up the telephone to alert his boss to this wrinkle when a call came in on his emergency line reporting the disappearance of Dr. Clark.

It was 12:30 in the morning.

Probably too late, he thought, *but pretty soon it'll be too late to not call.* He waited a heartbeat and then punched in the number.

"I need Diak Hodell—yes, now! Tell him it's real urgent," said Vincent23—fully aware that he was not only waking the boss, but also violating protocol by calling direct and using the German's full name. But his information couldn't wait for a noon conference call, so he decided to take the initiative and bypass the standard procedure of leaving a coded message. Regardless of the consequences, the diligent contractor had made his decision. He'd called Flagstaff, contacted the Hotel Monte Vista directly, and now he must await the verdict.

"You did right," Diak assured him. "I will take it from here."

"I'm guessin' the treasure and both targets is pretty much long gone," Vincent23 sighed, explaining that he'd been focusing so diligently on the professor that he'd neglected to adequately shadow the pilot.

"Not to worry," said Diak. "We might have hoped for more notice, but the fault lies with the pilot who failed to honor our agreement. Still, I know where they are bound and, with luck, I will catch them. If not, I will find the girl. Now read me again the description of the toolboxes and the locks and do it quickly!"

Armed with Vincent23's descriptions, the German hastily telephoned the cross-town Walmart and ordered a toolbox and padlock.

"Gray—not red—not black," he repeated. "Do you understand me?"

"Yes, sir," the nervous clerk squeaked. "And the padlock?"

"Anything with a key—something cheap," Diak instructed. "I'll be at customer service to pick everything up in fifteen minutes and my purchases had better be ready or your manager will hear from me."

"Yes, sir. Absolutely I..."

Diak ended the call and reached for his trousers.

Chapter 43

Popping his cell phone into a zippered pants pocket, the German continued dressing and let his mind churn as he tried once again to get inside the professor's head. Dr. Clark was romancing two dangerous customers, but he had only one artifact to sell. By closely monitoring the professor, Diak had learned that the merchandise in question was a rare Clovis point. One Clovis, two buyers, it was a dilemma which the German firmly believed Clark intended to resolve by selling the artifact to the Russians, while stiffing the Saudis.

So, where exactly was this precious Clovis?

Vincent23's report of locked toolboxes held the answer. The minute he learned of that wrinkle, Diak understood that the Clovis had already been smuggled out of Tucson. Clark had used the geocaching exercise as a cover to safeguard the treasure. The conniving professor had made his move long before the incident at the ranch house and before being whisked away by the Saudi's pilot. The German was convinced that the smuggled artifact now lay securely hidden somewhere in Colorado. It was inconvenient that Clark himself had vanished, but Diak was on the scent and—with good fortune—he'd yet corral the illusive man. Gathering up essential supplies, Diak took a hasty inventory and headed for the door. Rushing down the carpeted hallway, he summoned the hotel's ancient elevator. When, precious seconds later, the sluggish car failed to arrive, he shouldered through the fire door and rushed down three flights of winding stairs, his mind continuing to roil.

Think, he commanded himself. *What is Clark up to? Why does he feel the need to hide the Clovis and why is he running now?*

Only one answer made sense. Clearly the calculating professor was playing both ends against the middle. Without tipping off either buyer, Clark must have somehow convinced both the Saudis and the Russians that they alone were in the running to purchase the artifact. He was trying to keep both factions off balance—and managing to stay alive in the process—by making certain that neither buyer could put the corporeal body of C. Arnold Clark and the Clovis together.

How had he accomplished this maneuver with my surveillance teams watching his every move and I myself monitoring the man's email and especially his smartphone?

"The gap," he said aloud. "The damnable gap!"

For too long, access to Clark's smartphone had brought Diak little comfort, because the unpredictable man had made little use of the device. The last intercepted communication was the professor's daredevil conversation with the Russians, a ploy which alerted the German to Clark's down payment demand. Then the link had dried up. After the down payment call, the only action on Clark's smartphone had been two incoming calls, probably from the girl. But both had gone to voicemail and, owing to a limitation of his phone tap, Diak could only have monitored the messages if Clark had picked up on his end, which he did not.

Has Clark discovered that his smartphone is compromised?

Clark's failure to use his device had created a gap in Diak's surveillance and it must have been during this lapse that the fickle man concocted, and somehow communicated, an amended scheme. Clark had used his smartphone to demand the down payment, then seemed to deliberately avoid using the device. Days passed, then came the first unheard voicemail, immediately after which the German's man had spotted a diminutive visitor arriving at the conniving professor's ranch house. The watcher had recorded the visitor's arrival and the police had burst onto the scene before Diak's man could make any sense of the encounter.

Reaching the bottom landing, the German forced open the ground-level exit door, sounding an alarm as he stumbled out into the predawn darkness. With no traffic to impede his way, Diak sprinted across North San Francisco Street, where he triggered a second alarm on the security door leading to Flagstaff's subterranean parking structure. As he rushed downward, his footfalls echoed in the concrete stairwell, while his thinking percolated with each descending step.

Probably Clark's midnight visitor had been the man whom the Brotherhood insisted on sending for a second look at the Clovis. Diak had been listening when the frustrated Russians set that condition, so he'd learned the man was coming, but not the timing of the so-called inspection.

"Inspection," he scoffed aloud.

Knowing the Brotherhood, the German concluded that any Russian agent dispatched this late in the game was being sent to intimidate Clark—probably to obtain the artifact and kill the troublesome professor. It's what Diak would have done and it was something a brutal buyer might be expected to do when a potential seller was acting erratically. All things being equal, trying to extort two million dollars from an army of Russian mobsters was—to put it mildly—a risky venture. Clark was lucky to be alive. Hypothetically, during the time when Diak was out of the communication loop, the Brotherhood might well have killed the professor, snatched up the Clovis, and completely derailed the German's plan to hijack the transaction.

And yet, somehow, Clark had managed to turn the tables on his visitor, survive the confrontation, flee to meet the pilot, and make good his escape. But 'escape' wasn't the right word because, although Diak believed that Clark planned to leave the country eventually, he suspected the professor wasn't quite ready to go just yet. By accepting the Saudi's help in the form of their on-call jet, he was furthering the Russian transaction while also keeping the Arabs on the hook. What cock-and-bull story he'd told the Saudis to convince them to cooperate was anyone's guess, but clearly the professor had his own agenda.

Think, Diak repeated his self-admonition.

With the Clovis somewhere in Colorado, Clark's first priority would be to retrieve the smuggled artifact. Then he'd tell the Russians where to look and collect the balance of his money. How would he pull off that miracle with the Saudis watching his every move? The answer had to be that they weren't watching. Somehow Clark had charmed or bullied the Arabs into believing he could be trusted to honor their agreement. As far as the Saudis knew, Clark was being ferried north to pick up the Clovis which he was hiding from the Russians and which he promised to bring back to the waiting pilot and jet. The Arabian fools must still believe their wandering professor would return, climb aboard the jet, and bring the treasure to them.

"Good luck with that," Diak said aloud as he reached the bottom of the stairwell, pushed through the final door, and rushed across the concrete parking surface. Sprinting to his sedan, he fired it up. He roared up the ramp, squealing tires as he zigzagged through the tight corners of the parking structure. Reaching the top, he gesticulated angrily at the hapless night-guard who struggled to raise the exit bar just ahead of the speeding car.

"Next time," he shouted as he sped past and glared at the guard, "when you hear me coming, this gate had better be open!"

"Yes, sir," the guard yelled, "I..." But his explanation, no matter how valid it might have been, was lost to Diak as he wheeled into San Francisco Street, skidded onto Milton Road, and pushed through successive amber lights that conspired to slow his progress to Walmart. As he drove, he used voice commands to activate his GPS navigator, repeating the northern Arizona coordinates twice as he barked impatiently at the dilatory device. Reaching the 24-hour store, he rocketed through the deserted parking lot, dashed in and out, and was back behind the wheel in less than eleven minutes.

Hurtling through town, he pressed the accelerator and activated the blue strobe lights mounted on his dashboard as he sped toward Highway 89. The roadways were deserted, and it seemed unlikely that anyone would challenge his hard-charging sedan. Meanwhile, any driver he overtook would feel pressured to pull over and give him room. As for law enforcement, he'd have to risk attracting attention, believing he could outrun pursuit as needed.

He had no choice.

He had to master 130 miles of pavement in record time. Cursing the unreliable pilot, Diak sighed and settled in for the race of his life, thankful, at least, to know his destination. Having been lavishly bribed, the pilot had readily revealed the location of the primitive airstrip, pinpointing the spot where he was obligated to deliver the professor at some future, unknown date. But the pilot was also under orders to alert Diak's network when the journey commenced. The pilot had failed to apprise his benefactors of Clark's departure and Diak could only hope that the young traitor hadn't lied about the location of the airstrip. Faced with the pilot's duplicity, the German's only choice was to reach Page as soon as humanly possible and to do so he needed speed—only speed could help him now.

As he rushed north, Diak sought to calm his anger by resuming his thoughts about Clark and his buyers. Thinking it over, the German soon convinced himself that he'd encounter no Saudis on this particular treasure hunt. The squeamish Arabs were attempting to manage their vision of the Clovis transaction from afar, keeping their hands clean, using surrogates like their young pilot. The Russians, on the other hand, were in for a penny and in for a pound (if he recalled the idiom correctly) and liable to be prowling around and might get in the way. Diak decided he would burn that bridge when he came to it. Clark had a jet at his disposal and a head start, but the German knew where the pilot was headed, and he might just overtake the pair in time. With luck, he'd intercept the professor at Page and force the troublesome man to reveal the treasure's location.

Without slowing his pace, the German cradled his cell phone in the sedan's dashboard caddy. Using voice commands, he activated his tracking system and opened a connection. If Clark used his smartphone, Diak would be listening. Cell service would probably be spotty as he traveled across the isolated Navajo Reservation, but the signal would be strong close to Page when he needed it most. He was relying on the smartphone and betting that, sooner rather than later, Clark would be calling the Russians to divulge the location of the Clovis. In Diak's estimation, Clark would give the Russians first crack at the treasure. What he planned to tell the Saudis was anyone's guess. Double-crossing the Arabs would be a challenge and dangerous.

Almost as risky as lying to the Russians, but after all, someone was going to get screwed because there was only one...

"Ach," Diak exclaimed aloud—why hadn't he considered this before?

The professor was a talented archaeologist and perfectly capable of creating a *duplicate artifact*—one unlikely to fool an expert but passable enough to deceive the average messenger boy. Maybe Clark planned to collect from both of his customers. If so, which buyer was going to get the genuine Clovis and which one would be stuck with the worthless duplicate? Diak thought about that dilemma for a moment and then decided it was Clark's problem to appease his dangerous buyers. Whatever Clark did, the German would find a way to possess the genuine merchandise.

"Ich hoffe es ist so," he said aloud, hoping it was so.

And yet, as Diak roared through the night, his confidence wavered. The further he penetrated into the darkness, the less certain seemed the prospect of gaining the treasure. With Clark on the run, the German's ability to learn the whereabouts of the genuine Clovis was complicated. Finding the thing was like trying to spot a pea in a classic gypsy shell game. As a boy he'd run the deliciously efficient scam countless times when he and his mates hustled gullible gamblers in the mean streets of East Berlin. Clark's scheme was a parallel venture although, instead of three walnut shells and a single pea, Clark's game was shuffling a dozen toolboxes. Any of the boxes might contain a false Clovis and one undoubtedly held the genuine treasure.

Clark was a trickster, and yet the professor was new to the world of espionage, and—moreover—he was an American consumer. Given these realities, chances were good that Clark would convey the genuine Clovis to the Russians—feeling obligated to sell it to the buyer from which he'd received the down payment. The professor might distrust the Russians, but the man's consumer mentality would betray him. 'Half-down, half on delivery,' that was a compact which the average American would be likely to honor.

The Saudis had put up nothing in the way of earnest money. With the Arabs, it would be all or nothing, no down payment, no special arrangements other than an insistence that Clark will hand them the artifact and they will give him the money. Diak tried once again to put himself in the professor's place. Could Clark trust the Saudis to honor such a bargain? And, even if they did, how likely was Clark, a middle-aged overweight scientist, to believe that he'd be content living in exile in an Arab nation?

"Shite!" Diak exclaimed as he gripped the steering wheel.

Without warning, the glimmer of a yellow dog had appeared in the sedan's headlamps and the animal was fortunate to veer away at the last second, because the German had no intention of swerving or braking. He drove on without a second thought for the creature. The Reservation was literally crawling with abandoned canines, skinny and feral mongrels, homeless and pathetic and expendable. Such wandering animals, omnipresent on the Reservation, would be unwelcome in the Kingdom of Saudi Arabia, which forbade the importation of domestic pets, and Clark would likely get similar treatment.

Years ago, Diak had entertained the idea of dealing with the Saudis, but he'd been reluctant to trust them. In the German's experience, the Arabs overdressed for the weather and bowed and smiled with an outstretched hand while concealing a curved blade beneath their copious robes. Of course, Diak also had reasons to distrust the Brotherhood—even hate them—but he doubted if Clark could make the leap from dealing with the pseudo-Western Russians to trusting the exotic Saudis. Clark, he believed, would have made a calculation that Russia was a large country and diverse enough to offer him sanctuary. There were cities on the Black Sea where a man could live in a temperate climate surrounded by semi-familiar art and beauty. Diak himself had his eye on a comfortable villa there.

On the other hand, there were few Edenic paradises in Saudi Arabia, even presuming the Saudis would relocate the professor to their home country. Saudi cities were livable and cosmopolitan enough, if one could tolerate the heat and the pickpockets, but more likely the Arabs would deposit their new fugitive in the remote outback of a contiguous country. Probably Clark would end up in someplace like Yemen, with its vast semi-arid regions, devoid of tall buildings and trees. The Arabs would place Clark somewhere they could keep an eye on him. But, all things considered, Diak was convinced

that Arabia held no appeal for the scheming professor. Clark was manipulating the Saudis, much as he was using Anne Scriptor, to further his plans to sell
the Clovis to the Russians. He'd use others and then, when it was convenient,
abandon them. Driving on, the German wondered for a heartbeat whether
he was projecting too much of his own cynicism onto an evaluation of Clark's
motives and likely behavior.

Think, he again implored himself.

The professor had proven elusive, but Diak was certain that Clark's seemingly erratic behavior wasn't random at all. Instead, he saw Clark's actions
as having settled into a predictable groove, into a broad and steady channel
which would inevitably carry him toward Russia, not Arabia. In any event,
whichever way the professor decided to jump, Diak was determined that
Clark would achieve neither destination. Unfortunately for the fugitive,
the moment Clark called the Russians to reveal the location of the genuine
Clovis, Diak would be listening and poised to steal the treasure.

The German would outmaneuver both the Saudis and the Russians, leaving Clark stranded between two dangerous customers. With Diak in possession of the Clovis, the professor would be unsuccessful in his desire to board a
jet to Moscow or anywhere else. His jilted buyers would suspect the professor
of duplicity and, instead of the money he expected, Clark would receive a
Russian bullet. Either that or the Saudis would learn of his betrayal, then
hunt and kill him. Whatever happened, without the Clovis as a bargaining
chip, Clark would be a dead man. Diak would have the Clovis and Clark
would die—it was that simple.

Once the German possessed the object of everyone's desire, anyone wishing to buy would have to deal with him. Instead of an amateur purveyor of
priceless antiquities, prospective buyers would be faced with a soulless adversary as ruthless as themselves. With Diak in charge, the cost of doing business
in the Clovis trade was about to increase exponentially.

The intermittent flashing of his unofficial blue strobes and the dull glow
of his mounted cell phone combined to bathe the sedan's interior in an eerie

light, casting his face in a ghoulish, pulsating pallor. Taking his eyes off the road for an instant, he glanced at his wavering reflection in the rearview mirror.

"Dem Tod ins Gesicht sehen," he said aloud—*to look death in the face.*

Diak needed the Clovis and the fortune that precious treasure would bring him. He was tired—deathly tired—of staring at his ruined face. He was tired of spasms of pain shooting without mercy through his mangled visage, tired of the cruel numbness in his shriveled loins. He was tired of living in the shadows, tired of the intrigues, tired of the never-ending work.

Since leaving the Brotherhood to strike out on his own, the German had established a freelance extortion and murder-for-hire enterprise and, through it, had amassed a modest fortune. He was far from poor, but he wasn't wealthy. When the money flowed, it was good, but there were always expenses —mostly in the form of equipment and salaries and, of course, he also had to finance inevitable bribes and kickbacks. He lived frugally, but there was never enough money. Maintaining his organization was expensive and the stress of holding the enterprise together was taking its toll. Selling the Clovis would bring him enough to walk away from everything.

With sufficient money, he could retire and fulfill his fondest wishes. With enough money he could bring his face back into the light. Achieving that miracle would be expensive and the best clinics demanded cash up front. With enough money, he could stroll down any street in the world without causing passersby to recoil in horror. With enough money, he would take any path he wished and have any woman he desired, because with enough money even his damaged loins could be restored and, with that repair, his manhood.

Such were the heady dreams that compelled the German onward. Heedless of sharp curves in the narrow two-lane highway, he pressed on the accelerator and rushed headlong toward the salvation he so desperately desired. He would live again. He would love again. He would be whole again, if only he could reach his destination in time.

Chapter 44

Diak didn't catch the professor, of course.

To facilitate sudden departures, his sedan was always packed with traveling clothes, rations, and equipment, including an assortment of weapons and explosives. When he leased his parking space in Flagstaff's premier underground parking garage, he signed a liability contract pledging not to store paint and other flammables in his vehicle. But no one mentioned a grenade launcher, benign packets of C4, various blasting appliances, a bazooka, and other ordnance. So, he was technically in compliance.

Under ordinary circumstances, he'd have fired up his well-stocked vehicle and been on his way in a matter of seconds. But his desperate dash across the Reservation had called for extra supplies. His hurried trip to Flagstaff's all-hours Walmart to pick up a toolbox and padlock had cost him precious minutes. He'd purchased these extras on instinct and, during his drive northward, he'd devoted a portion of his thinking to finalizing a plan to use them. All he knew for certain was that it would involve explosives.

In the end, though he'd driven like a man possessed and traversed the early-morning route in record time, he'd arrived too late to intercept Clark at the Page airstrip. Given his tardiness there'd been no alternative but to kill the pilot, steal the Mustang, fly to Delta City, and find the girl.

As Diak slumbered in the cockpit of the speeding jet, the miles flashed by and his radio was silent for forty minutes before he awoke to the sound of chatter. There was an unmanned beacon below in the dark and a mechanical voice hailed the Mustang as the aircraft soared overhead.

"Dove Creek. 8V6," was all it said, but that was sufficient to confirm that he was dead on course. The German yawned and stretched, seeking to clear the memories which had coursed through his sleeping mind as he resumed control of the aircraft. Moments later, he turned a few degrees northeast and flew on, avoiding not only mountains but also manned towers by flying in between Hopkins Field and Telluride.

At 4 a.m. on July 15, he entered the airspace west of Delta City. He descended and followed the visible sheen of the Gunnison River for a few miles until he spotted runway lights and touched down at West Window Airfield. As he taxied the jet around the asphalt loop, he spotted the Toyota 4Runner he'd requested. Positioned in the short-cropped scrub grass with a line of stubby gray hillocks for a backdrop, the camouflaged Toyota was nearly invisible. The sturdy vehicle was parked right where it should be, in the pit area between two small propeller aircraft, and he made a mental note to add a bonus to Conroy14's usual delivery fee. He guided the jet into the pit and tied it down. It was still dark, but at least one rooster was awake.

"Cock's-crow," he said aloud as he plucked the key-fob off the topside of a rear tire and started the Toyota.

The highway was a stone's throw from the airfield. Within minutes, the German was on Colorado 50 and heading toward Delta City. He'd taken a chance flying this far north. Soon he would learn whether his gamble paid off. He'd roll through town and see if his legendary luck was once again with him.

Chapter 45

As Diak drove southward on Highway 50, a faint sliver of the coming dawn flared into view, igniting the eastern horizon, and framing the dark silhouette of Grand Mesa. The German glanced in that direction, then turned his attention back to the highway ahead. Meeting no other cars on the dark roadway, he grew weary and the isolation seemed to amplify his thoughts as his mind strayed to his checkered past and the ebb and flow of fate.

As a youth, Diak Hodell's fortunes had looked bleak. He was only a boy on the night the Berlin Wall fell, but he was no freer the next day. He was apprenticed then to the Scarlet Brotherhood and his trainers were fond of reminding him that his attachment was a lifetime commitment—a loyalty which transcended changes in the geopolitical landscape. He'd not planned to end up in Berlin, but there he was on account of what had befallen his mother. It was a sad story and one which she'd often told her son at bedtime, sometimes weaving events from her own life into the plots of classic fairytales. After she died and the German grew to manhood, it took him years to separate fact from fiction—perhaps he never did. He could still recall his mother's voice.

"Times were hard during those early days, before your birth, and during the bleak winter of 1945," his mother had told him, her voice rich with articulate diction which reflected her opulent upbringing and belied the reality of their poverty-stricken existence as East German refugees. "My family was trapped in the fighting as Russian troops poured into the Polish countryside. The Nazis were targeted, but many innocents were caught in the crossfire during those last days of the Second World War. In the indiscriminate bombing, my parents and older sisters were killed."

His mother would pause as tears filled her eyes and constricted her voice. Sometimes she could go no further, but ultimately, she managed to convey the entire story. With her family murdered, six-year-old Lavinia, alone and terrified, fled into the forest. She survived there in the company of other orphaned *wolfskinder*. Soon, the so-called wolf children gained an unsavory reputation, some of it deserved, much of it imagined. When the fighting in Europe ended at last, Lavinia was footloose and feral. She found it impossible to assimilate into the hodgepodge of ethnicities that swirled in Poland's postwar cauldron. As a displaced German and aristocratic Gypsy besides, she was out of context and ill-equipped to join any of the disparate political factions whose shifting allegiances vacillated between Lithuanian, Ukrainian, and Polish.

One vivid image of that bleak time of Soviet occupation remained with Lavinia and it was a story she often repeated to Diak, her only son. His mother had just turned eleven and was living with other homeless waifs in a hovel directly across from a train station. She was earning money by operating an illicit gambling pool in the multi-ethnic city. The betting called for wagers to speculate what language the ever-vacillating street signs would display on a given day. The Soviet authorities were not amused, and they placed the girl under surveillance which is how they learned that Lavinia was among a handful of ethnic Germans whom the Communists had yet to expel. That night, the Soviets curtailed her unsanctioned enterprise and threw her into a cattle-car bound for East Germany.

East Berlin was equally inhospitable, and Lavinia was quickly initiated into a street gang that dressed like American teenagers but acted like new-age Nazis. His mother had been vague about the details of her initiation, but Diak later learned from his own experience that the 'ceremony' must have included a brutal gang rape. There was never a father in the picture and considering her variety of attackers, Lavinia could have been impregnated by any one of a dozen virile gang members. She lived with the amorphous gang for years and survived several abortions until one day she refused the procedure.

She was shunned the moment her pregnancy began to show and thus Diak was born in 1984 in an indigent clinic to a 35-year-old unwed mother with few prospects. To survive, she turned to prostitution. While his mother walked the streets at night and slept most of the day, Diak was raised by a variety of surrogates—some indifferent, some cruel—in what passed for a nursery in the sordid second story of an urban brothel.

Despite her nocturnal liaisons and daytime slumbering, Lavinia never failed to say good morning and good night to her son and hold him and tell him she loved him. He remembered his mother as a thin woman. Not pretty, but proud and always very sad. He was five years old when she was murdered. Deprived of his mother's income, the brothel owner turned the boy out, whereupon Diak was soon absorbed by the same neighborhood gang that had deflowered his mother a decade earlier.

He ran with the gang until 1998 when the others began to shave their heads and turned from the practical pursuit of legitimate paying crime to senseless and profitless political violence. It was not that Diak was opposed to violence. Feeling alienated and being poor made him just as angry as the next street urchin. But he had no intention of remaining in poverty, so he immigrated to Russia, took charge of his own destiny, and channeled his anger into making for himself, not merely a living wage, but a luxurious one.

A handsome young man, Diak auditioned for an escort service operated by the Scarlet Brotherhood. Soon he was extracting favors and secrets from rich Communist widows and the neglected wives of Soviet diplomats and, in turn, he began blackmailing a constantly expanding catalog of jilted lovers and cuckold husbands. Ultimately his intrigues led him from the streets back to the brothels and then upward through an ever-improving series of Moscow bed chambers. But his prospects collapsed one crisp autumn evening when he tried to shake down a legendary Russian air force officer. The next morning, the enraged officer sent men to kidnap the would-be blackmailer. The soldiers beat Diak, then stuffed him into a corporal's uniform, and shipped his impertinent ass to the Caucasus.

At eighteen, the Russian forces in Chechnya evaporated and he found himself fighting as a mercenary. Working with a patchwork of official and unofficial forces, he showed a superb talent for clandestine operations and a native aptitude in all things mechanical. Later, when pilots were needed, he was pulled from the streets and sent to flight school. When he escaped the Caucasus at age twenty, the Brotherhood found new uses for him. It was the Brotherhood that launched him into a new, extremely dangerous, but also highly paid profession as assassin and bomb-maker.

His specialty was dispatching targets by rigging time fuses. To perfect his craft, he spent hours designing so-called 'pencil detonators.' The purpose of these ingenious devices was to trigger a bomb blast over a range of precise times, from a fraction of an hour to a full day after activation. His mechanism was a simple copper tube, about the diameter and length of an ordinary pencil, which was inserted into a lump of plastic explosive. The 'pencil' had a glass vial on one end and a percussion cap on the other. In the center was a striker bullet, held in check by a thin wire. When one end of the copper tube was crimped by pliers, the glass vial shattered, setting in motion a process that proceeded over time and step-by-step, like a deadly Rube Goldberg contraption. The shattered vial released a slow dissolving acid which would eventually corrupt the wire. The dissolved wire released the bullet, propelling it the length of the tube to ignite the percussion cap and spark the explosion. The timing depended upon the gauge of wire and the volume and potency of the acid, so the exacting German found it necessary to experiment using these variables.

Diak was never certain who had contaminated his work materials. He only knew that it was not he who had been so careless and that the sabotage had been intentional. Perhaps it was a rival criminal gang, perhaps it was one of his own Scarlet brothers who had grown jealous of his success. Or maybe it was nothing more sinister than an outraged husband seeking revenge. Whatever the cause, there was a catastrophic explosion in the young bomb-maker's tiny laboratory. When Diak came to his senses, he was lying in an East German hospital with half his face a mangled wreck and his loins reduced to a shattered husk.

Someone was going to suffer for this treachery and Diak had no interest in sorting through a pile of disparate theories or grasping at threads to unmask a conspiracy. The Russians were sponsoring him. The Russians were using him. The Russians were responsible for security at his lab. The Russians had not protected him. So, the Russians were to blame, and they would have to pay.

Chapter 46

As Diak drew nearer Delta City in the dissolving darkness, he turned his thoughts from his hatred of the Russians to contemplating their desire for the Clovis. If Dr. C. Arnold Clark was to be believed, the tremendous value of the artifact stemmed from the notion that its existence proved the obscure Solutrean Hypothesis. That ambiguous archaeological theory had drawn the German into Clark's scheme, or rather Diak had been attracted by Clark's belief that the theory could be proven. His own detective work had revealed that the Solutrean Hypothesis was a fanciful mixture of history, scientific speculation, and wishful thinking.

In the 1860s, a French field scientist had dug exploratory trenches near the base of the Rock of Solutre. Soon the soil surrounding the ancient limestone escarpment yielded a treasure trove of artifacts and ancient bones. Working tirelessly, the Frenchman unearthed prolific evidence of prehistoric habitation and his discoveries brought acclaim to the name of Henry de Ferry. The famed geologist, archaeologist, and paleontologist must have been something of a hero to the young Iowa rock-hound who grew up to become C. Arnold Clark, PhD. While monitoring Dr. Clark's dark web activities, Diak noted that the professor cited the long-dead de Ferry numerous times in a glowing abstract which outlined the provenance of the treasure he was peddling.

Diak slowed the Toyota as his headlamps picked out a pair of deer on the shoulder of the highway. He braked to let them cross, then he pulled into a turn-out and left the motor running while he took an unsatisfying leak in a knot of roadside bushes. Threading his zipper home, he heard rather than felt the Saudi cell phone vibrating in his pocket.

"Your whereabouts?" the text message asked.

"Awaiting passenger," Diak typed.

"Understood," was the reply.

I am gratified to know that someone out there thinks he understands, the German thought.

He felt no qualms about deceiving the Saudis, but his declaration that he was awaiting a passenger hadn't been a lie. As needed, the jet would be a handy way to whisk the apprehended professor or the girl or both back to Arizona—along with the treasure, of course. Diak would retrieve the jet eventually. It was much too valuable an asset to leave behind. The jet would be his ticket out of the wild Western Slope of Colorado. Meanwhile, he'd proceed at ground level.

Walking back to his idling vehicle, he could see the lights of Delta City looming in the distance. He yawned and rolled down the window, allowing the brisk night air to wash over him as he continued down the highway.

Stay alert, he told himself as he sought to occupy his fatigued mind by turning his thoughts once again to the Clovis and how he'd first learned of Clark's desire to market the artifact.

The German was a patron of the dark web and his interest was piqued when he noticed that someone had posted a curious advertisement:

Physical proof of Solutrean Hypothesis for sale to the highest bidder.
Opening bid $6(ka x ka). Serious inquiries only.

Clicking on the inquiry link in Clark's ad took a prospective bidder down a meandering cyber rabbit hole. To discourage casual inquiries, the would-be customer was bounced through a myriad of global servers before arriving at an anonymous encrypted email address. It would have taken a diligent and patient searcher to traverse such a tortuous pathway. No ordinary Joe or Jane or Juan or Jules or Jacque would have the chops to do it, but Diak had managed to break through and he knew that certain governments would also have the needed expertise: The United States, of course, along with Great Britain, Russia, Israel, Japan, China, and Saudi Arabia.

Such nationalities might be capable of comprehending Clark's offer, but only if they knew their science. By using the technical abbreviation for *kilo annum*, Clark had established the opening bid using a code which would only have meaning to certain people in the overlapping worlds of geology, paleontology, and archaeology. In those scientific communities, *k.a.*—meaning a thousand years—was a common abbreviation. Thus, the formula $6(ka x ka) could be translated to read a thousand times a thousand—in other words, a million—times six.

Clever, Diak had to admit, *but who, in their right mind, would pay six million dollars for what turned out to be a sliver of rock?*

Reading the details of Clark's claim, the German was compelled to conduct further research. His exploration was partially motivated by intellectual curiosity, but mostly he sought to confirm that Clark's miraculous Clovis was not only important but also valuable. To aid his inquiries, Diak set up two computers, using one to monitor traffic to and from Clark's supposedly impenetrable email account and employing the other to learn all he could about the Rock of Solutre, Henry de Ferry, and the Solutrean Hypothesis.

He soon discovered that de Ferry was not the author of the controversial hypothesis. After the Frenchman died young, other scientists coined the term 'Solutrean' in order to place his site on a continuum of prehistory as having been active some 21,000 years ago. Still other researchers theorized a so-called 'Solutrean Industry' and postulated a population of prehistoric humans who produced distinctive tools and other artifacts. Included in their handiwork were unique and delicate projectile points which might have been used to kill birds but were more likely to have been ceremonial or decorative.

Monitoring Clark's online activity, Diak soon deduced that the Solutrean proof the professor was peddling came in the form of a unique Clovis projectile point. It seems that any fool can splinter a rock to produce a primitive scraping tool or spearhead or hand blade, but only an artisan and—if some authors are to be believed, a prehistoric Frenchman—can produce a distinctively delicate and symmetrical projectile point. And somehow—in what Diak could only articulate as a miraculous stroke of luck—one of these perfect points had fallen into Clark's hands. Then the opportunistic professor had parlayed his discovery into a kind of archaeological missing link and proceeded to market his find as the solution to the puzzle of how a Clovis point from the Solutrean site in faraway France had ended up in prehistoric North America.

Clark's vision was a rehash of an original concept based on a similar anomaly. The idea was first proposed in 1970 when an ancient mastodon trunk and a Solutrean blade turned up together on America's Eastern Seaboard. That find intrigued researchers, who postulated that ancient humans from France's prehistoric Solutrean region had somehow crossed the Atlantic to carry the blade to North America. Thus, the Solutrean Hypothesis was born.

Descending a sweeping hill, the German encountered the first vehicle of his early morning drive. He dimmed his headlights, then reignited his high beams as the truck passed.

"Let there be light," he said aloud.

Returning to his thoughts, Diak recalled his deduction that either the Solutrean believers were absolutely correct or irredeemably crazy. Whichever the case, the veracity of Clark's claim, along with the state of the professor's sanity, mattered little to the German. Diak didn't care if Clark was crazy, or if the inscrutable professor was deluding himself, or if the Solutrean Hypothesis was fact or fantasy. All that mattered to the calculating German was that Clark himself believed he'd found proof and that Clark's reputation as a scholar was strong enough to convince certain well-heeled people that his theory was plausible.

Regardless of whether the theory was credible or complete bunk, Diak had no interest in the academic discussion. He was inextricably drawn to the scheme for one reason, and one reason only. He'd entered the hunt to pursue the possibility that millions might be in play.

To prime the pump, the German had nudged the professor with an offer to purchase the Clovis—an overture which was rudely rejected. Undaunted, Diak continued his surveillance while remaining acutely aware that convincing a buyer to swallow the hypothesis might be a long shot. Reviewing the literature, Diak understood that many of Clark's colleagues refused to accept the idea that early Europeans had crossed the broad Atlantic to reach North America.

These critics dismissed the notion that adventurers bearing Solutrean tools had arrived ahead of all others by dodging their way around, over, and across daunting floes of oceanic ice. Instead, opponents of the Solutrean Hypothesis clung steadfastly to the widely held scientific belief that North America's first settlers had crossed over a broad land bridge which once joined what is now Alaska with the northeastern edge of the Asian continent. Such detractors saw no need to explain how Solutrean tools had materialized in North America, suggesting by their dismissal that the out-of-place artifacts were inconsequential.

Studying the controversy, Diak was struck with a captivating observation. Although the popular land bridge theory and the maligned Solutrean Hypothesis each postulated differing versions of the peopling of North America, the two ideas had one thing in common. Both theories disregarded traditional Native American beliefs that the ancestors of modern tribes were indigenous to the New World, having emerged from underground at the beginning of human time to populate the surface. Despite his cynical nature, Diak preferred to believe the legend.

"Not East or West, but Below," he said aloud as he reached the outskirts of Delta City.

The competing visions were all about who came first and from which direction. Either ancient Asians came from the west, or Native American ancestors ascended from below, or ancient Europeans came from the east. Those who held the latter view embraced the Solutrean Hypothesis and such believers were decidedly in the minority. Yet here was a professor who claimed to have proof of that controversial notion—proof which he was offering for sale. Moreover, Clark was demanding an astounding opening bid so, at the time, the question still remained. *Would anyone in their right mind pay six million dollars for a tiny artifact that purported to prove a dubious theory?*

Diak had decided to wait and see.

Within a month, his patience was rewarded when an offer emerged. Noting the source, the German was mildly surprised to see that his former employer, the Scarlet Brotherhood, had submitted the bid and he was amused to note that the crafty Russians were attempting to low-ball the greedy professor. Negotiations ensued with the Russians balking and Clark bombarding them with profanity-laced emails. The professor's unorthodox strategy seemed to be to ask for six million and reject a Russian bid for three while attempting to bully the price up to four. Clark appeared unable to comprehend how dangerous the Brotherhood was. For Diak, the reckless professor's disregard of the risk conjured up an amusing image. He envisioned a tight-fisted merchant haggling over the price of a set of nesting dolls at a Moscow street market while the increasingly annoyed customer stood in the stall holding a loaded pistol.

Diak watched the bargaining for a time, then decided to intervene. He reached out to the Brotherhood and convinced them to take him on as an ally. He reminded the Russians of his former service to the cartel. Marketing himself as an agent who possessed insights into the American mind, he informed the cartel that he had a network of contractors already in place in the Western regions of the sprawling nation. Scheming from the first to double-cross the Brotherhood, and wishing to keep the field clear of competitors, Diak tried to convince his ex-employers not to send Russian agents to the States. Despite his offer to assist, and knowing the Brotherhood as he did, the German assumed his advice would be ignored. So, he secretly swore that any cartel agent who interfered with his plans to hijack the process would pay a price.

After a period of tense negotiations, during which Diak worked behind the scenes without the professor's knowledge, the German nearly managed to persuade the Russians to swallow Clark's demands, including the requested down payment. Perhaps because of Diak's intervention, or maybe as a result of Clark's relentless pressure, the deal was struck and it looked like smooth sailing until the professor secretly re-opened the bidding and the Saudis jumped in at the last minute with a preposterous bid of their own.

Eight million dollars? the German asked himself.

Once again, Diak considered this unexpected wrinkle and reaffirmed his decision that the Saudi bid was a distraction. He reasoned that Clark would entertain, but ultimately reject, the Saudi offer in favor of the Russians. How could Clark do otherwise? The Russians had placated the demanding professor by agreeing to that uniquely American concept—the down payment. Besides—with the exception of the double-crossing pilot whose sole job, it seemed, was to fly Clark wherever the professor wished to go at the drop of a hat—the Saudis had no presence in America.

Diak felt that he knew the Saudis—or did he?

In his closing days with the Scarlet Brotherhood, Diak had briefly served in Saudi Arabia. In fact, as a 15-year-old minion with the Russian cartel, he'd literally held the coats of the 9/11 hijackers, checking their jackets and keeping the garments safe as they attended a final meeting in Jeddah before embarking on their destructive missions. It was true that he had no current contacts among the Saudis, but nevertheless he was convinced that the prospective Arab buyer who'd submitted the last-minute bid was unqualified. The man was a disaffected prince, a remnant of the out-of-favor house of Saud. Though technically royalty, he was living in exile and was, at best, a nameless offspring of one of the deposed king's forty-some wives. So, chances were good that the forgotten prince lacked sufficient funds to back up his outrageous offer.

Eight million dollars?

Diak found the sum an absurd fantasy. He could more readily believe that the Brotherhood could afford half that amount. So, he chose to ignore the Saudis and concentrate instead on infiltrating Clark's scheme to sell to the Brotherhood. In his mind, the Russians were the only legitimate buyers and if any of the Brothers got in his way, he would simply eliminate them. Meanwhile, the German would proceed with his plans, including the need to cover his tracks.

Just last night, before retiring and in anticipation of soon being in a position to steal the Clovis, Diak had sat at his computer obliterating all traces of his online search history. He'd gathered up the multiple emails which represented the geo-political intrigues that the professor had spawned with his Clovis scheme. One by one, he'd transferred all the evidence to his laptop's recycle bin. At last, he emptied the bin and heard the satisfying 'pfft' sound which simulated the cybernetic obliteration of simulated trash. The Solutrean Hypothesis, the French archaeologist, the professor's tangled internet transactions, the secretive bidders, and their motives, all such evidence was electronically shredded.

Every encumbrance was efficiently out of sight and out of mind as Diak crossed the river bridge and rolled into Delta City in hopes of locating the blue Volkswagen of Anne Scriptor.

Chapter 47

On the morning of July 15, two Navajos on horseback had been following fresh tire tracks when they stopped to examine a new sedan sitting empty and apparently abandoned behind a tangle of rabbit brush.

Then they rode further and noticed the sun glinting off something in the distance. They followed the light until they reached an abandoned airstrip. There they found a young man lying on the runway with a pool of blood encrusted on the ground at the base of his neck. He was dressed like a pilot, but there was no sign of his airplane and on his lapel, shining in the morning light, was a metal pin in the shape of wings.

Part IV: Detours

Part IV: Defines

Chapter 48

July 15, Predawn
Page, Arizona

Unaware that the intrepid German had narrowly missed intercepting him, Dr. C. Arnold Clark sped away from the isolated Arizona airfield. He was showing off for the young pilot, but his celebration was short-lived. Once clear of the landing strip, he killed the light-bar and used the Rubicon's navigation system to steer toward a 24-hour coin laundromat on the outskirts of Page. Last evening, he'd located the vacant place for sale on a real estate website and noted its remote location along with the fact that it had been on the market without an offer for two years.

Reaching the isolated building, he pulled off the pavement and parked the Rubicon out back in a nest of tumbleweeds. Borne by persistent westerly winds, the weeds had accumulated in such numbers and to such an astonishing height that they intertwined with lower branches of mesquite trees to form a nearly impenetrable hedge. He squeezed out of the jeep, brushed through the prickly weeds, forced the flimsy backdoor lock, and entered the laundromat carrying his duffle bag. He sat the bag down on a dusty table and then, taking no chances, he walked to the front door and flipped the sign to say 'closed.' Next, he made sure the front door was locked and used a wooden bench to barricade the back door from the inside. Then he closed the venetian blinds, propped up his flashlight, and fashioned his bombs.

Relying on his past military training and following contemporary instructions he'd obtained on the internet, he found it a simple matter to extract the green plastic from the candy wrappers and mold a thin layer of the pliable explosive into the lid of each toolbox. He added a tripwire so that each box was rigged to explode upon opening. Then he carefully closed both toolboxes and used combination padlocks to secure them.

Cautiously wrapping each box in a blanket, he carried them one at a time to the Rubicon, and gently placed them in the cargo bay. With the toolboxes secure, he started for Colorado. It was nearly sunrise and he planned to cross the Navajo Reservation, drive into the nearest corner of the neighboring state, and pick up the Clovis point from the cache site near Cortez. Then he'd travel higher to Lizard Head Pass and replace the empty toolbox there with one of his own deadly caches. Once the bomb was in place, he'd get a good night's sleep then inform the Russians of the Lizard Head GPS coordinates, plus the padlock combination, and let the chips fall where they may.

The Saudis had supplied him with burner phones and he still had one left. He'd been using the throw-away devices to communicate with the Arabs and also to irritate the Russians. However, when he called the cartel to deliver the coordinates, he'd use his personal smartphone. To avoid spooking the Brotherhood, it'd be better to use a device which—on their end—would display his familiar smartphone number.

When it came time to acquire the booby-trapped toolbox, the Russians would be anxious to secure the treasure. Henchmen dispatched to collect the cache may or may not have enough discipline to keep from opening the box in the field. But, eventually, someone was going to spin the combination dial and lift the lid and meet their maker. As a precaution, he'd rigged two toolboxes. He may or may not need a second bomb, but it might come in handy should Russians be near.

Penetrating the predawn darkness, Clark headed for Cortez. Taking a moment to set the Rubicon's cruise control, he smiled. The act of dictating the speed reminded him that he was in charge—punch in the speed parameters, pull the strings—both actions were manifestations of control. Take, for example, his recent interactions with his anxious Russian buyers.

A few days ago, the Brotherhood had telephoned him on his seldom used landline to arrange for their representative to come to his Tucson ranch house, supposedly to reexamine and photograph the Clovis. It was true that the cartel had set this condition, but in a bold countermove, he'd sensed an ambush, turned the tables on his visitor, and disappeared. Then, an hour ago, as he and the young pilot flew north, Clark had used a burner phone to call the Russians and plant the idea that he'd hidden the treasure somewhere in the vast Four Corners region. Leaving the Brotherhood dangling, he'd abruptly ended the call and destroyed yet another burner. Soon the Russians would be looking for him, but they'd be searching an area so vast that they'd need months, not hours, to find him. Meanwhile, in less than forty-eight hours, the slippery professor intended to disappear again.

It might have been rash to tell the Russians so much. But he was sure that their attempts to trace his call would fail to pinpoint his exact location. At best, they'd be able to place him somewhere in northern Arizona. He'd baited them on purpose and their trace, though incomplete, would verify that he was indeed in the Four Corners neighborhood. Clark's call and his well-crafted half-truths would give the Russians a general, though hazy, idea of where he was. He would likely be free from interference, but it was best to be cautious.

He suspected that his nervous Russian customers might be on the prowl. If he was right, he and they would be traveling through a vast area of Western America while he went about his Colorado business and there was always a chance of crossing paths with the dangerous Brothers. The odds of an encounter were slim, but an extra bomb might come in handy.

Having taken precautions, Clark felt confident as he rolled along the vacant highway. After several miles without encountering another vehicle, he increased his speed. Rounding a sharp corner, he nearly collided with a large yellow dog which stood placidly in the center of the highway. Swerving and cursing, he took the corner too fast. Behind him, in the Rubicon's rear compartment, he seemed to hear the toolboxes slide. Plowing into the deep dust of the narrow shoulder, he kept the Rubicon running as he pulled his pistol from his bag and chambered a round. Kicking the door open, he leapt from the Rubicon, intent on plugging the brazen dog, but the mangy cur had disappeared. Unloading the pistol and pocketing the bullet, he put the weapon away and checked his cargo. The boxes hadn't moved at all. Nevertheless, he decided to make them more secure. It wouldn't do to have the boxes explode prematurely. They were, after all, intended for the Russians.

As he worked to secure the boxes, eerie howls arose from the surrounding darkness. The disembodied wailing seemed to come from both sides of the highway—a canine call and response. Shivering, he closed the Rubicon's rear compartment, sprinted for the cab, and eased back onto the highway, resisting the temptation to speed away.

"Crud," he told himself aloud as his thoughts raced. *What next, I wonder? Russian wolves pursuing me across the tundra? With Dobry's avenging ghost leading the pack?*

Any moment now, his dangerous customers might become a vindictive posse. Despite his claim of innocence in Dobry's death, word of their deceased comrade would eventually percolate through the Russian organization. When the news reached the Brotherhood's rank-and-file, the image of their diminutive pal sprawled on the floor of his Tucson study probably wouldn't sit well. It was bad enough that Sasha and the rest of the listeners knew Dobry was dead. They at least might be willing to accept the loss of the little man as a cost of doing business. But the news would spread rapidly and there was no telling how the field toughs might react. Clark was certain that Fyodor, for one, would be itching to avenge his little brother and he didn't relish a hostile reunion with that formidable man.

Of course, this was all speculation.

For the time being Clark was alive and, as far as the professor was concerned, only two things were keeping him that way. First, although the rank and file of the Scarlet Brotherhood might doubt his story and want Clark's head on a pike for what happened to Dobry, the cartel leaders would continue to hold their subordinates in check while the Clovis was still in play. Secondly, nobody who wished him harm knew exactly where the itinerant professor was.

But, just in case, he'd rigged two boxes. Better safe than sorry. The Four Corners was a vast region and it was doubtful the prowling Russians would spot him. If such an unlikely event occurred and it wasn't convenient or plausible to talk his way out or shoot the bastards, Clark had created an option. If cornered, he'd simply surrender a booby-trapped box. Then he'd caution the recipients not to open it and run like hell.

Naturally, however things went down, it would only take one explosion and the Russian deal, which was already on shaky ground, would utterly dissolve. One little explosion and Clark could forget about expecting any further payment from the cartel, or any mercy either. Once the fireworks started, the betrayed Russians would quickly drop their role as participants in a somewhat civilized treasure quest and rapidly evolve into a pack of feral wolves. Howling for blood, they'd launch a vicious manhunt and Clark would be their prey.

Getting efficiently and safely in and out of Colorado would be dicey, but he reminded himself that the mountains were his best option. There were too many eyes in Arizona and those prying eyes were connected to muscular bodies which could wield God-knows-what in the form of weapons. Forced to put the dangerous desert behind him, Clark would take his chances in the sheltering mountains.

Chapter 49

The highway leading across the Navajo Reservation to the Arizona-Colorado border was an adventure. More accustomed to urban streets and broad avenues, Clark didn't care for the narrow pavement, paper-thin shoulders, and roller coaster swells of the undulating roadway. The motion made his stomach queasy and his churning gut sent conflicting signals to his brain. Competing for attention, a gnawing gag reflex sought to cancel out an urgent reminder that he was starving.

The internal tug-of-war was touch and go, but the hunger won.

The professor glanced at the digital clock on the Rubicon's dashboard—5 a.m. his usual breakfast time. Keeping one eye on the unpredictable road, he continued driving as he rummaged through his pockets until he found a package containing a half-crushed breakfast bar. Using his teeth, he extracted the bar and wolfed it down, nearly choking on the dry leftover before he found and drank from his canteen. Still hungry and feeling drowsy, he managed to activate the radio and searched through a jumble of country-western music and late-night preachers until he found a decent station. He turned up the volume, peered through the bug-splotched windshield, then felt a sudden urge to glance over his shoulder.

Useless, he thought as he caught himself indulging in what was probably an unnecessary precaution. *Who the hell would be following me out here in hell and gone? Nobody is who.*

The Navajo Reservation is enormous, encompassing over 27,000 square miles—a stark and haunting landscape which includes the only spot in the lower forty-eight where the borders of four states meet. 'Four Corners,' the locals call it. There was a marker there, but Clark and everyone else that mattered, suspected the extravagant display was in the wrong place. The states met alright but probably not right next to the gift shop. Meanwhile, the Reservation itself overlapped three of the four states, extending into Arizona, Utah, and New Mexico. Navajo Land stopped at the Colorado border where the Ute Mountain Tribe's reservation began.

For the time being, Clark was on good terms with the Navajos—with the Colorado tribe, not so much. He wondered how curious the Utes would be when he crossed the border and stopped for breakfast by boldly parking his Navajo Nation police cruiser in their casino lot. Disregarding the disposition of tribal loyalties and state and reservation boundaries, Clark pressed on, embracing his role as a resolute midnight traveler committed to his mission and determined to traverse the region. Out here, boundaries were meaningless. There were no barriers out here. As sure as the coming sunrise, U.S. Highways 160 and 491 would take him where he wanted to go.

In the dark, everything looked the same.

Clark's stomach growled again. The quavering radio lost its signal entirely and he switched it off. To distract his mind from his hunger, he turned his thoughts to something that had been puzzling him ever since he'd launched his scheme to market the Clovis.

Clark could comprehend why ultra-right-wingers would be interested in the artifact and he'd been expecting bids from those fringe sectors. But he couldn't imagine what earthly use his competing buyers, the Saudis, or for that matter the Russians, would have for the artifact. The motives of the Arabs were—like the people themselves—inscrutable. As for the Russians, he had a hard time believing that the purposes of rabid Reds, or even lapsed Communists, aligned with the interests of white supremacists—let alone neo-Nazis. Of course, those misguided ideologies—bitter enemies in the past—had been pretty cozy during the Cold War when their desires to curb the West overlapped. During those uncertain times, he wondered how many mutual schemes—sinister joint-ventures aimed at America and her allies—had been hatched in East Berlin, Poland, and other countries languishing in the grip of the Soviet Bloc. So maybe the Brotherhood and the neo-Nazis shared occasional patches of common ground. And regarding the Arabs...

Clark frowned. Thinking about politics made his stomach hurt even more.

"Screw 'em all," he said aloud.

Probably his competing buyers had no immediate use for the Clovis. Probably they planned to re-sell it to yet another purchaser or hold the thing for ransom, threatening to either trumpet its existence or destroy it if their victims didn't pay.

Then Clark had a deliciously ironic thought.

Suppose word has reached NAGPRA, he speculated. *Suppose tribal interests with deep pockets have gotten wind of the Clovis and suppose they are willing to pay big to obtain the artifact and suppress its existence. Was it possible that tribal buyers—using the Russians and Arabs as intermediaries—would pay through the nose for the privilege of grabbing hold of the Clovis and sticking the benighted thing back in the ground? Wouldn't that be sweet revenge?*

The more he thought about it, the more he liked the idea. The more he embraced a scenario which had the Clovis going full circle—from rock to crafted artifact and back to earth again—the better he liked it. It was a soothing belief and one which calmed his queasy stomach.

"Sweet," he said aloud as he turned his attention to the highway.

Chapter 50

Clark made it across the Reservation with the toolboxes and his nerves intact. Dawn was breaking as he drove into Colorado. He stopped for gas, then parked at the Ute Mountain Casino to take advantage of the all-you-can-eat 24-hour buffet where he wolfed down a king-sized breakfast. Despite his apprehensions, absolutely no one seemed to notice either him or his conspicuous vehicle.

After breakfast, he drove a few miles further to the outskirts of Cortez. Turning onto a rural road, he parked the Rubicon and fired up his GPS device. Then, with the morning dew still fresh on the cheatgrass, he strolled through a fallow field toward the banks of McElmo Creek. It was an easy walk over flat ground to reach Anne's first cache and, as he approached the sound of rushing water, he wondered what she'd thought about placing toolbox number one so close to the road. Whatever her frame of mind might have been, he was pleased and totally unsurprised to see that, as instructed, his dependable graduate assistant had placed the precious cache precisely at the GPS crosshairs.

His students, of course, would judge Clark's use of his GPS to locate the box as dishonest. Every term, in a stern pre-fieldtrip lecture, he'd cautioned his classes that any student using shortcuts would be graded down, maybe even expelled from the program. But such rules didn't apply to Clark. He was on a quest which left no time to consult map and compass and certainly no time to fool around with a protractor.

He gathered up the toolbox and left nothing in its place. Carrying the box back to the Rubicon, he positioned it in the rear compartment. Reasoning that removing the artifact would unnecessarily expose it, he kept the treasure box intact. If anyone was lurking around and a search ensued, they'd be more likely to find the treasure in his pocket than to discover its ingenious hiding place.

Having retrieved the Clovis, Clark drove further north, hiked four miles, and replaced the Lizard Head cache with one of his rigged toolboxes, turning that isolated site into a deadly trap. It was late morning and growing hot by the time the exhausted professor reached the lofty spot. Nearly out of breath, he stood for a moment mopping his brow with his kerchief and regretting that he'd instructed Anne to place this particular cache so far away.

Reaching this spot had undoubtedly been a routine jog for the athletic girl, but the distance and vertical climb had proven a formidable challenge for her over-the-hill and overweight mentor. Huffing and puffing his way along the trail, his only solace was to remind himself of the reason for the distance. This dangerous box had potential for mayhem, so the further away from innocent bystanders the better. His goal was to destroy Russians, not some random vacationer.

After resting a moment, he double-checked to make certain the bomb box was properly placed. Then he picked up the other toolbox, carried the empty container to a deep gully, and tossed it over the edge. When he didn't hear it strike the bottom of the ravine, he leaned forward to make certain it had cleared the slope.

It was then, as he edged close to the precipice, that he lost his footing.

Chapter 51

Clark's tumble sent him over the edge and down a steep and muddy slope. Unable to check his fall, he descended rapidly, sliding face-up, feet-first, and powerless to stop. Falling was bad luck and yet, careening downward, he somehow managed to avoid colliding with any of a dozen unforgiving boulders which protruded from the muddy slope.

When his feet slammed into the floor of the ravine, he lay still for a moment with his back pressed against the slope. He'd survived the sudden descent without injury but, having reached the bottom, he was unable to catch his breath. Panting like a geriatric racehorse, he remained motionless until his breathing moderated.

After several minutes, he mustered enough energy to raise his chin, tilt his head back, and examine the sheer incline down which he had plummeted. No chance of spotting the missing GPS which had slipped from his hand as he fell and no chance of climbing back up.

"No exit that way, genius," he grumbled. How could he have been so careless? How could he have made such a rookie mistake? Leaning over a precipice? Hiking with no water? Losing the GPS? Leaving his cell phones in the Rubicon? Obviously, he'd been away from the field much too long. "Stupid-in-the-forest," he labeled himself. "Stupid!"

With effort, he stood up, teetered in place, and took a personal inventory. In addition to the missing GPS, he'd lost his cap in the fall and his backside was covered with mud, but nothing seemed to be broken. He took two tentative steps, tripped over the errant toolbox, and fell hard on the pitiless ground. Lying there, he cursed at the top of his lungs and the repetition of his profanity washed over him twice before the echoes were swallowed by the immense emptiness of the ravine. Struggling to his feet again, he prepared to kick the box, then thought better of it.

"Stupid-in-the-forest breaks his toe kicking his inanimate opponent," he cautioned himself. "Not today," he decided. "Now, how do I get my worthless carcass out of here?"

He found his cap lying nearby, put it on, and studied his surroundings. There was no climbing out the way he had arrived, and the opposite bank was just as steep. Abandoning the idea of scaling the precipitous sides, he considered both ends of the ravine. To the west, the narrow bottom seemed to go on forever. The eastern end was choked with weeds and partially blocked by a rockslide. Tilting his head far back, he looked up to check the position of the sun and decided. The sky was darkening. It might not rain, but, then again, it just might.

"East it is," he sighed as he faced the rockslide. It would be best to head downstream and, anyway, he was positive he'd left the Rubicon somewhere in that direction. As he trudged forward, thunder sounded, and it began to sprinkle. Seconds later, the modest drizzle enlarged to a drenching downpour.

"Just perfect," he growled as he picked up his pace. He was angry at his predicament and—despite being short of breath—he continued to chastise himself by attempting to narrate his situation. "Here I am," he wheezed as he ran, "trapped down here with steep sides and a narrow bottom. Marooned in an absolutely perfect conduit for a flash flood and being pelted by raindrops the size of watermelons with absolutely no earthly chance of climbing out on this side of the rock fall! So, I'd better move my sorry butt!"

He stopped talking then because he needed to save oxygen to fuel his ungainly run. As the rain pelted down, he jogged toward the rockslide, pawing the air with one hand, and using the other to hold up his trousers. Wishing he'd worn suspenders and suddenly thankful for his primitive surroundings, he was grateful that no one was present to witness the unlovely flopping of his flabby pectorals and bouncing belly. When he finally reached the tumbled rocks, he discovered the barricade to be too tightly woven to allow a robust man to pass through.

"Peachy," he scowled. "So, it's up and over I guess."

For an hour, as the downpour soaked him to the skin and filled the ravine below, Clark labored upward, clawing his way from boulder to boulder until the rain abruptly ceased. He was panting heavily, struggling to find purchase on the wet boulders, and nearing the top of the jumble when he came level with a narrow game trail which hugged the opposite slope of the ravine.

"Wrong side," he protested. "That figures." He looked across the ravine but could see no corresponding path on the other slope. He was still far below the upper rim of the ravine and the game trail seemed his only option. "Like it or not, dipstick," he told himself, "this looks to be your exit."

The game trail led tantalizingly upward, but it was criminally narrow, and Clark felt like a man balancing on a high wire as he shuffled along. As one shoulder rubbed along the ravine wall, he was forced to walk heel-to-toe with barely enough room on the slender trail to place either foot. A sheer rock face on his right and a sheer drop to his left, this was no pathway for a fat man. Then, just when he was about to despair and let gravity carry him over the side, the constricted trail unexpectedly widened, and he struggled to the top.

To the top, yes, but the top of where?

Looking around, he could see nothing but rock.

"Crud!" he shouted, and his voice echoed across the barren landscape. Giving full throat to his anger left him coughing spasmodically until he bent double and sought to recover his breath. When he straightened up, there were tears in his eyes, but that was all the moisture he could muster. Unable to roar his displeasure a second time, he could only croak plaintively as his parched throat seemed to shrivel like an overcooked steak. The rain had soaked his cap and jacket and kerchief and, manipulating his wet garments, he managed to squeeze a little water into his dry mouth, but those few drops were not nearly enough.

He glanced at the sky. In the wake of the storm there was not a cloud in sight and this clear sunny July day was just getting started. Soon it would be noon and blistering hot and he was on the wrong side of a seemingly endless ravine. To get back, he was going to need a way across or around and, in order to accomplish either, he would need a lot more water.

Keeping the rocky Lizard Head formation over his shoulder, he walked along the rim of the ravine staying well clear of the edge. First things first—he would figure out a way to conquer the ravine eventually—but for the time being he needed to search for water. If he recalled his geology correctly, this area consisted of a combination of volcanic and sedimentary deposits—a hodgepodge of somewhat solid and decidedly crumbling rock. That was okay. He was looking for holes—pockets in surface rocks, anywhere rainwater might collect. It would be risky to drink water in the open, but dehydration was riskier still and dehydration could set in quickly in this dry climate and at this altitude.

He was hoping to find captured rainwater. He was not disappointed.

There were literally hundreds of palm-sized dimples in the rocks and each indentation held a dollop of fresh rainwater. Without ceremony, he crouched on all fours and crawled over the rocks, pressing his lips against the pockets and slurping out liquid as he advanced over the ground, his head skimming over the rocks like an overweight sheep munching its way across a pasture. When he'd drunk his fill, he picked a few grains of sand out of his mouth, wiped his chin, and sat on a lonely boulder to survey his surroundings. He had to get to the other side and yet he could see no way across the ravine. He could follow it for miles. But that would only make a bad situation worse because, with each step, the chasm grew deeper and also steadily curved in the wrong direction, leading him further away from where he was certain he'd parked the Rubicon.

He'd have to find another route.

The flat topography which bordered the ravine extended to his right until it met a thick forest. Abandoning the ravine meant he'd be trading easy walking to take his chances in the trees. That might work. Among the trees he'd search for a draw or stream and follow either one downhill, no matter where it took him. Eventually such a downward path would lead him off this high ground to a point where he might stumble across a roadway or trail. If he ended up too far from the Rubicon, he'd simply have to make up the misdirection by walking back. It was a chancy proposition, but anything was better than spending the night on the exposed rim of the ravine.

Taking to the woods would mean leaving the water pockets behind. And no matter how clear a running current might appear, there was no way he was going to risk beaver-fever by drinking from a mountain stream. He was all too familiar with the manner in which microscopic giardia parasites could infect a hapless human with raging diarrhea. Much good it would do to hydrate with stream water, only to puke away gallons of body fluid. As for finding drinkable liquid, there would be dimpled rocks along the streambed, and he would likely find enough rainwater to get by. Clark took a final look at his surroundings. The sun was riding high and it would be much cooler among the trees.

That notion settled it.

Abandoning the ravine, the questing professor sidled toward the woods and, arriving there, he'd only traveled a hundred feet before he heard the unmistakable trickle of a healthy stream. Bushwhacking toward the welcome sound, he found the descending water, but saw that both banks were a tangle of brush. To avoid the thickly wooded banks, he'd have to wade in the current. The clear rushing water would be icy cold, but there was no choice.

He'd wade and like it.

To keep his hiking boots dry he took them off. Then he rolled up his pant legs, tied the boots around his neck, and splashed in. Proceeding in his stocking feet, he slipped periodically on slick moss and rounded rocks. Continuing downstream, he kept up a steady pace, pausing now and then to drink whenever he spotted a likely rain reservoir along the bank.

He was making good time. Then his luck changed.

After traveling a good mile, he decided to save time by cutting across a slow-moving eddy. Entering the broad pool, he was feeling his way when he lost his footing and reached for a streamside bush to recover his balance. Unfortunately, he grabbed a handful of brambles which impaled his palm and wrist and, in letting go, he lurched awkwardly and plunged his foot into the deep current. As his leg went under, he instinctively shifted all his weight to the submerging limb. Sinking to his waist, he lost control of his leading foot as his floundering ankle slid between two submerged rocks, descended into a narrow underwater crevice, and lodged there.

Balancing unevenly in the pool with one foot pinned in the crevice and the other on the streambed, he tried to pull free, but it was no use. The trapped foot and ankle had gone neatly in, but they refused to come out again. He splashed in the pool, rocking from side to side in a blind fury.

Shouting at the top of his lungs, he spewed a string of profanity. Echoes washed over him as he calmed down for a moment, then raged again, and finally hung his head and wept in despair.

"This is not good. This is very not good," he repeated over and over.

A moment ago, this streambed had seemed a convenient highway which he was convinced would lead him inexorably out of his dilemma. Now he realized that it was an extremely poor place to be trapped. The water was icy, and he was up to his waist in it. Never mind the possibility of hypothermia, another rainstorm and the flow would be over his head. Even if he survived the cold and inevitable flood, who knew what formidable creatures coveted this waterway as a nocturnal hunting ground. A bear or a cougar would be the last living creature he'd wish to meet after dark with his leg stubbornly pinned to the bottom of this confined streambed.

"Gotta get out," he decided. "Gotta get out."

Desperate to free himself, he bent over and wrapped both hands around his trapped leg. He shifted his weight to his free foot, got a firm grip just above the pinned ankle, gritted his teeth, and pulled.

Chapter 52

At dusk Clark awoke lying beside the stream between two moss-covered boulders, pain clouding his mind, and his body curled up into the tight cramp of a fetal position. Hours ago, he'd managed to pull his leg free from the stream bottom but not without trauma. To escape from the rocks which imprisoned his foot, he'd been forced to sacrifice considerable patches of skin and endure the hyper-extension of his ankle, not to mention losing one sock in the process.

After pulling his leg free of the rocks, he'd endured waves of pain and watched helplessly as the current carried his dislodged sock away, accompanied by a wafting skein of blood. Then, even though his badly scraped foot and twisted ankle hurt like hell, he managed somehow to limp toward shore. Reaching the stream's edge, he tumbled through a break in the bushes and onto a sandy spit where he pulled himself out of the current. He lay on his stomach with his injured foot throbbing until he mustered enough energy to move further away from the rushing water. Crawling as far as the boulders, he collapsed in agony until exhaustion and pain rendered him unconscious.

When at last he regained his senses, he had to look at his watch four times before he managed to comprehend how late it was. It was nearly dark and what little light remained was already muted by the canopy of dense brush and overarching trees which lined the stream bank. In the dimness, an army of mosquitoes were having a field day with Clark's exposed body, but he couldn't summon the strength to combat them.

He groaned and rolled onto his back, dimly realizing that he was still wearing his cap. He centered it on his aching head, then sat shakily up and stared down over his crotch in the direction of his legs. His boots lay a few feet away, sprawled on the sand and still tied together. Apparently, they had remained around his neck until he flung them aside in a desperate attempt to reach dry land. Looking closer, he could see that his route from the water to the boulders was marked by a dark stain of blood leading from his ankle and back across the tawny sand toward the stream beyond.

No wonder he'd blacked out. Even allowing for the absorbent sand, it looked like he'd lost a gallon of blood.

"Nothing left for you greedy vampires!" he shouted at the mosquitoes. "Get lost, you blood-suckers!" He removed his cap and swatted ferociously at the unseen insects, but only managed to ineffectively sling the cap toward the stream and spawn a vibration that reached his injured leg. He flailed his arms like a drowning swimmer, then lay back, exhausted. "I gotta get up," he told himself. "Gotta get up."

His chest heaving, the injured professor took several deep breaths and mustered his courage. At last, with considerable difficulty, he managed to sit up, bend forward, and reach out awkwardly to remove and wring out his remaining sock. Then he gingerly slipped the damp sock onto his injured foot and secured it in place with his bandana. With his foot swathed in a make-shift bandage, he grunted and wheezed until he had both boots on, laced-up, and tied as tightly as he could endure. He rose unsteadily and stood on one leg as he grappled with a pile of driftwood to dislodge a suitable limb. At last, heedless of the mosquitoes, he stripped off his jacket, molded it to the top of the driftwood, and tucked the improvised crutch into his armpit.

"Forward, march!" he yelled as he set his cap and started along the bank, pushing brush aside, and moving clumsily downstream with the aid of his primitive crutch.

Progressing slowly, he struggled through streamside brambles until he found an opening and was able to climb up the bank to reach higher ground. The wind was howling there and, though the breeze chilled him, at least it drove the mosquitoes away. By the time he emerged into open country, it was fully dark, and he'd entirely lost his bearings. No sense flailing through the dark. He'd have to seek shelter for the night. Stumbling along with the sound of the stream steadily fading behind him and the moonlight guiding his steps, he chanced upon an overhang of rock with evidence of habitation. Even in the dim light, he could discern that the underside of the chalky overhang had a blackened canopy—a sure sign that someone, at some time, had nurtured a fire there. The rain hadn't reached beneath the overhang and it only took the famous archaeologist a few moments to gather the necessary material to construct a primitive fire starter.

Exhausted, traumatized, and cold, he was operating on instinct—a humanoid, alone in a vast wilderness, a man reduced to his essence, a survivor.

In tackling the essential task of building a fire, Clark had a decided advantage over his prehistoric ancestors. Since his undergraduate days he'd religiously worn a belt holster which contained his trusty multi-tool. He was never without this ingenious combination of pliers, awl, knife, saw blade, scissors, bottle opener, and miscellaneous other devices. With the aid of this modern miracle, the professor was able to quickly saw a length of mid-sized tree limb in half and sharpen one end into a pointed wooden drill bit. And he had no trouble creating a suitable fireboard base by gouging a bit-hole into a slab of bark.

Constructing the bow to drive the make-shift wooden bit was also easy. The floor of the overhang was littered with sturdy branches—a selection of fir and spruce. The greenest of these made a superb bow and one of his leather shoelaces made an excellent bow string. Having assembled his primitive tools, he gathered handfuls of dry tinder and kindling. Then it was merely a matter of wrapping the bow string around the drill bit and working the bow back and forth in a rapid horizontal motion. Powered by the moving string, the bit rapidly chafed against the fireboard, which created enough friction to get the tinder smoldering. Blowing on the smoking particles generated sufficient sparks to ignite the tinder. As nascent flames appeared, Clark added kindling and soon had a blaze going. Warming his hands, the professor added more fuel and couldn't suppress a broad grin. Despite all the foolish mistakes he'd made that day—including not carrying matches—he'd still managed to create fire. Thus, he'd met and easily conquered a wilderness challenge which might have buffaloed a lesser outdoorsman.

"The struggle is real," he said aloud.

It was a phrase which his younger students were fond of using when they wanted to downplay the difficulty of accomplishing a seemingly insurmountable task. In practice, the phrase had a double, and therefore opposite, meaning. It was a cogent bit of millennial sarcasm. As such, it meant that certain so-called impossible struggles were imagined and hence *not real*.

For Dr. C. Arnold Clark, the struggle to create fire was extremely not real. Setting him in the wilderness and betting on him to start a blaze from scratch without the aid of matches was a sure thing. Whereas, hobbling an unknown distance in the dark on a bum leg with nothing to support his weight but a driftwood crutch was not. So, the professor did what he could. He built a fire and stayed put and tried to focus on the chancy task of keeping the flames going throughout a chilly night while also catching snatches of sleep. He was a lost hiker, but no one would be looking for him and, in the morning, he'd still be on his own. He struggled to keep his fire lit. He tried to sleep.

But, in the end, both he and the fire went out.

Chapter 53

Waking at dawn to a pile of smoldering embers, Clark was cold and stiff. He rekindled his fire, curled into a ball, and slept again. He awoke at noon and sought his bearings by reminding himself that he was Dr. C. Arnold Clark and the date was July 16. At last, though reluctant to endure the pain of movement, he gathered strength and set out.

It took the tottering professor most of the waning day to hobble from his primitive shelter to a road, then along that road to the spot where he'd parked the Rubicon. Sadly, his injury required him to invest another miserable hour and a half to the task of getting into his vehicle without further aggravating his wounds. When at last he was sitting in the driver's seat at an awkward angle to favor his bum leg, he gritted his teeth, started the Rubicon, and headed back to Cortez.

Following directions gained from a passerby, he found Mildred Road. Pulling over, he parked the Rubicon out of sight. Then, although it pained him to do so, he hobbled for two blocks to the facility. Arriving there exhausted, he leaned on the doorbell at the Southwest Urgent Care Center until someone came outside and helped him into a wheelchair. The swelling in his ankle had subsided and the physician's assistant on duty carefully removed the boot and Clark's make-shift bandage, then expertly cleaned and dressed the sizable scrapes on his foot.

"You're lucky," said the p.a.

"In what way, I wonder?" asked Clark.

"These scrapes are nasty, and you've got quite a bruise in the soft tissues from your instep to the bridge of your right foot, but you haven't broken anything. And that's real lucky considering there's over two-dozen bones in the human foot not counting thirty plus joints—all of which appear undamaged. Can't talk you into an X-ray, I guess."

"If it ain't broke," said Clark.

"I hear you," said the p.a. as he proffered a bottle of pills. "Take one of these now for the pain and another one at bedtime. Now you'll have to excuse me because I've got an emergency hook waiting."

Clark was curious to know what constituted an 'emergency hook,' but he needed to be on his way. Having already spent two and a half hours at the clinic, he was feeling exposed. To become a patient, he'd been obliged to flash his new license before he was ready to share it with the public. At the professor's request, the Saudi's skilled craftsmen had manufactured a photo ID that featured a bald and clean-shaven Clark. It was a great idea, except for the fact that he hadn't yet altered his appearance to match.

As a result, he endured a series of doubtful looks while the medical staff struggled to reconcile the clean-cut pinkness of the license photo with his present sunburned, bearded, and disheveled self.

"It's me," he declared and then, in an attempt to explain his changed visage from hairless tadpole to bewhiskered Santa, he added, "I lost a bet."

Being obliged to produce identification had been a nuisance, but his untidy appearance and his distinctive aroma after spending thirty-six hours in the woods probably combined to help him remain, if not anonymous, at least inconsequential. He'd arrived on foot looking homeless and so forlorn that the clinic staff would probably assume he was a down-on-his-luck transient. Anyway, absolutely no one would be looking for a Mister Leonard William Fischer of Newton, Iowa—his Saudi-supplied alter ego. In any event, he'd already lingered long enough at the clinic and he didn't relish further exposure, so he rolled down his pant leg, replaced his boot, and limped to the check-out desk. As Clark paid with cash, he scanned the waiting room until his eye landed on an embarrassed-looking man who was sitting awkwardly in an uncomfortable plastic chair with his head down. The man was dressed in a flannel shirt and cargo pants and he had one hand cupped over his ear.

This had to be the hook emergency, Clark decided. Recalling how many times he'd snagged his own ear while fly-fishing, the professor's thoughts went out to the victim: *I've been there, pal, and I feel your pain.*

It was pitch dark outside and, in case anyone was watching, Clark resisted the temptation to limp directly back to the Rubicon. Instead, he took a circuitous route and the exercise seemed to do him good. As he walked, his pain moderated, and he reviewed his options. Thanks to his adventure in the ravine, he was running behind schedule. By rights, he should have already called the anxious Russians to reveal the Clovis coordinates. But the sun was down, and he was tired and could feel the pain meds kicking in. Not the best formula for thinking clearly, so he decided to lay low for the night, get up early in the morning, and make the call then.

July 16? July 17? What did it matter?

The Russians had given him a deadline, but he'd let them stew a bit longer. A few more hours of worried waiting would make the cartel all the more anxious and reckless in their pursuit of the treasure. The bomb wasn't going anywhere. Tomorrow would be soon enough to make his call. In the morning he'd fire up his smartphone, which had gone unused for days. He'd make the call and give the Russians, and whoever else might be eavesdropping, the magic numbers they'd been longing to hear. Then, after making that long-anticipated call, he'd drive like blazes, using the Rubicon's lights, and siren too if he could manage it, as he rushed back to Lizard Head at breakneck speed. He'd hurry to the high pass in order to find a good vantage point where he would wait for the fireworks.

And there would be fireworks.

Clark had no regrets about his plan to bomb the Russians. From the first, the Brotherhood had tried to low-ball him and then they'd gone out of their way to annoy and belittle him, not to mention hatching a plot to kill him. So, he was going to take perverse satisfaction in knowing that he'd bilked the odious Brotherhood out of two million bucks and knowing, moreover, that they had fallen for his toolbox trap. As a bonus, depending on who won the race to Lizard Head Pass, he might even snare the troublesome detective whose minions had been spying on him for over a year.

Either way, somebody was in for a surprise.

Whoever responded to his call, Clark had every confidence that, the instant his intended victims were in possession of the Lizard Head coordinates, they would break their greedy necks rushing toward the mountain pass.

How long would it take them to get there?

Thanks to Clark's imperfect disclosures, the Russians already knew that 'the treasure' was hidden somewhere in the vast Four Corners region. Based on that information, they might be strung out anywhere from Utah to New Mexico.

Then again, they could be much closer.

If the Russians did their homework, they might narrow their search to the route associated with the university's traditional geocaches. In that case the treasure hunters could already have boots on the ground in Colorado, cruising conspicuously back and forth in their extremely noticeable Bentleys. He hadn't spotted them, but that didn't mean they weren't on the prowl. The Brotherhood might be searching in all four states or only one. Either way they'd be seeking a very small needle in a very big haystack. The simple truth was, without knowing the exact coordinates, the Four Corners region was far too much territory to cover.

Or was it?

Clark's mind was beginning to swirl. He'd hobbled away from the clinic convinced that the Russians were far afield. But, by the time he reached the Rubicon and started it up, the professor was entertaining other thoughts which gave him pause. Maybe the searchers were in Colorado after all and maybe he hadn't encountered them this far south because they were further north and looking for Anne.

Was she in danger?

He hastily reviewed his calculations. Getting Anne to the mid-point of her caching assignment hadn't been an arbitrary goal. He'd intentionally waited until she was halfway through her route before disappearing. He wanted her to have a generous head start so that, by the time anyone thought to follow her, she'd be far away and heading north. With luck the Russians would miss her entirely. Even in the unlikely event that one of the Brotherhood intercepted the girl, what would they find? She was carrying empty toolboxes. If they questioned her, what could she tell them? She knew nothing whatsoever about the Clovis and no one, including Anne, had the least idea where Clark was. Not even his pilot knew. The pilot's only instructions were to return to the airfield when summoned and Clark had every expectation the young shave-tail would do exactly that. Mulling things over, he drove downtown and, by the time he'd ordered a take-out pizza at a neighborhood bistro, his mind seemed to clear. Waiting for his supper to emerge from the joint's oven, he told himself that his escape route was solid, and Anne was safe.

Everything's okay, he convinced himself.

Arriving at his motel, he wolfed down the pizza, lay back on the bed, and closed his eyes. When he was injured in the wilderness, he feared he'd never see the Clovis again. Now it was at his side, secure in its concealing box, lying on the bedside table. Knowing it was safe, he conjured up a mental image of his treasure, envisioning the artifact clearly in his mind's eye.

It was a perfect specimen, and everyone wanted it. It was worth far more than the Russians had offered and even more than their unknown rivals the Saudis were willing to pay. Eventually, whoever owned the Clovis would be able to resell the priceless artifact for a figure beyond reckoning. The money it generated would be enough to finance the most impossible dream, the most boundless ambition, or the most fearful nightmare. Whatever somebody did with the Clovis or the money, it was none of Clark's concern. His only desire was to punish the Russians, do business with the Saudis, and earn enough to spend his twilight years in the lap of luxury.

In the morning, when he made his call and the coordinates were known, all comers would race to the high pass. The instant the toolbox exploded, the hunt for the treasure would descend into a frantic search for the professor. That would be a great time to disappear again, which is exactly what Clark intended to do. After the explosion, he'd instantly call for his jet, then rocket back to Page with siren wailing and lights flashing. He'd skid onto the airstrip, ditch the Rubicon, tip his hat to the pilot, and reboard the Saudi aircraft, Clovis in hand, to make good his escape. He would...

Clark's eyes flew open and he suddenly felt ill as he stumbled to the bathroom and vomited vociferously. After sitting on the tile floor straddling the commode and feeling absolutely miserable for twenty minutes, he got unsteadily to his feet and peeled off his clothes. He took a shower, carefully re-bandaged his foot, then made sure the motel room door was locked and chained. He took his night pill and, in the darkened room, looked once again to make certain the Clovis box was on the table next to his bed. Then he set his alarm for 5 a.m. and, once again, closed his eyes.

Chapter 54

The sedatives had done their work all too well. Clark slept through his alarm and far into the afternoon before he awoke. The maid's unwelcome knock on his motel room door pulled him back into the land of the living. Resisting the urge to strangle the woman, Clark begged her to come back later. When she was gone, he reached through the partially open door, hung the 'do not disturb' sign, and went back to sleep. Unconcerned about the time and feeling much better, he arose for good an hour later, dressed, and drove to a convenience store where he bought coffee and donuts. It was then that he saw the newspaper and learned of Anne's death.

With the Rubicon idling in the parking lot, he was immobilized—stuck in a recurrent loop of shock and grief as he read and re-read the article. So, he'd miscalculated. The Russians had found Anne after all. He buried his chin in his chest and wept.

No one tapped on the window to ask if he was okay. No one called the cops. For all they knew, sitting there in his Navajo Police vehicle, he *was* the cops.

Recovering at last, he crumpled the newspaper, wiped his tears, and peeled out of the parking lot. Wheeling through the streets of Cortez, he sped north until he reached Rico, a tiny burg a few miles downriver from Lizard Head Pass. The place seemed deserted, so he stopped alongside the highway, activated his smartphone, punched in the number, and glanced at his watch. He was calling much later than he'd planned, but so be it. The Russians could like it or lump it. After two rings he delivered his tersely worded message. Then, remembering that the phone could be used to track him, he immediately terminated the call.

He stepped out of the Rubicon, planning to place his smartphone in the path of the front tire in order to drive forward and crush it. But rather than destroying the device, he hesitated and glanced back through the jeep's open door as he considered the last of his burner phones which lay in its packaging on the passenger seat. The burners were probably okay as telephones, but that was all they were good for. His smartphone on the other hand could perform a wide range of functions as a navigation device, conduit to the internet, and storage device. In many ways it was the electronic equivalent of his multi-tool. Without it he'd feel helpless.

His smartphone held a host of contact numbers. It also contained countless photographs plus certain sentimental voice mails that he'd saved over the years. One particular file documented the silky voice of his former lover professing her undying love. Her pledge had been a lie, of course, but he hadn't the heart to erase it. Besides, he'd stored a boatload of images on his smartphone, including a candid shot of Anne whimsically posing next to her tiny car, and he was reluctant to surrender those mementos. He tried to convince himself that he'd soon be making new contacts, taking new photos, and creating new memories, but he knew he couldn't part with the things which resided on his personal smartphone. So, he pocketed the versatile device—promising himself to use it sparingly—and climbed back into the Rubicon.

Then he put on his seatbelt, checked his rearview mirror, switched on the roof lights, and ignored the speed limit as he raced up to Lizard Head. He'd get there well ahead of his victims and find a spot with an unobstructed and safe view of the cache site. The Russians would pay for what they did to Anne and he was looking forward to annihilating the bastards.

Part V: Anne Redux

Chapter 55

July 15, Midnight
Near Delta City, Colorado

Unaware that her professor was lying injured in the Lizard Head wilderness, Anne Scriptor made her way on foot from the outskirts of Lavender, intent on walking all the way to Delta City. She'd sacrificed her VW and this overland trip was her punishment. Her destination didn't appear far away, but she made scant progress as she struggled to traverse an undulating terrain known locally as the 'dobies.

The slang was a variation of the word 'adobe' and it adequately described the malleable obstacle which stretched before her. Left behind millions of years ago by a retreating, and now-vanished, primordial inland sea, acres of ancient clay and shale had been sculpted by wind and water into sizable mounds. To reach the city she was obliged to scramble over a seemingly endless expanse of bleak dirt knolls, less steep than Old Goat Trail but no less muddy. It was a daunting task and one made all the more challenging in the aftermath of the evening's soaking rain.

"Doggone mud again," she grumbled.

Climbing up each hill was bad enough but trying to get down the other side without falling was impossible. Soon she gave up the idea of descending gracefully. Choosing a more direct, if undignified route, she balanced at the crest of each rounded top, then squatted and sledded down on her butt. As she slogged onward, far to the right—westward as she reckoned it—Anne could see the headlights of an occasional car snaking its way along a distant divided highway.

"That'll be Colorado 50," she said aloud to no one in particular. "Nice flat pavement, which is tempting, but too risky for a fugitive."

As she struggled on, the hills grew less muddy until she slid down one last slope and landed on a hard-packed dirt road which was surprisingly dry. Apparently, the rain had not reached this far. The dirt road ran parallel to the highway but not near enough to invite attention, so she followed it toward the still distant lights of Delta City. The roadway ran perfectly straight and for several miles she walked along with her eyes closed, feeling suddenly very tired, vowing that she'd only open them if she sensed the road was curving or heard a vehicle coming. Trudging along, her thoughts turned inward. She'd been on a dark road like this before.

Years ago, on the night she left Bisbee, she'd walked for days through the Arizona darkness, sleeping in the open in isolated fields and beside rural roads. Orphaned at thirteen, Anne had decided to reinvent herself. Reaching the next county, she'd changed her name and boarded a bus bound for a new school. She had a vague idea of what she'd do when she arrived there and, if that nascent plan failed, she'd figured she could always make a run for it.

As it happened, she'd pulled it off. Lying about her age—a ruse assisted by her independent nature—she finished high school early and matriculated at The University of Arizona before turning eighteen. The university admissions officers had raised an eyebrow when they examined her incomplete school records and borderline test scores. Explaining the missing transcripts, she'd told the university the same half-truth she'd told the registrar on the day she caught the unfamiliar bus and rode to her newly adopted high school.

"There was a fire," was what she'd said, and, for effect, she pretended to tear up.

"*Oh, honey,*" was the usual response—that and a predictable referral to a counselor.

As time passed, Anne got by on the strength of her good looks and a sob-story that was only a bit contrived. There had, in fact, been a fire—a spectacular fire in which her father perished.

The place burned down on a Saturday morning. Anne had been away. Pretending she had her father's permission, but without bothering to ask the old man, she'd ridden from school with a friend to take part in a Friday night sleep-over in a neighboring town. The next day, the girl's parents drove her home. Sitting in the backseat with her friend, Anne watched impassively as the driver pulled over to allow several fire trucks and an ambulance to pass.

"Somebody's life is changing," the mother said.

When they came in sight of the still-smoldering shell of her house, Anne didn't give the place a second look. With a sincere lie, she convinced the father they'd made a wrong turn and asked to be dropped off in front of another house three miles away. She got out of the car, thanked her hosts for a lovely visit, hoisted her backpack, and pretended to walk up the nearby driveway. As soon as the family was out of sight, she crossed the road, climbed a fence, and disappeared. She didn't return to her old school. She changed her last name and lived on the streets of Bisbee for a month. She didn't attend her father's funeral, and no one seemed to miss her. A rumor spread that she too had died in the fire and she did nothing to discourage that falsehood. She cut her long hair, vowing never again to grow it to the length 'Daddy likes.' Eventually her wanderlust carried her on foot to Sierra Vista where she adopted a new school and embarked on a life built on lies.

Think about something else, she told herself as she trudged on through the predawn darkness.

The road did not curve, and no vehicle materialized, and Anne kept her eyes shut for several more minutes, opening them only when she heard a honking horn. She was prepared to abandon the road until she realized that the sound came from far ahead. Stopping, she rubbed her eyes and drank from one of her water bottles.

"Almost empty," she frowned. "But nearly there."

It took another hour of steady walking, but the city lights were no longer a faint glow on the rim of the dark horizon. She could pick out distinct points of illumination. As the land continued to level out, she perceived the silhouettes of tall structures. She spied a tower pulsating from top to bottom with a vertical spine of red flashing lights and she could see similar lights outlining the upper reaches of a distant grain elevator. Next visible were streetlamps and finally she saw the subdued lights of homes and the garish glow of business signs. Flickering headlamps and taillights appeared and disappeared as meandering vehicles tracked through unseen streets. A siren sounded somewhere in the dark.

She had reached civilization.

Anne glanced at her watch. It was 3 a.m. If the sidewalks of Delta City hadn't been made of unbending concrete, they would have been rolled up long ago. The downtown traffic signals had ceased to cycle through their full sequences and were instead flashing red and amber. There appeared to be nothing open, which was fine with her. All she wanted was sleep. For a split-second she toyed with the idea of returning to the Starlight Budget Motel, but she was certain somebody would either be watching the actual motel or virtually monitoring her debit card. How much cash did she have? Not enough, that much was certain. In the morning she'd risk getting more money, but now she needed rest. She wasn't certain exactly how far she'd walked since leaving Lavender Hill Farm, but she guessed it was at least fifteen miles.

As the weary woman trekked steadily onward, she heard the rushing water before she reached it. This had to be the Gunnison River and there would be a bridge on this side of town. Drawing closer to the crossing, she saw people walking on the far side, but the figures seemed to vanish before they reached the bridge. She stopped, momentarily wondering where they'd gone, until she realized they must have descended the riverbank. She hadn't expected to encounter anyone, so she'd thrown her cottonwood club away while struggling through the muddy 'dobies. Her weapon was gone, and she was beginning to wish she'd kept it.

"Morning," the voice from behind startled her and she turned to see a kid in a sock-cap.

"Good morning," Anne said. She didn't like to think what she must look like after slipping and sliding her way through the muddy hills. She was glad it was dark.

"Too late for Abraham," the boy sighed.

"I guess," Anne agreed, even though she had no idea what the kid was talking about. *Is he referring to himself in the third person? Just my luck to run into a tweaker,* she thought.

"Abraham Shelter's closed," the boy explained. "So, it's the bridge for we'uns I reckon," he suggested. "T'other side is for girls, you know."

Anne didn't know that whatever space lay beneath the bridge was divided by gender—females on one bank of the river, she presumed, and males on the other—but it sounded like a sensible arrangement.

"See ya," the boy said as he started down the near bank.

"See ya," Anne responded as she crossed the bridge.

Descending the far bank, Anne moved among slumbering bodies, found a dry spot, and slept beneath the bridge until dawn.

Chapter 56

On the morning of July 16, Anne treated her five bridge mates to breakfast at McDonalds and learned that a southbound bus would be leaving Delta City that morning at 9:30. After buying meals for her new friends, she had fifteen dollars left which would, they assured her, get her as far as Telluride—which was two counties away.

After buying her ticket, Anne was broke, but she didn't want to use an ATM so close to Lavender. There was a chance her debit card was already cancelled, but she wouldn't risk using it until she was further away.

She caught the bus and, once on board, she made one last phone call. She spoke briefly to the manager of her Tucson credit union, a man she knew well. Anne turned on the charm and talked him into sending the entire contents of her savings account—all $3,500—online in multiple batches to the Telluride Western Union outlet. She could hear him typing on his computer as he completed the transaction and gave her the address.

Then she hung up. The call was probably traced, but she wished whoever might be listening good luck getting a fix on her in a moving bus surrounded by towering mountains. The bus was a mid-sized vehicle with comfortable seats. Anne sat next to the window and watched helplessly as the bus sped past the caches she'd placed near Olathe and Montrose. She'd have to forget the idea of retrieving caches along the bus route. No chance of asking the driver to stop for hours while she hopped off to retrieve a box or two. That would be not only inconvenient but also unforgivably suspicious. Anyway, she was certain that the three sites nearest to Lavender would soon be crawling with searchers.

That was her fault.

In her haste to flee from the farm, she'd foolishly left her route map behind. Even though it didn't show exact GPS coordinates, the map contained enough information to help her pursuers calculate approximate cache locations.

When the bus stopped to unload passengers in Ridgway, Anne glanced out the window and gazed wistfully at the town park where a few days ago she'd enjoyed a late supper. After Ridgway, the bus passed Last Dollar Road and she craned her neck, longing for a glimpse of the meadow where she'd spent an idyllic afternoon among the flowers and the bees. She stared until the bus rounded a sweeping curve and the trees closed in. Still, she turned her head, looking desperately back, knowing she couldn't actually see the spot, but afraid she might never see it again. Abandoning her gaze at last, she turned in her seat to find the woman across the aisle staring in her direction.

"Thought I saw an owl," she offered this feeble excuse then—when the woman seemed poised to launch a conversation—Anne put her head down and pretended to search through her pack. When her neighbor lost interest, she positioned her pack on the empty seat beside her, improvising to create a 'do not disturb' barricade. She was on the run and couldn't afford to talk to strangers. Turning toward the window, she closed her eyes. Soon she was fast asleep and unable to appreciate the spectacular scenery whizzing by just outside the bus window.

An hour later they arrived in Telluride and only the prodding of the impatient bus driver compelled her to abandon her comfy seat. Stumbling off the bus, Anne went straight to the Main Street Bank and picked up the Western Union transfers, grumbling under her breath at the exorbitant fees the union and the bank charged. Then she threw caution to the wind and walked around to hit every ATM in town until she had nearly depleted her checking account and accumulated another $1,000—all in twenties. Somehow, she managed to beat the account freezers and left them nothing to play with but an account balance of $7.43. Added to her extracted savings, the four thousand and some dollars she accumulated was all she had in the world and it would have to be enough.

Flush with cash and for no particular reason, she surrendered to an impulse and went shopping for junk food and even purchased a couple of Archie comic books from a convenience store. Then she paid for a motel, enduring the third-degree and stink eye of an inquisitive clerk who was overly curious why this disheveled person, who wanted to check-in early, was covered in mud. Why did she insist on paying in cash? Why was she traveling with no vehicle and no luggage except a pair of equally mud-covered packs? As the officious man droned on, Anne smiled on the outside while on the inside she was thinking, *if only I still had my cottonwood club.*

Anne survived the clerk's unwelcome interrogation and steamed up her motel room by spending an hour in the shower. Turning the spigots on full blast, she scraped off mud until the teeny-tiny bar of motel soap was reduced to an insubstantial wafer. Then she simply luxuriated in the cleansing ecstasy of the cascading water. Feeling squeaky clean, she walked to the motel pool and risked swimming in her sports bra and everyday panties. Luckily the only other prospective swimmers, a young couple, seemed to have their hands full with three rambunctious children, so no one seemed to notice, let alone object to, her unconventional swimwear.

Returning to her room, she took another shower, then filled the bathtub and dawdled there in the enveloping steam. Eating potato chips and other junk food, she stayed put and read her comic books until the water turned tepid. She emerged from the tub chewing on a Slim Jim and studied her reflection in the bathroom mirror.

"On the run I see," she said to her towel-swathed self. "Yeah," she scowled, flaunting the Slim Jim like a cheap cigar. "What of it, Copper?" She sneered at the mirror as she pretended to scatter ashes all over the bathroom floor. Then she brandished the unhealthy shaft of meat, salt, soy, wheat, and corn like a pistol as she added, "Pow, pow, pow. Take that, you filthy animal."

Switching the television on, she crawled under the sheets, and lounged in the king-sized bed until, although it was not yet three in the afternoon, she fell sound asleep.

Chapter 57

Sprawled on the floor of his hideout and under the influence of half a dozen beers, Diak Hodell drifted languidly into a deep slumber, anticipating that the professor's long-awaited call would wake him. But no call came. Instead the German slept like the dead, entirely missing most of July 16. By the time he struggled to his feet, it was nearly dusk. Stumbling out the back door, he took a ragged leak, which he imagined rather than felt. Then, sensing he'd done all this before, he zipped up his trousers and drove toward Lavender Hill Farm. He passed the archway but did not turn in. He doubted that the emergency responders from the previous evening were still there, but it was best to be cautious. He drove further until he found a different hiding place for his 4Runner. No sense using the same spot as yesterday.

Repetition draws attention, he told himself.

He parked, grabbed his rifle, loaded the magazine, and walked overland to the lavender field. He slung the weapon across his back and, as he'd done the day before, he again knelt and crawled along a furrow until he was satisfied with his progress. Reaching a point where he could see not only the scene of the Bentley explosion but also the farm buildings below, he stopped to reconnoiter. Both sites seemed unoccupied. The field showed no sign of yesterday's army of investigators and no one seemed to be stirring at the farmhouse. Diak unslung his rifle and threaded his left arm through the sling to create a steady position. Then he lay prone and propped himself up on his elbows. Looking through the ocular lens of his telescopic sight, he examined the scene of his bomb-work. The wreckage of the Bentley was gone, of course, no doubt hauled away to a distant forensic lab.

He wished them luck assembling that jigsaw puzzle.

From this low angle it was difficult to appreciate the size of the crater which undoubtedly memorialized the spot where the doomed automobile had once rested. But the crime scene tape was still in place, so it was possible to estimate how far yesterday's blast had hurled the Bentley. He judged it to be about thirty feet—nine meters—not a bad distance. Moreover, judging from the lack of damage to the surrounding lavender plants, it looked as though the airborne car had jackknifed cleanly backwards and landed more-or-less exactly on the roadway.

Diak smiled with satisfaction.

A day after setting his coordinated charges, the German evaluated the scene objectively and pronounced his work quite acceptable for an improvised field detonation. The blasts had been crude but also effective. He'd used rough explosives—a meat cleaver if you will—to create yesterday's havoc and Russians had died. Today he'd use the scalpel of well-aimed bullets to settle remaining scores with the girl and her partner. Whatever her knowledge and whatever his role in this affair, they'd be next.

Turning his attention to the farmhouse, the German judged the distance to be about two-tenths of a mile—within the accurate range of his rifle—but he moved closer. Heedless of damaging the crop, he left the furrow and crawled across the lavender rows, holding his breath as he advanced. Fighting the aroma of the crushed buds, he continued rummaging through the plants until he was near the road which bisected the field. Stopping there, he used his scope to look again.

"Interesting," the German whispered under his breath.

He couldn't quite comprehend what he saw, but he hadn't come this far to abandon his task. It was time to flush out the occupants. He'd fire a series of preliminary shots, creating noise to draw spectators into the open. Then, he'd pick them off. If no one stirred, he'd forsake his cover and go down to investigate the curiosity he'd spotted in the farmyard. Diak chambered a round and took aim through his telescopic sight. He had no need to adjust the windage or elevation settings. His scope was perfectly calibrated, and his single eye eliminated the need to compensate for the quirks of bifocal vision. No need to close his hollowed-out eye. He could not have been more locked in on his target if he were looking straight through the barrel. He aimed for the center of the farmyard where a tin drinking cup hung on a hook beside the handpump. He stilled his breath and squeezed off a round. The ping of the rifle was barely audible, but not so the instantaneous racket which erupted as the wounded cup clattered noisily to the concrete well pad. Seconds passed, but no one emerged from the house to investigate the cause of the noise.

Just to be sure, Diak shot the cup a second time and watched and listened as it flew into the air and rolled further across the driveway, clattering madly, and bouncing like a thing possessed. Then he waited a full twenty minutes until he was certain no one was home. At last, he stood up and walked through the field and down the gravel road, keeping his rifle at the ready. It was a bold move, but his luck held, and no shots rang out and no one challenged him. When he reached the farmyard, he put on gloves, retrieved the cup, and placed it back on its hook. Eventually, someone would notice the holes, but not soon enough. With the cup in place, he knelt to examine the burnt hull of the Volkswagen.

"A lovers' quarrel?" he mused aloud as he took a closer look at the curiosity he'd first seen from far away. "This was perhaps the noise I heard in the night."

There was a blackened suitcase on the backseat of the VW and, when Diak pried open the front bonnet, he discovered the scorched remnants of six empty toolboxes. The German walked up the front steps, pointed the muzzle of his rifle at the entrance, and rang the doorbell. When no one stirred inside, he turned the knob.

Unlocked—such trusting Americans, he smiled.

Inside, in the front hallway, he found a pile of fragmented padlocks and a pair of bolt cutters. Contemplating the meaning of this debris, he paused to count the number. They totaled six—evidence confirming his suspicions that the girl had, in her mission to stash twelve caches, reached the halfway point. A rapid inspection of the ground floor took him into a home office which appeared to be in disarray. He found no laptops or paperwork. Someone had packed everything up and had done so in a hurry.

"Perhaps not so trusting," he said aloud.

Searching further, he discovered a narrow pasteboard box wedged sideways in a desk drawer and apparently forgotten. The box had been emptied of the business cards it once held, but the printer's proof was still taped to the lid.

"Trinidad Sands, Private Detective," he read the printing out loud. *The name and title sound contrived, he thought, and the card may or may not be a fake, but suppose it is genuine.*

The German smiled. Having two detectives on this job might make for an interesting competition. Returning to the front hall, Diak lingered at the base of the stairwell, looking up and listening.

He decided not to go higher.

It would be too easy to get trapped upstairs should he hear a vehicle approaching or detect unexpected movement on the ground floor. It would be dark soon and, if challenged, he might not get a clear shot from above. Besides he could see there were no back stairs and, if he was forced to flee, he wouldn't be in favor of a two-story jump.

With a combination of regret and irritation, Diak decided to postpone his ambush. He was about to depart when he paused in the hallway and knelt to examine the bolt cutters. This was a tool he might well need but hadn't thought to bring along. As bolt cutters went, this was a fine pair with reinforced jaws and short handles. It was a compact tool, small enough for a man to carry in a belted holster. Would it be too daring to take the cutters? What sort of message would that send to Herr Sands?

"Katze und Maus," he said aloud. "The cat toys with the mouse."

If this rival detective noticed the missing bolt cutters, it might present the German's adversary with a riddle at a time when the man was probably already overtaxed with puzzles. Smiling to himself, the German left the farmhouse. The long summer afternoon was fading, and his two pigeons had flown. Calculating his next move as he walked toward the setting sun, he carried his rifle in one hand and the purloined tool in the other.

Chapter 58

Anne awoke before dawn and took a moment to remember the date and where she was.

I'm in Telluride, San Miguel County, she recalled. *It's July 17th, not yet sun-up, and I'm sleepily gathering wool in a cheap motel—far from Lavender but still a long way from home.*

The television flickered in the darkness. It'd been running all night and the programming had deteriorated. She'd been half-watching a mellow vintage movie before she fell asleep. The movie had ended hours ago, and, in its place, an obnoxious infomercial invaded her motel room. She watched the glowing screen through half-closed eyelids, absently listening to the audio.

According to the grinning TV pitchman and his equally toothsome female partner, everyone in their viewing audience absolutely, positively needed a Super-Rind Lemon-Lime Slicer. As Anne stared blankly, the effervescent announcers tried to persuade her that she needed not one, but two of the lame 'labor-saving' devices.

How, she found herself wondering, *can this insufferable pair smile so broadly while simultaneously spewing their endless palaver? It should be anatomically impossible to grin and talk at the same time, and yet...*

Suddenly the sales team shifted into a frantic 'buy now, time is running out' routine and a digital countdown clock appeared onscreen, with each passing second accompanied by throbbing staccato music. Anne could stand it no longer. Fumbling with her sheets to locate the remote, she pounded buttons until the power was extinguished. Then she fell back and pulled the covers over her head. After a fruitless half-hour spent trying to recapture sleep, Anne got up, dressed, and went for a run.

It was chilly outside and pitch-black. The bright moon of the previous night was obscured by a thick layer of clouds, but streetlights illuminated her path. As she ran along Telluride's deserted avenues, she vaguely wondered whether—dressed as she was in dark leotards, black jacket, and sock cap— she might be mistaken for a cat burglar. But she encountered no people or cars or cats for that matter and it was fortunate that she wasn't a housebreaker since she was far from invisible. Reflective strips on her leggings and shoes made her conspicuous from the waist down and, for added safety, she paused a moment to reverse her jacket, putting the lighter side out.

As she ran on, predawn clouds dissolved and the moon reappeared, its sheen making the chartreuse fabric of her inverted jacket glow incandescently. The moonlight also dogged her steps and spawned a stark pulsating shadow that mirrored each quickening stride. Leaving downtown behind, she took a winding side road, grinning as gravel crunched beneath her running shoes. With each energetic tread, her contentment increased. She accelerated her pace. It felt good to run. She'd missed her routine. Sprinting to the outskirts of town, she came to an intersection where she paused and jogged in place.

Crossroads, she thought. *Picking which way to run is easy—left or right— uphill or down. But my other big choice ain't so simple. Come on, kiddo. You've come on this run to make up your mind, so, once and for all, what'll it be? Do I retrieve the caches or just go home and abandon them?*

When she'd boarded the bus to Telluride, her immediate thought had been simple: she needed to put distance between herself and Lavender. Arriving at the resort town, she'd pursued another immediate need by securing all the cash she could muster and then she'd become...

"Side-tracked," she said aloud as she turned right and headed uphill, regretting how she'd wasted most of yesterday lounging in the tub and shower, eating junk food, reading comics, swimming in her underwear, watching television—in short doing anything to keep from facing up to her responsibilities. Climbing upward, she was soon far enough from the lights of Telluride to appreciate the unblemished night sky. Stopping abruptly, she glanced aloft, relishing the ocean of stars that stretched above her.

"Second star to the right and straight on 'til morning," she told herself as she ran on.

Leaving the crossroads far behind and running resolutely, Anne continued to ascend the right-hand road, vowing to keep going until she reached Peter Pan's mythical Neverland or sprinted back into reality, whichever happened first.

Yesterday, lazing in her motel room, she'd been indulging in fantasy, trying to avoid what—in her heart—she knew must be done. And this morning, given a choice, she might have slept the day away. Only a sheer force of will had compelled her to don her running togs and stumble into the darkness. She'd been trying to avoid the idea of undoing her assignment. Vacillating and procrastinating, she'd been unwilling to commence the unwelcome task of erasing what she'd accomplished just a few days ago. How many days? So much had happened that she couldn't quite recall.

Her internal clock, once so reliable, was shot to pieces and, as she labored uphill, she discovered that her running stride was also ragged. Having covered less than two miles, she was beginning to tire, but she had no intention of stopping. Instead she pushed herself harder, cresting the hill and rounding a corner at full speed until she came upon an open-air stairway.

Curious, she marked time at the base of the unexpected staircase, unable to see the top, but discerning that it led dramatically upward through a stand of close-packed aspen trees. After a moment's hesitation, she sprinted up the metal steps. Taking two at a time, making a terrible racket, and breathing lustily, she scrambled up, ignoring the possibility of losing her footing. Gaining a second wind, she burst over the topmost step with an impromptu shout.

The sudden noise roused a brace of neighborhood dogs, as she ran on, leaving a chorus of barking in her wake. Hitting her stride, Anne relished the sensation of running free. What if she kept running? What if she just kept going and never stopped? How far could she run? Would it be far enough? Once again, her mind filled with doubts and, despite her best intentions, she found herself beginning to backslide.

Forget the caches, she thought as she powered through another dark intersection, *what possible difference will it make if I retrieve them? What's the point?*

Anne tried to convince herself that she'd done her best to fulfill her assignment—at least the first part had gone well. She'd hiked through scenic wilderness to cache toolboxes and, after placing each, she'd turned around and sprinted all the way back to the trailhead. No one told her to run. She did that on her own. Two days ago, she'd hiked one way six times and six times she'd run back, feeling unbridled as she blissfully sprinted through spectacular wilderness scenery. Inspired by the percussion of her strides and the rhythm of her measured breathing, each run had filled her with unconcealed joy, because the only thing she loved more than being outdoors was running in the open.

One-foot, two-foot, red-foot, blue-foot, she told herself over and over. It was a rhythmic cadence she'd employed when running cross-country in school. She was not the fastest in her class, but she was the most dogged—regularly placing in, and often winning, marathons.

"What's your secret?" the cub reporter for the school paper had asked her years ago as he struggled to conduct an interview while running beside the energetic girl.

"It's a simple strategy," Anne told the boy. "First I get out front and then I keep everybody else behind me."

In high school, on the caching trails, and now again on the streets and byways of Telluride, she measured her breathing and set a steady pace. That's how she'd accomplished it, how she'd completed the first half of her assignment. She'd done it by taking one step at a time. She was proud of having mastered the task's physical challenges and also the accompanying brain work. Placing each toolbox had required her to expend physical effort but setting out the caches had also required an intellectual investment.

On 3x5 cards carried in the broad pockets of her cargo shorts, she'd jotted several paragraphs of cleverly worded hints to guide the searchers. For each cache site, she'd designed landmarks and invented ingenious clues—creating a series of waypoint instructions designed to entertain and bamboozle the student seekers.

A week from now, when the fieldtrip students were supposed to arrive to search for her caches, she'd been certain the class would be in for a significant learning experience. She was convinced the searchers would have needed to possess not only exemplary orienteering skills but also a certain amount of instinct and not a little luck. The success of her professor's field assignment depended entirely upon her performance. If she failed to place each box precisely and didn't cleverly describe its location by fashioning a challenging matrix of well-crafted directions and hints, Dr. Clark's entire assignment would be ruined.

Anne swerved to avoid a cluster of roadside pebbles and the near mishap brought her firmly back to the present as she admitted that, despite her best efforts, Dr. Clark's assignment was well and truly screwed. She'd done her best, but it was pointless to celebrate the past. Nothing could alter the fact that she'd failed to place all twelve caches. She'd done an incomplete job and was poised on the brink of undoing even that.

It was annoying to think of retrieving her work and more bothersome still to realize that some of the caches were going to fall into the wrong hands. Still, she wished everyone luck because—although they had her map—they'd be searching for the caches without the benefit of the precise coordinates or her written clues. Anyone else would struggle to find the cleverly hidden boxes, whereas finding them would be easy for her, if only she could convince herself that the effort was worthwhile.

"Oh, man," she said aloud, "just do it!"

In an ideal world, she'd have completed her assignment, but that was impossible now. Her only option was to accept the reality of having to reverse her work. She'd embarked on her Telluride run hoping to convince herself to do what needed to be done. And it had taken five miles of sucking oxygen and pumping adrenaline to nail down a rationale for retracing her steps.

It all boiled down to a sense of duty.

She'd do what was necessary to honor her professor, her chosen profession, and herself. Deciding to pursue archaeology as a field of study had been an important choice—the most momentous adult decision she'd ever made—and she stubbornly refused to accept the prospect of failing to pass the first real test of her professional tenacity. Dr. Clark had entrusted her to complete her assignment and, if she couldn't finish the job, at least she could limit the damage. She'd tried to convince herself to give up, admit defeat, and slink home with her tail between her legs. But her dash through the Telluride darkness had gotten her juices flowing. With each running step, her resolve to see things through grew stronger. The burst of pure exercise had tapped into her ornery streak and rekindled an obstinate desire to retrieve what caches she could, even though the effort was destined to be incomplete.

The re-energized woman ran another mile and then, as the sky began to lighten, she made a wide circle and turned back toward Telluride. The run had done her a world of good. Reinvigorated, she pushed her doubts aside and dashed back. Feeling confident and determined, she sprinted through the darkness until she reached the steep stairway.

"Easy does it, jack rabbit," she cautioned herself.

She stopped at the crest and stood for a moment with one hand on the metal bannister, measuring her breath. The dogs aroused earlier by her impromptu war-whoop were silent now. Somewhere a rooster was crowing. The bannister was moist with morning dew. Jazzed but mindful, she decided not to chance breaking her neck with a pell-mell plunge down the slick steps.

Determined to be neither a careless Jack nor a tumbling Jill, she sauntered down, assuming a prudent and majestic stride. Keeping one hand on the bannister, she used the other to affect an unhurried parade-wave. She descended gradually, pretending to be a debutant, and acknowledging the adulation of an unseen audience, until she safely reached the bottom. Then she instantly skipped forward and resumed her run. Heading back toward downtown, she shelved her regrets and sought to embrace the future, seeking to accept her fate with a mixture of pride and sorrow.

She was proud of having done an exemplary job in placing her initial caches, but sad that her work was incomplete; proud that she had faithfully followed her instructions, but sad that Dr. Clark's assignment was blown; profoundly proud of her resolve to retrieve her caches, but also profoundly sad to think that—with her professor missing and no searching students on the horizon—there'd be no one to appreciate her work.

Part VI: End Game

Chapter 59

July 17, Dawn
Telluride, Colorado

After escaping from Lavender and landing in Telluride, Anne had been refocusing her energy with a predawn run through the dark streets and by-ways of the mountain town. And she might have run forever had her pride not compelled her to return. As she sprinted back through downtown, the sun was rising and morning mist swirled around her until she abruptly stopped, stood on the sidewalk, and stared at a newspaper.

The paper was folded in half and pressed up against the glass door of a sidewalk vending machine. She could only see the paper's masthead, the lead headline, and a single photograph, but that was plenty. It was the headline which caught her eye: 'Spectacular Lavender Fire.' In the same instant she'd noticed the photo.

She'd never liked that picture.

Luckily it was an old image. But why publish that one? What was the point of using her old sorority photo? Her hair had been lighter in those days, an adolescent experiment, chemically altered to achieve an artificial shade of spun gold. Given the sharp contrast to her present and natural brunette, it was unlikely anyone would connect the beaming blonde in the newspaper photo with the dour brunette standing on this foggy corner in downtown Telluride. It was almost as if whoever released that photo had no interest at all in finding her.

She could see her reflection in the window of the vending machine. Her mirror image shimmered in the thin slab of smoky glass that separated her from the newspaper. For an instant, her image hovered there, seeming to overlap with the newspaper photo. She reached up to finger a strand of her raven-black hair—black as the finish on those Bentleys that pursued her, black as—she couldn't think of another example. Using the vending machine as an impromptu mirror, she grasped the wayward strand and pushed it back under her cap while, beyond her current reflection, lay that sheepishly grinning and very blonde image of her younger self.

What was the point of publishing such a dated photo?

Obviously, the authorities must have deduced that her body didn't burn up with the Bug. That conclusion would have been obvious with so many first responders and forensic experts available just uphill from the VW's funeral pyre. How much time had it taken them to realize that she was not there? Apparently long enough for her to get where she was now—two counties away from the scene.

Was that far enough?

Well, it was what it was. Fleeing from Lavender, she'd reached Delta City on foot. She'd slept in the open before riding the bus to Telluride where she spent the night in a motel bed, then wallowed in procrastination until finally galvanizing her thinking with a brisk morning run. And she'd indulged in this marathon of frenetic activity only to end up on this street corner to discover her picture—inaccurate though it may be—on the front page of the *Denver Post*.

She knew that the *Post* was a statewide paper, but she was equally certain that the dateline heading for the Lavender story would read 'Delta County.' If so, chances were that, after a glance, folks here in San Miguel County would care less. Thinking it over, she decided that, if folks in these parts were disinterested, the incident would draw even less attention as she continued further south. Somehow, she'd have to get through Colorado, over the border, and back into Arizona, a state away, where a fire, however spectacular, would cease to be front-page news. Then she'd be well beyond the reach of the story and traveling back to Tucson—back to something resembling reality.

However, she was not in Arizona yet and to see exactly where things stood, she needed to read the Post. But getting to the newspaper was going to be a problem. It was early morning and nearby businesses were closed and the vending machine required four quarters and—once again, just like at the Lavender carwash—Anne had nothing but folding money. Remembering the carwash and the quarters made her think of Trinidad. Remembering the master of Lavender Hill Farm made her think of the kiss they had shared and the beautiful tune he'd played on his harmonica after supper and...

Think about something else, she admonished herself.

Anne had encountered no one on her morning run and she was alone on the sidewalk. Even if someone appeared, she'd be reluctant to attract attention by asking a stranger for change. So, she just stood there, dollar bill in hand, staring at her reflection and fingering her hair.

"Pretty." The voice was so near that Anne jumped. "Sorry," the voice continued, "I didn't mean to startle you."

The old woman was short, almost doll-like, and she was dressed in a vintage outfit that might have been all the rage in 1940. She wore a feathered cap and an ancient fur-collared coat with a hem so long that it obscured not only her ankles but her feet as well—creating the impression that she levitated above the sidewalk. Anne shook her head, trying to dislodge the image of a floating woman.

Get a grip, Anne told herself.

She and the woman seemed frozen in time as morning clouds rolled in and it began misting rain. Shivering, Anne turned up her collar and pulled her sock-cap down to cover her ears. It was cold. She missed her scarf.

"You were admiring your reflection," the woman said. "And why not? Such a pretty face. Now, you'll excuse me, I'm sure."

Anne stepped aside as the woman unsnapped an old-fashioned pocket-book, dug out four quarters, fed them into the vending machine slot, and opened the lid.

"Do you want one, dear?" the woman asked as she held the lid open and inclined her head in Anne's direction.

"I only have this dollar," said Anne in a voice so small and helpless that it took her by surprise.

"Oh, my dear, no worries." The woman used her gloved hand to pluck a newspaper. "I'll trade you," she said. She took and pocketed Anne's dollar, handed a paper to the young stranger, took another one for herself, and carefully guided the glass lid back into place. Then, in response to Anne's quizzical look, the old woman added, "No harm done. I'll put extra quarters in next time."

"Thank you," said Anne as she gripped the newspaper with both hands but avoided looking at it. Though burning with curiosity, she resisted the temptation to immediately unfold the paper. No sense appearing over-anxious. She wanted to avoid attracting attention and this corner was much too conspicuous. People were beginning to appear on the sidewalk and cars were passing. She needed to move. If the old woman lingered, Anne would walk unhurriedly away and find a quiet spot to read the article.

"Well, thanks again and good morning," Anne said, and she was about to turn away when the woman spoke again.

"Oh my," said the woman as she studied the front page. "Oh my," she repeated, and she clicked her tongue and shook her head. "Such a shame and so young. Such a pity, don't you agree?"

The woman waggled her paper and gazed pointedly at Anne, seeming to see her for the first time and appearing to be sizing her up. Fearful that she might be recognized, Anne quickly unfolded her newspaper and held it up to obscure her face. As she did so, her attention was instantly drawn to the caption below her photo. Inhaling sharply, she found herself tangled in a web of disbelief as she read that, according to authorities, the young woman pictured there—her younger self—had tragically burned to death.

Chapter 60

The old woman who'd helped her buy the newspaper might have called out, but Anne didn't look back as she spun around, rushed from the corner, and sprinted down the block. She ran in a daze, clutching the newspaper and ignoring curious glances from a growing number of early morning pedestrians and motorists.

So, I'm dead now, Anne thought.

Despite her intention to keep a low profile, the instant she'd read her own name and the words 'burned to death' in the same sentence, an image of her girlhood home in flames clouded her senses and she could think of nothing to do but run.

Gripped in a panic of full flight, Anne sprinted around a corner where her abrupt appearance startled a dog-walker. Swerving to avoid a collision with the man and his trio of energetic poodles, she dropped her newspaper, voiced an apology, and knelt down to recover the fluttering sheets. Bending to assist her, the flustered man tangled the leashes, creating a churning jumble of people, paper, and animals. In the confusion, the stridently barking dogs broke free, bursting through cascading pages of newsprint and scampering away in different directions while the distraught man howled with indignation.

Seeking to escape the chaos, Anne bolted from the scene and raced toward an alleyway where she turned sharply, lost her balance, and fell hard. She stayed face-down on the asphalt for several minutes trying to regain her composure, until she felt pain in her right hand. Remaining prone, she turned her head and glanced at her palm. It was bleeding. She stood up and heard bits of glass crunching under her feet.

"Fine," she said aloud.

She found her circumstances almost laughable. This pristine mountain community was legendary for its litter control, and yet, somehow, she'd managed to fall—and fall spectacularly—into one of Telluride's few piles of trash. Thinking of litter, Anne recalled dropping the newspaper into a herd of dogs. Sighing, she envisioned the aftermath and pictured a blizzard of renegade pages swirling through the town's otherwise unblemished streets. She could imagine the disassembled publication meandering unchecked through spotless neighborhoods, like a flock of sluggish seagulls. Dropping it had been accidental, of course. She hadn't meant to litter. But how long before the town's polite but firm patrol officers would be on her trail? How long before she was surrounded by alpine police, riding mountain bikes, decked out in helmets, crisply starched uniforms, and shorts? Not long, she imagined as her anxiety over being discovered caused her to visualize a mob of indignant citizens marking her trail.

"That way, officers, the dang litterbug went that way."

Convinced that having to talk her way out of a littering citation would most certainly ruin her day, Anne hurriedly improvised a disguise. Pulling her cap further down, she reversed her jacket, putting the dark side out again. Then she wrapped the remains of her handkerchief around her bleeding hand and took her bearings. She was in an alleyway, a narrow pavement partially filled with trash dumpsters and lined on both sides with the rear entrances of downtown businesses. The street number and name of each shop was neatly stenciled on its back door and she walked quickly down the alley until she discovered what she was seeking. The door was unlocked, so she slipped inside and found herself in a busy kitchen.

"Sorry," she said as she sidled past workers who were dunking pots and pans into steaming sinks. "Sorry, excuse me." The dishwashers looked up briefly before resuming their tasks, apparently indifferent to her passage. She slipped by a trio of busy cooks who were similarly apathetic until she reached a set of swinging doors where she encountered a frowning waitress.

"Well," said the waitress.

"Sorry," said Anne.

"Sit at the counter," the waitress sighed with an exasperated tone. "And next time, honey, use our front door instead of trying to buck the line."

The place was crowded. Every table was full, and several prospective diners were waiting their turns on comfy chairs in a brightly lit alcove near the restaurant's front windows. The walls vibrated with noisy conversations and sporadic laughter as people hailed one another across the broad dining room. This was obviously a local hangout and luckily, if the waitress' reaction to her was any indication, it was a place where Anne could blend in. Even if the law was seeking her outside, they'd never find her in here. An empty stool at the counter seemed to beckon. Crossing the room, she sat down, ordered coffee and breakfast, and tried to calm herself.

Thankfully, the coffee wasn't long in coming.

The newspaper, her dash through the streets, the poodle disaster, and her fall in the alley had unnerved Anne and her hands were still shaking as she raised the steaming cup to her lips. Blood was soaking through her handkerchief. She prayed no one would notice.

She hadn't intended to end up in Telluride. It was just where the bus took her. Back in Lavender they had her map and they'd be expecting her to double-back on her route, so they were probably watching all the towns along the way. But this town wasn't on her itinerary. Driving her VW north a few days ago, she'd bypassed Telluride entirely as she cached a toolbox west of this isolated mountain town. To reach her out-of-town caching spot, she'd parked near Sawpit, crossed, and re-crossed the San Miguel River, then continued on. Even with the aid of her map, they wouldn't be looking for her here.

'They,' she thought. *Have I already reduced Trinidad to a personal pronoun—or rather an impersonal one? Have I already condensed him into an amorphous 'they?'*

Despite the tension that had simmered between the two of them these past few days, she felt they'd connected. There'd been a spark and she believed he'd felt it too and there'd been something else, something even more important than a flicker of sexual attraction. Being with him had compelled her to suppress the past and remain grounded in the present. To her, that inspiration to 'be here now' was a gift beyond measure. If only she could have trusted him. If only he'd trusted her. For Anne, it was all about trust. It was hard to think of Trinidad as undependable but, try as she might, she could no longer muster confidence in him. Remove trust, take away confidence, and what was left?

Think about something else, she told herself, *Or, better yet, forget the past and think about where you are right now.*

Was she safe in Telluride? She'd thought so until she saw this morning's newspaper. Now she was uncertain. Cautiously, she scanned the dining area. At least a dozen people were reading newspapers. Feeling suddenly exposed, she swiveled on the counter seat to put her back to the crowd. Despite the disparity between the newspaper photo and her present appearance, someone might recognize her. If she was spotted in this town, she'd be trapped here, because she was literally boxed in. Unless a person could fly, or had a four-wheel drive and a death wish, there was only one road in and out of Telluride.

After breakfast, she'd need to be on that road and gone.

She'd flee south, retrieving toolboxes as she went, which meant she needed transportation. The bus which had carried her to Telluride yesterday would be passing through again this afternoon and it would retrace her caching route, taking her back over Lizard Head Pass and on south to Cortez. She could certainly afford a ticket, but public transportation wasn't going to cut it. She'd have to buy a car. She had money and she was one step ahead of whoever was trying to convince the rest of the world that she was dead. By now those same people would have frozen her bank accounts and be poised to trace her cell phone. But they'd be too late to do either because Anne was about to get busy.

After hiding out in the Telluride restaurant long enough to eat a modest breakfast and grab a newspaper left by one of the diners, she finally read the article. It alleged that she was dead, the victim of some as yet unknowable tragedy. The implication was that no one in law enforcement would be looking for her, but she had her doubts.

Since arriving in Telluride, she'd been sleep-walking, believing that she was somehow clear of the chaos swirling around her. She'd indulged in childish excesses, lounged around, and ignored her mission. She'd toyed with the possibility of hiding out in Telluride and had nearly abandoned the notion of retrieving the toolboxes before her morning run reignited her resolve. Even then, she'd deluded herself into thinking she was out of danger until the newspaper threw her a curve.

Bottom of the ninth, she told herself. *How many strikes left? Time to swing for the fences—time to get a move on!*

She downed a final cup of coffee and left the newspaper behind, minus the front page which she ripped off and pocketed. Then she edged to the cash register to pay her tab plus a modest tip. She'd have preferred to leave a more generous amount, but she decided it was best to remain a less memorable diner.

"Ten dollars," the waitress would tell the authorities. "You bet I remember that girl!"

Needing to pee and also anxious to tie-up loose ends, Anne walked briskly to the ladies' room. Safely seated in a locked stall, she made sure her remaining cash was well-distributed between her jacket and pants pockets. For good measure, she stuffed a wad of twenties under her sock cap. She had no intention of blowing her entire bundle on a used car, so she wouldn't diminish her chances of striking a bargain by showing too much cash at the start of negotiations.

She unrolled enough toilet paper to make a more absorbent wrap for her injured palm and put on a glove to keep the makeshift bandage in place. Next, she unrolled enough squares to finish her business. Then she rolled off enough to blow her nose and secured another handful to put in her pocket, just in case. Flushing the commode, she exited the stall, washed and dried her free hand, stuffed paper towels in the bathroom sink, and turned on the tap.

Other than calling Tucson days ago and using her cell phone yesterday to call the bank, she'd kept it powered off hoping to make it harder to trace. Just to make certain, she'd sacrifice the device. When the sink was nearly overflowing, she used her good hand to submerge her cell phone. After holding it underwater for a moment, she unstopped the sink, wrapped the compromised phone inside a nest of paper towels, and stuffed everything into the nearest trash receptacle. Maybe she should have tried calling Dr. Clark one more time, but what was the point of leaving a voice message to say she'd failed? He'd know that soon enough when she showed up in Tucson, dragging the remaining toolboxes behind her. She dried her hand, put on her other glove, and walked back to the motel, where she retrieved her packs and went looking for a used car lot.

Twenty minutes later, she was sitting in the cramped and dingy and overheated office of Creekside Motors. You'd be surprised what an attractive female can buy, for cash-money, at a small town used car lot, especially if she chooses the salesman carefully and unbuttons enough to bare a little cleavage. Anne was coquettish as she displayed sufficient cash and just enough flesh to dispense with such formalities as providing identification, proof of insurance, or residency.

The old Nissan pickup truck she wished to purchase had a manual shift, could she drive a stick, the salesman asked?

Yep.

Paying cash?

Yep.

Wouldn't she prefer the company's finance plan?

Nope.

No trade in?

Nope.

Test drive?

Unnecessary.

"Kind'a in a hurry, ain't cha, honey?" the balding salesman asked Anne with an unvarnished leer.

"Got a sick kid in New Mexico," she lied. "Ten years old with leukemia and needing his mama."

"I know what you mean," sniffed the salesman. Apparently, she'd struck a nerve with her mama-and-kid story because the salesman instantly shifted from flirting to parenting. "Okay then. Temp sticker's in the back window.

The tank is full. Tires will carry you for now, but don't wait too long to replace them. Here's your paperwork—title and bill of sale. And that insurance card in your wallet might work if the cops pull you over, but—like I said—get an updated one ASAP. Now, here's one set of keys, truck box key included—there's another set in the ignition. Don't forget to use your seatbelts and drive careful."

He's concerned, she thought, *and gullible. He'll remember my sob-story and remember New Mexico and the sick kid when Trinidad's gang or the Bentleys come asking after me, and maybe that'll throw them off my trail for a time. Meanwhile the 'burned to death' story might keep the public at bay, but that might be a mixed blessing because, if I get in trouble, who's going to lift a finger to help a dead girl?*

"Miss?" the salesman asked. He must have been attempting to continue their conversation but—lost in thought—Anne hadn't responded. Had he asked a question?

"Sorry," she said. "I was miles away."

"I just asked if everything was okay," he explained. "Is it?"

"Couldn't be better," she lied.

As she climbed into the battered truck and started it up, she waved goodbye to the salesman. He tipped his hat to her and that bit of Western chivalry conjured up thoughts of Trinidad and caused her to wonder once again whose side her attractive but untrustworthy companion was on.

"Think about something else," she said aloud.

Chapter 61

Carefully adhering to the speed limit, Anne had no intention of getting a ticket as she drove through the afternoon sunshine and out of Telluride. She was traveling west and taking the only conceivable exit out of town. When she was certain she was not being followed, she continued on to the tiny burg of Sawpit where she parked, grabbed her GPS, and sprinted three miles. She moved quickly to cross the San Miguel River, hopping from rock to rock to avoid getting wet, ignoring the primitive beauty of the area as she rushed to retrieve cache number three which she'd placed there two days ago. She found the toolbox exactly where she'd left it, well above the water line and nestled in a tangle of downed tree limbs.

Anne paused long enough to drink from one of her water bottles. Then she picked up the toolbox and hiked back along the cascading current, ignoring the beautiful river. Crossing the rushing water again, she climbed the steep bank to reach the road, waited out of sight until there was no traffic, and sprinted over the pavement. She placed the retrieved toolbox in the truck bed, made a U-turn, and doubled-back to pick up Colorado 145 heading south.

Still heedless of the spectacular alpine scenery and looking constantly over her shoulder, she followed the ascending pavement up into the San Juan Mountains, which even the most jaded visitors compared to the Swiss Alps. The vistas were breathtaking, but the alpine beauty was lost on her. Driving the VW this way a few days ago, she'd stopped to take a selfie with towering

mountains looming in the background and both arms outstretched like
Maria von Trapp in the opening moments of 'The Sound of Music.' Then
she'd stood in awed silence, drinking in the majesty of the alpine scene. Now
she was on a mission and the topography which had so recently captivated
her had become a blur.

Would she ever be free again to celebrate Nature?

Reaching the lofty pass, she left the highway, parked behind a screening hill, and began her four-mile run through acres of moist green tundra to
recover the Lizard Head toolbox.

Chapter 62

C. Arnold Clark, PhD, lowered his field glasses and leaned against the fender of his Rubicon trying to regain his bearings in the growing chill of late afternoon. He was disoriented and struggling to catch his breath as he tried to make sense of what he was seeing. Since using his personal smartphone to call in the treasure coordinates, he'd been parked for hours at Lizard Head Pass, watching the trailhead, and waiting for the Russians to show. He'd been expecting to see black Bentleys, so it was with mixed emotions that he watched the arrival of an old canary-yellow Nissan truck.

An instant later, he stared in astonishment as he saw a familiar figure emerge from the parked vehicle and set off in the direction of the Lizard Head cache. Everything happened so fast that, before he could stop her, Anne Scriptor was sprinting toward the rigged toolbox, running full speed directly toward the bomb he'd so recently, and with such great personal exertion, planted there. Even if he'd wanted to halt the energetic girl, she was much too far away. In any event, he was immobilized by indecision.

What in the blind world was going on? Why was Anne here and not the Russians? What in blazes was keeping them? And how was she even alive?

Her last telephone message had come to his smartphone days ago from the little burg of Lavender. When he heard her voicemail, he'd looked for the place on the map. It was a dinky settlement, less than twenty miles from Delta City, which was the halfway point of her caching assignment. Based on her message, he assumed she'd stop in this Lavender place briefly and then continue on to cache the remaining toolboxes—performing activities which should have taken her further north and well out of harm's way. These were his assumptions until earlier this afternoon when he saw the newspaper report of her death. And he was just beginning to get his head around that shocking news when the girl herself miraculously appeared at Lizard Head, minus her Volkswagen, but apparently unharmed. On one hand, he couldn't believe his eyes, on the other, he'd been distracted and had nearly missed seeing the girl arrive.

Moments before Anne drove back into his life, the professor had been several yards away from his vehicle and pacing across the mountainous terrain in search of a phone signal. A desert dweller and unused to the fickleness of alpine cell service, he'd miscalculated. The Saudis required that he call every day. If he failed to check-in, there would be no jet waiting to whisk him to Denver and no connecting flights to New York and on to his Arabian sanctuary. To keep his customers happy and his exit open, he needed a cell signal.

After frantically waving his last remaining burner phone at the unapologetic sky and tilting his torso at awkward angles, he'd finally found an iota of coverage and used the uncooperative device to leave a message assuring the Saudis that all was well.

Completing his call, he was returning to his jeep when he saw the unfamiliar truck leave Highway 145 and roll to a stop on the far side of the broad alpine meadow which stretched below his elevated position. Looking across the wide gap which separated his vantage point from the far trailhead, he'd sighted Anne and his mind seemed to freeze. Seeing her alive was the last thing he'd expected, and the shock left him both jubilant and perplexed. For a feverish moment, it was all he could do to restrain himself from leaping into the Rubicon and rushing over to welcome her back to the land of the living. But by the time he'd entertained that notion, she was already running across the undulating tundra.

"You go, girl," Clark said aloud and, watching her vigorous stride until she disappeared, he smiled.

The running figure was far away, but it was Anne all right. Even at a distance there was no mistaking her energy. She ran like the wind, so he couldn't
have overtaken her even if he wanted to, and he wasn't certain he did.

Regardless of his personal feelings for the girl, he was too deep into the
end game of his scheme to risk contacting her. So, partly out of curiosity,
but also to serve his own self-interest, he decided to wait. It would take her a
couple of hours to innocently retrieve the bomb and yet there was no danger
unless she opened the box. She wouldn't open it—would she?

Chapter 63

The afternoon was steadily advancing as Clark sat in his jeep on the edge of a broad alpine meadow which lined both sides of Highway 145. His position was elevated, overlooking the meadow on his side, the paved highway, and the far meadow as well. Using his field glasses, the professor studied the faraway scene as he waited for Anne to return to her unusual vehicle. The Lizard Head trailhead was distant. The yellow truck appeared no larger than a thimble. He found it difficult to believe that the girl was alive and that his expected victims hadn't shown. But she was not merely alive. By the look of her stride, she was flourishing.

As for the whereabouts of the Brotherhood, he was certain he'd called the correct number.

Hours ago, gripped by a mixture of emotions, he'd stopped south of the pass in the tiny village of Rico, where cell service was still relatively strong, and made his call. As promised, he'd used his personal smartphone and he had the Russians on speed-dial, so he was positive he'd called the right number. It rang twice and he hadn't waited for someone to say hello. He'd simply read the coordinates and the combination code for the padlock and then repeated the numbers.

"Got that, you Commie bastards?" Clark had asked.

"Yes," said a voice on the other end and the thick Slavic accent made Clark smile. Apparently, the smooth-talking Magar had already been replaced.

He'd made his call and momentarily contemplated destroying his smartphone. But he just couldn't extinguish the familiar device. So, he'd made the call and kept his phone and yet the treasure-hungry Brotherhood had not converged on Lizard Head. Not a single Russian had arrived from any point of the compass to give Clark the satisfaction of watching his hoodwinked buyers get blown to pieces. Not one Russian had taken the bait and come rushing to Lizard Head to feel the sting of his vengeance for the abuse he'd endured from his cantankerous buyers and their role in Anne's death. Instead, his faithful graduate assistant herself had shown up—very much undead—and rushed up the trail to collect the deadly box.

What the hell-fire is going on? he asked himself.

A few days ago, he'd sent Anne to Colorado to cache a dozen toolboxes, including toolbox number one with the priceless Clovis point. Although he hadn't heard from her for days, her most recent phone messages had confirmed that she was at the midpoint of her assignment and was on her way north with the exception of an unscripted stop in some hole-in-the-wall called Lavender. So, naturally, when Clark had boarded the Saudi jet in the wee hours of July 15 and flown toward northern Arizona, he'd believed that Anne was safe. He'd continued to think she was safe when he recovered the Clovis from McElmo Creek. Even as he fell in the wilderness and struggled to make his way back to his jeep and while he twiddled his thumbs in the urgent care clinic and even as he slumbered in Cortez, he'd continued to believe that Anne was safe.

But that dogged belief had been abruptly shattered earlier this afternoon when he read that she'd been killed. As he struggled with a mixture of grief and anger brought on by the devastating news of Anne's death, he'd summoned the Russians. And yet, the Russians hadn't come. Instead, the girl was here and, although her unexpected appearance had certainly relieved him, it also caused him to rethink things. Suddenly he began to suspect that something was not quite right, and he needed to take inventory.

Think!

Since arriving in Colorado, Clark had been operating under several assumptions, but now things were changing, and he found himself wondering what was real. He'd believed Anne was safe and then he'd believed she was dead, but now she was safe again providing she didn't open the Lizard Head toolbox. Meanwhile, he himself had recovered the McElmo cache and so it should follow that the Clovis was in his possession, even though he hadn't checked to make certain the treasure was there. All at once, these introspective exercises led him in a vast circle until his thoughts became muddled and he experienced a sinking feeling.

He'd come so far and endured so much and yet...*did he in fact have the Clovis?*

Anne would be gone for hours and he had to know. In a kind of panic, he hurriedly extricated himself from the driver's seat, limped around the Rubicon, and opened the rear door. Taking a deep breath, he centered what he hoped was the treasure box on the cargo floor and instinctively reached for the key.

"Dang it," he said aloud.

He'd purposely left his special key behind in the Saudi jet in order to keep it and the Clovis box separate. It was one of his 'just in case' measures and the precaution had seemed like a good idea at the time. Now he wasn't so sure.

Can I pick the padlock? he wondered as he reached for his multi-tool.

For fifty years, since his undergraduate days, he'd faithfully carried the versatile tool, which folded neatly into a small holster on his belt. Two days ago, the device had probably saved his life when he'd used it to manufacture a campfire from scratch. He was never without the thing and today was no exception. He extracted it, then paused. He had to be certain the Clovis point was there, but he needed to slow down and take a moment to think about what he was doing. Acting impetuously could damage the artifact. He flipped through the multi-tool but couldn't find the right utensil for such a delicate operation.

"Thinner," he said aloud. "I need a..."

He put the tool aside, left the box where it was, and hurriedly scanned the ground.

"Come on," he growled as he searched the terrain surrounding the Rubicon. "Do you mean to tell me that I've chanced upon the one and only place in conspicuous-consumption-consumer- America that..."

He left that thought unfinished because he spotted what he needed. Bending down, he retrieved the dusty strip of aluminum and rushed back to his jeep. As he hurriedly used his multi-tool to fashion the sliver of metal into a makeshift key, he considered the irony.

Is this ironic? he wondered.

He could never remember how you knew for certain whether something was ironic. Maybe what he thought of as irony was merely an ordinary twist of fate. Whatever he felt while he worked, his thoughts turned to the past.

With a nostalgic smile, he recalled how often he'd arrived at the site of an American archaeological dig to find the ground littered with vintage pop-top beer cans. He remembered too that, wherever old discarded beer cans accumulate, they are inevitably accompanied by additional litter in the form of throwaway ring-tabs.

"Pop the top and toss it," he said as he worked. "Then drink the suds and toss the can. Repeat. That's the predictable agenda of countless rural beer bashes. That's the tried and true American littering habit—a pervasive after-hours ritual, which leaves behind mountains of trash."

In truth—and maybe this was the ironic part—the pop-top technology was over half a century old. It was a chronology which suggested that the metallic bones of discarded beer cans and their ubiquitous ring-tabs could be considered relics in their own right. As he labored to fashion a substitute key, it seemed only fitting to Clark that he was making use of a vintage ring-tab artifact to liberate an ancient Clovis one.

After a few more moments spent reshaping the pliable aluminum, the professor examined his work. Slowly inserting the crude key into the padlock, Clark took a deep breath, gently turned it counterclockwise, and felt the mechanism give way.

'Think outside the box,' he'd often challenged his students to adhere to that maxim. He wondered if they ever paid attention. He wondered if Anne had guessed that one of the unassuming toolboxes which she'd so dutifully cached included a false mechanism—a bogus hollowed-out padlock which did double duty as the hiding place for his priceless Clovis point.

Yes, the point was that small—so small that it could be bundled in a tiny square of gauze and stuffed into a false compartment inside a standard pad-lock. Clark had formed the compartment by hollowing out the slot where the blade of a key was ordinarily inserted. With the Clovis in place, he'd used a false plug to seal the space.

Carefully extracting his improvised key, he pulled the plug free. Remov-ing the gauze, he held the precious point in his palm. After a moment's reflec-tion, he rewrapped the Clovis, repositioned the artifact, and clicked the plug back into place. Then he threw the ring-tab away. Whatever happened now, the treasure was once again secure and concealed in the last place anyone would look.

The lock was such an ingenious hiding place, and the special key that opened it was so vital, that Clark had elected to keep the two items strictly apart until the last moment. So, he'd taken the precaution of purposely leav-ing the key behind on the jet, taped to the bottom of his passenger seat. Then he'd retrieved the Clovis toolbox and deposited it in the rear of the Rubicon with the padlock in place. He'd taken these extra measures not because he feared the Scarlet Brotherhood and not because he didn't trust the Saudis.

He'd instituted these safeguards in hopes of deceiving the German detective.

For weeks, Clark had been aware that, in addition to the Russians and the Saudis, there was another competitor who longed to possess the Clovis. Somehow, a rogue detective had gotten wind of the priceless artifact and his efforts to insinuate himself into Clark's affairs had been subtle at first and then bold enough to arouse suspicion. For months, Clark had sensed that he was being watched. Then the Saudis had noticed something too and it was they who confirmed Clark's misgivings.

Returning to the Rubicon's cab, he settled inside and looked across the distance that separated him from the yellow truck. He would watch for Anne, mirroring the actions of others who, in turn, had been keeping an eye on him. Sitting there, waiting for a glimpse of the returning girl, he recalled the moment when the Saudis had called him to communicate their concerns. Clark had just talked the Russians into a down payment and he was sitting at his computer, watching the two-million trickle into his bank account, when one of his burner phones rang.

"Dr. Clark, is that you?" His Saudi contact, who went by the name of Hamza, had been speaking in a voice so diminished that his words were scarcely audible on the phone.

"Yes, but I can barely hear you," said Clark.

"You should be aware that you are being watched," Hamza whispered.

"Watched? When? Where?" Clark decided to feign surprise, even though he'd already become aware of the watchers.

"At all times. At your home and on your campus."

"So pretty much all day and everywhere," Clark said, confirming what he already knew. But there was one thing he didn't know, and he asked, "So, who's watching me?"

"Not the Brotherhood and not us. But there is another who has been watching you for many weeks. He slipped in before the Russians came and went, and before our arrangement."

"Before...?" Clark asked. His mind mulled over this chronology. *Before the Russians? Have they been watching me that long?* "Who...?" he asked aloud.

"We do not know his exact nationality," Hamza continued. "Some say German, although he uses a diversity of...."

"Are you saying this is one man?" Clark interrupted.

"One man—a rogue detective—who employs certain others."

"Sounds pretty vague," Clark complained. "Does this man have a name?"

"A birth name only." There was a pause and then, in a voice even smaller than his original whisper, a voice no louder than snow striking a tombstone, Hamza intoned the name, "Diak."

"You sound worried," Clark said. "How worried should *I* be?"

"Even I do not know the true nature of your treasure, but my superiors are convinced that this resourceful man has somehow ferreted out that knowledge. He knows what you possess, and he knows its value. Therefore, until you have safely arrived on our end," Hamza whispered, "you should take every precaution. We suggest you devise a means to slip away undetected."

"Disappear you mean?" asked Clark.

"That would be advisable."

"Any idea how I can manage that?" asked Clark.

"We will provide transport. The details and the timing we leave to your well-known intellect," whispered the Saudi.

"Glad you have such faith in me."

"We presume that our generous offer will motivate you. Good day, Doctor."

Hamza was right. Eight million dollars was one gigantic motivator.

As soon as Hamza's warning call had ended, Clark did what he did best. He conducted a cavalcade of research. Discovering that the enigmatic Diak was a detective of sorts, the professor learned that he used such a variety of surnames that it was prudent to assume he had none. What he did have was a reputation as a soldier of fortune and treasure hunter whose flexible scruples allowed him to sometimes work with the police, and sometimes against them. Rumors persisted that he was disfigured in some way—an accident for which he blamed the Russians. Despite his deformity, or perhaps because of it, no useful photographs of him existed. Clark's research uncovered only a single blurred image, apparently taken of a man in motion and at extreme distance using a powerful telephoto lens.

As for the man's elusive nationality, some sources reported that Diak had a Gypsy heritage and that he spoke multiple languages and could imitate a wide range of accents. Despite uncertain data and although he had to admit Diak was unique, Clark decided to think of the mystery man as nothing more exotic than German.

Having consistently avoided capture and cheated death scores of times, this Diak seemed to possess more than nine lives and he was rumored to be a master of disguise. Perhaps even his so-called deformity was a ruse. A combination of luck and deceit seemed to explain how the resourceful detective managed to insinuate himself into the tightest of private circles, to slip undetected through the most densely woven security, and to learn—and profit from—the most closely guarded secrets.

Before Hamza's last-minute warning, Clark's plan had called for the Russians to find the bomb. He'd intended the rigged toolbox as a nasty surprise, an unexpected wrinkle which would keep his erstwhile customers off-balance while he winged his way to Arabia. When he learned of the existence of the mysterious Diak, the professor decided that a well-placed bomb might also be a convenient way to eliminate the troublesome detective.

Dealing with the Russians was risky enough, but it made Clark particularly nervous to think of a sinister man lurking about, filching secrets, and waiting in the wings to interfere with his plans. No one seemed to know exactly how Diak managed it, and yet the German detective continually worked his magic to such perfection that he seemed always to be one step ahead of his victims. Clark had to assume the worst. He had to assume that whatever he communicated to the Saudis or the Russians, and whatever those entities told him, would inevitably find its way to the ears of this resourceful interloper. It would follow then that, once Clark made his call to the Russians, once he revealed the GPS coordinates and the padlock combination, he'd have to assume that the detective would also know these details.

Fine, he thought, *let the Russians and the detective race one another to reach the cache site. In the battle to be first, the winner will get more than he bargained for.*

The professor's planning called for a sudden stampede toward Lizard Head Pass, a headlong race which would follow in the wake of his phone call. He pictured something like the Oklahoma land rush with a crowd of treasure seekers rushing pell-mell to locate the prize, only to encounter his secretly rigged toolbox. He was convinced that the hunters would break every existing speed record in their frantic pursuit of the hidden cache. He was equally certain that—whoever won the contest—the overeager victor would be unable to resist opening the box on-site. The dramatic climax Clark visualized encompassed an enormous explosion with a smoldering crater left behind to mark the finder's doom.

And he truly desired to witness that destruction.

But, for whatever reason, none of his intended victims had taken the bait—no Russians and no German—and it seemed there was nothing he could do about it. Reluctantly, he decided to forget his missing victims and concentrate on matters at hand.

Satisfied that he had the Clovis and still perplexed that Anne had the bomb, Clark pulled out his field glasses and again peered across the broad terrain that separated his hiding place from Anne's garish truck. The girl hadn't yet returned, and the sun was well past its zenith.

"What in the world are you up to, Anne with an 'e,' Scriptor with and 'o'?"

Chapter 64

The evening of July 17 was about to commence. Though it was not yet dusk in less elevated terrain, the sun slipped behind the lofty Lizard Head formation and the pass grew darker.

The Russians had given Clark a deadline to reveal the GPS coordinates and that had given the professor just enough time to disappear, travel north, retrieve the Clovis, and plant the bomb. And of course, he had to do all this without being followed. To disappear he'd needed to stage a robbery and, to accomplish everything in the time allotted, he had to leave Tucson quickly.

So, he was pleased that the Saudis were willing to supply a pilot and a jet and, if his proposed destination had raised any alarms with his new Arab allies, they didn't say so. Clark had convinced them that his trip to the Navajo Reservation had something to do with what they and the Russians were both calling 'the treasure.' Once again, the professor reminded himself that lower echelon Russian and Saudi foot soldiers didn't understand what the treasure was, nor had they any idea of its phenomenal value.

The Clovis was priceless and yet Clark had entrusted the artifact to Anne because—well, because he trusted her. He could have sent the bomb with her as well, but he had just enough scruples left not to take that particular risk. She'd be the unsuspecting courier of the hidden Clovis and several empty boxes, nothing more. His plan didn't include intentionally putting her in danger. Her role was to place the caches and move on. Believing the girl safely out of the way, Clark had followed behind her and collected the Clovis. Then he'd planted the bomb to eliminate the Russians, the detective, or anyone else who understood the significance of the coordinates.

Why go to all this trouble? Why not just keep the Clovis point in a locket around his neck, wait for the bids to roll in, pick the highest one, and board an airplane to exotic places to collect his prize money? Why use the girl in the first place? Why bother with the toolboxes?

For one simple reason: because, even before the Saudi's gave him a name, Clark had discovered that he was being watched and he was thoroughly convinced that his every movement was being monitored and recorded by a determined foe. It's not paranoia if you keep noticing the same people that don't belong on the hills above your house, or in the hallowed halls of your campus. It's even more convincing when you see these same out-of-place people every other day—a phenomenon which Clark interpreted as conclusive proof that he was not only being watched but was being systematically scrutinized on a factory scale, complete with alternating work shifts.

At first, he'd suspected the Russians, and then the Saudis, until he learned that the surveillance was being orchestrated by this Diak character, a conglomerate of races—a mongrel Slav and wandering Gypsy, who might also be German. Could this mysterious character be the anonymous emailer who, months ago, had tried to low-ball Clark by offering to purchase the Clovis for pennies on the dollar? Hadn't the final message from that passing correspondent been written in German? 'Pleased to meet you' might have been an innocent remark, but at the time it had sounded like something a cat might say before devouring a mouse. Even then, that phrase had struck him as a threat masquerading as a pleasantry. With each passing day, it seemed even more ominous.

Mindful that his movements were being scrutinized, Clark had been cautious. Someone was out there and, whoever was watching, the professor was convinced that any break in his routine would be noted and catalogued. So, he'd established a routine and kept it going, ad infinitum.

Every morning, the watchers would expect to see him arise before dawn, walk to his mailbox to get the early newspaper, and eat breakfast (inside if the weather was inclement, otherwise outside on the patio.) Then he was expected to dress and wait for a taxi to carry him to the University. He never operated a car. As far as the watchers knew, he was incapable of driving. Every weekday at 10 a.m. he would be on campus in the departmental lecture hall to teach a graduate class. At precisely 11:30 a.m. he would hold office hours until 1 p.m. Then he would eat lunch in the faculty cafeteria and host an afternoon seminar for post-doctoral students. Promptly at 3 p.m. a taxi would arrive to transport him back to his remote ranch house, stopping always at the same small storefront restaurant no later than 3:45 p.m. to pick up a take-out meal. Upon arriving home, the predictable professor would collect his mail, then work in his study with the blinds open until 6:15 p.m. Then he would eat supper in the kitchen, read a book in his study, and retire upstairs at 9:45 p.m. Without fail, the light visible in his bedroom window would snap off at 10:30 p.m. On weekends and holidays, he would stay home and follow a similar boring and mind-numbing routine.

How many times can I trim these same orange trees? he asked himself. *And how many times can you nosy interlopers bear to sit on your stupid hill and watch me as I do it?*

He pictured his bored watchers, tired of writing the same things over and over again in their surveillance logbooks. Might they be tempted to merely photocopy one day's log and reuse it for succeeding entries, having only to change the date each time? Clark had no visitors at the ranch house, and he interacted with no one on campus except his faculty colleagues and students.

Every fourteen weeks in the spring and fall and once in mid-summer, he met with a graduate assistant—usually a man and sometimes a woman—in order to finalize the details of his traditional geocaching experience. It was something he did every session. Eventually, on one completely predictable morning, he and the grad assistant would load the cache boxes into the student's vehicle and the student would drive away. Like Clark's other habits, this particular practice never varied.

Until it did.

A few days ago, Anne Scriptor's departure with the summer session caches had seemed routine with one small exception, which Clark believed would go unnoticed. This time, for the first time ever, the cache boxes had been padlocked. It was an addition made necessary by Clark's need to conceal and smuggle the Clovis out of Tucson. Previously, when he'd dispatched the caches, someone had followed the student but, like Clark's routine on campus and at home, what happened out in the field was always the same, so the watchers had ended that aspect of their surveillance. They knew what would happen out there in Colorado. The boxes would be left somewhere along a familiar route. A week later, a posse of students would set out, armed with the tools of orienteering, to locate each cache and trundle their prizes back to campus. To observers, it would be just another day at the office.

Steeped in recollections of the past, Clark had allowed his attention to drift, but he abruptly ceased his musing when he detected movement at Anne's truck.

Chapter 65

As Anne walked toward the Nissan, she paused to study the heavens. By the time she'd retrieved the Lizard Head cache, stars were visible in the steadily darkening sky. Following her established pattern, she'd have preferred to run back to the trailhead. But the caching order was reversed now, so that—having sprinted uphill—she'd arrived at the lofty site exhausted, then been obliged to slow to a walk as she carried the toolbox down. Returning at last, she unhinged the tailgate and climbed wearily up into the bed of her newly purchased pickup. Kneeling awkwardly, she locked cache number two next to cache number three in the truck box.

So, she thought as she stood up, *that's two down and one to go.*

With the recovered toolboxes secure, she sat in the cab and reviewed in her mind what she had experienced since fleeing from Lavender. She'd sacrificed her VW and narrowly missed being ambushed by a cougar before walking overland to Delta City, then riding the bus further southward. She'd taken the bus even though doing so left her unable to retrieve several toolboxes.

Remembering those abandoned caches, Anne recalled her missing map. The cache coordinates were programmed into her GPS and she'd visited all six sites in person and also written up detailed directions, so she'd get by without the map. Nevertheless, leaving it behind had been a mistake. Sitting there in the growing darkness, she was positive that Trinidad and his allies—the so-called good guys—would be using the map to anticipate her movements. Her only consolation was that he and his gang would probably choose to follow her route systematically by starting from Lavender and working their way south. If they conducted their pursuit methodically, she'd be able to stay ahead of them.

As for the Bentley gang, if there were any left, they had no map and, presuming they too were seeking toolboxes, their only option was to find and follow her. She remembered what Trinidad had said. Bentleys had been driving north and south and trying to catch her in the middle—the sugar cubes converging on her from both directions. Apparently, they'd intended to confiscate the boxes she hadn't yet cached and force her to reveal the location of the rest.

She shuddered to think how close she'd come to being caught in that trap. Only her impulsive decision to head down Old Goat Trail had saved her—that and Trinidad, of course. Though she remained suspicious of the handsome detective's motives, she had to admit that he'd already saved her twice. Once from the man in the Bentley which rolled past the pancake house covered in mud and again when the pair of thugs chased her through the lavender field. Trinidad had rendered those men unconscious, but apparently someone had dragged them back to their Bentley and blown them sky high.

Who did that, she wondered? Then more basic questions cascaded into her mind. *What the hell's so important about a cluster of empty toolboxes? And why are so many people so anxious to find them—willing to kill for them—and why the padlocks?*

She had no answers to those mysteries, but at least she was absolutely sure of one thing. She was certain that all the trouble had started in Colorado. Trinidad, the Bentleys, the explosions—every troublesome event had occurred after she crossed the border. Now that trouble was pursuing her southward and keeping ahead of it would take all the luck she could muster. If she reached the remaining caches before the Trinidad gang, and managed to avoid being spotted by the Bentley gang, maybe she'd make it home in one piece.

Apparently, neither gang would stop until they found what they were looking for. Whatever they were after, she was certain the answer was connected to her first six caches. This had to be so because she'd seen with her own eyes that toolboxes seven through twelve were empty. Besides, those half-dozen boxes were history. She'd turned them into ashes, along with her Bug.

Meanwhile, between them, both gangs would soon locate the toolboxes she'd been obliged to skip over and that might be a good thing. Maybe they'd find what they were looking for and leave her alone. Then again, they might discover more empty boxes and keep looking. Either way, she planned to be a moving target. She had the advantage. She had a head start and first-hand knowledge of the GPS coordinates, so chances were good that she'd continue to outmaneuver the others.

In a moment, she'd drive to Cortez, buy some batteries, and use her flashlight to secure the last remaining cache—good old box number one. Then she'd take the retrieved boxes back to Tucson, where she'd track down her missing professor and thrust the pesky things back into Dr. Clark's hands. Her professor would know what to do. He'd explain everything and, if her luck held, she'd accomplish all this before either gang closed in.

Why call them gangs?

She decided it was a suitable description. Just because the Bentley bunch drove fancy cars and dressed to the nines—albeit in retro outfits and identically—that didn't mean she couldn't think of them as a gang. They carried guns like ordinary gangsters, and they seemed to love violence, so there was a chance that most of the Bentleys were already dead or in jail. Either way, she didn't trust them. Thinking it over, she had to reluctantly admit that she also equated Trinidad's allies with a gang. Some of them had dual identities, like Trinidad and Madge. Some might wear official uniforms, like the sheriff she'd yet to meet—but try as she might, she didn't trust that bunch either. If either gang managed to overtake her, she was convinced there would be trouble and she had no intention of being caught.

She glanced over her shoulder. She was a good distance from the pavement and out of sight. The two caches she'd retrieved so far were secured in the truck bed and, despite her curiosity, she had no intention of opening either box. 'I have the key,' Professor Clark had told her. They were his caches. He should be the one to open them.

"So," she sighed aloud, "here I am in the middle of nowhere again, immersed in yet another fine mess, and a missing man has the key to unlock a dwindling number of boxes which I have faithfully stashed across the wilderness. And suddenly everybody—simply everybody—wants what's in the boxes, but the damned things are empty. Isn't that peachy? What was the point of caching nothing? And why are so many people interested in chasing nothing?"

She tried again to puzzle it out.

She knew of a few instances in archaeology where devotees buried empty caskets in one place and secreted the actual bodies of their beloved idols elsewhere in order to thwart grave robbers. Maybe the toolboxes were false caches meant to deceive someone. If so, to deceive whom and to what end?

All at once Anne shuddered and sat bolt upright as a chilling possibility crossed her mind. What if there was a *third gang*? Not the Bentleys. Not Trinidad and his allies. But another set of searchers more ruthless than the former, more lawless than the latter. Someone had caused those explosions and if it wasn't the Russians and it wasn't the law...

Suddenly, her feelings of safety began to vanish, replaced by a growing sense of dread. Her assumption that the Bentley gang was either disorganized or dead or incarcerated had made her feel relatively secure. As had her belief that the Trinidad gang was plodding along behind her, working methodically, but ultimately too slowly to overtake her. But suppose there was another searcher, an unpredictable wild card? At the rate Trinidad was going, he'd be too far away to catch her, but also too far away to help.

Did she need his help?

Anne began to feel dizzy and feverish as her thinking swirled in unresolved circles. Dr. Clark had warned that setting out the Colorado caches would require her to exercise at altitudes far above the Tucson desert. She'd only half-listened when cautioned to take it easy and admonished to drink copious amounts of water. She hadn't paid attention when advised to take precautions to counteract the altitude sickness which typically afflicted the uninitiated flatlander.

Instead, she'd been running for miles in the thin mountain atmosphere and that vigorous activity had undoubtedly complicated things. Already, she'd experienced two fainting episodes and the topography surrounding her at the moment was anything but flat. At more than 10,200 feet, Lizard Head was one of the highest spots on her itinerary. Exercising at this altitude and lingering here while she mused about caches and gangs had been a mistake. With so many people pursuing her, Anne could ill-afford to make mistakes and she had a nagging feeling that she'd made more than one, and recently.

As she sat in the growing darkness, it suddenly occurred to her that there was something odd about the two toolboxes she'd retrieved today. Was it her imagination or was one of them missing its number? And was one of the padlocks different? She'd found both boxes exactly where she expected them to be and, upon retrieving them, she'd merely glanced at each. She needed to leave this isolated spot and drive to a lower altitude. She needed to catch her breath and clear her head. Most of all, she needed to find someplace with better light to take a closer look at her cargo.

No question about it.

She had to get off this mountain.

Hurriedly, Anne gulped down the last of her water, put the key in the ignition, and grew increasingly groggy as she tried to start the truck. At first the vehicle balked and then it sputtered until it clicked and fell silent.

You'd be surprised what a piece of crap an attractive female can buy, for cash-money, at a small town used car lot.

Chapter 66

Time had passed and there'd been no explosion. At twilight, Clark had spotted Anne again. She was walking back toward her battered truck. She looked exhausted. Hadn't he cautioned her about running at this altitude? She had the toolbox. She had the bomb.

Once more, his instinct was to warn her, and he was on the verge of blowing his cover and driving down there to take the box away. But again, he hesitated as he peered in the darkness and tried to guess Anne's next move. His field glasses proved unreliable in the failing light, so Clark put them aside and scanned the terrain below with his naked eyes. Then he heard something. Listening intently, he peered into the gathering darkness and realized what had happened.

"She can't get her old truck started," he decided.

He laughed and then took a deep breath realizing that he felt a great sense of relief. The Nissan's failure to start might be a problem for Anne, but, in his view, it was good news. Seeking to take advantage of the malfunctioning truck, Clark made his decision. In a half hour, when it was thoroughly dark, he'd fire up his Rubicon and return to the main highway. He'd pass her truck as it sat disabled and far from the pavement. The distance was significant. She wouldn't hear or see him drive by.

"Good girl," he murmured as he looked through his field glasses and saw just enough to approve of the way she'd positioned the truck to make it invisible from the highway. Whether doing so on purpose or randomly, she'd been efficient in choosing her location, which meant he'd be able to roll by unnoticed in the darkness. There was a slim chance she might walk out to the highway and try thumbing a ride on this remote stretch of mountain pavement. But, after going to all the trouble to retrieve the Lizard Head toolbox, Clark believed she'd be unlikely to abandon it. Why she was retrieving the box at all was a mystery, but he convinced himself it didn't matter.

The newspaper article must be somebody's idea of an intentional ruse. He had to believe that an army of folks were looking for her and he guessed she knew these things too. So, it seemed unlikely she'd walk to the highway and risk flagging down any vehicle in the dark, let alone one which looked as official as his Jeep Rubicon. The impressive vehicle was on loan from the Navajo Nation Police and equipped with all the conspicuous lights and sirens and bells and whistles of law enforcement. He was absolutely certain the last thing Anne would do was flag down a cop.

As he sat there waiting for dark, Clark relaxed, put his field glasses away, and took a moment to admire all the trappings of his borrowed vehicle. Some of the Rubicon's equipment was unfamiliar, but he recognized radios, computers, and cameras—all dormant and password-protected, of course. He surveyed the empty weapons rack which, when full, must hold quite an arsenal. Meanwhile, all this equipment was surrounded by the jeep's solid exterior of laminated armor. It was a finely appointed vehicle and, given his present situation with bad guys on the prowl, Clark was more than happy to be driving what amounted to a high-tech tank.

It paid to have connections on the Reservation and there'd been no questions when the tribe had received his faxed request to have the jeep standing by at the northern Arizona airstrip. The mantra, "It's for Clark," still carried weight in Navajo Land and, if everything went as planned, it would continue to do so, at least for a few more hours. After that, no Navajo or any other Native American would have anything to do with Professor C. Arnold Clark. By this time tomorrow his name would be reviled and his character forever tarnished, but he would also be extremely wealthy. Clark could live with that. He was more than willing to sacrifice his reputation so long as his goal to acquire his millions proceeded according to plan.

And so far, things were proceeding splendidly.

It was true that there had been a few missteps, but Clark had handled them and moved on. It'd been inconvenient that his initial buyers, the sanctimonious and miserly Russians, weren't able to match the Saudi's higher offer. At least Clark was pretty sure the Russians wouldn't pay more. He'd never know for certain, of course, because he didn't intend to ask the Brotherhood. He'd planted the bomb and informed his Russian customers of the coordinates fully expecting them to take the bait and get blown to bits for their trouble. It might be unsporting to kill his initial buyers. But an extra eight million dollars from the Saudis were sufficient motivation to change customers and the fireworks would've killed enough Russians to baffle the rest. If the Lizard Head explosion had come off, Clark would have had the satisfaction of knowing that the blast had thrown the Russian mobsters, who were already confused by his disappearance, into complete chaos. Add an unexpected explosion to the mix and things would've become hopelessly jumbled. With his former Russian associates in disarray, he'd have made his exit.

"Dance with the one that brung you," his grandma used to say, but Clark was inclined to amend that old maxim into something more practical. He preferred to go with a more realistic saying—one that allowed him to dump the tight-fisted Brotherhood in favor of a new dance partner who offered the most cash.

Of course, now that the Russians had neither appeared nor exploded, and now that Anne had unexpectedly retrieved the deadly box, Clark was rethinking things. He reached up and stroked his beard then ran his fingers through his long white hair. 'Santa Claus' the undergraduates called him. Shaving his face and head would be a major sacrifice but, when it was done, he would match his new passport picture and nobody, absolutely no one, would tie his newly altered visage to his former self. After blowing up the Russians, he'd intended to return to Cortez, eat supper, and alter his appearance. Then he'd planned to contact his pilot and rush southward to reconnect with his jet.

Anne's unexpected arrival had temporarily muddled his end game. Never mind, he'd soon resolve things. His solution was simple. He'd forget the

Russians and assume they'd been too stupid to interpret the coordinates. As for the inscrutable Diak, perhaps Clark had been mistaken—maybe the German hadn't been eavesdropping after all. So, he'd have to forego the thrill of the explosion and abandon Anne at Lizard Head. He would sneak past the girl and leave her behind, but would that be enough?

Ah wait, he thought. *Here's a better solution.* For good measure, and also for Anne's protection, Clark would take one additional precaution. *I like this idea,* he praised himself.

Once he was clear of Lizard Head, he'd call the local cops and report her. He'd tell them she had a bomb and where to find her. She'd get arrested of course and have some explaining to do but, to tell the truth, she didn't know that much. She had no idea how lucky she was to be uninformed. Blowing up Russians was one thing, but Clark didn't relish the idea of harming Anne. She was loyal and he liked her and, if her persistence—however misguided—had become a problem, it was a problem he was about to solve.

Jail was the safest place for his earnest young graduate assistant and the cops would absolutely have a way to disarm the rigged toolbox. She'd thank him if she understood what was going on, but whatever happened, she would soon be behind bars, completely out of his hair, and safe. There would be no explosion, of course, but having her and the bomb in custody would hand the cops a puzzle and, by the time anyone sorted out her story, Clark would be long gone. The cunning professor would wait a few more minutes in order to drive away in total darkness. In the meantime, he sat still as the long summer twilight lingered. Feeling content, he lit a cigarette and thought about Miss Anne Scriptor. It was likely he would never see her again. Meanwhile, the last thing he expected to deal with at this late hour was the erratic behavior of the girl.

"Ha!" he said and laughed aloud. "Wouldn't she just take me to task for calling her a *girl*?"

"How'd you like it?" Anne had been fond of complaining. "What would you say if I called you part of the old boys' network? How would that feel?"

He'd apologized, although in truth he secretly felt that he didn't mind being thought of as a *boy*—old or otherwise. And yet he was more than willing to admit that Anne was a remarkable young woman. She'd always been a reliable student—a precocious senior who'd earned her bachelor's degree ahead of schedule with honors and was about to enter her second term of graduate school. Clark sighed as he remembered how eager Anne had been to help with his caching assignment and he felt a wave of regret. It pained him to imagine how disappointed she'd be when she learned the details of his sacrilege. He found it strangely unnerving to think that he could stomach the recriminations of his colleagues and the enmity of every North American tribe, and yet he was heartily glad that he wouldn't be around to see the sadness in Anne's eyes. He shook his head and lit another cigarette.

Poor Anne, he thought. *She'll be disheartened, but she'll get over it.*

She was loyal, but she was tough too, and already an accomplished archaeologist. She was also an excellent GPS navigator and she'd been well on her way to completing her task of caching toolboxes when she'd unaccountably deviated from her itinerary. She'd telephoned and left a voicemail to say that she'd taken an unsanctioned detour, which had the potential to disrupt Clark's timetable. But the detour hadn't mattered, because her sudden trip to this Lavender place had turned out to be nothing but a fluke.

What was she even doing there in the first place? he wondered.

He knew much about Anne, but in many ways, she remained a puzzle. He had to admit he wondered why the normally dependable girl had stopped phoning-in with regular progress reports. Since the call from Lavender, he'd received no further voicemails. Had news of his disappearance somehow reached as far as Colorado? Then too, he wondered about the fire in which Anne had allegedly perished and he was equally curious about why the newspaper reporting her death had chosen to publish such a dated photo.

All irrelevant, Clark decided.

Some sort of misunderstanding he imagined, so he stopped thinking and yawned. He'd managed a catnap on his flight from Tucson and endured a restless night in the wilderness plus a fitful night in his Cortez motel but, in truth, he hadn't had a decent sleep since leaving home. He snubbed out his cigarette, reclined the Rubicon's plush seat, and closed his eyes.

Chapter 67

Daylight had faded, and a cold wind cascaded down from the dark shoulders of Lizard Head Peak. It was late. Waiting for sundown, Clark had momentarily closed his eyes. An hour passed and, when at last he opened them again, it was pitch dark and the luminous dial of his watch told him it was time to go. He put the Rubicon in gear and drove cautiously down the steep hillside until he reached Highway 145. He pulled onto the pavement, picked up speed as he neared the spot where Anne was hidden, and roared past without a tinge of conscience.

"A cold night alone will do her good and anyway she'll soon have company," he decided as he switched on the radio and tuned into a country-western station. "She'll be okay," he told himself.

An hour ago, with something like trepidation, he'd watched her handle the bomb and put it into her truck. Was she in danger? Not really, he convinced himself. He was certain he knew Anne well enough to predict what she would and wouldn't do.

"There's no way she'll open that box," he said aloud. "No way," he repeated.

Nevertheless, the instant he left the pass he was feeling anxious—so anxious that he pledged to use the last of his burner phones to call 911 and tell the dispatcher where to find Anne. When he reached the outskirts of Rico and drove into steady cell service once again, he stopped to make the call, but the burner's battery was dead. Reluctantly taking a chance that someone might trace his location, he grasped his smartphone and punched in 9-1-1.

Although he didn't hear a ring, he sensed that someone had picked up the line. Hurriedly he described Anne and her truck, gave her location, and closed his spiel with a final comment: "The last name is Scriptor with an 'o,'" he said. "She has a bomb in the lockbox of her truck and I'm sure you'll find she's wanted as a material witness in an arson case."

"Understood," the voice said and was it his imagination or did he detect a foreign accent?

Clark shrugged, hung up, and placed his smartphone in the dashboard caddy, once more thinking he ought to get rid of it. But again, he reminded himself that he'd stored up a ton of visual and auditory mementos on the device—many with irredeemable value. A less sentimental man might have crushed the thing and then cast the fragments as far as possible out into the darkness. But Clark knew he'd regret doing anything to compromise those memories. So, he kept the phone and continued southward toward Cortez and supper.

Forty minutes later, he was drinking beer at the 'Rado Inn and watching a Colorado Rockies baseball game on television as he waited for his steak to arrive. The place had a wide screen television which covered one wall of the tiny bistro and Clark was sitting so close that the picture was basically a blur. As he half-watched the distorted images flicker and listened indifferently to the garbled sound, his relaxed mind converted the media into the soundtrack of an imaginary confrontation between the tardy Russian mobsters and their irate superiors.

"You found no box! You retrieved no treasure!" the superiors would shout.

"We did not understand the numbers," one might squirm as a Brotherhood torturer shoved yet another hot poker up the underling's ass.

"We are not good with numbers," another might plead as screws tightened on his thumbs.

"Screw 'em all," Clark said aloud.

Misunderstanding Clark's outburst as a comment on the game, the place's only other late-night patron yelled, "Right on, man!"

Clark saluted the man with his empty beer bottle, ordered another, and then addressed his audience of one by declaring, "Drinks all around!"

"Don't mind if I do," said his neighbor.

"Sweet," Clark proclaimed as his meal arrived.

He ate his dinner at a leisurely pace, ordered yet another beer and then dessert. The Rockies won in extra innings. It was past eleven o'clock and his drunken companion was snoring like a buzz-saw when the slightly tipsy professor left the restaurant, walked across the street to his motel, and paused a moment to make sure his jeep was securely locked. The light over his door seemed to have burned out. He was fumbling with his room key when he heard a noise behind and turned just enough that the blow intended for the back of his head glanced off his shoulder.

"What the fuc..." Clark began. but a second blow struck his temple and knocked him unconscious.

Chapter 68

It was well past midnight when Trinidad removed his reading glasses and rubbed his eyes. If he'd been alone in the nondescript office, he'd have reached for his harmonica and played a tune to help gather his thoughts, but he wasn't alone. He and Jack were standing together, elbow to elbow, in the sheriff's cramped command post in downtown Delta City. The attention of the two men was focused on a crumbled Colorado map.

"No coordinates, I notice," Jack complained as his smartphone beeped to tell him the calendar had advanced to July 18. "And no time to lose," he added.

"We can make do with these markings," Trinidad growled as he stared at Anne's route.

They had her map, but the document didn't include GPS coordinates, only general indications of the cache drops, each location loosely marked with a cluster of three triangles.

Tri-Deltas, Trinidad thought.

"Hmm," Jack said. "Looks like you guessed wrong on this one, Slick."

Trinidad was silent as his thoughts turned to Anne. He had to admit that, where Miss Scriptor was concerned, he'd totally miscalculated. He'd been wrong to believe she accepted his role as white-knight-to-the-rescue and wrong to believe she'd meekly surrender the GPS coordinates. He'd underestimated her loyalty to her professor and her assignment. It had to be loyalty, what else could he call it—pride maybe? How else to comprehend her astonishing actions? How else to explain her exploded car and sudden disappearance? He should have taken the earnest young woman into his confidence, should have told her everything. If he'd made her an ally from the start, she might not be missing, might not be in danger. He'd been wrong to think that Anne would submit to melting into the background while he did the heavy lifting. He should have known, from the moment he found her covered head-to-toe in mud—should have realized that she wasn't one to shy away from dirty work.

"Dirty work," Trinidad said aloud.

"You got that right," agreed Jack. "How do you want to do this?"

"Our Russian in custody—the guy I cold-cocked the other day—what's his name again?"

"Vlad, if it matters," said Jack.

"It matters," said Trinidad. "Some of the Scarlets specialize in disinformation."

"How about our guy?" Jack asked.

"This Vlad's a low-level foot soldier on his first assignment and looking to cut a deal—that's how I make him."

"Good for us then," said Jack.

"So far," said Trinidad. "But Citizen Vlad only knows a piece of what's going down. He speaks little English, but he told the Fed interpreters the Brotherhood was waiting for map coordinates, so maybe the remaining caches are still untouched."

"So, this Vlad character is sure the university toolboxes are involved?" asked Jack.

"He knew about the boxes," said Trinidad, "but not where they were or what was inside. He only knew something general about a broad search area for some so-called treasure. So, how about your people start with these three?" The detective pointed to the site near Olathe and indicated two more, one south of Montrose and the other along Lost Dollar Road.

"Those are close by," observed Jack.

"Yes," said Trinidad. "So, I'll leave them to you."

"Okay," Jack agreed, and Trinidad noticed the sheriff was lost in thought.

"What is it?" Trinidad asked.

Jack paused for a moment more before he said, "Comrade Professor Clark's been on the loose for more than thirty-six hours. He could be anywhere but, thanks to the Navajo Nation Police, we know he ain't fled the country. If it wasn't for their help, we'd all be lookin' for Clark someplace else. Good thing they told the FBI about the jeep and the jet. I'm just sorry our Washington friends didn't pass on the Navajo tips right away, otherwise we might've nabbed our slippery professor days ago."

"Unfortunately, dropping the ball was just the Feds being the Feds," said Trinidad. "But we're still ahead of the game because the Navajos have the dead pilot and they have the airstrip staked out. No idea who took the missing plane, or where it ended up, but chances are good that our wandering professor will be coming back that way."

"So, who killed the pilot and where's the dang plane?" asked Jack.

"I have my suspicions about the killer," said Trinidad.

"You thinkin' what I'm thinkin'?" asked Jack.

"Maybe," said Trinidad.

"Well, anyway," said Jack, "thanks mostly to Washington's delay, Comrade Clark got clean away and we still got no idea what in blazes our unpredictable professor is up to. Why go to all the trouble of disappearin' in Tucson to get on a jet and fly up this direction instead of just takin' it on the lam?"

"In my opinion, there's only one reason the professor would risk coming north," said Trinidad. "His merchandise must be here in Colorado and chances are it's in one of the caches."

"Well, there ain't many caches left to find," said Jack. "Your little girlfriend blew up a half-dozen. And, as far as the others, if we have this figured right, the professor'll be callin' the Russians any time now and givin' out coordinates that'll lead the Brotherhood to a toolbox that could be in six different places. And not right next to the road neither. These caches look to be miles away from pavement."

"All except the Cortez site," observed Trinidad.

"Yeah," said Jack, "that's a puzzle alright. Maybe your girlfriend knows the answer. Anyways, I wish we could eavesdrop on the conversation when

Comrade Clark telephones his Russian pals." Then the sheriff added, "And hey—you know—I'm sorry about those 'girlfriend' cracks."

"It's okay," said Trinidad. "But, as far as Clark's phone call is concerned, my guess is he'll be leading the Russians to a dead end."

"So, you think Comrade Clark plans a double-cross?" asked Jack.

"I'm sure of it," said Trinidad. "And I think we can leave off referring to our professor as *Comrade* Clark. I don't think his Russian pals would appreciate the honorific."

"Noted," said Jack. "But what makes you think it's a double-cross?"

"The Federal techs traced a meandering line from two million in Russian cash to Clark's bank accounts. And those same techs are convinced there's another Russian two million waiting in the wings."

"So, with the Russians it's a two-mill down and two on delivery deal," Jack speculated.

"Undoubtedly that's what the Brotherhood thinks, but my guess is Clark has other plans," said Trinidad.

"Keep the down and blow off the balance?" Jack whistled through his teeth. "That's cold. If the old fox is willin' to risk screwin' those bloodthirsty Russian mobsters, he must have one peach of a back-up offer."

"You haven't seen the latest," said Trinidad as he handed a spreadsheet to the sheriff.

"Hmm," said Jack as he studied the report. "Seems like the techs believe our professor also has somethin' goin' with a Saudi bunch too. And, if I read this correct, it looks like Clark's back-up offer could be twice what the Russians are willin' to pay. So, old Clark figures it's two million down from the Russians and eight million more bucks from the Arabs—which is a chunk of change, but I suppose it's possible."

"It's possible. Who else do we know that has that kind of cash lying around?" asked Trinidad.

"Right," said Jack as he took a final look at the spreadsheet, then set it aside. "So anyway, where are we? We seem to have got a handle on the money, and the buyers, but no line at all on what Clark is peddlin'. Got any ideas on the particulars of this mysterious merchandise of his? What's this treasure everybody's so keen on? What's so dang special that both the Russians and the Saudis want it so bad?"

"Well, Citizen Vlad seems to have no knowledge of what the treasure is, and he knows nothing about Saudi involvement. Plus, he tells us that Clark has been under close surveillance for more than a year," said Trinidad. "And not just being watched by the Russians but also by a renegade group of Germans."

"Germans? So, we're right to think that Herr Hodell is involved?"

"Up to his deformed neck probably," Trinidad agreed. "When the Feds reported that first explosion the other day at the barricade, it got me thinking. So, I rigged up a disguise and played a hunch at the pancake house and Vlad didn't even blink when he saw me. So, he seemed to be expecting our German friend."

"Expectin' him?" Jack asked.

"Yes," said Trinidad, "and planning to ambush him probably. Among the things he told the FBI interrogator was the details of two radio calls from his comrades. First, they called to say they'd spotted someone matching Diak's description at the roadblock and that the stranger was acting suspicious. Then they called again to say they had the treasure in hand and then the transmission went dead."

"And all this right before that bunch was killed in explosion number one," Jack deduced.

"Exactly," agreed Trinidad.

"Well," said Jack, "that jives with what my Tucson police contacts have told me which was that—right after they got word to keep an eye on the professor—they took a close look and found the university campus and the Arizona hills crawlin' with eastern Europeans and other strangers. They spotted out-of-place people on foot and on bicycles and drivin' inexpensive heaps—all of which adds up to the frugal Germans and their American cronies. Plus, they also spotted gangster-types ridin' around town in expensive black Bentleys."

"And those Bentleys would be carrying the big-spender Russians," Trinidad guessed.

"Correct," said Jack. "So, I reckon that gives us a pretty good idea of who all's involved: certain Russians in plain sight and certain Germans in plain sight—not countin' that ghost, Diak, who nobody's actually spotted—plus an unknown number of absentee Saudis. Quite a crowd for this little treasure hunt."

"That's for sure," Trinidad agreed and the two stood silently for a moment.

"So now," said Jack, "about this merchandise that old Clark is peddlin', the chatter the Tucson cops intercepted from all them local watchers seems to confirm one thing, which is that Clark didn't deliver no kind of treasure to anybody before he up and disappeared—at least nothin' noticeable. So, Slick, what's got our German's attention and what's worth the gabazillions the Russians and the Saudis are willin' to pay?"

"I'm convinced that the professor's mystery merchandise is something sexier than the usual black-market stuff," said Trinidad. "It's something unique—something that piqued Diak's interest and which the Russians and even the Saudis only refer to obliquely as 'the treasure.' My working theory is that Clark's merchandise is exceptional—so exceptional that a dishonest professor of archaeology would be sorely tempted to peddle it to strangers."

"Some kind'a missin' link do you mean?" Jack speculated.

"Yes, something like that—something extremely important and rare," said Trinidad. "And, given Clark's past preferences as a collector of antiquities, and the inability of a host of watchers to spot it, it's likely to be something extremely small."

"Twelve million bucks small," said Jack. "Or anyway, small enough to fit in a toolbox maybe."

"I hear the lab boys plan to go over the toolboxes pretty thoroughly," said Trinidad and his pained expression suggested that he immediately regretted broaching the subject.

"The boys tell me they'll use hammer and tongs and contraband-sniffin' dogs and x-rays and even spectral analysis," said Jack.

And they might be wasting their time because the boxes I inspected were totally empty, Trinidad thought, and the detective's wistful expression made the sheriff raise an eyebrow.

"Well, anyway, we're ready and willin' to give them boxes a good going over," said Jack. "Assumin' if we ever manage to get our hands on one."

Trinidad remained silent, hoping his friend would drop this particular subject, because the last thing the detective wanted to talk about was the six empty boxes he once had sitting in his hallway. A trove of evidence, sitting there for hours bold as brass before he lost them and lost Anne. But Jack cleared his throat and it was apparent the sheriff was going to go there.

"Now I seem to recall that all the boxes which ended up at your farmhouse was not only just empty but also blown sky-high," Jack said as he smirked, then turned serious. "Listen, forgettin' them boxes aside for a moment, me, I'm inclined to follow the evidence we got, and, to me, the evidence is pretty darn clear. I'm convinced that the girl has whatever this-here so-called treasure is, or soon will have it the minute she gets the rest of them boxes together, which is probably what she's up to right now. So, it's either that or..."

"You're right," said Trinidad holding up a hand. "Okay. You're sort of right, but here's the thing: either Anne has the treasure without knowing what she's got, or Clark has already picked it up sometime between now and when he disappeared in Arizona."

"You're forgettin' one other possibility," said Jack. "The possibility that Clark and the girl are in this together—the possibility that before we know it, those two'll both be on their way to a life of luxury in your Middle East or your Russia or wherever that boatload of money takes them. Meanwhile, here we sit with our thumbs up our asses and bein' played for chumps. Look, tell the truth, Slick, don't that business of her torchin' her VW seem fishy to you?"

"It does seem extreme," admitted Trinidad. "Either she was being a thorough partner in crime by destroying evidence, or something else was going on."

"What else?"

"Maybe she was just confused and scared," Trinidad suggested.

"Hmm—maybe," said Jack, although he sounded skeptical. "Meanwhile, I just don't trust her."

"But I do," Trinidad insisted. "Remember this: I tried to trick her into vouching for Clark's lies when I showed her pictures of the midget lying dead in his ranch house. If she was in on the professor's deception, why didn't she go along with the idea that the little guy was Clark? And I also appeared to her in disguise and gave her a chance to recognize Diak, so I'm convinced she's not working with the German."

"Okay. Okay. I guess you know what you're doin'," said Jack. "Lucky for us you've had a gander at this German creep and got a notion of what his mangled face looks like. Which is a lot more than the Feds have in their files—they don't even have a decent snapshot of the guy. At least you've seen him once."

And once was enough, Trinidad thought as he recalled his one and only chilling glimpse of the German.

The brief sighting happened on a dark night two years ago when the fledgling detective was helping Jack with a kidnapping case. Trinidad had been hiding no more than ten feet away in the shadows, eavesdropping on a conversation, when the German's companion lit a cigarette. For an instant, before the match had flickered out, Diak's ruined face was illuminated. Trinidad had been under orders not to spook his targets, so he'd remained hidden as the German and another man finished their talk, walked into the darkness, and disappeared. It was an unsettling memory, seeing that ghoulish face in the dark.

Remembering the incident, it took Trinidad a moment to return to the present and Jack had to prompt him.

"Are you with me, Slick?" the sheriff inquired.

"Yeah," Trinidad answered. "And, whatever you say, I still say I believe her."

"Okay...I was in love once myself," said Jack and, when Trinidad started to protest, the sheriff cut him off and added, "So, like I say, how do you want to go about this?"

"Well, we need the woman, but there's no point in chasing her from cache to cache with the head start she has," said Trinidad.

Jack was grinning from ear to ear because he realized what an effort it must be for Trinidad to say 'her' and 'the woman' instead of 'Anne.'

"Go on..." Jack prompted.

"Meanwhile we've already released the story of her perishing in a fire, along with sending the newspapers her old photo. With luck, those deceptions will convince the Russians to stop looking for her. Assuming there are any Russians left to do the looking. To tell the truth, I'm beginning to suspect that the last of our local mobsters died in my lavender field."

"You could be right there," Jack agreed. "We've racked up quite a Scarlet Brotherhood body-count and nobody's spotted a single Bentley since the Lavender blow-up."

"Speaking of Lavender Hill Farm," Trinidad noted, "has your crew been back to my place since I cleared everything out and moved my workspace to your building?"

"Not that I know of," Jack answered. "Why do you ask?"

"Just curious," said Trinidad. "I went home earlier today to pick up my bolt cutters and couldn't find them."

"No idea," said the sheriff.

"Probably not important," Trinidad shrugged. "So, anyway, I figure that this treasure hunt has narrowed now, so it's down to her and us."

"Us and her and maybe Clark and maybe a Saudi or two and probably that devil, Diak," Jack corrected.

"Right," Trinidad agreed. "So, we'd better get a move on. Your team can hit the two local caches and then head straight to Dollar Road."

"You're not comin' with us?" asked Jack.

"Nope," said Trinidad. "I've decided to think outside the box."

Jack gave his friend a quizzical look and was about to comment, but Trinidad continued.

"I'm hitching a ride on a Federal jet to get ahead of the woman. I'm going to retrieve cache number one in Cortez, then I'll work my way north, while you and the rest work south. With luck we'll find her in the middle. Meanwhile, all of us will need to keep an eye out for Russians, and for Clark."

"And for Diak," Jack reminded him.

"Yeah," said Trinidad as he strapped on his pistol. "With any luck that cockeyed villain has given up the hunt. Or maybe there'll be one lone Russian out there who'll ambush the weasel and save us the trouble. But, just in case, you and I will absolutely need to keep an eye out for Diak."

Chapter 69

Unable to sleep as the FBI's sleek jet winged southward, Trinidad opened his eyes and consulted his cell phone—2:00 a.m. The six agents assigned to accompany him were apparently acclimated to the early hour, because all were fast asleep. Even the K-9—added to the group as a precaution to detect explosives—seemed to be slumbering. At least the animal's eyes were closed, although her ears seemed wide awake. Thoughts were racing through Trinidad's weary head and, to tame them, it was either pull out his harmonica or talk to the dog.

"Come, Cozy," Trinidad whispered, and the dog opened her eyes, stood alertly up, and padded down the narrow aisle to lean against the detective's leg. "Good girl," he said as he petted the sociable shepherd. "I wonder if you'll experience a conflict of interest if we ask you to bite down on a fellow German."

The dog tilted her head and yawned, then stretched out on the floor in front of Trinidad's no-frills jump seat. The FBI agents were sitting in cushioned passenger seats, leaving no illusion as to who was in charge of this operation. The Feds—each dressed identically in an expensive suit—were running the show. This might be an inter-agency venture, but, to the officious agents, local law enforcement consisted of little people and Trinidad, a civilian, was considered even smaller. Still, Trinidad couldn't help liking the dog and he wondered whether this whole operation might be improved with a slight adjustment. For example, things might go better if, instead of a half dozen imperious Feds and a single dog, this so-called reconnaissance team had been assembled to include six dogs and one agent. He laughed aloud at the thought and Cozy stirred briefly while the agents slept on.

Trinidad glanced out the window and thought of Anne. She was down there somewhere, alone in the dark, maybe in danger, and that was entirely his fault. Why, in the midst of all the meaningless banter he'd used to deflect her questions, hadn't he mustered enough courage to tell her the truth? It was no good trying to justify what he'd done—or rather what he'd failed to do. It was no use saying it was complicated—even though it was. No use pretending any more. The hum of the jet was hypnotic, and the detective closed his eyes. How simple it had all seemed when Jack first approached him with the idea.

"Doing anything this comin' week?" the sheriff had asked as they sat in Stacy's Coffee Shop sharing a morning table.

"My lavender crop is in good shape. Pruning's done for now," Trinidad answered. "And peak bloom time is still around the corner—why?"

"I could use your help for a few days," was all Jack said.

"A case?"

"Yeah—a big one," Jack said. "Can you get Cruz and the rest to tend the field?"

"I suppose," said Trinidad. "Is this a paying gig?"

"Are four figures enough—a five and three zeroes?"

"Wow," Trinidad said, and he whistled through his teeth. "Five-K? Where'd your office come up with that kind of dough?"

"Federal bucks," Jack said.

"Is what you're doing even legal?" Trinidad asked.

"Probably," said Jack. "You interested?"

"I could call Cruz right now and get a crew lined up if..." Trinidad began and then paused.

"If...?" Jack prompted.

"If you tell me what exactly I'm getting into."

Jack invited Trinidad to ride along to Delta City where the two had a confidential chat in the sheriff's office. He told the detective what he could, which turned out to be plenty. The federal agency in charge of protecting

Native American gravesites had been alerted to some traffic on the dark web. Someone was offering an important artifact for sale. Although they couldn't discover exactly what the merchandise was, the agency was convinced the object was a funeral article.

"No specifics," Jack explained. "Just persistent rumors that somethin' big was goin' down."

"Big enough to generate a budget and hire a starving detective," Trinidad noted. "But apparently not big enough to call in the Famous-But-Incompetent."

Jack smiled to hear Trinidad use the local law enforcement's unflattering interpretation of the illustrious initials: F.B.I.

"The antiquities trade ain't exactly in the Bureau's wheelhouse," the sheriff observed. "To get the Feds involved, somethin' would have to explode, or terrorists—foreign or domestic—would have to start comin' out of the woodwork. Right at this moment, all we've got is some nervous bureaucrats at NAGPRA and an Arizona crackpot who drinks too much."

Jack immediately regretted his comment about Dr. Clark's alcohol problem, but if Trinidad was offended, he didn't show it. Or did he?

Hearing the unfamiliar acronym, Trinidad had given Jack a quizzical look and the sheriff was relieved when the detective asked, "NAG-PRA?"

"Native American Graves Protection and Repatriation Act," Jack clarified. "The pencil-pushers there have a hard-on to nail some uppity professor in Arizona..." Jack pulled out a file. "Clark Arnold Clark, PhD—it says here. A guy with three first names and somebody who was apparently born into a family that lacked imagination when it came to christenin' their kids. Anyway, he's a special ops veteran who served a stint in Vietnam—trained as a sniper of all things and dabbled in explosives. Now he's a famous professor of archaeology with shady habits." The sheriff slid the thick file across the cluttered desk and Trinidad picked it up.

"Hmm," the detective said as he studied the contents, which included a glossy photograph. "A healthy paunch, I see. He looks like Santa Claus."

"Yeah," agreed Jack. "He stands out in a crowd all-right and—with what most people don't wear in the summertime heat around here—he shouldn't be too hard to find in mid-July."

"Does he need finding?" Trinidad asked.

"Well," said Jack as he looked at the calendar, "as of early this mornin'—in the wee hours of July 15—he went missin.'"

"Missing in Arizona you mean?"

"Missin' in Arizona and headed, we think, to Colorado and leavin' behind a stiff on his living room floor with pockets stuffed full of Dr. Clark's identification documents and no fingerprints."

"A giant stiff I presume," said Trinidad as he glanced again at the professor's photograph. "And what do you mean 'no fingerprints?' No prints in the room? No prints for the stiff? Or no prints for this missing professor?"

"All three," said Jack. "And the stiff ain't no giant. If anythin' he's a midget." Jack passed another file folder to Trinidad—a thin one this time.

"I don't get it," said Trinidad as he examined the folder which contained images of a man who was clearly not a body double for the missing professor. Then he looked closely at a macro-photo of the dead man's hands. "Ugh," he said. "That must've hurt."

"All evidence of arches, loops, and whorls chemically removed—even the palm was fixed," said Jack. "Makin' the midget's hands soft and smooth as a baby's bottom."

"So, the stiff had no prints, but you said, 'all three,'" Trinidad reminded the sheriff.

"Well," said Jack, "the professor's ranch house where the body was found was full of prints—all from the same individual—but no matching records anywhere."

"Anywhere?" Trinidad asked.

"Not nowhere, no-how," said Jack.

"So, our elusive Dr. Clark—whose prints I presume must be all over his place of habitation—might as well have a pair of hands which are also smooth as a baby's bottom," said Trinidad and he was unable to suppress a laugh. "Because, technically, Santa Claus doesn't exist."

"One doozie of a coincidence," Jack observed, "to have a Russian who's technically invisible laying stone-dead in the house of a missin' American who is also technically invisible."

"So, the stiff is Russian," Trinidad speculated. "No name of course, but—given his chemically altered paws—probably a member of the Scarlet Brotherhood."

"Has to be," said Jack. "So, now you know why I need your help, Slick. Your past dealin' with the Brotherhood makes you our local expert and the only one here-abouts who knows these characters. So, what's your educated guess? Do you know of any other bunch that forces its hatchet-men to erase their prints with acid?"

Trinidad knew the answer to that, and he wished he could forget the last time he'd tangled with the murderous Scarlet Brotherhood.

It'd happened two summers ago when the detective was on a midnight stakeout while helping Jack with a kidnapping case. Trinidad had been tailing a suspect through the dark expanse of a Grand Junction railyard when a muscular Russian mobster attacked from behind. The detective had tried to forget the memory of that night, because his legendary luck had nearly forsaken him. A long freight train was lumbering past and Trinidad hadn't heard the assailant approaching. But he'd detected the stench of hydrochloric acid just in time to turn and ward off the man's initial blows.

He'd learn later that the ambusher was in the final weeks of an excruciating process of enduring an acid treatment to eliminate his fingerprints. But all Trinidad knew that night was the man's coarse hands stank and his fingers, though badly burned, were sufficiently strong to wrap menacingly around his would-be victim's throat. The scuffle had been a desperate one because the detective had been drinking and his reflexes were impaired. And yet, it may have been Trinidad's drunken state which saved him. As the Russian pressed his advantage, the ambushed detective went suddenly limp, dropped to his knees, executed an impossible pirouette, and elbowed his assailant in the groin before flattening the powerful man with an uppercut.

"Has to be the Brothers," was all Trinidad could manage to say.

"Sorry," said Jack, realizing what his recovering friend must be feeling. "This conversation stirs old memories I guess."

"No worries," said Trinidad, "I lived, and I'm two years sober."

"Yeah-boy" said Jack. "Well, anyway—fingerprints or not—this Clark character was already on NAGPRA's radar. So, when these dark web rumors began to circulate, they got suspicious enough to call in some favors. Do you want to hear all this?"

Jack looked at Trinidad, whose interest seemed to be waning.

"No, go ahead," the detective insisted. "I was thinking about something else."

"A woman or I miss my guess," Jack said, and his contagious laugh drifted into the corridor, which caused Deputy Oxford to poke her head into the sheriff's office.

"What's the joke?" Madge asked.

"Our friendly neighborhood detective can't keep his mind on the task at hand," Jack said with a wink in Trinidad's direction.

"I know what goes on in that handsome head of his," said Madge.

"Hey, Ox!" shouted a colleague down the hall. "Let's go! This jury ain't gonna escort itself to the courthouse."

"Hold your dang horses," Madge shot back. "And you two," she eyed Trinidad and Jack with a critical gaze, "try keeping your eyes on the ball!"

"Yes, ma'am," the two said in unison.

"You know my deputy—she's got a crush on you," Jack said when Madge was out of earshot. The sheriff reinforced his jibe with a broad grin.

"Hard being an idol," Trinidad said, and added a grin of his own.

"Okay, Slick. That's enough cop banter. You'd better take notes," Jack said. "I don't want to repeat all this."

Trinidad took out his pocket notebook and listened and jotted down pertinent data as Jack reviewed the NAGPRA case. The agency had been reeling from some botched attempts to repatriate two dozen Native American artifacts which had been languishing in a roadside museum near Kingman, Arizona. But they hadn't moved in a timely manner to prevent the owner from skipping town with the objects and the trail had gone cold. Needless to say, the Hualapai Tribe was not pleased, and a Congressional hearing stopped just short of resorting to tar and feathers. So, when rumors began circulating that NAGPRA's poster child for confiscation, Dr. C. Arnold Clark, was putting out clandestine feelers about marketing a rare artifact, the agency asked the FBI to investigate.

But the Bureau demurred, overtly citing jurisdictional limitations and covertly harboring profound indifference. So, NAGPRA officials went shopping for investigative assistance. They tried the National Park Service, the Bureau of Land Management, and a couple of other federal organizations. They were seeking help from agencies which, in the past, had assisted with the repatriation of sacred tribal objects. But the alleged sale of an unknown artifact to as yet unidentified buyers carried little weight. It looked like the whole thing would have to be shelved, until an enterprising bureaucrat in the Government Accountability Office figured out a way for NAGPRA to issue a grant to itself, thereby generating a pot of money to conduct their own investigation.

"So, there's our investigation budget includin' your five thousand bucks," said Jack, apparently convinced that he'd explained all that was necessary. "Any chance you could use five thousand bucks?"

"When do I start?" was Trinidad's instant reply.

Jack brought Trinidad on board just as the case began popping-up on everyone's radar. Soon, the sheriff was coordinating a task force which included NAGPRA wonks along with Arizona constables, police officers, and deputies. Things moved into high gear when Clark disappeared, and a foreign agent turned up dead in the professor's Tucson ranch house. An inventory of the last people to interact with Clark in Arizona turned up a young pilot—also missing—and the professor's young graduate assistant, whom he'd dispatched to Colorado. Additional rumors suggested that Diak Hodell might also be involved.

So, Trinidad quickly became part of an ever-widening investigation as Jack assigned his friend to look for the missing persons. Working on his computer, the detective had been unable to trace the pilot or nail down Diak's whereabouts, but he quickly compiled a file on the woman whom everyone knew was somewhere in Colorado. There were suspicions that she was acting as the professor's partner in crime—assuming there was a crime involved—or playing cozy with the Russians. Possibly, she was acting as an accomplice of the shadowy German operative, or maybe in league with an obscure Saudi prince.

The whole case was beginning to smack of international intrigue and Trinidad had only been on the job a few hours when FBI agents—who'd gotten wind of NAGPRA's end-run around their jurisdictional stonewall—flooded into Colorado. Russians, Saudis, and German rogues? The Feds couldn't be more delighted with this cast of characters. So, they took up positions in Jack's already crowded building and sat at their identical laptops and spun out a dizzying array of plausible and fanciful scenarios.

The agents had reviewed the limited facts available and that glimpse had been enough to convince the Bureau that something was up with the professor's caching assignment. As a result, somebody in Washington decided the best course of action was to interrupt the professor's traditional caching route. The plan was to create a mythical construction project near the isolated settlement of Lavender, hastily put up a roadblock, and see what happened.

The Feds spent forty feverish minutes creating their roadblock and then disappeared as suddenly as they had arrived. An hour later, they came pouring back when their roadblock exploded in a hail of wood, sand, Bentley components, and Russian body parts. Instantly the Bureau developed a keen interest in all things Clark and the pace of the investigation quickened.

Assisting the FBI while also following his own line of inquiry, Trinidad was inspired to quickly dress up as Diak Hodell. He suspected the German was behind the bomb carnage and the detective's intention was to determine if Diak and the woman were in league together. To complicate matters, Trinidad was also charged by the sheriff to be on the lookout for any members of the Scarlet Brotherhood who might wander into his wheelhouse.

"And what exactly constitutes my wheelhouse?" Trinidad had inquired when Deputy Madge Oxford briefed him regarding the parameters of his investigative mission.

"Lavender and Lavender alone, Mr. Halloween, and hold still," commanded Madge as she put the finishing touches on his eye prosthesis.

Moments later, Trinidad met the lovely Anne Scriptor and, even though he'd been instantly attracted to the playful woman, he nevertheless continued his deception. One lie led to another, as he tried to convince himself that his investigative ethics justified deceiving Anne with half-truths and blatant falsehoods.

Investigative ethics, he told himself, *as if that flimsy excuse justified my wrong-headed behavior.*

Suppressing his growing feelings for Anne, he'd been relieved to discover she had no idea who Hodell was. His relief turned to dread with the second explosion in his lavender field. The bombings confirmed his suspicions that the German was involved. Fearing for Anne's safety, he'd been about to tell her everything when she vanished.

During the few hours they'd spent together, the detective's duties had continually collided with his emotions. Marching hand-in-hand with his deductions and deceptions had been his growing affection for Anne. He couldn't help himself. He was inexorably drawn to the lovely young woman, who seemed to be innocently caught up in her professor's plot to sell a priceless artifact to a dangerous pack of unsavory buyers. It was a scheme made all the more precarious by the apparent interest which another detective—namely, Diak, a shadowy and infamous rogue—had shown in the transaction. Trinidad was in a quandary. With each passing moment, he found himself falling more in love with his subject. He muddled on, trying to moderate his growing affection, and with no clear idea if his passion would be reciprocated.

As he basked in the sheer joy of Anne's company, the interests of NAG-PRA, the concerns of the FBI, the schemes of the wayward professor, the expectations of the professor's buyers, the bad intentions of Diak Hodell, and even the wishes of the sheriff and his deputy—all these disquieting and competing factors fell away. The only thing left, the one thing that mattered to Trinidad was Anne—her desires, her wishes, and her safety.

Nothing else should have mattered.

Thoughts of Anne pulled Trinidad out of the past and back to the jet, to the dog at his feet, and the ache in his heart. He should have told Anne everything. If he'd trusted her from the start, he might have gained her confidence and together they'd have tried to make sense of things. Even if his honesty had done nothing to clarify events, at least they'd be facing the unknown together. As it was, he'd failed Anne. She was alone now and in danger.

Desperate to make amends, Trinidad was trusting his instincts by flying south. It was a gamble which might pay off—a chance to get ahead of her. In another hour, the anxious detective and the reluctant Feds would land in Cortez, pile into waiting pursuit vehicles, and rush northward, retrieving caches as they went. If the detective's legendary luck didn't desert him, they'd locate Anne and make her safe. He'd give anything to see her again—to hear her voice—to touch her.

"Anne," he whispered as the jet winged southward and his canine audience perked up her ears.

Chapter 70

The instant Clark sought to telephone his Russian customers to divulge the treasure coordinates, his call was routed to Diak's cell phone and the German eavesdropped. Apparently under the mistaken impression he was in exclusive communication with the Scarlet Brotherhood, the unsuspecting professor rattled off a cascade of numbers, then paused.

In the pregnant silence which followed, Diak could hear the professor breathing, but said nothing. The others too were silent. When Clark asked if his information was understood, Diak responded with a mumbled reply and the professor hung up, unaware that his Russian buyers hadn't said a single word.

The German remained on the line, knowing the Russians were there. Had Clark realized what was happening, he might have been puzzled by the reticent Russians, whereas Diak understood their silence. For days, treasure hunters had crowded into Western Colorado. Now, only the German remained. He let the Russians stew a moment before he spoke.

"Hello, Comrades," Diak put his cell phone on speaker, freeing his hands to unfold his map and begin plotting the location of Clark's coordinates. "I know you are there. Please respond."

"Herr Hodell," a voice answered—the words bitter.

"Magar," the German guessed. "So good to hear your voice." In the silence which followed, Diak wondered how the vanquished Brothers would react to the reality of his intervention.

I have consigned to hell six of their number, and a seventh is missing, presumed dead. We are fresh out of local mobsters, and no substitutes have appeared. The rest are too far away to interfere. They are without options—the field is clear.

"What are your terms?" Magar asked—his tone a mixture of defiance and resignation.

"I'm leaving just now to secure the treasure," Diak announced. "And my terms are ten million dollars. I will be in touch shortly. Can I reach you at this number?"

"As you wish," said Magar, irritably.

The instant the call officially ended, Diak dialed the Saudis and brought them up to speed, making certain they understood the concept of same-Clovis/new-vendor with the opening bid increased to ten million. When the Saudis suggested they needed to speak to Clark, he told them the professor was dead, which would eventually be true, one way or another.

Having set that pot boiling, the German grabbed his map, fired up his 4Runner, and began his joyful journey by programming the Lizard Head coordinates into his navigation system. At last, his dreams would be realized. Relishing his good fortune and anticipating his victory, he sped southward. Feeling unbridled, he pressed the accelerator. Soon he was rushing headlong, mere hours away from seizing the Clovis and remarketing it for millions. The Toyota hummed, the pavement whizzed by, and Diak was making excellent progress, until fate intervened.

Barreling past the sleepy town of Olathe, the questing German ran afoul of a local patrol car. Pursued westward, he rocketed through unfamiliar country, switching from pavement to dirt roads and back again, startling livestock by wheeling through pastures, and finally hiding in the dark recesses of a grain elevator to evade capture. By the time he managed to elude the police, the sun was approaching the horizon.

Returning to the highway, the German resumed his journey feeling flustered but also philosophical. He'd wasted hours dodging the police and yet his confidence was unshaken. It was true that night would fall before he reached the pass, but time and circumstances were on his side. Despite the delay, he took comfort in the realization that absolutely no one else was in a position to claim the Clovis.

His explosions had distracted the law, his competing detective had turned tail, Clark had pulled up stakes, the Russians had surrendered, the Saudis remained impotent, and the girl had vanished. For all intents and purposes, he was alone in the vast wilderness of Western Colorado and soon the treasure would be his.

Moderating his speed, Diak traveled southward, buoyed by a sense of destiny, savoring each passing roadside attraction—a tree, a shrub, a rock, a mile-marker, as an instance of delicious foreplay. Without further incident, he rolled through Ridgway, bypassed Telluride, and climbed toward Lizard Head. Cruising through the final mile, he approached the isolated pass with soaring hopes, but no sooner did he arrive at the trailhead than his optimism evaporated at the sight of a vehicle sitting there. In the dark, he'd driven into the well-concealed parking area, totally unaware and with no time to react.

If this is a trap, the German told himself, *I am dead already.*

Expecting the worst, Diak kept his head down and spun the steering wheel, blocking the exit. His tight turn kicked up rocks and dirt, temporarily obscuring the constricted parking area from view. When the dust cleared, his headlights illuminated a battered yellow truck. Annoyed to see the vehicle, and unhappier still to see that it was occupied, the German cursed under his breath.

What now? he asked himself.

The truck's headlamps remained dark and, when the driver didn't try to flee, he guessed the vehicle was inoperable. There was a chance its being here was pure coincidence. The occupant might be a bystander with engine trouble, a person in the wrong place at the wrong time. Whatever the case, there was clearly someone sitting in the cab and this unexpected witness would have to be eliminated. Rapidly considering his options, Diak remained in his idling 4Runner.

He was still alive, so he presumed the interloper to be unarmed. Watching the truck for movement, he took a moment to decide whether his knife or his pistol or some other means would be required to deal with the situation. Selecting his most subtle weapon, he emerged from his vehicle and walked in front to position himself between the Toyota's headlights. Concealing a syringe at his side, the German used his empty hand to wave for the other driver to join him. Seconds passed, then the truck's headlamps suddenly illuminated, and he was on the verge of ducking out of the light when the yellow door swung open and the occupant stepped out.

"Ah," he said aloud. His fabled luck hadn't deserted him.

Anne Scriptor stood beside her truck for a tantalizing moment. She seemed to be hesitating and curious, but not afraid. Instead, she looked directly at the German's battered face, seemed to recognize him, and started forward. Disarmed by her unexpected openness, Diak involuntarily took a step back. He was simultaneously surprised and a little amused to have discovered the troublesome girl alone at the trailhead, far from the highway, and apparently stranded. He'd been astonished to encounter her and even more amazed when, upon seeing him, she didn't instantly leap from her truck and bolt into the darkness.

Anne moved a step closer before stopping with a bemused look on her face. They stood in the darkness a few paces apart—each seemingly astonished to see the other. Then abruptly the spell broke. Her face suddenly clouded and she began to turn away, but before she could run, Diak rushed forward to block her escape. Quickly overpowering his confused victim, he subdued her with an anesthetizing inoculation. Emitting a stifled cry, Anne collapsed in his arms. He lifted his petite prisoner with ease and carried the unconscious woman to his Toyota where he placed her in the passenger seat and secured her seatbelt. Then he rapidly searched her vehicle and confiscated two toolboxes from the claptrap truck's lockbox.

"Endlich," Diak said aloud as he placed the purloined boxes in the 4Runner's cargo bay and switched on the rear dome light. "Finally."

Here at last, he told himself, *are the inscrutable toolboxes. But why two boxes and what are they and the girl doing just now on this dark mountain? If I set aside the question of the boxes, there are only two possible reasons for the girl to be here. Either she has come to spirit the treasure away—a daring double-cross of her professor and the Brotherhood. Or she is working in league with Clark, has had the treasure all along, and is here to place it at the revealed coordinates. A puzzle, yes, but what does it matter if the girl is coming or going? What matters is...*

As Diak tried to organize his thoughts, he wolfishly eyed the boxes. Caution suggested that he wait to open them, but anticipation was bubbling over. Surrendering to his curiosity, the triumphant German reached for his stolen bolt cutters. Intent on forcing the locks on both boxes, he positioned the jaws around the shank of the nearest padlock and took a deep breath.

Happily-ever-after, he told himself as he exhaled expansively while muscles in his shoulders, arms, forearms, wrists, and fingers flexed in anticipation of the energy needed to fracture the metal. But, before he could make the cut, his phone vibrated as Clark's call to 911 was redirected.

Dropping the bolt cutters, Diak swiftly took the call, concealing his identity, speaking little, and listening intently, the German played the part of an emergency operator to perfection as Clark reported that one of the girl's boxes might contain a bomb.

A bomb? Diak thought. *So, it seems that great minds must think alike.*

The moment Clark ended his call, the German dismissed the idea of opening the boxes. Instead, he expertly secured his potentially hazardous cargo, closed the Toyota's rear hatch, and hurried to the driver's seat. Diak had no idea where Clark was, but he trusted that the oblivious professor would keep his smartphone activated. Instantly, his faith was rewarded as he located Clark's signal, activated the 4Runner's tracking system, and set out in hot pursuit. The German needed answers and the professor and the girl were going to provide them.

With his female prisoner strapped-in and unconscious in the 4Runner's passenger seat and the boxes safely stowed, Diak tracked Clark's signal southward on Colorado Highway 145 as it followed the course of the Dolores River. Descending through the tiny settlements of Rico and Dolores itself, he drove on until he reached Cortez where he traced the signal to a solitary vehicle parked at a roadside motel. Observing the conspicuous Rubicon in the otherwise empty lot, and immediately comprehending the Navajo connection, he was certain he'd located the elusive professor's vehicle. It was the work of a moment to consult the pilot's note and verify the jeep's license plate number.

Rapidly evaluating the scene, Diak deduced the location of Clark's room from the jeep's position in front of the only unit with closed curtains. Knocking and ascertaining that the room was empty, he unscrewed the single light bulb above the door. Then he parked the 4Runner in an alleyway and waited nearby in the shadows until he saw the professor limping across the street. The German had another syringe which was handy and already primed with diazepam. As Clark neared the motel, the rotund man paused to open the rear hatch of the Rubicon and look inside.

Remaining in the shadows, Diak unzipped his syringe case. It'd been efficient to inject the astonished girl at the pass and the German could follow the same procedure to pacify the professor. But Clark's unpredictable behavior had been annoying. So, when Clark locked his vehicle and started toward his room, Diak left the syringe behind. Moving swiftly and silently, he used the butt of his pistol to knock the irritating professor senseless.

Loading the overweight man into his 4Runner, he further incapacitated Clark by administering an injection. With the unconscious man stretched out across the rear seats, he rummaged through Clark's pockets until he found the Rubicon key-fob. A quick search of the professor's jeep increased the German's puzzlement exponentially.

"Two more boxes," he whispered to himself as he added them to his growing collection. "The puzzle enlarges."

The motel and its surroundings were deserted and Diak managed to remain undetected as he started his vehicle. Reversing course to return to Lavender, he drove northward through the darkness, carefully adhering to speed limits as he pondered the meaning of the four toolboxes, the girl's presence at the pass, and Clark's 911 call about a bomb. His initial reaction to Clark's warning had been to presume the evasive man was lying about the explosives and using them as an excuse to inspire law enforcement to pick up the girl.

But the police were not coming—Diak had seen to that by intercepting Clark's call before it reached the authorities. Furthermore, the German's reliable nose had detected an anomaly and a closer examination of his new acquisitions confirmed his suspicions. Trusting his senses, he found the evidence to be crystal clear. One box from the girl's truck and one of those in the professor's possession exuded the unmistakable odor of almonds. Plastic C-4 was Diak's conclusion—had to be—although he couldn't comprehend the purpose of the bombs.

Have I stumbled onto a plot to ambush the Russians? he asked himself. *If so, why would Clark endanger his buyers? And why lure the treasure hunters to Lizard Head? If Clark had his way, his unsuspecting buyers would have congregated at a remote mountain pass, only to encounter the girl and her bomb, not to mention having to deal with a flock of police—again why?*

Thinking back to Clark's recent call to the Brotherhood, Diak now considered it odd that the professor had revealed the coordinates but made no arrangements to receive the balance owed. Given subsequent events, that omission suggested a double-cross and, viewed in the context of the bomb and the summoned authorities...

Diak shook his head. Clark's motives and those of the girl seemed hopelessly muddled. The German's logic seldom failed him, but he had to admit to a bewildering inability to get inside the minds of his adversaries. He could feel a headache building behind his missing eye as he bypassed Olathe and slipped around Delta City. When he reached his Lavender hideout in the wee hours of the morning, he was not only weary and feverish but also perplexed. Turning off his ignition, he sat in the Toyota, closed his good eye, and considered the curious outcomes of his busy evening.

Hours ago, he'd rushed to Lizard Head Pass expecting to take possession of the priceless Clovis. His exuberant haste had nearly gotten him arrested, but he'd survived that challenge, only to stumble upon a puzzle consisting of four toolboxes and two captives. The professor remained unconscious—his corpulent mass stretched full-length across the back seat—his hollow breathing reminiscent of some great slumbering beast. The respirations of the girl in the passenger seat beside him were milder until she suddenly gasped and stirred, indicating she was beginning to awaken. Unbuckling her seatbelt, he forced his dazed prisoner to walk and guided her into the basement where he gagged Anne and tied her to a chair.

Returning to his vehicle, he took time to make certain the toolboxes were secure before using all his strength to carry the comatose professor inside. Binding Clark like a Thanksgiving turkey, he left the troublesome man on the cold basement floor. Next, as the semi-conscious girl watched him trudge up and down, he carried each toolbox carefully into the basement and made a final return trip to secure the bolt cutters. With his prisoners secured, he turned his attention to the four boxes lined up on a dusty table.

Examining them closely, he could see the boxes were similar but not identical. Two had keyed locks. One of these had the number '1' painted on its lid and the other was numbered '3.' Box number one had been in Clark's possession and he'd found number three in the girl's truck. The remaining boxes were secured with combination padlocks. Neither of these had a number. To avoid confusion, he used a marking pen to carefully sketch an 'X' on the boxes retrieved from the professor's jeep in order to distinguish them from those extracted from the girl's truck.

Four potential bombs, he thought.

Starting with the numbered boxes, he carefully picked up box one and held it at eye level. He visually examined all four sides as well as top and bottom. Returning box one to the table, he picked up box three and systematically repeated the process. His nose confirmed that neither numbered box smelled of almonds. That distinct odor was limited to the pair of unnumbered boxes, each secured with a combination lock.

And now, down to two potential bombs, he concluded.

He mused for a moment more, then made his decision. He'd trust his senses and his luck. Carefully moving the unnumbered boxes to one side, he picked up the bolt cutters, took a deep breath, exhaled, and severed the shanks of both keyed padlocks. Placing the bolt cutters aside, he took a moment to settle his breathing. Then he opened the lids on the two numbered boxes, fully expecting to discover the Clovis in one or the other. Finding both boxes empty, he frowned and went back upstairs to think.

Exhausted by his 300-mile round trip to Cortez and back again, Diak surrendered to his mounting headache, sucked down a dose of Jackpot, lay down on his bedroll, and nodded off. As he slept, his unconscious mind continued to gnaw at his puzzle. On the basement table were four boxes. His sense of smell had given him confidence to open the numbered boxes, both of which proved to be empty. In the German's estimation, this meant that one of the unopened boxes was rigged to explode, while the other was laced with C-4, but not wired.

So, his slumbering mind deduced, *my Clovis will be found within which-ever toolbox is safe to open—but which is which?*

It was a stubborn puzzle which remained unsolved at 3 a.m. when Diak—suffocating in the stuffy confines of his Lavender hideout—coughed himself awake. Rising unsteadily, he walked to the top of the basement stairs and peered into the darkness below, listening for sounds of movement. Hearing nothing, he stumbled outside to take an unsatisfying leak. He was standing in the bushes behind his hideout when he had an inspiration. Zipping his fly home, he gazed into the darkness.

To the northwest, just visible in the moonlight, the dark outline of Grand Mesa stretched across the horizon and he felt strangely drawn there. Dismissing the notion that the middle of the night might not be an ideal hour for sightseeing, he impetuously decided to take a drive.

He wanted to see for himself if the rumors were true.

The German had only been a week in Western Colorado, but already he'd grown accustomed to the region's sprawling pastures, its vast fruit orchards, and bleak dirt hills. In contrast to these lowlands, it was said that the elevations of Grand Mesa boasted an immense forest and many lakes. Diak sensed that a trip to the top and back again would help him collect his thoughts. In the past, he'd relied on Nature to calm his mind. Perhaps the Mesa's lofty atmosphere would help solve today's puzzle. Convinced that his prisoners were secure, he left them in the basement and fired up his SUV. Guided by his intuition, which often defied logic but had never steered him wrong, he drove through the sleeping streets of Lavender to reach the highway.

Arriving at the base of Grand Mesa, he pressed on his brakes as his headlights picked out the glowing eyes of a roadside creature. Gliding to a stop, he watched as a feral fox boldly crossed the pavement, pausing to gaze at him through the SUV's bug-splattered windshield. Sighting a fox, his mother had once told him, could serve as either an omen of good luck or a dire warning of impending misfortune.

"Time will tell," he said aloud while the seemingly unfazed animal lingered a moment more in the headlights before it casually sauntered to the edge of the highway and vanished.

The journey was not far and soon the German was sitting high on the Mesa in the dark on a narrow bridge. Below him trickled a lively stream, a narrow current flowing onward to feed a distant lake. The German's eye tracked the motion of the stream, his mind embracing the perpetual melding of water and darkness. With unceasing motion, the tumbling current flowed into the broad lake, merging smoothly into a single dark expanse framed by a shadowy border of towering pines.

Save for the perpetual music of the stream, it was absolutely quiet.

Overhead stretched a dark canopy, a vast dusky sea ranging from horizon to horizon. Countless stars suspended there—a universe of glimmering sailboats floating in a boundless black ocean. Among these endless pinpoints of light, rode the distant moon—a gilded sphere, past its zenith, but still undisputed ruler of the predawn sky. Streaming down from the heavens, moonlight etched a bright ribbon upon the lake's placid surface, forming a shimmering borderline which seemed to bisect the dark water.

"This," he said as he gestured toward one side of the divided water. "Or that," he added as he pointed to the other. "A choice of two—the very image of my puzzle."

The night-world of Grand Mesa seemed crystal clear and surprisingly cold for July. Glad for his jacket, Diak sat cross-legged on the bridge, watching the glistening moonlight on the lake, listening to the passing stream, and contemplating his puzzle. The flowing current seemed to bear away his troubles and the lake beyond to absorb and diminish them. His sense of the present steadily dissolved until his thinking, so tangled in the maze of his current puzzle, began to stray into his well-remembered past. Perhaps a solution lay there. He measured his breathing and his mind relaxed as his thoughts turned to his boyhood and his mother's stories of her days as an orphaned child, homeless and hungry, forced to survive in the woods.

On a night such as this, years ago, in the closing months of World War II, his mother and other *wolfskinder* children would have been sleeping beneath the stars in a distant European forest. Mourning their murdered families, the children would huddle together to keep warm, surrounded on all sides by dark trees and dense brushwood.

"Weren't you frightened," the boy Diak had asked his mother.

"Of course," she'd answered as she tucked him in. "But not in the way you think. The woods did not frighten us. Even the animals failed to frighten us. The men—the men with guns—this is what we feared."

Diak sighed and looked aloft toward the distant stars. Steeped in tales of his mother's misfortunes, he'd vowed never to be reduced, as she had been, to a target. When she died, he hardened his heart and turned his mother's nightmare on its head. His solution was simple. To escape the ranks of the hunted, he became the hunter. Even so, his mother's voice reached him from beyond the grave.

"You must not be afraid," she'd told him. "The past is gone and now you and I are here and safe and warm. So, sleep well, my son, and H.E.A."

"H.E.A." her son had agreed. But even then, he'd wondered if he'd ever attain the safety and contentment encapsulated in that hopeful abbreviation.

Pondering these bittersweet memories, the German allowed himself a brief smile. He hadn't thought about that three-letter combination since—how long had it been since his mother died? The Communist authorities had conducted a cursory investigation, but he'd refused to believe their verdict of suicide. Though their existence had been bleak, his mother loved life and she would never have abandoned her only son. As evidence of her love and her indomitable spirit, he recalled that, while she lived, the letters H.E.A. had been a secret code which united them—a conspiracy of optimism which he and his mother had shared, until that fateful morning when she did not return.

H.E.A. stood for a hopeful tagline to her many tales, something positive and soothing his mother said at the close of her bedtime stories, something she always said when she kissed his forehead before leaving to walk the streets of East Berlin. When he was a boy, the two of them had made a private game of the initials, writing the three letters on scraps of paper and leaving the paper in a pocket, or beneath a cereal bowl, or under a pillow, where the other would be sure to discover it. One day young Diak had created a bauble for his mother by scratching the letters onto a beer bottle cap. To his delight she'd threaded the metal onto a delicate chain to fashion a crude necklace which became her most prized possession. The fact that the necklace had been missing when they recovered her body convinced Diak she hadn't jumped like they said. She would never have parted with the locket voluntarily. Someone had taken it. Someone had pushed her. Why or how wasn't clear. As a boy of five, all Diak knew was this: his mother and her necklace were gone and, with them, his happiness.

"Happily-ever-after," he said aloud, wistfully deciphering the abbreviation he'd shared with his late mother. "Happily-ever-after," he repeated, his breath fogging in the cold, the words seeming to suspend in the pure mountain air.

H.E.A. presupposed an outcome which had eluded his poor mother and left her young son to struggle on alone. Now, with the Clovis so near, happiness seemed to be, at last, within his grasp. It'd taken him three decades of blood, sweat, and tears to reach tonight's opportunity of achieving his childhood fantasy of a happy ending. Blood, sweat, and tears to be sure—although, in truth, there had been considerable sweat and few tears. Mostly there had been blood.

Think on something else, he told himself as he sat on the bridge and tried again to focus his thoughts. Something about his sitting position triggered another memory, this one more recent, and he followed that thread in search of peace.

Unconsciously, he'd positioned his legs in a yoga pose and he sought to recall the breathing exercises which his earnest teacher had once tried to drum into his wooden head. A vision of Greta in her sensual leotard seeped into his thoughts. When whole and virile, he'd had many women, but Greta, slim and beautiful and kind, had been his truest and—as it happened—his final love. After the accident, there was no facing the sensual woman, let alone pleasuring her. She'd written many letters seeking explanations—seeking closure—but he'd burned them all and fled to America. In his former life—

his life as a whole man—and on such a night as this—thoughts of Greta Dove should have stirred his loins. As it was...

Think on something else, he chastised himself.

The past was gone. He needed to focus on the dilemma which had been presented to him. Seeking solitude, he'd driven to the Mesa, hoping to immerse himself in Nature, hoping to cleanse his thoughts and, thereby, solve his puzzle. The mountain serenity had been calming, yes, but it had also pulled him into the past. As a result, he was spinning his wheels and, literally, sitting on his ass as he wallowed in the throes of ancient history.

His mother was dead, her necklace and her love were beyond his reach, never to return. Greta was gone, pushed away. He'd wasted too much time reminiscing about the past when he ought to be embracing the present and moving forward to secure a brighter future. Cursing his inaction, he struggled to stand erect, finding his legs stiff from sitting overlong. He'd been mired in the past, an indulgence which had pulled him far from his present puzzle. He needed to reawaken his tingling legs and rekindle his thinking through deliberate movement. Placing one foot in front of the other, he left the bridge behind, found a path, and followed the stream toward the distant lake, walking briskly, his progress aided by an abundance of gleaming moonlight.

He needed to refocus his divided attention. Much had happened and he must sort it out. Wrapped in the dark beauty of Grand Mesa, Diak walked along the descending trail. Taming his restless mind, he forced himself to consider the perplexing dilemma which Clark's unexpected behavior had wrought. The German's legendary luck and his ability to monitor the professor's smartphone had allowed him to capture the rotund man and the bothersome girl and confiscate caches from both. Through a combination of good fortune and clever detective work, he'd drawn tantalizingly close to grasping the treasured Clovis. Even when informed that the boxes might contain bombs, his confidence had made him bold. Trusting his instincts, he'd acted decisively to force two locks, found both boxes empty, and been momentarily flustered. The two empty toolboxes left two unopened, both of which smelled of almonds. He needed to think—needed to approach things systematically—needed, as his mother would say, to organize his trouble-some ducks.

"Deine Enten in einer Reihe bekommen—ducks in a row," he said aloud.

Increasing his pace, he took several steps then abruptly halted on the trail, which seemed to fade beneath his feet. Looking aloft, he found that clouds had obscured the moon, causing the once-visible pathway to disappear from view. Having strayed far, it would be dicey to make his way back to the 4Runner without the aid of moonlight. To judge the distance, he turned and glanced back. He'd left his Toyota on high ground, parallel to the edge of an elevated parking area. Seen from a distance, the car should have appeared as a shadowy hulk on a dark hill, but instead a glimmer of light shone from the vehicle's rearmost windows.

"Shite!" he exclaimed as he sprinted headlong back in the direction of his SUV.

Heedless of the darkened terrain, he crashed over uneven ground. Keeping his vehicle in sight, he willed himself to remain upright. He ran with abandon, trying not to fall and hoping he was wrong. Earlier that night, while stashing confiscated toolboxes at Lizard Head Pass, he'd manually activated the Toyota's rear dome light but failed to switch it off. He could see the bulb glowing faintly as he struggled uphill.

Reaching the parking area, he used his key-fob to unlock the 4Runner while he dashed toward the vehicle and skidded to a stop on the compacted dirt. Swearing an oath, he yanked the rear hatch open, extinguished the light, and angrily slammed the hatch shut. Instinctively, he glanced at his watch and then aloft. Time had flown and the dark sky was beginning to lighten. Lamenting his negligence, he climbed into the Toyota and pushed the starter button, but the engine wouldn't turn over.

Verdammt!

Seeking solitude on the Mesa and leaving the 4Runner's dome light burning while he frittered time away with his foolish ruminations had been a mistake. The Toyota had been in storage for months. The weak electrical system was a malfunction waiting to happen until the burning dome light conspired with the Mesa's lofty altitude and chilly predawn temperatures to kill the battery. When all this was over, Diak would severely reprimand his Grand Junction contractor for not keeping the vehicle's battery charged, but the thought of administering future discipline held little consolation at the moment. Despite the contractor's oversight, it was the German himself who'd been careless, and the results of his inattention left him stranded high in the dark forest with dawn approaching and miles separating him from his treasure.

Inexcusable! he told himself as he stepped out into the night and, in that instant, recognized the solution.

His luck had not deserted him. The Toyota sat on an incline. Still muttering under his breath, Diak scrambled back inside and placed the SUV in neutral. Opening the door, he jumped out again, took a firm stance beside the stalled vehicle, and began pushing. Immediately the heavy machine started rolling downhill. He dove inside, jammed in the clutch, and popped the car into gear. The Toyota lurched and bucked as the engine caught hold. Blaspheming in the darkness, the German steered back onto the highway and sped away.

He'd abandon this hypnotic forest with its mesmerizing streams and lakes. He'd forsake the past and rush back to Lavender, unravel his present puzzle, and embrace the future. He'd confront his prisoners, force Clark to open the treasure box, and—at long last—secure his prize.

As he rushed down the highway, though it was not yet fully light, the German defiantly, and in deference to his splitting headache, fitted his sunglasses onto his throbbing face, and pressed on the Toyota's accelerator as he rocketed back toward Lavender.

Chapter 71

Deputy Madge Oxford was lying on her back and sweating profusely in the station gym as she did one final rep. In less than an hour, she'd have to report for her morning assignment. Sighing, she stripped extra plates off the barbell and stacked each one on its corresponding peg, putting everything in order for the next lifter. The women and men—mostly men—who frequented the county's exercise room always knew when Madge had been using the free weights, because whatever she left in her wake was organized and in its proper place.

Madge ran her fingers through her moist hair then wiped off the bench and grabbed a fresh towel. Disrobing as she walked, she stripped off her gym outfit and headed for the showers. As usual, the water in the county locker room was scalding and she had to ratchet up the cold to make it tolerable. Moments later, standing in a cloud of steam with water dripping off her shoulders, the deputy used her palm to clear a place in the mirror.

"Hopeless," she said.

As usual her hair was a mess. Using both hands, she tried to mold it in place. At last she decided her kinky locks were sufficiently tamed to be covered by her service cap, so she focused on her face. Leaning her head back she could see two troublesome hairs nestling just under her chin. With some effort, she grasped them one by one with her short fingernails and plucked them out. Then she turned her head from side to side and considered her eyes.

"Nope," she said aloud. "Not gonna try *that* today."

The last time Madge had experimented with eyeliner and mascara, the result had been exactly that—an experiment. That particular trial-run had left her disfigured with a lopsided face resembling something a near-sighted mad scientist might have concocted in a monster movie laboratory.

Ignoring her eyes, she moisturized her ruddy face, slathered on deodorant, and got dressed. With her uniform in place, she adjusted her cap, centered her image in the mirror, and sighed. She was what she'd always been, what she would always be: a big-boned and big-breasted gal. Much good the breasts did her, because her face, she knew, was rough-hewn and angular, as if arbitrarily chiseled out of living rock. When she smiled, which was not often, her face was appealing enough—to small children and animals—but seldom to men.

Madge sighed again.

Sighing was her thing, although she mostly did it in secret. To the world—and especially while on duty—Delta County Deputy Sheriff Madeline Oxford was a gruff and no-nonsense colleague, a stout woman who traded insults and taunts with her male comrades. In private, she mostly sighed. A final glance in the mirror revealed that her name plate was crooked and, sighing once again, she took pains to straighten it. OXFORD, M. the brass name plate declared. If she hadn't been tired of sighing so much, she would have repeated the emotion as she recalled her first day on the job.

"Hey, Ox!" a posse of deputies had taunted seven years ago when they passed her in the hallway. "Yo, Ox!" her new mates shouted across the cafeteria. They waved for her to join them and she did. What else could she do? Everyone in the department had a nickname—everybody except Sheriff Jack of course—and, given her size and surname, her handle was a natural. So, she rolled with it.

"Okay, Ox," she told her reflection, "let's go kick some ass."

She secured a riot gun and her Glock pistol from the weapons locker, holstered the pistol, and double-checked the ammo in her belt magazines. Then she walked to her patrol car with the shotgun in her left hand and a nagging feeling that she was forgetting something. She checked her jacket pockets with her free hand and was relieved to find the folded image. Opening it as she walked, the deputy beheld the likeness of the smiling woman. Contemplating that wholesome image, Madge was about to sigh at Anne Scriptor's breathtaking beauty. But before she could indulge her thoughts, the sheriff interrupted by nearly colliding with his deputy.

"Sorry, didn't see you there," said Jack as he rushed into the corridor carrying a helmet and wearing a ballistic vest. "Sorry," he repeated the apology and she grunted her acceptance. "I'm just headin' out. You good to go, Madge?"

Unlike the others, Jack always used his deputy's given name. Undoubtedly, he was aware of her nickname and, probably, for her sake, he consciously avoided using it. "You all set?" he asked again and, seeing the photo in Madge's hand, he added, "I see you've got the picture."

"Yes, sir," said Madge.

"That's the real one," said Jack. "She's a brunette."

"I get it," said Madge.

"Good huntin'," said Jack.

"Good hunting," Madge responded as the two officers turned to travel in opposite directions.

The sheriff and four deputies were heading south in search of Anne Scriptor's nearest caches and the woman herself. A handful of FBI agents and a brace of bomb-sniffing dogs were joining them. Trinidad and more agents and one dog were flying still further south with the idea of getting ahead of the Scriptor woman. The search was on and Madge had wanted to go along, but she was, according to Jack, "needed elsewhere."

Earlier that morning, the sheriff had assured Madge her job was important.

"It ain't likely you'll spot our girl anywheres near Lavender," Jack had said as he handed her a recent photo of Anne—one showing her winning smile and current hairstyle. "But there's always a chance she might double-back, plus—just like the rest of us—you'll need to watch for this professor character and the German. And also, you'll need to stay alert in case you spot any of them black Bentleys. But it's really the girl we're after at this point, and you've met her in person, so that makes you the one most likely to recognize her."

Not counting Trinidad, Madge had thought, because she was thoroughly convinced that the handsome detective had more than his share of firsthand knowledge of the lovely Anne. The deputy had nothing against the beautiful young woman, except she envied Anne's good looks, resented her college education, and was jealous of her effect on Trinidad. With effort, as Jack gave her a quizzical look, she'd managed to curb her jealous thinking and forced herself to ponder something else.

"So," Madge summarized in an attempt to focus on her assignment, "I know what this Scriptor gal looks like alright and I've seen a Bentley before and you say the professor looks like Santa Claus, beard and all, so he'll be easy to spot. But do we have a picture of this German guy?"

"No picture," Jack had said. "But, believe me, he stands out. He's an ugly devil and only got the one eye, so he'll look pretty much like Trinidad did in his pancake house getup."

Madge had recalled the ridiculous disguise which she'd helped Trinidad concoct a few days ago. Plus, she also remembered how she'd allowed jealousy to cloud her brief interaction with the attractive graduate student who shared breakfast with the handsome detective. Regretting her behavior in urging Anne to leave town, the deputy had started to apologize again for this lapse, but Jack stopped her.

"What's done is done—that's water over the dam," he'd told her. "That little incident at the pancake house is old news. This Scriptor girl, she has an effect on people, so at first glance you either love her or hate her."

"Which is it with you?" Madge had asked. She was convinced that Trinidad had fallen under Anne's spell and she was curious to know if the sheriff was equally smitten.

"I'm on the fence," said Jack.

Now it was two hours later, and Jack may or may not be off the fence. But rather than ask the sheriff where he stood regarding the charms of the wily Miss Scriptor, the deputy walked on in silence, as her boss headed down the opposite hall. Soon Jack would be traveling south with his troops in search of toolboxes, the illusive Anne, and other assorted characters. As for Madge, she was traveling in the opposite direction to do her duty and as usual, she was going it alone. Refolding Anne's picture, the deputy buttoned it into her pocket as she walked out back to grab her vehicle.

She found the parking lot empty except for her patrol car and the county's tactical tank. For a moment she wondered why the seldom-used tank hadn't been called into service. With the explosions in Lavender and the FBI on the job, it was all hands on-deck, which meant that the sheriff's office was short-staffed, and it seemed to her like a great opportunity to road-test the tank. But Madge had her assignment and so, with a forlorn glance at the rolling fortress, she fired up her less spectacular vehicle and headed toward Lavender.

She was still twelve miles out when the call came in.

Someone had collided with a deer on the southern flanks of Grand Mesa and needed assistance. Madge was close and she told the dispatcher she'd take a look. The deputy had traveled five miles up a dark stretch of Highway 65 when she recognized young Katherine Lock driving down. Seeing the patrol car, Kate pulled over. The deputy turned on her beacon flashers and crossed the pavement to park in front of the dented vehicle. Emerging from her patrol car, Madge could see that the front fender and a portion of the Kia's grill were awkwardly crumpled.

"Dang, girl," said Madge as she walked forward.

"I couldn't stop. It just ran right into me," Kate sobbed. The unhappy woman exited her damaged compact and leaned heavily against the driver's side door, still clearly shaken from the recent collision.

"You hurt?" asked Madge.

"Just my heart," said Kate as she held a trembling hand to her breast and struggled to keep her balance. "There was a fawn and I hit the mother and she was still kicking, and I called 911 and..." Her voice trailed off and she slumped forward as the deputy moved quickly to keep the distraught young woman upright.

"Easy, kiddo. Don't forget to breathe and focus on me. How far up?" Madge asked as she steadied Kate and got eye contact.

"About three miles, I guess," said Kate.

"Breathe," said Madge.

"Two more curves up," Kate gulped as she took a deep breath and managed to stand erect.

"You okay to drive down?" Madge asked.

"Yes, I think so, yes," Kate answered. "I'm okay."

"Good," said Madge. "You go home. I'll take care of things up here." The deputy waited as Kate steered her bruised car back onto the highway and headed downhill. Then Madge called in her location and drove slowly up the highway with her roof beacons flashing. Steering with one hand, she used the other to manipulate the patrol car's spotlight, sweeping the darkness as she went.

After three miles, she spotted the fawn. It was a fresh young thing with a tawny coat and distinctive spots. Obviously stressed, the quivering animal stood slack-legged and wide-eyed on the pavement, its slender limbs awkwardly straddling the center stripe. The fawn did not bolt but remained in the middle of the road, seemingly transfixed in the stark glare of the deputy's spotlight. It made no sound, only shivered, and swayed and inclined its head toward the highway's downhill shoulder.

Madge killed the spotlight and eased her patrol car to the opposite side of the highway. She radioed her location, designating the nearest mile marker and instructing the dispatcher to notify Cody at Colorado Parks & Wildlife that a distressed fawn would need attention. Switching off her roof beacons, she left the engine running and set her front fog lights and rear taillights flashing. The deputy exited the patrol car slowly as the fawn watched her every move.

"Easy, honey," Madge cooed. "Easy now—it's okay."

The once-clear night had turned cloudy. It was dark on this edge of the secluded Mesa with only the patrol car's intermittent flashers to illuminate the scene, but Madge left her cumbersome flashlight behind. She'd search for the mother without it. She'd have to make do with light from the flashers and, besides, she might have to move quickly to evade a wounded doe. The mother might be down, but she was just as likely to be ambulatory and poised to protect her fawn by challenging a would-be rescuer.

Just one less thing to carry if I'm forced to draw my weapon or make a run for it, the deputy thought. *No sense having to juggle a flashlight if an angry doe charges out of the darkness.*

The fawn's movements seemed to point Madge in the right direction as she skirted around the frightened animal. Sidestepping across the pavement, the deputy continued to eye the young deer until she reached the far shoulder of the highway. She stopped there and listened intently, feeling certain the doe must be near. The mountain stillness seemed absolute and she was about to search elsewhere when she heard a flurry of sounds.

Turning away from the fawn, she heard the noises more distinctly: labored breathing followed by a sharp cough and unmistakable rustling in the road-side foliage—then silence again. Madge took a deep breath and placed her hand on the grip of her weapon as she inched forward. The patrol car's lights continued to flash off and on, causing her surreal surroundings to pulsate between pitch-black and semi-darkness. Peering ahead, she followed the curve of the roadway until she spotted something and moved in for a closer look.

The mother was there, near the edge of the road, and just visible—the downed animal's bulk forming a crease in a clump of tall grass. The deputy approached cautiously. With a fawn close by, even an injured doe would be a handful and Madge had a healthy respect for the sharp hooves of a protective parent.

She pulled her Glock and moved ever closer.

Dawn was approaching. The sky was clearing, and stars were beginning to fade as Madge drew near enough to distinguish the doe in the evaporating darkness. The animal lay on its side, its feet toward the highway. When the deputy took two more steps, the doe raised her head with effort and then let it roll back again. Madge could smell blood and feces and, even in the pale predawn light, she'd managed to catch a glimpse of the doe's glazed eyes and protruding tongue. The deer was puffing stridently, unable to regain its feet, and the deputy didn't need to examine its injuries to know the creature was in pain and dying.

She chambered a round but hesitated.

Madge was certain that firing her weapon would make the fawn bolt. She also knew that the young deer wouldn't run far and would eventually return to languish near its mother's carcass. The fawn would stay by its mother until it was rescued or until a motorist struck and killed the grieving animal. The doe stirred again and raised her head high enough to look Madge directly in the eye, as if pleading for the deputy to do what must be done. Madge sniffed, aimed true, and fired a single clean shot to the head.

Over her shoulder, she heard scrabbling on the pavement and turning to look toward the highway, she could see the fawn was gone. Convinced the young animal would remain nearby, Madge holstered her weapon, crossed the highway, and opened the patrol car trunk. Searching for flares, she took four, lit them in turn, and set them out—two on each highway shoulder and spaced apart. That array would alert drivers to reduce speed as they approached this sweeping curve from either direction. In the steadily increasing morning light, the deputy crossed the road to check the position of the doe a final time, making certain the body was clear of the highway. Then she surveyed the scene. Time was passing and she needed to take up her post in Lavender. The red flares sputtered. They might burn for another twenty minutes, but dawn was at least an hour away. The sky was lightening, but the roadway would remain dark and, as soon as she left the Mesa, Madge was certain the fawn would return.

She couldn't go yet, not without doing her best. A few moments spent totally securing the scene might save the fawn's life.

She searched her trunk again and found two LEDs—good for ten days the manufacturer claimed. The sleek flameless flares were expensive, and the county comptroller was constantly harassing officers and construction workers who used the precious items for everyday traffic control. She'd come back and pick them up later if she could. For now, no matter the cost, she'd set out the longer-lasting flares as insurance to keep the fawn safe.

With the LEDs in place, she closed the trunk, got back inside her patrol car, killed the flashers, and was about to make a U-turn when a speeding SUV came out of nowhere. The careening vehicle was heading downhill, and it barely made the corner. The driver seemed not to notice her or the flares.

Madge wheeled her patrol car around and was about to give chase when the radio blared.

"Oxford, what's your 20? Are you in position?" It was Jack's voice.

"On my way," Madge answered.

"Wait—what?" Jack sounded exasperated.

"Was called to a deer collision. Nobody hurt. I'm minutes out."

"Dang it, Madge, stop screwing around," said Jack, "and do your job."

"Roger that," said Madge. "Out."

Highway 65 snaked down the side of Grand Mesa and she could see the lights of the SUV as the vehicle continued downhill. The speeder was forging ahead, heedless of the curves, weaving through the switchbacks far below her. She'd gotten a good look at the camouflaged 4Runner when the driver raced through her accident scene. She'd remember the distinctive vehicle when she saw it next. For now, she had other work to do.

"You are one lucky speeder," she said aloud as she steered down. "Any other time and your butt would be mine."

Fifteen minutes later, Madge reached the base of the Mesa, passed through the undulating 'dobies, and crossed over the creek bridge to enter the outskirts of Lavender. She was rolling slowly through the village when she spotted the reckless 4Runner. The heavily camouflaged vehicle was parked next to a small house which sat between two towering grain elevators.

"Well, lookie here," Madge said. She killed her lights, eased onto the shoulder, and parked in a grove of trees. Watching the spot through binoculars, she saw the shadowy figure of a man emerge from the house, extract a pistol and holster from the SUV, and return to the building. This wasn't the girl she was looking for and it wasn't the professor who was a dead ringer for Saint Nick and, whoever it was, they sure as heck weren't driving a Bentley. But the coming dawn had provided just enough light and Madge caught a glimpse of a ruined face, which convinced her that she'd located one of the people she and the sheriff and the FBI and Trinidad were searching for. "Gotta be our German," she told herself.

She waited a heartbeat more and then, as the sun continued to rise, she called for back-up.

Chapter 72

When Clark came to, he was lying face down on a cold hard floor with his hands and feet bound behind him. As his mind cleared, he heard a rooster crowing.

"Dawn or dead," the professor muttered.

"Dr. Clark?"

He hadn't expected to hear Anne's voice.

"Anne? Anne, are you here somewhere?"

"Here in the dark," she whispered. "We're stuck in a basement. It's probably daylight, but the windows are blocked off. And I've tried calling for help, but we must be pretty isolated because no help has come..." Her voice trailed off.

"Are you—are you okay?" Clark asked.

"Yes. I was tied up is all—and drugged and gagged—but I worked the kerchief loose and I'm okay now," she whispered. "The question is—are you okay?"

"My head aches and my foot hurts, but I think I'm okay. So, why are we whispering?"

"I think he's nearby," she said.

"Who?" Clark asked.

"The man with the scar. He found me at the pass. He arrived in a cloud of dust and I thought he was someone else, so I opened the door. Big mistake. He stuck a needle in me, and I dropped like a sack of rocks."

"Probably the same little creep who slugged me," whispered Clark.

"Probably, although I wouldn't call him little, because he managed to carry you all the way downstairs on his own—no offense."

Clark laughed at his student's thinly veiled reference to his rotund size. "None taken. So, you're probably thinking I owe you an explanation."

"Do you?" she asked.

"Hmm," said Clark. "Oh!"

A bright light flared, and the sudden glare startled the captive pair. A single bulb illuminated the scene and, for a moment, by turning his head awkwardly, Clark managed to catch a glimpse of Anne across the room. She was tied to a wooden chair which sat in the shadows of a cubby-hole beneath a wooden stairway. The top of the stairway was hidden in darkness. Between the two of them was a long table and on it he saw a pair of bolt cutters and four toolboxes.

Clark recognized them instantly. Two were the boxes he'd brought from Tucson, the pair he'd rigged in the laundromat—each with deadly contents primed to explode and their combination locks still closed. The other two were original caches, including the precious Clovis box from his Rubicon. The lids on both original toolboxes were standing open and their keyed padlocks had been fractured. Clark saw that the body of the padlock containing the Clovis was still intact, which meant the hidden projectile point remained undiscovered on the table. He and Anne exchanged a hurried glance, then a voice came from the head of the stairs.

"Awake I see." The voice echoed in the cavernous basement. "And, young lady, why am I hearing your voice? You have been a naughty prisoner. Your gag is not as it should be. Shall I come down and silence you?"

"You leave her the hell alone!" shouted Clark.

"Ha! So noble, Dr. Clark. If only she knew of the danger in which you have so selfishly placed her." The man spoke confidently and with an accent Anne couldn't place, but the professor was certain the unseen man must be the renegade German whom the Saudis feared. Clark held his breath in anticipation of having to face this mysterious interloper, but the man remained hidden, apparently choosing not to descend the stairs.

This one has a sense of the theatrical, Clark thought, *very dramatic— purposely playing the mystic with disembodied voice.*

"But my time is limited," the voice continued, "so I will come to the point. The girl's life for the treasure. That is my offer. I will leave you two to discuss the details. When I return, Herr Professor, you will give me the Clovis."

The lights went off again and they could hear footsteps, then an upstairs door slamming shut, then silence.

When Anne was certain they were alone, she spoke again. She should have been frightened, but instead she was curious and a little angry as she whispered, "What Clovis?"

"It's a long story," Clark sighed. "And apparently, we have little time, so I'll say only this: I came across a singular Clovis point—so small that I was able to hide it in one of our padlocks..."

"Our padlocks?" Anne whispered.

"Yes," Clark confirmed. "And you would not believe how special it is... how definitively it verifies the hypothesis..."

"Oh, my God," Anne interrupted as the clever student of archaeology instantly guessed what her professor had discovered, "The Solutrean Hypothesis!"

"Yes, without a doubt this Clovis will prove the hypothesis. And I'm ashamed to admit that I was planning to sell it to some very bad people for an obscene amount of money. I was a fool and now it's over and I'm going to call him back and..."

"Wait," he heard Anne whisper, but her voice didn't come from across the room. She was somehow at his elbow. Then he felt her fumbling in the darkness, trying to loosen the knots on the rope that held his wrists behind his back.

"How..." he whispered.

Anne was working feverishly on the knots. "It's a long story," she whispered as she labored, "but I'll tell you this: our captor may be a psychopath, but he's also a gentleman. When he started to tie me up, I pleaded with him not to leave me on the icy floor, so he sat me in a chair. I told him I'd cut my palm— which is true—and I held my hands out in front of me with my knuckles pressed together and, as I hoped, he didn't pull the knots tight. Then he roped me into the chair, gagged me, and pushed me under the stairs. When he left, presumably to drag you down here, I...what is it with these knots?"

Over-stimulated by a combination of anxiety and adrenaline, Anne was talking non-stop as she struggled to loosen Clark's bonds and recounted the details of her near escape. With a measure of pride, which was totally out of keeping with their situation, she boasted that earlier, as soon as the stranger had left her alone, she'd immediately relaxed her tensed-up hands and wriggled free. She'd removed the gag and easily slipped out of the clumsy loops which her captor had so obligingly wrapped too many times around the chair. She'd hurriedly unsnarled the knots that held her ankles and was about to climb the stairs to escape when she heard the man returning. Rushing back to her chair, she draped the ropes over her, repositioned the gag, and prayed he wouldn't check her closely. She barely had time to sit before the lights had come on and she'd watched the muscular man carry Clark downstairs and tie him tightly.

"Almost there," she whispered as she grappled with the stubborn knots. "Anyway, after the guy left you on the floor, it got really weird when he made four trips back and forth carrying those toolboxes. It was puzzling to see how he man-handled you but not the boxes. He carried them down one at a time and placed each one carefully on the table—it was like he thought they were made of glass or something—very strange. Anyway, he cut two of the padlocks, then he went upstairs again and was gone for a long time and—ugh—I can't get these knots..."

They heard footsteps on the floor above as Anne scampered back to her chair and hastily repositioned herself before Diak started downstairs.

"You win," said Clark. "Untie me and let the girl go and I'll give you the Clovis."

"I accept your offer," said Diak as he reached the basement floor, glanced briefly at Anne, then crossed the room. "But the girl stays." The German carried a pistol, and kneeling beside his helpless prisoner, he pressed the barrel to the professor's temple. "Now there is a mark—just here—where I struck you last night. It will leave a scar, but I have only to pull this trigger and a bullet will explode in your skull which will, I assure you, make a much deeper and more permanent impression. In making this prediction, I speak from experience. So, I am going to untie you, but if you make a single false move, I will shoot you first and then the girl. Understood?"

"Understood," Clark answered.

"Das ist gut," said Diak. He shoved the pistol back into his holster and produced a knife to slice the ropes restraining Clark's feet and hands. The German worked rapidly, and he was none too careful about it.

"Ouch!" Clark winced as the blade raked across his knuckles.

"Stand up, Santa Claus," Diak commanded while he deftly re-sheathed his knife and pulled his pistol.

Clark got unsteadily to his feet, stumbling as Diak shoved him against the table, forcing his captive to face in Anne's direction.

"Look there at your young student," Diak instructed him. "And understand that her life is in your hands. Now, do not move."

Diak walked around the table as he trained his pistol on the teetering professor. Then he stopped on the far side and stood erect with his back to Anne and his attention riveted on Clark.

"Eyes up," said Diak.

Clark raised his head, looked at his captor for the first time, and realized the man was wearing sunglasses. He only had a moment to stare, but the professor seemed to see the edge of a scar protruding below one of the lenses. Then Clark saw his own haggard face reflected in the sunglasses and he looked away.

"Give me your attention," said Diak as he reached across the table to grasp Clark's chin with his powerful hand. The German's grip was firm as he turned Clark's head and forced the professor to look directly at him. Diak held Clark fast and repeated his threat. "If you fail me, I will shoot you both. First you and then I have only to turn and shoot the girl. And, trapped as she is beneath the stairs, I am unlikely to miss. Now, let us review what we have here before us. These are the boxes which you and the girl had in your possession, so one of these must contain the illusive Clovis."

"I..." Clark began. Rapidly assessing the situation, the professor was absolutely certain that, should he reveal the location of the Clovis, this dangerous man would kill them both. He had to stall for time—had to think of something. "I..." Clark repeated.

"No speaking," said Diak. "I am not asking, I am telling. Understood?"

"Understood," Clark repeated.

"Good. I begin again. You can see I have already searched the obvious boxes by removing the padlocks—but as you already know, these are both empty. Now, pay close attention, because my faithful nose tells me that the other two boxes, the pair as yet unopened, contain plastic explosives. Yes, these two unassuming containers, with their unique tumbler locks and elusive combinations have, I suspect, been booby-trapped by you. And no doubt you have used vintage plastique because the aroma of almonds is unmistakable, no? But you and I know that only one of these boxes is rigged to explode. And, by process of elimination, the safe box must contain the Clovis. Meanwhile, my dishonest friend, you have manipulated this hunt so thoroughly that no one but yourself knows which box is deadly and which contains the treasure."

Diak released Clark and the professor reflexively reached for the nearest box.

"Take care," Diak cautioned. "I know a little something about explosions. You are perhaps thinking that you would like to kill me. You are maybe even thinking that you would sacrifice yourself. But you do not wish to kill the girl, of this I am certain. And opening the wrong box in these tight quarters would kill us all. Is that what you want?"

"No indeed," said Clark trying to make his voice sound steady as his mind searched frantically for an idea. "It's just that...well...you've mixed them up, see. And I need to examine the padlocks to determine the correct box."

"You know the combinations, I presume?" Diak asked.

"Of course."

"Memorized?"

"Hardly. I..." Clark reached for his shirt pocket.

"Whatever comes out of that pocket," Diak threatened, "it had better be a list of combinations. And those numbers had better match with your recent phone call."

So, Clark thought, *the villain was listening.*

"I...I assure you these combinations are genuine," Clark said aloud. He was improvising frantically and with good reason. He could see that Anne had once again slipped her bonds and he sensed from her determined posture that she was about to tiptoe forward to try grabbing their armed abductor from behind. He shook his head to discourage her and hoped Diak would not comprehend the intent of his gesture because, if the German turned and saw Anne loose...

"I don't think this is a good idea," Clark said, and he shook his head again, hoping Anne would understand that he was trying to warn her to forget the idea of wrestling with the muscular German.

"What are you saying?" Diak seemed about to turn.

"I said," Clark shouted to get the man's attention, "I don't think this is a good idea because I... I... I seem to have mislaid the list of combinations." Then, hoping Anne would recognize the message he intended to send, he quickly added, "So, why don't you go upstairs?"

Diak raised his pistol, evidently intent on striking the older man, but then he lowered it, removed his sunglasses, and smiled sardonically. The smile crinkled his face and caused the deep scar that ran from his forehead to the bottom of his cheekbone to writhe like a thing possessed. Clark gaped at the ruined face with its prominent scar and missing eye.

"I am tired of these games, Dr. Clark. You see before you a man who has high hopes of selling your precious Clovis to the highest bidder in order to pay whatever is necessary to repair this less than handsome face and the remainder of my mangled torso. And, once made whole again, to fulfill my dream to live a quiet life in obscene luxury. So, Dr. Clark, let us achieve my happy ending, let us proceed because, you see, I know what you are doing."

Go upstairs, Anne, Clark silently prayed. *Go now!*

"For example," Diak continued while he glared at Clark and used his pistol as a pointer, aiming it carelessly at the professor's chest, "I know that you do not have a paper in your pocket. How do I know this? I know this because, while you lay unconscious, I searched you thoroughly and I found the bullet, though what you hoped to accomplish by reaching for it just now, I cannot imagine."

In truth, Clark had entirely forgotten about the bullet he'd absently placed in his pocket days ago on the dark Reservation. It was only there because he'd abandoned his attempt to shoot the yellow dog. And yet, he was desperate for ideas to forestall Anne's unwise attack and the bullet might be just the distraction needed to enable her escape.

"That well-placed bullet is—uh—merely a reminder that we should aim for the goal of *getting out of this particular basement...*" he suggested, giving as much of a lilt to the final words as he could prudently manage—willing Anne to understand.

"Nicht!" Diak growled. "Spare me your foolish riddles. You are merely stalling for time and hoping for some miracle. Am I correct in this?"

"Yes, but if you could *just go upstairs...*"

"Enough! Take up the bolt cutters, Doctor. I know they are not as delicate as your precious laboratory tools, but they are very much like the garden shears you have used all those monotonous weekends to prune your Arizona orange trees, yes? So, take up this practical tool and, at long last, let us have the Clovis. Do it now!"

Grasping the bolt cutters, the professor allowed himself a furtive glance past Diak's shoulder. Anne was gone at last. While Clark stalled for time, she must have quietly stolen away, up the stairs and out of harm's way. Knowing Anne was safe made Clark feel suddenly bold. He made quick work of the nearest combination lock, neatly severing the padlock shank with a single cut. He pulled the disjointed parts free and let them fall noisily to the concrete floor. Then he made his decision and looked up.

"No need to open the other one," Clark said.

"Ah. Put the bolt cutters down if you please," said Diak. He began to back away from the table, unsheathing his knife with his free hand as he kept his pistol trained on Clark. "I think it is time now for the young lady to join us. I will cut her free and then, just to be certain, we will allow her the honor of opening the box."

Diak turned and, seeing Anne gone, furiously wheeled back to level his pistol, but fired too late. Clark already had his hand on the bomb box and, before the German's bullet found its mark, the professor had just enough time to open the lid.

Epilogue

July 18, 2018, Noon
Lavender, Colorado

Trinidad had returned to Lavender too late to rescue his damsel in distress. But not too late to offer her a cup of coffee and Anne had to admit she welcomed his attention. She and the apologetic detective were sitting on a pair of upturned buckets just outside a borderline of crime scene tape. Cradling their coffees, they watched Jack and the enthusiastic Feds pick through the rubble. The searchers had just unearthed the outline of the concrete basement where she and her professor had been imprisoned. All around the ruined house lay a blast zone of shattered wood. The rubble formed a broad circular carpet of debris, a layer of still-smoldering fragments, strewn like confetti between the sheltering sides of the grain elevators.

Bandages on Anne's arms and forehead covered a few small wounds she'd received when shrapnel peppered her as she ran from the erupting and now demolished house. She'd been pulled from the wreckage and wrapped in a silvery foil survival blanket. Each time she moved, the blanket buckled, and the fabric made a crackling sound. She took a sip of coffee and cringed as the blanket crinkled.

"Do I have to keep wearing this thing?" she asked.

"The guys tell me it prevents hypothermia," Trinidad explained.

"Yeah, who'd a thought a subterranean explosion would rupture a water main," she said.

"And don't forget the fire hydrant that landed on the roof of Madge's patrol car," Trinidad said. They sat in silence for a time until he added, "I was miles away when Madge contacted everyone to say she'd spotted our German here. We had no idea you were inside, but Madge kept watch, and it was Madge who pulled you from the wreckage."

"Good old Madge," Anne said as she tipped her coffee cup in Madge's direction. She was feeling woozy and giddy as her mind sought to process the trauma of the explosion and the shock of Dr. Clark's demise.

"Jack was next on the scene. He was closest," Trinidad continued.

"Good old Jack," she said as a paramedic interrupted their conversation to examine her pupils and check her pulse. The technician was satisfied with her condition and said so.

"Another shot of oxygen?" he asked.

"No thanks," Anne said. "More coffee?" She held out her empty cup and blushed to see both the paramedic and the detective reach readily out to serve her. *I must look a sight,* she thought, *but passable enough to arouse a pair of moonstruck males. My pulse is normal, but I can't say the same for these distracted suitors.*

"I've got this," said Trinidad and he stared at the paramedic until the man retreated.

Anne watched as her attentive detective hurried to the situation tent and returned lugging an entire urn of coffee, trailing the unplugged cord in his wake. He refilled her cup and settled in beside his bemused companion, picking up the conversation as if nothing had happened.

"And—well—anyway I'm just sorry I was so late getting here," said Trinidad.

"It couldn't be helped," she decided. "How could you know this thing would come full circle? Besides, I didn't make it easy for you."

"Neither did Clark..." Trinidad said, and he instantly regretted the sarcasm in his voice. "Sorry."

"Never mind," said Anne. She was beginning to come to terms with the emotional rollercoaster of thinking her professor dead, then missing, and now finally dead again.

Sensing her distress, Trinidad remained silent as Anne struggled to give voice to her feelings.

"I know…" she began, then faltered, and at last continued. "I know Dr. Clark deceived me and he did some reckless and completely unethical things, but he came through in the end. In a way, he's a kind of hero, to me at least. He intentionally made sure I was clear before he did it."

"Okay, and I'm glad he did what he did, however belated the gesture was, but I just wish I knew a couple of things," said Trinidad. "Do you feel up to answering some questions?"

"Try me."

"Well, we know about the money and all the bad guys Dr. Clark had swirling around him—the Russians, the Saudis, and that German creep, Diak. But we still have no idea what your illusive professor was trying to peddle. What's his merchandise? What's the so-called treasure? And where's it hidden?"

"As for the hiding place," said Anne, as she began to recover some of her spunk, "my guess is it was in plain sight all the time. Remember how Dr. Clark always said to think outside the box?" She looked over the rim of her coffee cup, held Trinidad in her gaze, and batted her eyelashes.

"Don't tell me!" Trinidad shouted and he laughed as the idea hit him. "Inside one of the padlocks! The only place we didn't look."

"Bingo," said Anne and she realized how much she'd missed matching wits with this handsome stranger. "And I'm guessing that, even if you examine all the padlocks, you still won't find the treasure. Knowing my professor, he would've kept it close, so I'm pretty sure it went up with the house and the hydrant."

"Would we even know what to look for?" Trinidad asked. "What exactly were we looking for?"

"Patience," said Anne, "I'm getting to that. Now, as to what the merchandise was, tell me, have you ever heard of the Solutrean Hypothesis?

"Suh-lew-tree-in?" Trinidad tried to repeat her pronunciation, "is that what you're saying?"

"Yes, Solutrean. Ever hear of it?"

"I have a feeling I'm about to," Trinidad frowned. "Is it a long story?"

"Somewhere between 17 and 30,000 years," she said and laughed aloud.

Trinidad, who suddenly realized how much he loved that laugh, looked at his watch and said, "Lucky for us, I just closed a big case and it just so happens that I'm free for the next thirty thousand years."

"Okay," she said. "Where shall we begin—your place or mine?"

```
UT │ CO
─────┼─────
AZ │ NM
     │
```

The Four Corners

A Note Regarding *The Four Corners Mystery Series*

Readers have wisely requested an explanation which ties together novels included in this series. For those who've read the introductory books, the following will serve as a refresher. For those new to the series, this information provides essential background. To supply further context, the final pages of this book list the upcoming titles and plot summaries of each novel in the series.

Set in Arizona, Colorado, New Mexico, and Utah, *The Four Corners Mystery Series* explores diverse regions which share a common border. Featuring breathtaking vistas of lofty mountains, high plains, and desert panoramas, the series chronicles the exploits of two fearless investigators.

Raised in a hardscrabble Arizona mining town, twenty-something **Anne Scriptor** has survived a troubled childhood to become a skilled archaeologist. She has no interest in solving crimes until she meets **Trinidad Sands**, a thirty-something Colorado native. He's a law school dropout and recovering alcoholic who channels his keen powers of observation into detective work while also managing a productive lavender farm.

Their paths first cross in *The Road to Lavender*, then merge in *A Lavender Wedding*. Book three is a prequel entitled *Spirits of Grand Lake* in which Trinidad relates the story of how he became a detective. More adventures follow as the couple continues to unravel mysteries which haunt the beautiful, often rugged, and sometimes deadly landscape of Western America.

Acknowledgments

As of this writing, having reached the venerable age of seventy-five, I find myself essentially unchanged—still nothing more or less than a kid with a crazy dream. Writing is born as a solitary endeavor which takes on life when shared and I've found that guiding a work of fiction from conception to finished product requires the work of many people. At the risk of leaving someone out, I'll acknowledge the support of folks I can recall, with the promise that—if I've inadvertently omitted a name—I'll correct that oversight in subsequent books. There are several more novels to come as my characters take on further challenges in *The Four Corners Mystery Series*. A complete list of upcoming titles appears at the close of this novel.

A word regarding **ANNE SCRIPTOR**, my troubled and spunky main character: she represents a combination of my late mother Carol Ruth Benjamin, her stillborn daughter Ann, and my late friend Tina Elisabeth Kjolhede. I like to imagine that my sister Ann, who never experienced life, would have grown into a dynamic and plucky woman with traits reflecting the finer qualities of my resolute mother and my unforgettable friend. Other family members have consistently supported my creative endeavors including my late father Leonard and my big brother Tom and his wife, my precious sister-in-law, Sharon, who was patient enough to read an early version of the story. The antics and good sense of their children, my spirited niece Pam (Watts) and daring nephew Bill Benjamin, inform the playful and heroic sides of my characters—as do the frolics of grand and great nieces and nephews too numerous to mention.

I acknowledge the work of anonymous judges for The Rocky Mountain Fiction Writers' 2019 Colorado Gold Contest. These intrepid volunteers collaborated with the finals judge—Jill Marr (a veteran agent with the Sandra Dijkstra Literary Agency)—to award selected passages from *THE ROAD TO LAVENDER* a third-place finish in the group's mystery genre competition. And a shout-out to the New Mexico Book Association which honored *THE ROAD* with a special award for cover design. Those recognitions are inspirational honors.

I am also indebted to several residents of my newly adopted hometown of Cedaredge, Colorado (population 2,231). Special thanks to my beta-readers who believed enough in my work to slog through early versions of the Lavender story: Stacy Malmgren, Randy and Pat Sunderland, Cecilia (Cissy) Norton, and Kim Taylor. Trudy and Phil Berghauser along with Skip Bethurum performed miracles with technical details about archaeology and jets, respectively. Mark Petterson supplied German language passages. Karen Grant did essential last-minute edits, then Wayne McKinzie and Reneé Janiece (the musical duo known as *Bittersweet Highway*) nailed down the final read. I am eternally grateful to my dear wife and intrepid collaborator, Donna Marie (Woods) Benjamin. She provided practical edits and fashioned an appealing cover design. She also exhibited a fountain of patience and good humor while overseeing the all-important formatting process. She is love personified.

My old college chum Linda Trzyna, Cedar Mesa friend Carol Bosco, Canadian pal Paul Lucas, New Mexico amigos Bo and Kathleen Miller, Reno residents Jack and Gretchen Casey, and my army buddy Ted Rosen and his wife Sharon buoyed me up with regular infusions of wit, encouragement, and common sense. Other authors provided valuable assistance as members of writing groups and production advisors. This generous group includes Alice Andersen, Barbra Campbell, Michael Ruchhoeft, Vicki Law, David Short, Kris Veigele, Julie Ann Helmick, and David M. Delo. Polly Letofsky of *My Word Publishing* provided valuable tips and support.

Last, but certainly not least, I discreetly omit the name of the charismatic woman who rocketed through my life in the summer of 2018. Her passion for life rekindled my creative spirit and inspired me to write this, the first of many novels. This book is dedicated to her better angels.

Thanks, everyone. I hope I made you proud.

Donald Paul Benjamin/July, 2020

The Four Corners Mystery Series

In paperback or Kindle on **amazon.com** and **barnesandnoble.com**.

Book 1: *The Road to Lavender*

A smuggled prize, bloodthirsty treasure hunters, a hungry mountain lion, and a budding romance--it looks like a busy summer for Anne Scriptor. Navigating through Arizona and Colorado, will the spunky young student of archaeology survive her journey on the road to Lavender? This debut novel received a 2020 award for cover design from the New Mexico Book Association and won third-place in the 2019 Rocky Mountain Fiction Writers' *Colorado Gold Writing Contest.*

Book 2: *A Lavender Wedding*

Contains adult subject matter and sexually sensitive topics. Anne Scriptor forms a working partnership with Detective Trinidad Sands by joining his investigative team. When the handsome detective proposes marriage, Anne says yes. The working couple explores the unsolved murder of Esau Koller, a prolific author and Colorado celebrity. And the clock is ticking as they strive to crack the case in time to orchestrate a lavender wedding.

Book 3: *Spirits of Grand Lake*

In this prequel, set years before Trinidad Sands meets his precocious wife, the footloose bachelor lands his first case. Working a seasonal job at Grand Lake Lodge, he befriends a local character, investigates a kidnapping, and risks the wrath of a vengeful arsonist. Will he be aided or hampered by the spirits which haunt the Colorado Rockies?

Book 4: *The War Nickel Murders*

The brutal murder of a local hermit entangles the husband-and-wife detective team of Trinidad and Anne Sands in international intrigue. Echoes of World War II unnerve the entire village of Lavender as a deadly assassin strives to claim the key to eternal youth and uncover a hidden stockpile of counterfeit nickels.

Book 5: *Rare Earth*

Detectives Trinidad and Anne Sands decide to take a vacation from sleuthing. Trinidad has received a generous offer to purchase his lavender farm and he focuses his energy on making a life-altering real estate decision. Anne gets a chance to apply her scientific skills when a trio of visiting Chinese archaeologists arrive to explore Colorado and neighboring Utah. But these seemingly unrelated projects soon overlap in a marathon of espionage, murder, and betrayal.

Book 6: *Walking Horse Ranch*

A Hollywood movie crew comes to New Mexico hell-bent on completing a feature film in record time. Things are looking up when they locate an ideal setting and the production schedule is rolling along until the star's stand-in is murdered. There are fifty-five eyewitnesses to the crime, not to mention camera footage from seven angles. But it will take a fresh look by Trinidad and Anne Sands to unravel the mystery of Walking Horse Ranch.

Book 7: *A Lavender Farewell*

It's time for Trinidad and Anne Sands to leave the mythical village of Lavender, Colorado. The catalyst for their departure is an unsolved murder perpetrated by a notorious villain who was earlier presumed dead.

About the Author

Donald Paul Benjamin is an American novelist who specializes in cozy mysteries and high fantasy. His writing includes elements of romance and humor. He also writes about Western Colorado history. He is the author of the *The Four Corners Mystery Series, The Great Land Fantasy Series and the Surface Creek Life Series.*

In addition to his writing career, he also works as a freelance journalist, cartoonist, and photographer. A U.S. Army veteran, he served three years as a military journalist and illustrator, including a tour in Korea. Trained as a teacher of reading, he has worked with a wide variety of learners from those attending kindergarten to college students. He also holds an advanced degree in college administration. He lived in Arizona and worked in higher education for more than three decades before retiring in 2014.

He now lives in Cedaredge, a small town on the Western Slope of Colorado, where he hikes and fishes in the surrounding wilderness. He and his wife, Donna Marie, operate **Elevation Press**, a service which helps independent authors self-publish their works (see info on the following page).

Email: elevationpressbooks@gmail.com
Studio Phone: 970-856-9891
Mail: D.P. Benjamin, P.O. Box 603, Cedaredge, CO 81413
Website: https://benjaminauthor.com/
Visit the Author's Facebook Page under: D.P. Benjamin Author
Instagram: https://www.instagram.com/benjaminnovelist/

The Four Corners Mystery Series
- **Book 1:** *The Road to Lavender*
- **Book 2:** *A Lavender Wedding*
- **Book 3:** *Spirits of Grand Lake*
- **Book 4:** *The War Nickel*
- **Book 5:** *Rare Earth*
- **Book 6:** *Walking Horse Ranch*
- **Book 7:** *Lavender Farewell*

The Great Land Fantasy Series
- **Book 1:** *Stone Bride*
- **Book 2:** *Iron Angel*
- **Book 3:** *Redhackle*
- **Book 4:** *Bindbuilder*
- **Book 5:** *Nachtfalke*
- **Book 6:** *Isochronuous*
- **Book 7:** *Ruth and Esau*

Surface Creek Life Series
- **Book 1:** *A Surface Creek Christmas: Winter Tales 1904–1910*

In paperback or Kindle on **amazon.com** and **barnesandnoble.com**.